my LITTLE
PONY
Friendship is Magic

COVER BY
Toni Kuusisto

SERIES EDITS BY
Megan Brown and Bobby Curnow

COLLECTION EDITS BY
Alonzo Simon and Zac Boone

COLLECTION DESIGN BY
Neil Uyetake

Special thanks to Tayla Reo, Ed Lane, Beth Artale, and Michael Kelly.

For international rights, contact **licensing@idwpublishing.com**

ISBN: 978-1-68405-685-9

23 22 21 20 1 2 3 4

IDW® Licensed By:

www.IDWPUBLISHING.com

Originally published as MY LITTLE PONY: FRIENDSHIP IS MAGIC issues #84–88.

I'm So Excited

WRITTEN BY
Christina Rice

ART BY
Toni Kuusisto

COLORS BY
Heather Breckel

No Fear!... Except One

WRITTEN BY
Mary Kenney

ART BY
Casey W. Coller

COLORS BY
Marissa Louise

And Then There's Maud

WRITTEN BY
Jeremy Whitley

ART BY
Kate Sherron

COLORS BY
Heather Breckel

The Draytona Breach

WRITTEN BY
Ted Anderson

ART BY
Tony Fleecs

COLORS BY
Heather Breckel

LETTERS BY
Neil Uyetake

art by Toni Kuusisto

NOW CLASS, I AM HAPPY TO ANNOUNCE THAT WE'RE ALMOST HALFWAY THROUGH THE SCHOOL YEAR.
WHICH MEANS IT'S TIME FOR—
MIDTERMS!
GROAN!
YOU KNOW WHAT THIS MEANS?
WE'RE GONNA HAVE TO SPEND THE NEXT COUPLE OF WEEKS MEMORIZING A TEXTBOOK FOR A TEST?
TIME TO BUST OUT THE PILLARS OF EQUESTRIA: TIME, PLACE, AND MEMORY!
YONA NO LIKE TO REMEMBER SO MANY PONY THINGS!
WHAT SHE SAID.
ACTUALLY, MEMORIZATION WILL NOT BE REQUIRED FOR THIS MIDTERM.
WHEW!
IN FACT, THERE'S NOT GOING TO BE A TEST AT ALL!
NO TEST?! YES!
THAT'S WHAT I'M TALKING ABOUT!

INSTEAD, I WANT YOU TO TAKE WHAT YOU'VE LEARNED AND BE CREATIVE!
...CREATIVE?
THAT IS NOT WHAT I'M TALKING ABOUT.
YONA NO UNDERSTAND CREATIVITY!
...WHAT SHE SAID.
EACH OF YOU WILL CREATE A PROJECT THAT CONVEYS WHAT YOU HAVE LEARNED ABOUT THE HISTORY OF FRIENDSHIP.
AND WHAT IT MEANS TO YOU.
IT CAN BE A POEM, PERFORMANCE, WORK OF ART.
ANYTHING YOU WANT, IN FACT.
AS LONG AS IT'S A REFLECTION OF YOU.
IN TWO WEEKS, YOU'LL PRESENT YOUR PROJECTS IN FRONT OF THE SCHOOL.
ANY QUESTIONS?
YES, SMOLDER AND GALLUS?
CAN WE MEMORIZE A TEXTBOOK AND TAKE A TEST?
I GUESS WE SHOULD GO TO THE LIBRARY AND LOOK UP BOOKS ON... BEING CREATIVE?
NO MEMORIZATION? NO TEST?
I DON'T EVEN KNOW WHO YOU ARE ANYMORE.

I JUST DON'T KNOW WHAT TO DO!
MEH. WE HAVE TWO WEEKS.
YOU'LL FIGURE SOMETHING OUT.
WE HAVE TWO WEEKS TO COMPLETE IT.
I NEED TO FIGURE OUT SOMETHING NOW!
I KNOW WHAT YOU MEAN! SHOULD I DO A SONG?
OR A PAINTING?
MOSAIC?
BOARD GAME?
DIORAMA?
I DON'T KNOW HOW I AM EVER GOING TO GET THIS—
DONE!
YONA FINISH CREATIVE PROJECT!
NO OFFENSE, YONA, BUT THERE'S NO WAY YOU'RE ALREADY DONE AND READY TO PRESENT TO THE SCHOOL.
YONA IS DONE!
YONA MAKE FRIENDSHIP BRACELETS, WOVEN LIKE YAK RUGS. BUT INSTEAD OF TRADITIONAL YAK COLORS—
—DIFFERENT COLORS ARE FOR HOMES OF DIFFERENT CREATURES. YONA'S FRIENDS!

AT PRESENTATION, YONA PERFORM OLD YAK CEREMONY BEFORE GIVING BRACELETS TO FRIENDS.
WOW, THIS IS AMAZING, YONA!
IT REALLY IS A REFLECTION OF YOU AND WHAT YOU'VE LEARNED ABOUT FRIENDSHIP.
THAT REALLY IS GREAT, YONA.
I GUESS YOU'RE MORE IN TUNE WITH YOUR CREATIVITY THAN THE REST OF US.
BRIEF HISTORY OF PO
BRIEF PONY HISTORY II
HAS IT OCCURRED TO YOU THAT YOU HAVE A BIGGER CREATIVE ADVANTAGE THAN THE REST OF US?
YOU'RE A ***CHANGELING.***
YOU CAN JUST CHANGE INTO FRIENDSHIP... THINGS.
THAT'S IT!
THANKS, SMOLDER!
YOU'RE... WELCOME?
BOLT

IT SURE FEELS GOOD TO CATCH SOME RAYS AFTER BEING COOPED UP!
I GUESS, BUT I'M REALLY WORRIED ABOUT OCELLUS.
HAS ANYONE SEEN HER LATELY?
YONA SEE OCELLUS!
WHEN?
NOW!
WHERE HAVE YOU BEEN LATELY?
WORKING ON MY MIDTERM PROJECT, OF COURSE!
AFTER SMOLDER SUGGESTED I USE MY CHANGELING POWERS FOR THE PROJECT, IT OCCURRED TO ME—
—THAT I COULD DO AN INTERPRETIVE DANCE ABOUT THE HISTORY OF EQUESTRIA—
—WHILE CHANGING INTO ALL THE KEY PONIES OF EQUESTRIAN HISTORY!
I'M SO EXCITED!
I REALLY DON'T HAVE TIME TO CHAT.
I'VE FINISHED WITH THE LIBRARY.
TIME TO WORK ON THE DANCE!
THAT'S... THAT ACTUALLY SOUNDS REALLY AMAZING.
IT DOES, BUT—IT'S ONLY A TEN-MINUTE PRESENTATION.
DO YOU THINK YOU MIGHT BE OVERDOING IT?
I DON'T THINK SO.
I JUST WANT TO DO MY BEST, AND THIS IS HOW I'M GOING TO DO THAT.
THIS IS NOT GOING TO END WELL, IS IT?
NOPE.

I DON'T THINK OCELLUS EVEN SLEPT IN HER BED LAST NIGHT! SHE WAS OFF REHEARSING HER DANCE.

I'M STARTING TO REALLY GET WORRIED.

NOT SURE WHAT WE CAN DO.

WE CAN'T EXACTLY STOP HER FROM WORKING HARD ON HER PROJECT.

AND DONE!

WHAT IS THAT?

IT'S THE TREE OF HARMONY MADE OUT OF ROCK FROM THE DRAGON LANDS.

OK... WHAT'S THE PRESENTATION GOING TO BE?

ME TALKING ABOUT THE TREE OF HARMONY WITHOUT EATING ANY OF THESE GEMS!

BUT WHAT ABOUT OCELLUS?

MAYBE WE SHOULD TALK TO HEADMARE TWILIGHT?

WE'RE ALL WORRIED, BUT WE ALSO HAVE OUR OWN PROJECTS TO COMPLETE.

THIS POEM AIN'T GONNA WRITE ITSELF!

BESIDES, YOU KNOW WHAT A PERFECTIONIST TWILIGHT IS.

THIS IS PROBABLY NORMAL BEHAVIOR TO HER.

AND OCELLUS WOULD PROBABLY BE REALLY UPSET IF WE WENT TO THE HEADMARE.

OUT OF THE WAY!

Z

?

WHERE IS IT? WHERE IS—
THERE!
OBSCURE TALES OF EQUESTRIA

OCELLUS?
NO TIME, SILVERSTREAM!
HAVE TO INSERT SOME MORE CREATURES INTO MY DANCE!
BUT APPLEJACK'S CLASS IS ABOUT TO—
NO TIME!
—START.

ONE OF THE HARDEST THINGS ABOUT HONESTY IS THAT PONIES, ER, **CREATURES** DON'T ALWAYS LIKE TO HEAR IT.
BUT SOMETIMES THEY NEED TO, FER THEIR OWN GOOD.
NOW SHOULD WE GO TO TWILIGHT?
ZZZZZ
SOMETIMES HE ROARS BECAUSE HE IS HAPPY TO SEE YOU, AND THERE'S NO REASON TO BE SCARED.
NOW FOR A DEMONSTRATION.
Z
ROAR
ZZZZZZ
MAYBE WE SHOULD GO SEE TWILIGHT NOW?
HOW ABOUT ***NOW?***
ZZZZZZZ
BOOM!

OCELLUS! WE WERE THINKING OF GOING FOR A FLYAROUND THIS AFTERNOON.
YOU SHOULD JOIN US!
SORRY, SILVERSTREAM. I'VE GOT TO KEEP REHEARSING FOR THE PRESENTATION.
BUT WE NEED YOU TO CHANGE INTO SOMETHING BIG WITH WINGS SO YOU CAN CARRY YONA.
I'M REALLY SORRY, BUT I CAN'T.
WE'RE ACTUALLY WORRIED ABOUT YOU.
YOU'RE FALLING ASLEEP IN CLASS AND YOU'RE NEVER AROUND.
YOU'RE PUTTING ***TOO MUCH*** INTO THIS PROJECT.
TOO MUCH?
THIS IS MY CHANCE TO SHOW THAT A CHANGELING CAN USE THEIR POWERS FOR SOMETHING GOOD AND BEAUTIFUL.
AND IT NEEDS TO BE PERFECT!
I'M SORRY IF YOU ALL DON'T UNDERSTAND THAT.
BUT YOU NEED TO RESPECT IT.
CHEERLEADING CLUB BIG AFTERGAME SHOW!
I NEED TO GO REHEARSE.

IT'S THE MIDDLE OF THE NIGHT, SILVERSTREAM!
WHERE ARE YOU TAKING US?
OCELLUS HASN'T COME BACK TO THE DORM AGAIN!
TWILIGHT GAVE HER PERMISSION TO REHEARSE IN ONE OF THE EMPTY CLASSROOMS.
IT'S TIME FOR AN INTERVENTION.
IT CAN'T WAIT UNTIL MORNING?
I WOULDN'T ARGUE. HAVE YOU EVER SEEN SILVERTREAM THIS SERIOUS?
YOU MAKE A GOOD POINT.
THERE SHE IS.
ARE WE READY TO GO IN?
NO! WHAT ARE WE EVEN GOING TO SAY TO HER?
HOW ABOUT, "GO GET SOME SLEEP, SO WE CAN, TOO"?
WE NEED TO LET HER KNOW THAT WE UNDERSTAND, BUT WE'RE HERE TO SUPPORT AND HELP HER.

GAH!
OOF!
SLAM
OCELLUS!

WHA— WHAT ARE YOU ALL DOING HERE?
GO GET THE HEADMARE.
WE'RE HERE TO HELP YOU.
HELP? I DON'T NEED HELP! I'VE GOT THIS UNDER CONTROL.
EVERY CREATURE IS GOING TO LOVE IT!
THEY'RE ALL GOING TO BE SO EXCITED TO SEE IT.
I'M SO EXCITED!
I'M SO EXCITED!
I'M SO... SCARED.

OCELLUS, YONA EXPLAINED WHAT'S GOING ON, BUT I'D LIKE TO SPEAK WITH YOU ABOUT IT.
IN PRIVATE.
WE'LL BE RIGHT OUTSIDE IF YOU NEED US!
THANKS.
WHEN YOU TOLD ME ABOUT YOUR PROJECT, I THOUGHT IT SOUNDED AMBITIOUS BUT STILL ACHIEVABLE.
I DIDN'T REALIZE IT HAD SPIRALED OUT OF CONTROL.
HOW MANY CREATURES WERE YOU PLANNING ON CHANGING INTO DURING THE TEN-MINUTE PRESENTATION?
THREE HUNDRED FORTY-SIX.
THERE IS SO MUCH FASCINATING HISTORY ABOUT EQUESTRIA AND HOW FRIENDSHIP TIES INTO IT.
I WANTED TO TRY AND PRESENT IT ALL AND NOT DISAPPOINT ANYPONY BY LEAVING ANYTHING OUT.
I WANTED TO SHOW HOW AMAZING THE CHANGELINGS CAN BE.
BUT IT LOOKS LIKE I'M FAILING AT IT.

YOU'RE NOT FAILING.
YOU'RE JUST TRYING TO DO TOO MUCH. IN FACT, IT'S MORE THAN ANY CREATURE IS CAPABLE OF.
WHAT WOULD YOU DO?
ME? WELL, I WOULD...
I WOULD TRY TO DO WAY MORE THAN I COULD HANDLE.
COMPLETELY STRESS MYSELF OUT.
AND FEEL LIKE A TOTAL FAILURE WHEN IT WASN'T PERFECT.
I KNOW I'M NOT A GREAT EXAMPLE IN THIS CASE.
BUT SINCE WE LAUNCHED THE SCHOOL OF FRIENDSHIP, I'VE BEEN TRYING TO PUT LESS PRESSURE ON EVERY CREATURE.
INCLUDING MYSELF.
THAT'S WHY I ASSIGNED THIS PROJECT. I HOPED IT WOULD BE LESS STRESSFUL THAN A MASSIVE TEST.
I GUESS I MESSED UP, HUH?
YOU DIDN'T MESS THIS UP!
I'M ACTUALLY IMPRESSED WITH YOUR VISION.
IT'S CERTAINLY CREATIVE!
BUT I CAN'T DO IT!
YOU MIGHT NOT BE ABLE TO CHANGE INTO THREE HUNDRED FORTY-SIX CREATURES.
BUT I BET YOU CAN PICK ONE SMALLER STORY TO TELL.
AND WE'LL ALL BE JUST AS IMPRESSED.
WELL, MAYBE YOU'RE RIGHT.
AND YOUR FRIENDS WILL BE HERE TO SUPPORT YOU.
I KNOW MINE ALWAYS ARE.
I KNOW YOU'RE RIGHT ABOUT THAT.
GOING FORWARD, WE BOTH NEED TO TRY AND GIVE OURSELVES A BREAK. OK?
DEAL!

SCHOOL OF FRIENDSHIP MID-TERM PRESENTATIONS
AND, UH, WHEN AT LAST THIS, UH, JOURNEY ENDS...
I'LL, UH, BE OK, IF I'M WITH MY, UH... FRIENDS.

EQUESTRIA SCHOOL OF FRIENDSHIP RULES!

CLAP CLAP CLAP
CLAP CLAP CLAP CLAP
CLAP CLAP CLAP CLAP

SCHOOL OF F
THANK YOU, GALLUS, FOR THAT ORIGINAL POEM ABOUT FRIENDSHIP.

CLAP CLAP CLAP CLAP
CLAP CLAP CLAP CLAP
CLAP CLAP CLAP CLAP
AND NOW FOR OUR FINAL PRESENTATION.
AN INTERPRETIVE DANCE PERFORMED BY OCELLUS!

YOU'RE OK?
YES!

OOHHHHH

FRIENDSHIP M -TERM PRESENTATIONS

THAT WAS AMAZING!

YONA LOVE INTERPRETIVE DANCE!

INCREDIBLE!

UDSHIP MID-TERM PRESENTATIONS

I OWE IT TO YOU ALL.

INSTEAD OF TRYING TO TELL THE HISTORY OF EQUESTRIA, YOU MADE ME REALIZE THAT I SHOULD JUST TELL **MY** STORY.

THE STORY OF WHAT FRIENDSHIP MEANS TO ME.

THAT CONCLUDES OUR MIDTERM PRESENTATIONS.

NOW, I'D LIKE TO INVITE ALL OUR STUDENTS AND TEACHERS TO TAKE A MUCH-DESERVED BREAK WITH THEIR FRIENDS!

The End!

art by Sara Richard

art by Casey W. Coller

ALRIGHT, APPLE BLOOM. YOU WERE PICKIN' APPLES, AND THEN YOU SAW WHAT, EXACTLY?
A GIANT FLY-DER! BIGGER'N YOU!
THAT DON'T MAKE ANY SENSE. FLY-DERS ARE ONE: TINY, AND TWO: ALL THE WAY OVER IN LUNA BAY.
BUT I SAW IT! WHY'D YOU COME HELP ME LOOK IF YOU DON'T BELIEVE ME?
'CAUSE I KNEW YOU WOULDN'T LET IT GO, AND GRANNY WOULDN'T LET YOU COME OUT HERE ALONE AFTER DARK. BUT I PROMISE, IT CAN'T BE A FLY-DER.
OH, YEAH?

NOW HOLD ON! I'M GONNA GET YOU DOWN!
HURRRRRY! I'M STUCK!

OOMMF!

I JUST DON'T GET WHAT COULD BE BIG ENOUGH TO MAKE THIS...
WHO CARES?! WE'RE STUCK FOREVER! IT'S GONNA COME BACK AND EAT US!
NO, IT AIN'T. NOW LOOK, YOUR PART OF THE WEB'S PRETTY THIN. IF YOU RELAX, I THINK IT'LL SNAP.

I CAN'T DO IT! I CAN'T GET OUT!
YOU CAN. IT'S JUST YOU'RE TOO SCARED TO DO ANYTHING—
I AIN'T SCARED!

IT'S OKAY TO BE SCARED, APPLE BLOOM. PLENTY OF THINGS SCARE ME, TOO.
NUH-UH.
YES, HUH. SEEMS WE AIN'T GOIN' ANYWHERE FOR A WHILE, SO I'LL TELL YOU ALL ABOUT IT...

YEARS 'N YEARS AGO...
YOU REMEMBER THE OLD WELL AT THE EDGE OF THE PROPERTY?
"ONE DAY, I DECIDED I ***HAD*** TO SEE HOW DEEP IT WENT. WHAT IF SOMETHIN' WAS INSIDE? MERPONIES? TINY LITTLE FISHIES?"
HELLOOOOO?! ANYPONY DOWN THERE?
HELLLLLLLLP!

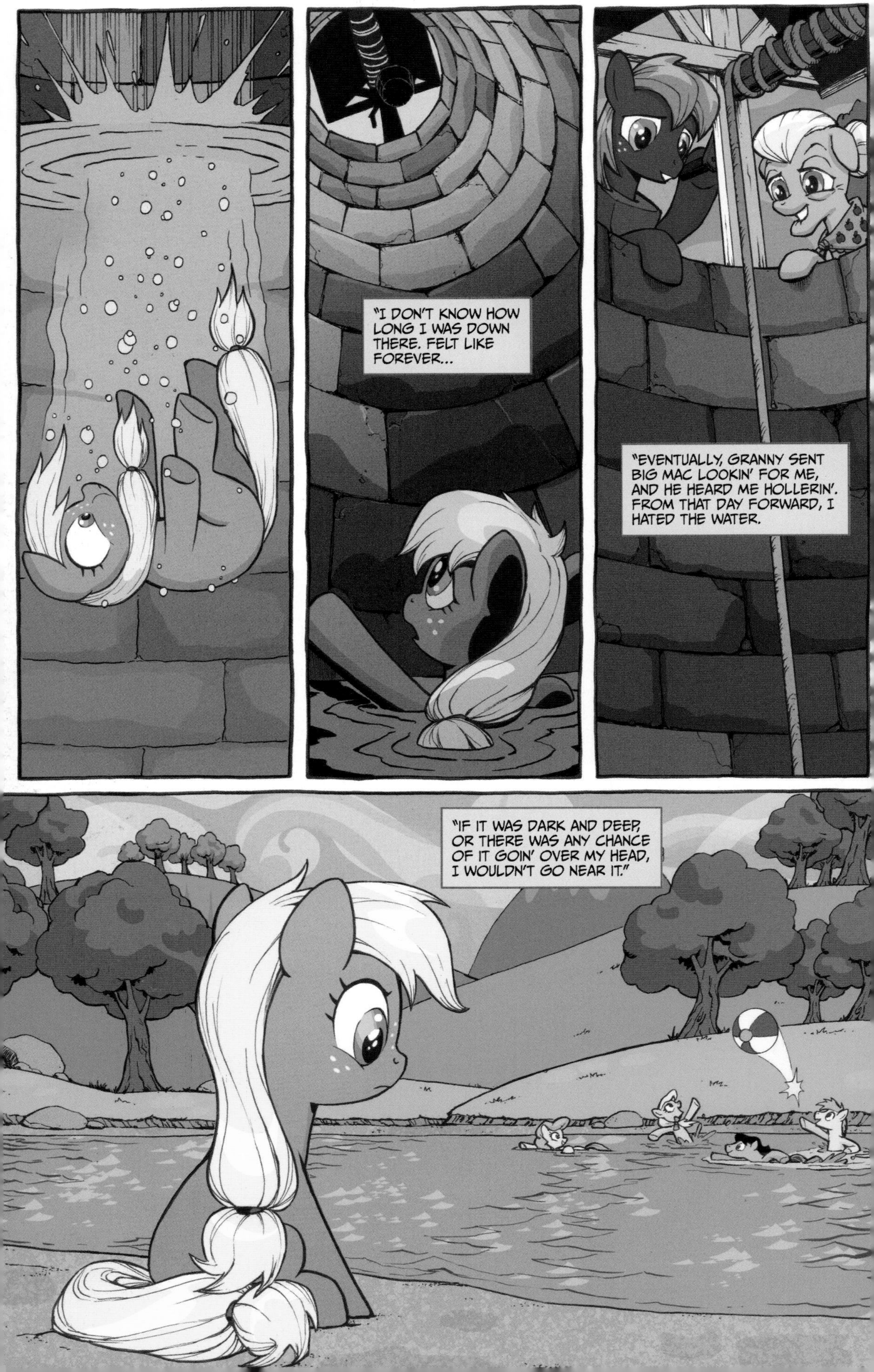

"I DON'T KNOW HOW LONG I WAS DOWN THERE. FELT LIKE FOREVER...

"EVENTUALLY, GRANNY SENT BIG MAC LOOKIN' FOR ME, AND HE HEARD ME HOLLERIN'. FROM THAT DAY FORWARD, I HATED THE WATER.

"IF IT WAS DARK AND DEEP, OR THERE WAS ANY CHANCE OF IT GOIN' OVER MY HEAD, I WOULDN'T GO NEAR IT."

NOW HOLD ON JUST A DARN MINUTE!
I'VE SEEN YOU GO IN WATER PLENTY OF TIMES! HECK, I'VE SEEN YOU SWIM! YOU'RE NEVER SCARED!
MAY I FINISH, PUH-*LEASE*?
FINE.

"THANK YA KINDLY.

"NOW, MY FEAR OF WATER CAME AT A REAL BAD TIME— IT WAS THE HOTTEST DANGED SUMMER YOU'D EVER FELT.

"AFTER WORKIN' IN THE ORCHARDS ALL DAY, WE'D GO DOWN TO THE LAKE TO COOL OFF 'N PLAY."

LAST ONE IN'S A ROTTEN APPLE!
C'MON, APPLEJACK, LET'S GO!
"WELL, THEY'D PLAY. I'D JUST SIT 'N WATCH. I WANTED TO JOIN 'EM...

"...BUT I WAS TOO SCARED."

C'MON, APPLEJACK!

AW, C'MON, NOT YOU TOO!
JUST 'CAUSE AJ'S NO FUN DOESN'T MEAN YOU GOTTA BE, BIG MAC!
YEAH!
WE CAME TO PLAY!

WANNA GO IN?
NO.
WHY NOT?
DO I GOTTA HAVE A REASON?

Y'KNOW, BEIN' BRAVE DOESN'T MEAN NOT BEIN' SCARED. IT MEANS FACIN' THE THING YOU'RE SCARED OF.

HOW DID— THAT'S NOT WHY I'M NOT GOIN' IN!
EEEYUP.
I MEAN IT! IT AIN'T ABOUT THE WATER AT ALL!
EEEYUP.
I AIN'T SCARED!

NOT EVEN A LITTLE.

LET'S PLAY PONY POLO! BIG MAC, YOU'RE PONY.
POOOONNNYYY...
POOOOOLOOOOO!
POOOOOLLLLLLLLOOOO!
POOOOLLLLLLLO!

C'MON, AJ! THERE'S ROOM FOR YOU!
WE NEED A NEW PONY POLO. BIG MAC'S NO GOOD AT IT.
HEY!

AAAA!
SLIP

"BIG MAC GRABBED ME BEFORE I COULD GO UNDER, BUT IT DIDN'T MATTER. IT WAS LIKE PROOF THAT I COULDN'T GO IN THE WATER, THAT I NEVER COULD. THAT I'D BEEN RIGHT TO BE AFRAID."

WHAT'S WRONG WITH HER?
I DUNNO, BUT SHE LOOKED... I DUNNO, LIKE SHE SAW A TIMBERWOLF.
WHY?
BEATS ME.
"I MADE A PROMISE TO MYSELF, THEN AND THERE."

I'M NEVER GOIN' IN THE WATER AGAIN!

NOW, APPLE BLOOM, DON'T MOVE.
WHY?
BECAUSE...

...I FOUND THE CRITTER THAT MADE THIS WEB, AND IT AIN'T A FLY-DER.
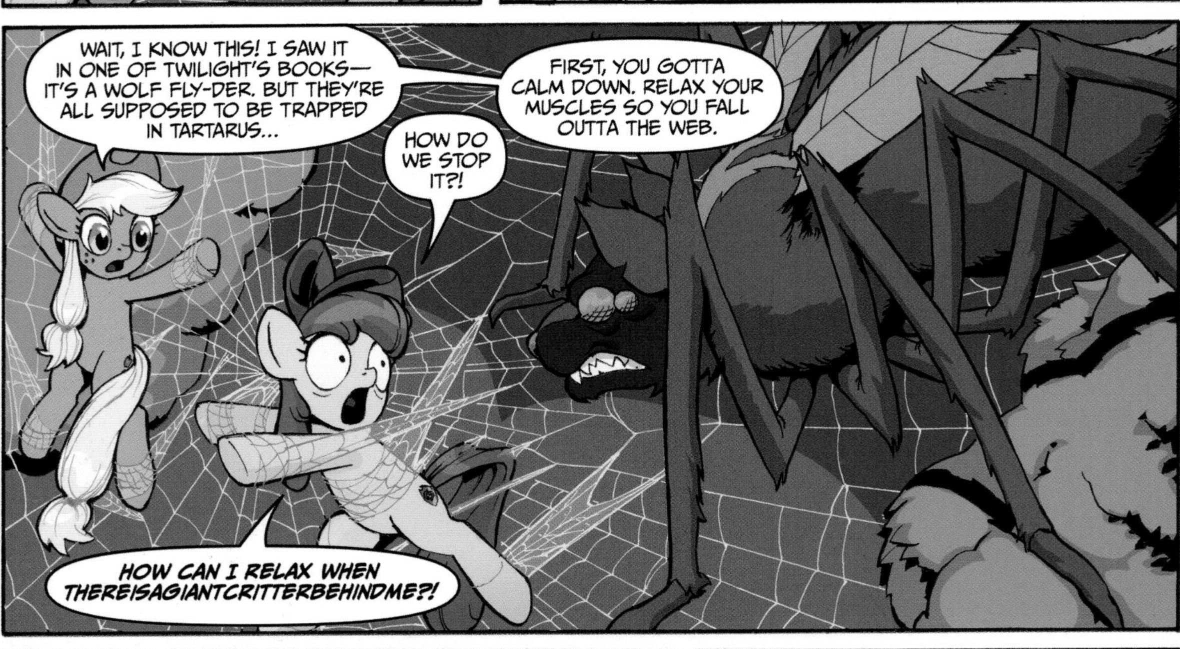
WAIT, I KNOW THIS! I SAW IT IN ONE OF TWILIGHT'S BOOKS— IT'S A WOLF FLY-DER. BUT THEY'RE ALL SUPPOSED TO BE TRAPPED IN TARTARUS...
HOW DO WE STOP IT?!
FIRST, YOU GOTTA CALM DOWN. RELAX YOUR MUSCLES SO YOU FALL OUTTA THE WEB.
HOW CAN I RELAX WHEN THEREISAGIANTCRITTERBEHINDME?!

HEY! WHY DON'T YOU PICK ON SOMEPONY AS BIG, MEAN, AND SCARY AS YOU?! GO ON, GIT!

WE'LL NEVER GET OUTTA HERE IF YOU CAN'T GET OUT OF THAT WEB. THE ONLY WAY TO DO THAT IS FOR YOU TO ACCEPT THAT YOU'RE AFRAID AND DEAL WITH IT.
I AIN'T SCARED, I ALREADY TOLD YOU! STOP SAYIN' I AM!
NO NEED TO LASH OUT.
I'M NOT!

"...ALRIGHT THEN. YOU MIND IF I FINISH THE STORY?"
"...SURE, GO AHEAD."
AW, C'MON, APPLEJACK. YOU'LL GO IN THE WATER AGAIN WHEN YOU'RE READY.
YOU STAY OUTTA THIS! I NEVER WOULDA GONE IN IF YOU HADN'T MADE ME!

"MADE" YOU? I SAVED YOU!
WHY DON'T YOU JUST LEAVE ME ALONE?!

YOU GONNA COME ALL THE WAY IN THIS TIME?
C'MON, IT'S STILL SUNNY, WE GOTTA GO PLAY!
WHERE'S HE GOIN'?
YOU OKAY, AJ?
"Y'SEE, I'VE GOT THIS HABIT, WHEN I'M AFRAID."
EVERYPONY JUST LEAVE ME ALONE!
"I TAKE IT OUT ON THE PONIES TRYIN' TO HELP ME.
"I WAS SO SCARED, AND SO MAD THAT I WAS SCARED, THAT I HURT THE PONIES I LOVED—
"—WHEN I COULD'VE JUST ADMITTED WHAT I WAS FEELIN'."

"BEIN' BRAVE DOESN'T MEAN NOT BEIN' SCARED." I AIN'T SCARED. I JUST GOT BETTER THINGS TO DO, IS ALL.
"(I DIDN'T.)
PLINK
"THEN, FOR THE FIRST TIME EVER..."
OH, NO...
"...I WAS SCARED FOR SOMEPONY BESIDES ME."

APPLEJACK! WHERE YOU GOIN'?
AIN'T YOU HEADED HOME?
STORM'S COMIN' IN FAST!
WHERE'S BIG MAC?
WE THOUGHT HE WENT WITH YOU.
IT'S GETTIN' SO DARK!
HANG ON, BIG M! I'M COMIN'!
WAIT, AJ!
IT'S NOT SAFE!

"THAT'S WHEN I KNEW WHAT IT REALLY MEANT TO BE AFRAID."

HANG ON, BIG BROTHER! I'M A-COMIN'!
"IT WAS LIKE BIG MAC HAD SAID. BEIN' BRAVE DOESN'T MEAN NOT BEIN' SCARED.
"IT MEANS FACING THE THING YOU'RE AFRAID OF."

"AND THE BEST WAY TO DO THAT?"
YOU WERE SO BRAVE!
THANK GOODNESS YOU WERE HERE, APPLEJACK!
YOU'RE OKAY!
"IS REALIZIN' THERE ARE WAY MORE IMPORTANT THINGS THAN FEAR."

JUST 'CAUSE YOU'RE AFRAID DON'T MEAN YOU GOTTA STAY THAT WAY.
AJ...
WHAT NOW?
IT'S BEHIND YOU.

AAAAA!

RELAX, JUST RELAX. RELAX RELAX RELAX...
SNAP
GIT AWAY! GIT OFFA ME!

OW...
EEEEEEEEEP!
THUD

I SAID GIT! DON'T YOU KNOW WHEN YOU AIN'T WANTED?
HISS!
HEY!
NOW LISTEN HERE, WE'VE HAD QUITE ENOUGH OF YOU LEAVIN' WEBS ALL OVER OUR FARM AND SCARIN' EVERYPONY!
SO HOW ABOUT YOU LET MY SISTER DOWN, CLEAN UP YOUR WEBS, AND GO SOMEWHERE DARK AND CREEPY. LIKE STRAIGHT BACK TO TARTARUS!
NOD NOD NOD

YOU'RE AWFULLY BRAVE.

The End!

art by Sara Richard

art by Kate Sherron
PARTY!
ROCK ON!

PINKIE, SPEAKING AS AN EXPERT IN THE STABILITY OF ROCK FORMATIONS, THIS CAKE APPEARS TO BE UNSTABLE.
AW, COME ON, MAUD, DON'T BE SUCH A NEIGHSAYER!
CRANKY AND MATILDA'S ANNIVERSARY IS TOMORROW, AND I HAVE TO MAKE SURE THAT THEY HAVE THE BESTEST, BRIGHTEST, SWEETEST, MOST AMAZINGEST CAKE IN ALL OF EQUESTRIA!
I'VE BEEN BAKING AND FROSTING ALL WEEK AND I'VE ALMOST GOT IT.
PINKIE, BOULDER HYPOTHESIZES THAT YOUR HAPPINESS FOR YOUR FRIENDS IS CAUSING YOU TO OVERESTIMATE WHAT IS PHYSICALLY POSSIBLE IN PASTRY PHYSICS.
OH, MAUD.
THIS CAKE IS HELD TOGETHER BY THE POWER OF FRIENDSHIP! THERE'S NOTHING STRONGER THAN—
PINKIE, HELP!
YELP!

GOTCHA!
WHAT DID YOU NEED HELP WITH, MAUD?
PINKIE, HAVE YOU EVER HEARD ME YELL LIKE THAT? IT WASN'T ME. IT WAS—
MARBLE!
GOSH, PINKIE. I DIDN'T MEAN TO! YOU ALMOST FELL OFF THE CAKE!

DON'T WORRY ABOUT IT, LITTLE SIS! BAKING IS A DANGEROUS LINE OF WORK.
YOU NEVER KNOW WHEN YOU'LL HAVE A CAKE CATASTROPHE OR A CROISSANT KERFLUFFLE OR AN EGG TART EXPLOSION.
OR PIE PERIL!
DO YOU FEEL IT, BOULDER? I'M ABOUT TO BE PULLED INTO A GROUP HUG. I DON'T KNOW WHY IT'S GOING TO HAPPEN, BUT I—
PIE PERIL! THAT WOULD BE A GREAT NAME FOR A BAND! WE SHOULD FORM A FAMILY BAND! I DON'T SEE YOU GUYS ENOUGH! COME HERE, MAUD!
I TOLD YOU.
WE SHOULD HANG OUT MORE! I LOVE MY SISTERS! MAUD ALMOST NEVER TAKES A BREAK FROM HER WORK AND MARBLE...
WHY ARE YOU HERE, MARBLE?
OKAY, SO, YOU REMEMBER HOW I TOLD YOU I WAS SHY AND DIDN'T HAVE MANY FRIENDS?
AND I SAID THERE WAS NO WAY, BECAUSE YOU'RE THE NICEST, MOST EXCITING PONY I KNOW?
YEAH... THAT.

WELL, I DECIDED TO TRY YOUR SUGGESTION OF HAVING A PARTY AND INVITING PEOPLE I WANTED TO BE FRIENDS WITH.
OOH, YES! DID YOU GIVE OUT FLYERS? DID ANYPONY RSVP?
WELL, THAT'S THE PROBLEM. IT WAS ONLY SUPPOSED TO BE A SMALL GET TOGETHER, BUT...
OVER TWO HUNDRED GUESTS RSVP'D.
THIS IS GONNA BE A GREAT PARTY! YOU MUST BE SO EXCITED!
BUT PINKIE—
I DON'T KNOW HOW TO THROW A PARTY! ESPECIALLY NOT FOR TWO HUNDRED PONIES! IT'S GONNA BE TERRIBLE!
WELL THEN, YOU'VE COME TO THE RIGHT PLACE! YOUR SISTERS ARE HERE TO HELP!
ALL I HAVE TO DO IS DELIVER THIS CAKE TO CRANKY AND—
CREAK
UH-OH.

PINKIE!
SMUSH!!
WHOOPS! I GUESS BOULDER WAS RIGHT ABOUT THE CAKE AFTER ALL.
POP
THAT'S OKAY. I'LL JUST NEED TO MAKE A NEW CAKE BEFORE WE LEAVE.
BUT PINKIE! THE PARTY IS TOMORROW NIGHT!
THEN I GUESS IT'S A GOOD THING YOU HAVE TWO SISTERS WHO ARE EXPERTS AT THROWING GREAT PARTIES, HUH?
DO YOU MEAN... MAUD?
EXACTLY! MAUD PLANNED MY FIFTH BIRTHDAY AND IT WAS THE BESTEST PARTY I'VE EVER HAD.
PINKIE, CAN I TALK TO YOU?
I KNOW YOU HAD A GOOD TIME AT THAT PARTY, BUT I THINK IT MIGHT BE BECAUSE YOU ARE EXCITED ABOUT EVERYTHING I DO FOR YOU AND NOT BECAUSE I PLANNED A GOOD PARTY.
WHAT DO YOU MEAN?

I INVITED ALL OF MY FRIENDS. THERE'S FLINT AND QUARTZ AND OPAL AND GRANITE AND OBSIDIAN AND—
THERE'S SO MANY! THIS IS THE GREATEST PARTY EVER!
—SANDSTONE AND DACITE AND BASALT AND PUMICE AND...
AND IT WAS THE GREATEST PARTY EVER! I WAS JUST TELLING RAINBOW DASH ABOUT PUMICE THE OTHER DAY!
BUT MARBLE ALREADY HAS REAL PONIES COMING TO HER PARTY. SHE NEEDS TO ENTERTAIN THEM. I AM MUCH BETTER WITH ROCKS.
I HAVE AN IDEA!
STREAMERS, PARTY HATS, BOARD GAMES, CUPS, PLATES...
OOH! SNACKS.
PINKIE?
SHHH! NOT WHILE I'M PARTY PLANNING.
OKAY, THIS IS A LIST OF EVERYTHING I'M GOING TO NEED TO THROW THE BESTEST BIRTHDAY PARTY IN THE WORLD...
...EXCEPT PARTY CANNONS. I'LL BRING THE PARTY CANNONS.
FOLD FOLD FOLD FOLD FOLD
MAUD WILL HEAD HOME WITH YOU TODAY AND HELP YOU GET EVERYTHING, THEN AS SOON AS I'M DONE WITH THE NEW CAKE, I'LL TAKE A TRAIN AND BE THERE TOMORROW AFTERNOON WITH PLENTY OF TIME TO HELP THROW THE PARTY.
IS THAT OKAY, MAUD?
I AM CAPABLE OF PURCHASING PARTY SUPPLIES, YES.
OH, THANK YOU, PINKIE! THANK YOU!

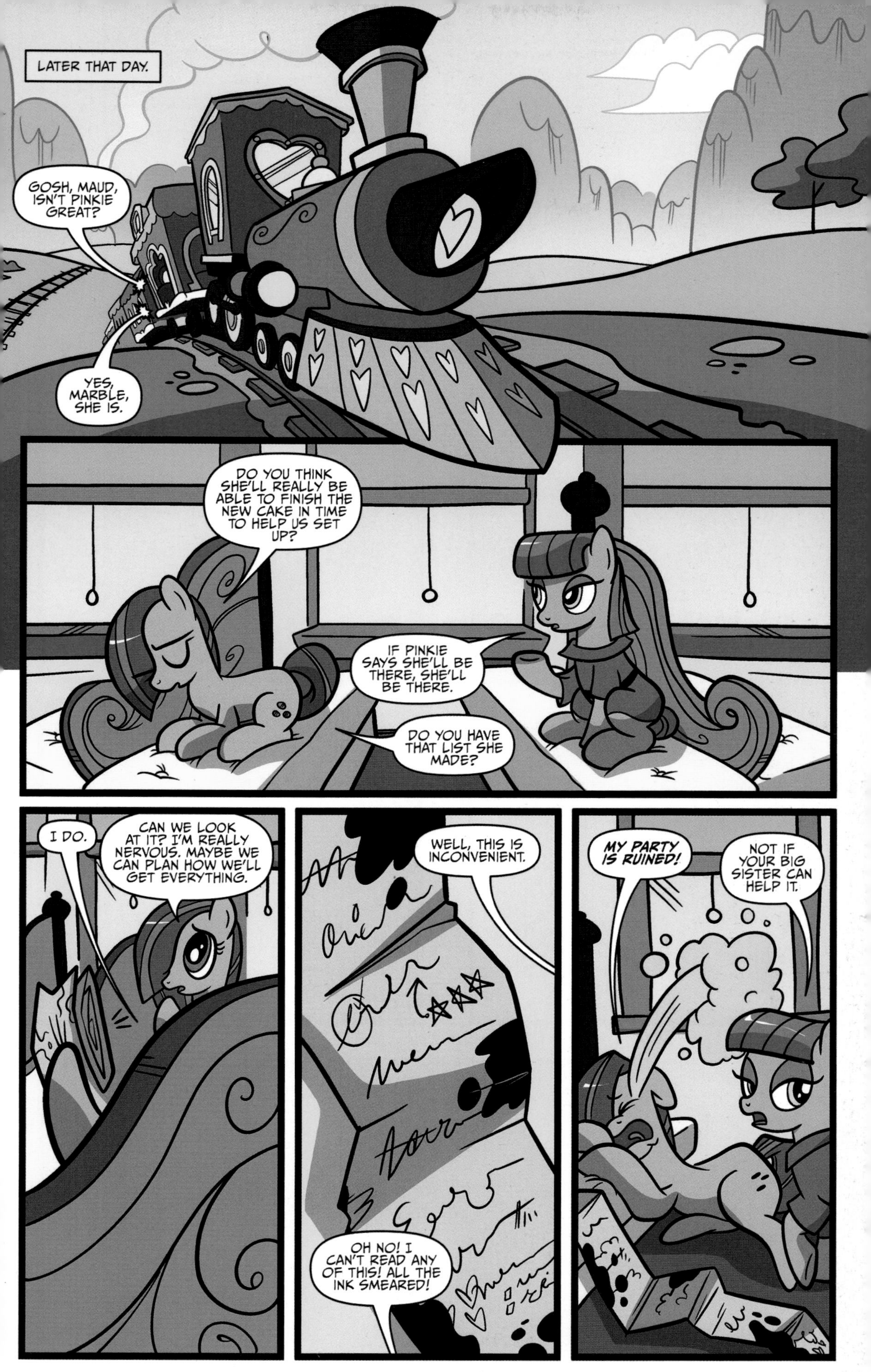

LATER THAT DAY.

GOSH, MAUD, ISN'T PINKIE GREAT?

YES, MARBLE, SHE IS.

DO YOU THINK SHE'LL REALLY BE ABLE TO FINISH THE NEW CAKE IN TIME TO HELP US SET UP?

IF PINKIE SAYS SHE'LL BE THERE, SHE'LL BE THERE.

DO YOU HAVE THAT LIST SHE MADE?

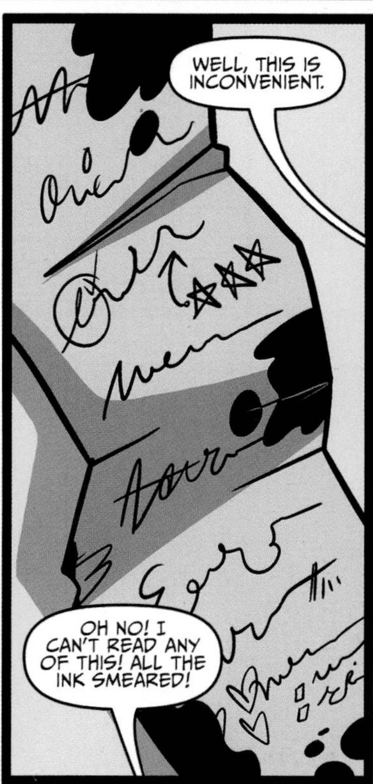

THAT NIGHT. THE PIE FAMILY ROCK FARM.
OKAY, BOULDER. THIS ISN'T SO DIFFERENT FROM GEOLOGY WHEN YOU THINK ABOUT IT.
DON'T SCOFF. I'M BEING SERIOUS.

THAT NIGHT. SUGARCUBE CORNER.
OKAY, GUMMY, IT TOOK ME A WEEK TO PUT TOGETHER THE FIRST CAKE.
NOW WE NEED TO REPLACE THE WHOLE THING OVERNIGHT.

CONSTRUCT AN ACTIONABLE HYPOTHESIS BASED ON PROVIDED EVIDENCE AND KNOWLEDGE OF THE SOURCE.

LET'S GET CULINARY.

scrape
scrape
scrape
scrape

THIS IS IT, BOULDER. WITH A CHALK RUBBING, WE'LL BE ABLE TO DISCOVER THE ORIGINAL IMPRINT OF PINKIE'S PEN.

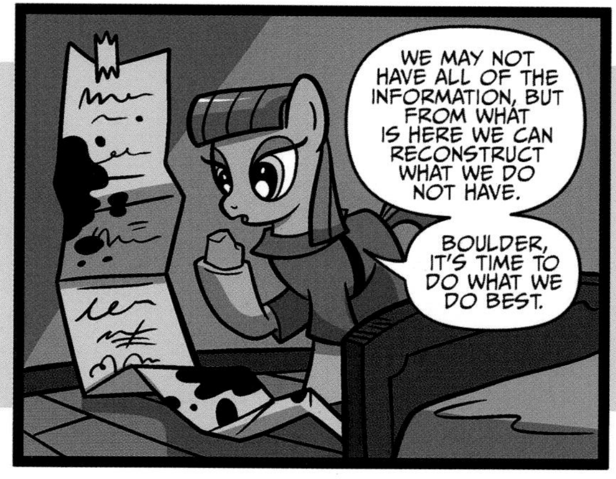
WE MAY NOT HAVE ALL OF THE INFORMATION, BUT FROM WHAT IS HERE WE CAN RECONSTRUCT WHAT WE DO NOT HAVE.
BOULDER, IT'S TIME TO DO WHAT WE DO BEST.

OBVIOUSLY, THE FIRST ONE DIDN'T WORK, SO WE HAVE TO COME UP WITH SOMETHING JUST AS AMAZING.
CRANKY AND MATILDA DESERVE A CAKE AND AN ANNIVERSARY THEY'LL NEVER FORGET!

IT SAYS "BALLOONS," BOULDER.
THESE ARE CERTAINLY TWO L'S AND TWO O'S.

MORE FLOUR! I NEED MORE FLOUR!

• BALLOONS
• PLATES

GUMMY! BRING ME THE DOWEL RODS!

THE NEXT MORNING.
YOU DID IT!
YES. IT TOOK ALL NIGHT, BUT I DID IT.
OH, THANK YOU, MAUD! I WAS SO WORRIED! NOW WE CAN GO SUPPLY SHOPPING BEFORE PINKIE GETS HERE.
ARE YOU COMING, MAUD?
shake
shake
shake
YES. YES, I'M COMING.
THE THINGS I DO FOR MY SISTERS.

OH, GOOD, PINKIE MUST HAVE LOCKED UP AFTER SHE FINISHED.
OH DEAR.
THAT IS A VERY LARGE CAKE.
Dear Cranky and Mathilda,
Sorry I couldn't stay for your anniversary party, but my sisters need my help. I hope you love the cake I made for you!
Your bestest friend,
Pinkamena Diane Pie
HOW DOES SHE EXPECT ME TO DELIVER THIS? IT WON'T EVEN FIT OUT THE DOOR.

I HOPE THEY HAVE EVERYTHING WE NEED.
I BELIEVE THAT PINKIE PROBABLY HAS THEIR INVENTORY MEMORIZED.
OH, HERE ARE THE BALLOONS!
IT DOESN'T SAY WHAT COLOR TO GET! MAUD, WHAT COLOR DO YOU THINK PINKIE MEANT?! I DON'T WANT TO GET THE WRONG ONES!
I'M SURE PINKIE WOULD...
MAUD?!
SORRY... I... I'M SURE PINKIE WOULD TELL YOU TO GET YOUR FAVORITE COLORS.
RIGHT!
wooble
wooble
wooble
OH! HERE'S THE NEXT THING!
THUMP
SOMEHOW, I DOUBT PINKIE IS THIS TIRED.

DID I TELL YOU I WAS PLANNING A PARTY FOR MY SISTER?
YES, MA'AM. YOU'VE MENTIONED IT THREE OR FOUR TIMES ALREADY.
NEWS
OH, SORRY! I WAS UP BAKING ALL NIGHT, AND I MAY HAVE SAMPLED SOME OF THE FROSTING, AND I'M FEELING VERY—
EXCITED—
FOR MY—
SISTER'S—
SCREEECH
WEEEE!
WHAT WAS THAT?!

SHE'S SUPPOSED TO BE HERE SOON! I CAN'T WAIT!
ZZZZZ
EXCUSE ME...
IF YOU ALL ARE WAITING ON THE PONYVILLE TRAIN, I'M AFRAID IT'S NOT COMING TODAY.
NOT COMING?! WHY?!
IT'S A ROCK SLIDE. AFRAID IT MIGHT BE DAYS BEFORE WE CAN GET THROUGH.
BUT I DON'T HAVE DAYS! MY SISTER'S PARTY IS TONIGHT!
WELL, I'D SAY YOU CAN WALK, BUT THAT'D TAKE TWO DAYS FROM HERE.
MAUD, PINKIE'S NOT COMING! WHAT DO WE DO?!
HMMM?
THAT'S WHAT YOU THINK, BUDDY, BUT MY SISTER NEEDS ME, AND I'VE EATEN A LOT OF SUGAR!
I'M COMING, MARBLE!

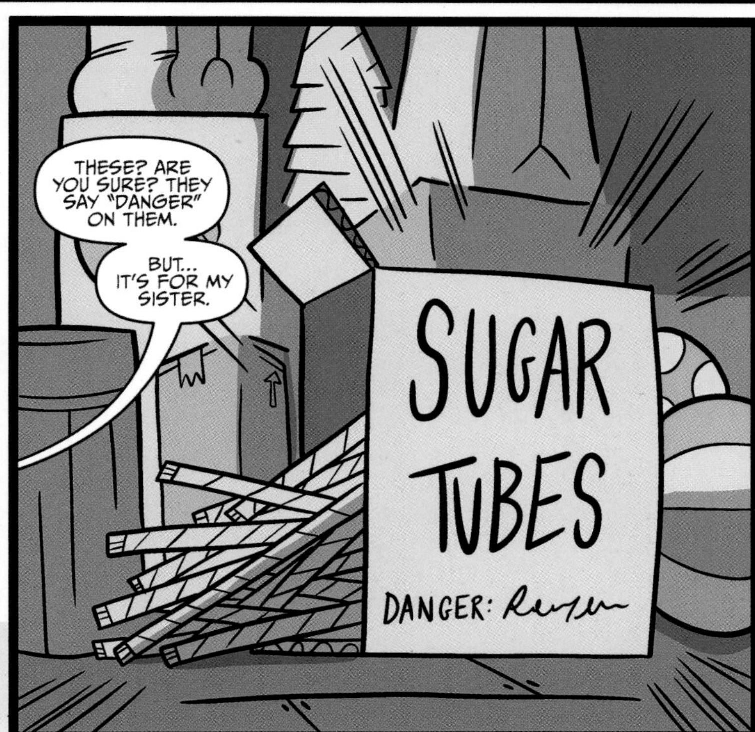

DANGER: PURE SUGAR CANDY

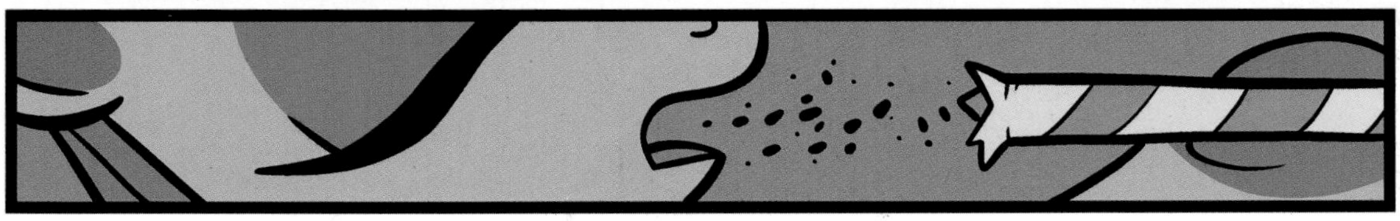

COME ON, MAUD. FIND YOUR INNER PARTY ANIMAL. DO IT FOR YOUR SISTERS.
BOINGY BOINGY BOINGY!
WAIT. THE SUGAR IS STARTING TO WORK! I...
LOOK OUT, BIRDY!
BEEP BEEP!
?!
I CAN SEE WHERE ALL OF IT GOES. I CAN SEE HOW IT ALL WORKS TOGETHER.
I FOUND MY INNER PARTY ANIMAL!
MARBLE, WE'RE GONNA SAVE THIS PARTY!
HAND ME THE STREAMERS AND LISTEN UP!

MARBLE, LIMESTONE, GET THOSE TABLES IN PLACE.
MA AND PA, THE DANCE FLOOR GOES THERE.
SUGAR... WEARING... OFF.
LOSING... ENERGY.
MORE BALLOONS! WE NEED MORE BALLOONS!
MAUD, WE DON'T HAVE THE PARTY CANNONS! PINKIE WAS SUPPOSED TO BE BRINGING THOSE!
I CAN STILL MAKE IT!
MY SISTERS NEED ME!
PARTY CANNONS ARE PINKIE'S THING.
BUT I'D NEVER THROW A PARTY WITHOUT INVITING SOME OF BOULDER'S FRIENDS.

LATER THAT NIGHT.
MAUD!
IS EVERYTHING GOING OKAY? IS SOMETHING WRONG?
EVERYTHING IS GREAT! IT'S SO AMAZING! I'VE ALREADY MADE TONS OF FRIENDS TONIGHT! HOW CAN I EVER THANK YOU?
YOU DON'T HAVE TO. YOU'RE MY—
—SISTER!
YOU'RE SO AMAZING! THANK YOU SO MUCH!
WELL, BOULDER, I GUESS WE DID IT. YOU WANNA GO WATCH FROM ABOVE, WHERE IT'S QUIET?
YOU'RE RIGHT. IT WAS A PRETTY NICE HUG. EVEN IF I DON'T USUALLY LIKE HUGS.

IT'S TOO BAD PINKIE MISSED THIS. SHE WOULD HAVE LIKED—
DID I MAKE IT? AM I IN TIME TO SAVE THE DAY?
PINKIE, I THOUGHT YOUR TRAIN WAS STUCK.
IT WAS, BUT I COULDN'T LET MY SISTERS DOWN. I HAD TO...
OOOOH!
WHAT ARE THOSE PRETTY LIGHTS?
THEY WERE BOULDER'S IDEA. WE SHONE SOME OF YOUR PARTY LIGHTS THROUGH REFRACTIVE CRYSTALS. IT WAS A WAY TO LIVEN UP THE PARTY.
WAIT...
YOU DID THIS, MAUD? YOU PUT THE WHOLE PARTY TOGETHER BY YOURSELF?
I WOULDN'T SAY THAT. I HAD TO ASK MYSELF, "WHAT WOULD PINKIE DO?"
THE SURPRISING THING WAS, I ALREADY KNEW THE ANSWER, BECAUSE I'VE KNOWN THE ANSWER FOR YEARS.
MY SISTER WOULD GO OUT OF HER COMFORT ZONE AND DO WHATEVER IT TOOK TO MAKE HER SISTER HAPPY. SO THAT'S WHAT I DID.

THAT'S EXACTLY WHAT I WOULD DO! I LOVE YOU, MAUD!
I LOVE YOU TOO, PINKIE.
SHOULD WE GO JOIN IN? I KNOW YOU DON'T LIKE PARTIES, BUT—
I CAN LIKE PARTIES FOR ONE NIGHT FOR MY SISTERS.
lean
BUT COULD WE REST HERE FOR JUST ONE MORE MOMENT? IT'S EXHAUSTING WORK BEING PINKIE PIE.
yawn
yawn
TELL ME ABOUT IT! YOU CAN'T IMAGINE THE DAY I'VE HAD.
WHY DON'T YOU TELL ME ABOUT IT WHILE WE REST...
WELL, FIRST THERE WAS A ROCKSLIDE AND THEN...
EIGHT HOURS LATER.
ZZZZZZZZ
The End!

art by Sara Richard

art by Tony Fleecs
20
5
AMH '19

SOMEWHERE DEEP IN THE DRAGON LANDS...
SNEAK
SNEAK
SNEAK
SNEAK
SNEAK
VWIP!
RUN
RUN
RUN

APPLEJACK! WAKE UP!
I NEED YOUR HELP!

MORNIN', RAINBOW DASH.
UP KINDA EARLY, AREN'T YOU?
NO TIME FOR CHIT-CHAT, AJ! I GOTTA GET TRAINING!

THE WONDERBOLTS GOT YOU TRAININ' IN THE OFF-SEASON NOW?
NOT THE WONDERBOLTS! THIS IS SO MUCH BIGGER!
I'M GONNA RUN IN THE DRAYTONA BREACH!

OH, MERCY.
THE DRAYTONA IS ONE OF THE BIGGEST RACES IN THE WORLD!
IT'S A COMPETITION NOT JUST OF SPEED—BUT ALSO OF ENDURANCE! STAMINA! AND GUTS!

IT'S A GRUELING TRACK THAT RUNS BETWEEN THE BORDER OF EQUESTRIA AND YAKYAKISTAN!
PERILOUS, MOUNTAINOUS TERRAIN! STEEP CLIFFS AND ROCKY TRAILS!
THE DRAYTONA IS A RACE FOR THE REAL COMPETITORS!

"IT ALL STARTED YEARS AGO, WHEN INTREPID PONIES WOULD CARRY CART-LOADS OF CIDER TO THE THIRSTY YAKS OF YAKYAKISTAN.
"THESE DARING DRIVERS WOULD HAUL THEIR PRECIOUS CARGO OVER THE TWISTY MOUNTAIN ROADS!

"EVENTUALLY, SOMEPONY GOT THE IDEA TO DO A RACE BETWEEN ALL THOSE AWESOME PONIES...
...AND THE DRAYTONA WAS BORN!"
7

OF COURSE, THESE DAYS, INSTEAD OF HAULING CIDER, THE RACERS JUST PULL WEIGHTED CARTS—
—BUT IT'S STILL THE SAME TREACHEROUS COURSE THROUGH THE MOUNTAINS IT'S ALWAYS BEEN!
OH, SURE, I KNOW ALL ABOUT IT.

WAIT— YOU KNOW ABOUT THE DRAYTONA?
WHY? DID YOU RUN IT?
NOPE! BUT SOMEPONY I KNOW REAL WELL WAS A RACER!

YOU RAN THE DRAYTONA BREACH?!

MY BEST FRIEND'S BROTHER RAN THE TOUGHEST RACE IN THE WORLD?!
TELL ME EVERYTHING! WHAT WAS IT LIKE? HOW'D YOU DO IT?

...
OKAY, FINE, YOU'RE NOT BIG ON TALKING, BIG MCINTOSH.

MAYBE YOU COULD MIME SOME ANSWERS FOR ME? ACT THEM OUT?
I JUST WANNA HEAR ABOUT THE RACE! ANY TIPS OR TRICKS?

PLEEEEEASE, BIG MAC!
I GOTTA RUN THIS RACE, AND YOU'RE THE ONLY CREATURE WHO KNOWS ANYTHING ABOUT IT!
ISN'T THERE ANYTHING YOU CAN DO FOR ME?

YEP.
91
VWIP!

GASP!
YOUR OLD TRAINING CART!
THANK YOU, MAC!

DRAYTONA 500
AW YEAH!
WOW, THAT'S A LOT OF CREATURES!
OH YES! RACE IS BIG EVENT ALL OVER!
YAKS LOVE RACE! PONIES LOVE RACE! EVEN GRIFFONS AND DONKEYS LOVE RACE!
ONLY DRAGONS NOT LIKE RACE, BECAUSE IT SO COLD UP IN MOUNTAINS.
YEAH, I KNOW THE FEELING!
THERE'S A FEW DRAGONS OVER THERE!
OH, YEAH... THEY'RE ALL BUNDLED UP.
I SHOULD ASK 'EM WHERE THEY GOT THEIR EAR MUFFS.
C'MON, LET'S FIND THE REGISTRATION DESK!
NOW THERE'S A FAMILIAR FACE!
HUH?
MCINTOSH! IS THAT YOU?

MY WORD, IT IS!
IT'S ME! YOUR OLD PAL SILVER STREAK!
I HAVEN'T SEEN YOU SINCE FARM SCHOOL!

WHY, YOU HAVEN'T CHANGED A BIT, MAC!
WHATEVER YOU'RE DOING ON THAT FARM HAS KEPT YOU IN TIP-TOP SHAPE, I MUST SAY!

YOU'RE A FRIEND OF BIG MAC'S?
HECK, I KNEW HIM BACK WHEN HE WAS CALLED LITTLE MAC!
WE WERE LIKE TWO PEAS IN A POD BACK IN FARM SCHOOL!

AND IF HE'S BACK NOW...
...MAYBE HE'S FINALLY READY TO FACE ME AGAIN.

• • •

BIG MAC?
HEY— WHERE'RE YOU GOING?

BIG MAC!
SNEAK SNEAK

BOSS?
HEY, MR. S! I'M BACK!
AS I'VE TOLD YOU, LUMPY...

CALL ME BY MY FULL NAME...
DOCTOR SACKS ROAMER!
FREELANCE ARCHAEOLOGIST AND ANTIQUITIES DEALER!

I THOUGHT YOU DIDN'T FINISH YOUR DOCTORATE?
JUST TELL ME WHAT YOU FOUND, LUMPY.

TH-THERE'S A BUNCH OF DRAGONS HANGING AROUND. I THINK THEY'RE HERE TO SEARCH THE RACERS.
THEY LOOK PRETTY ANGRY...
OF COURSE THEY'RE ANGRY!
I STOLE ONE OF THEIR OLDEST ARTIFACTS—

—THE MANGALESE DRAKE!
OOOOHH!

FRESHLY ACQUIRED FROM THE DRAGON LANDS, THIS PRETTY BAUBLE WILL FETCH A HIGH PRICE...
...IF I CAN GET IT ACROSS THE BORDER!

THE DRAGONS WON'T BE ABLE TO FOLLOW US INTO YAKYAKISTAN DUE TO THE COLD WEATHER!
I'LL MEET MY BUYER SAFELY ON THE OTHER SIDE OF THE MOUNTAINS!

AND THIS RACE WILL PROVIDE THE PERFECT SMUGGLING METHOD!
ALL I HAVE TO DO IS CONCEAL THE STATUE IN MY CART AND PULL IT TO YAKYAKISTAN!

THE DAY BEFORE THE RACE...
YOU'RE **STILL** TRAINING?
NOW'S THE **BEST TIME** TO TRAIN!
I CAN FINALLY RUN ON THE **ACTUAL TERRAIN** I'LL FACE IN THE RACE!
EEYUP.
OKAY, LET'S GIVE IT A **WHIRL!**
rattl rattl RATTL RATTL
HUH?
RATTL RATTL RATTL
RATTL RATTL
YOWP!
CRASH

RAINBOW DASH OKAY?
YEAH, I'M FINE!
I'M JUST NOT USED TO RUNNING ON ROCKS THIS HARD!

WHADDYA THINK, BIG MAC?
HMM.

TURN!

WHAT BIG MAC DOING?
HE'S GONNA DEMONSTRATE SOME ADVANCED RUNNING TECHNIQUES TO HELP RAINBOW DASH!

HOW SPIKE KNOW THIS? BIG MAC NOT SAY ANYTHING!
I'VE LEARNED HOW TO READ THE BIG GUY AFTER A WHILE.

LEAP!!!
NYOOOOM
HOP!
ZWIP!
SKIDDD!
clap
clap
clap
clap
clap
clap

CLAP
CLAP
CLAP
CLAP
CLAP
CLAP
BRAVO!
NOW *THAT'S* THE BIG MAC I *REMEMBER!*

THAT *SPEED!* THAT *STYLE!* JUST LIKE THE RACER I *USED* TO SEE!

WHY, REMEMBER, BIG MAC—WE USED TO RACE ALL THE *TIME!*
IT'S WHAT *BROUGHT US TOGETHER!*

I'VE NEVER HEARD BIG MAC TALK ABOUT YOU BEFORE.
I MEAN, HE DOESN'T TALK ABOUT MUCH OF *ANYTHING,* BUT STILL.
OH, WELL, I SUPPOSE THAT'S NOT TOO SURPRISING.

Y'SEE, THIS RACE IS *ALSO*...
...THE REASON WE *STOPPED* BEING FRIENDS.

WHY DON'T YOU SEE IF YOU CAN GET HIM TO TELL YOU WHAT *HAPPENED?*
THEN YOU'LL KNOW *JUST* WHAT KIND OF FELLER YOUR PAL BIG MAC *REALLY* IS.

ALRIGHT, MAC, START TALKIN'!
YEAH!

SOMEPONY WE'VE NEVER MET BEFORE JUST SHOWED UP AND TOLD US YOU'VE GOT SOME KIND OF PREVIOUSLY UNKNOWN BACKSTORY WITH HIM!
SEEMS TO HAPPEN A LOT AROUND HERE.

WHATEVER HAPPENED BETWEEN YOU AND SILVER STREAK—THIS IS YOUR CHANCE TO CONFRONT IT!
AND WE CAN HELP YOU!
FRIENDS HELP FRIENDS!

I KNOW YOU'RE NOT BIG ON TALKING, BUT...
...THERE'S GOTTA BE SOME WAY YOU CAN TELL US WHAT'S GOING ON!
MAYBE I CAN HELP!

HUH?
AFTER HANGING OUT WITH BIG MAC AND PLAYING OGRES & OUBLIETTES TOGETHER, I'VE LEARNED HOW TO UNDERSTAND HIS BODY LANGUAGE AND OTHER SUBTLE CLUES!
I CAN TELL YOU WHAT HE'S THINKING!

HOW ABOUT IT, BIG GUY?
LET ME HELP YOU TELL YOUR STORY!
nod!

"IT ALL STARTED BACK IN FARM SCHOOL...
"SILVER STREAK WAS ONE OF MY ONLY FRIENDS.
"HE LOVED RACING, AND HE WANTED ME TO TRY IT AS WELL.
"HE THOUGHT I'D BE A NATURAL AT LONG-DISTANCE RACING.
"AS IT TURNS OUT... I WAS.
"I WAS BETTER THAN HIM.
"MUCH BETTER.
1
"I DIDN'T REALIZE HOW MUCH I WAS HURTING HIM UNTIL IT WAS TOO LATE.
"WHEN I BEAT HIM IN THE DRAYTONA... HE SAID THAT WAS THE END OF OUR FRIENDSHIP.
"I LOST A FRIEND BECAUSE OF RACING.
"I SWORE I'D NEVER RACE AGAIN."
BIG MAC...
I'M SORRY, PAL.
I CAN'T BELIEVE YOU LOST A FRIEND OVER RACING!
SPIKE DO EXCELLENT IMPRESSION OF BIG MAC!
LOTS OF PRACTICE.
I GOTTA TALK TO SILVER STREAK!
"NO, WAIT!"

HEY!
SILVER STREAK!

MAC JUST TOLD ME YOU STOPPED BEING HIS FRIEND BECAUSE HE BEAT YOU AT RACING!
IS THAT TRUE?

HE STOPPED BEIN' MY FRIEND WHEN HE TOOK AWAY THE THING I LOVED MOST!
RACING'S THE THING I DO BEST! IT'S WHAT DRIVES ME!
AND THEN I LOST IT!

IT'S MAC'S FAULT, AND I WON'T FORGIVE HIM FOR THAT!
IT IS NOT HIS FAULT! HE ONLY RACED BECAUSE YOU WANTED HIM TO!
AND IF YOU COULDN'T HANDLE HIM BEING BETTER THAN YOU, THAT'S YOUR PROBLEM!

WELL, THEN, MAYBE WE OUGHTA SEE IF HE'S STILL BETTER THAN ME!
AND IF HE IS, THEN YOU GOTTA FACE UP TO WHAT YOU DID TO YOUR BEST FRIEND!

FINE!
GOOD!

SO... UH...
I MAY HAVE JUST SIGNED YOU UP FOR A MARATHON AGAINST YOUR FORMER BEST FRIEND?
SORRY ABOUT THAT.

BUT YOU TWO CLEARLY HAVE SOME ISSUES TO WORK OUT...
...AND IT SEEMS LIKE RACING IS AT THE HEART OF THEM!
THIS MIGHT BE YOUR BEST CHANCE TO MAKE UP WITH SILVER STREAK!

EE-
YUP.

AWRIGHT!
THAT'S THE SPIRIT!
HOORAY FOR RACING!

NOW LET'S GET YOU REGISTERED FOR THIS THING!
SNEAK
SNEAK
SNEAK

23
16
2
5
11
8
KEEP OUT
RACE CREWS ONLY
76
SNEAK, SNEAK..

NOW, **REMEMBER,** LUMPY—
FIND MY CART WITH **THAT NUMBER** AND SLIP THE STATUE INSIDE!
72
91
YEAH, YEAH...

AND STOP PICKING YOUR **EARS!** IT'S **DISGUSTING!**
PICK PICK

HMM...
91

91
91
AHA!

SCAMPER SCAMPER

THE DAY OF THE RACE!

FILLIES AND GENTLECOLTS! CREATURES OF ALL SIZES!

WELCOME TO THE DRAYTONA BREACH!

DRAYTONA

THE RACERS ARE LINING UP AT THE STARTING LINE...

GO, RAINBOW DASH! GO, BIG MCINTOSH!

WOOO!

91
IF THE STATUE IS IN CART NINETY-ONE, THEN—
THERE! I'LL HAVE TO SWITCH CARTS WITH HER DURING THE RACE!
16

A-ARE YOU SURE YOU CAN DO IT, DR. S? SHE LOOKS FAST!
I'LL HAVE TO! MY PAYDAY IS IN THAT CART!

YOU READY TO RACE FOR OUR FRIENDSHIP, BIG MAC?
ON YOUR MARKS...

...
GET SET...

GO!
AND THE RACE IS ON!
TWANG!

AND THIS YEAR'S DRAYTONA BREACH HAS BEGUN!
WE'VE GOT AN INCREDIBLE RACE TODAY, SPORTS FANS!
OUR COMPETITORS HAVE JUST STARTED THE GRUELING TREK TOWARD THE BORDER TO YAKYAKISTAN!
GO, BIG MAC!
GO, RAINBOW DASH!
LEADING THE PACK IS LAST YEAR'S CHAMPION, SILVER STREAK!
BUT CLOSE BEHIND IS THE WONDERBOLT WUNDERKIND, RAINBOW DASH—
—AS WELL AS A FACE WE HAVEN'T SEEN ON THE TRACK IN A LONG WHILE, FORMER RACING PHENOM BIG MCINTOSH!
YOU'RE GOIN' DOWN, GUYS!

ISN'T THIS GREAT, BIG MAC?
THE TWO OF US, RACING AGAIN! JUST LIKE THE OLD DAYS!

WE CAN FINALLY FINISH OUR RIVALRY FROM FARM SCHOOL!
RIGHT HERE, ON THE RACETRACK—
NYOOM!

CAN YOU RUN AS FAST AS YOU TALK, SILVER?
WHA—HEY!
I'M TRYIN' TO HAVE AN EMOTIONAL CONFRONTATION WITH MY OLD FRIEND HERE!

PANT PANT PANT
WHY ARE THE OTHER RACERS—
PANT PANT
—SO DARNED FAST?

I THINK YOU'RE CATCHIN' UP TO 'EM, BOSS!
QUIET, LUMPY!
IT'S YOUR FAULT I'M IN THIS PREDICAMENT!

AND THE PACK IS ENTERING **TOOTHROCK CANYON...**

IS TINY CREATURE **SUPPOSED** TO BE THERE?

MAYBE HE'S A **RACE OFFICIAL?**

STOMPITA STOMPITA STOMPITA

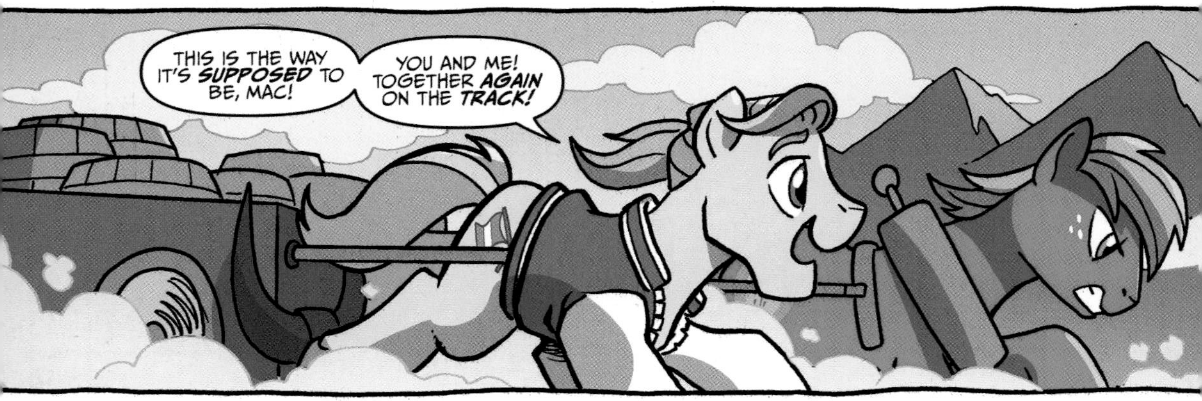

THIS IS THE WAY IT'S SUPPOSED TO BE, MAC!
YOU AND ME! TOGETHER AGAIN ON THE TRACK!

BACK IN FARM SCHOOL, I KNEW YOU'D BE A GREAT RACER!
I ALWAYS WANTED TO TEST MYSELF AGAINST YOU!

NOW I FINALLY GET THE CHANCE!
I CAN FINALLY PROVE I'M THE BETTER RACER!
SO WHAT?

RACING IS THE REASON YOU TWO STOPPED BEING FRIENDS!
YOU WANTED MAC TO RACE—BUT COULDN'T HANDLE IT WHEN HE WAS BETTER THAN YOU!

YOU LOST A FRIEND BECAUSE YOU CARED MORE ABOUT WINNING!

TH-THAT'S NOT TRUE!
I JUST WANTED BIG MAC TO BE HIS BEST!
HIS BEST? OR YOURS?
MAYBE BIG MAC DIDN'T WANT TO RACE! MAYBE HE JUST WANTED A FRIEND!
HE ONLY TRIED RACING BECAUSE OF YOU!
ASK YOURSELF WHAT'S MORE IMPORTANT—
RACING? OR YOUR FRIENDS?
CAN YOU TWO KEEP IT DOWN? WE'RE TRYING TO RACE HERE!
AND OUR RACERS ARE COMING UP ON HARE-PIN TURN—THE BANE OF MANY A COMPETITOR!
SILVER STREAK AND BIG MAC ARE PULLING AHEAD! THIS IS A RACE FOR THE AGES, FOLKS!
WHAT A RACE!
HEY, WHO ARE YOU GUYS ROOTING FOR?
WE'RE NOT HERE FOR THE RACE.

WHAT DRAGON MEAN?
WE'RE HERE ON THE TRAIL OF A STOLEN ARTIFACT—A GOLDEN STATUE CALLED THE MANGALESE DRAKE.
WE THINK THE THIEF IS ONE OF THE RACERS, AND MAY EVEN HAVE THE STATUE WITH THEM!
A GOLDEN STATUE? LIKE THE ONE IN RAINBOW DASH'S CART?

YOU FOUND THE DRAKE?!
YEAH! DASH ASKED ME TO CHECK HER CART BEFORE THE RACE, AND IT WAS IN BACK UNDER THE TARP!
AND YOU DIDN'T REPORT THIS?
I DIDN'T KNOW THERE WAS ANYTHING WEIRD ABOUT IT!
I THOUGHT ALL THE CARTS HAD GOLDEN STATUES IN THEM!
BUT WHY WOULD STATUE BE IN DASH'S CART? DASH IS NO THIEF!

WE'LL HAVE TO FIGURE IT OUT LATER!
RIGHT NOW WE NEED TO STOP THEM!
SIR! WE NEED TO SHUT DOWN THE RACE!

WHAT THE—ARE YOU NUTS?
THEY'RE RUNNING OVER DANGEROUS TERRAIN! IF WE TRY TO STOP THE RACE, IT COULD BE CHAOS!
PLUS, THE SPONSORS WOULD BE FURIOUS!
WE CAN'T AFFORD TO WAIT!

ACROSS THE FINISH LINE IS YAKYAKISTAN—IT'LL BE TOO COLD FOR US TO CHASE THE THIEF!
SO WHAT CAN WE DO?
EXCUSE ME—CAN YONA BORROW?
AH HA!
SMALL FUNNY CREATURE IS HEADING FOR RAINBOW DASH!
SAY WHAT?

I SEE HIM! HE'S NOT A RACER—HE'S CHASING DASH!
HE MUST BE THE THIEF!

WE'VE GOT TO GET HIM AWAY FROM DASH!
BE CAREFUL!
WE'LL COME WITH YOU!

EMERGENCY PARACHUTE
CAUTION

RAINBOW DASH IS FALLING BEHIND—A POOR SHOWING FOR THE SPRINTING SPEEDSTER!
RMBL RMBL RMBL

DANG! I'M BEHIND THE MAIN PACK!
GOTTA POUR ON THE JUICE!

DASH!
WAUGH!
YOU'VE GOT TO STOP!

A STATUE GOT STOLEN FROM THE DRAGONS, AND SOMEHOW IT GOT INTO YOUR CART, AND WE NEED TO GET IT BEFORE YOU CROSS THE BORDER OR ELSE—
WHOA, WHOA—YOU'RE NOT MAKING ANY SENSE, SPIKE!
91

JUST PULL OVER! DON'T FINISH THE RACE!
NO CAN DO, LI'L BUDDY! RAINBOW DASH STOPS FOR NO CREATURE!

TELL ME AFTER THE FINISH LINE!
BUT THAT'LL BE TOO LATE—!

RRGH!
STUPID TINY WINGS!

NYOOM

HEY! YOU!
HRGCK!

YOU'RE THE FUNNY GUY! I MEAN, THE THIEF!
WHO, ME? I'M NOBODY! I'M NO THIEF!
I JUST WORK FOR THE THIEF!
WAIT, THAT'S THE WRONG THING TO SAY.

OKAY, OKAY!
HIS NAME IS DOCTOR SACKS ROAMER!
HE'S A, YOU KNOW, ANTIQUITIES DEALER!
YOU MEAN HE STEALS ARTIFACTS AND SELLS THEM?
YEAH, THAT'S THE TICKET.
WHERE IS HE? WHAT'S HE LOOK LIKE?
HE LOOKS LIKE, UH—
—AN ESCAPE ROUTE!
HEY!
PHOOEY TO THIS THIEVING STUFF!
I'M GOIN' TO JOIN THE CIRCUS!
SO LONG, SUCKERS!
Wee Hee Hee Hee!
HENCHMEN ARE SO WEIRD.

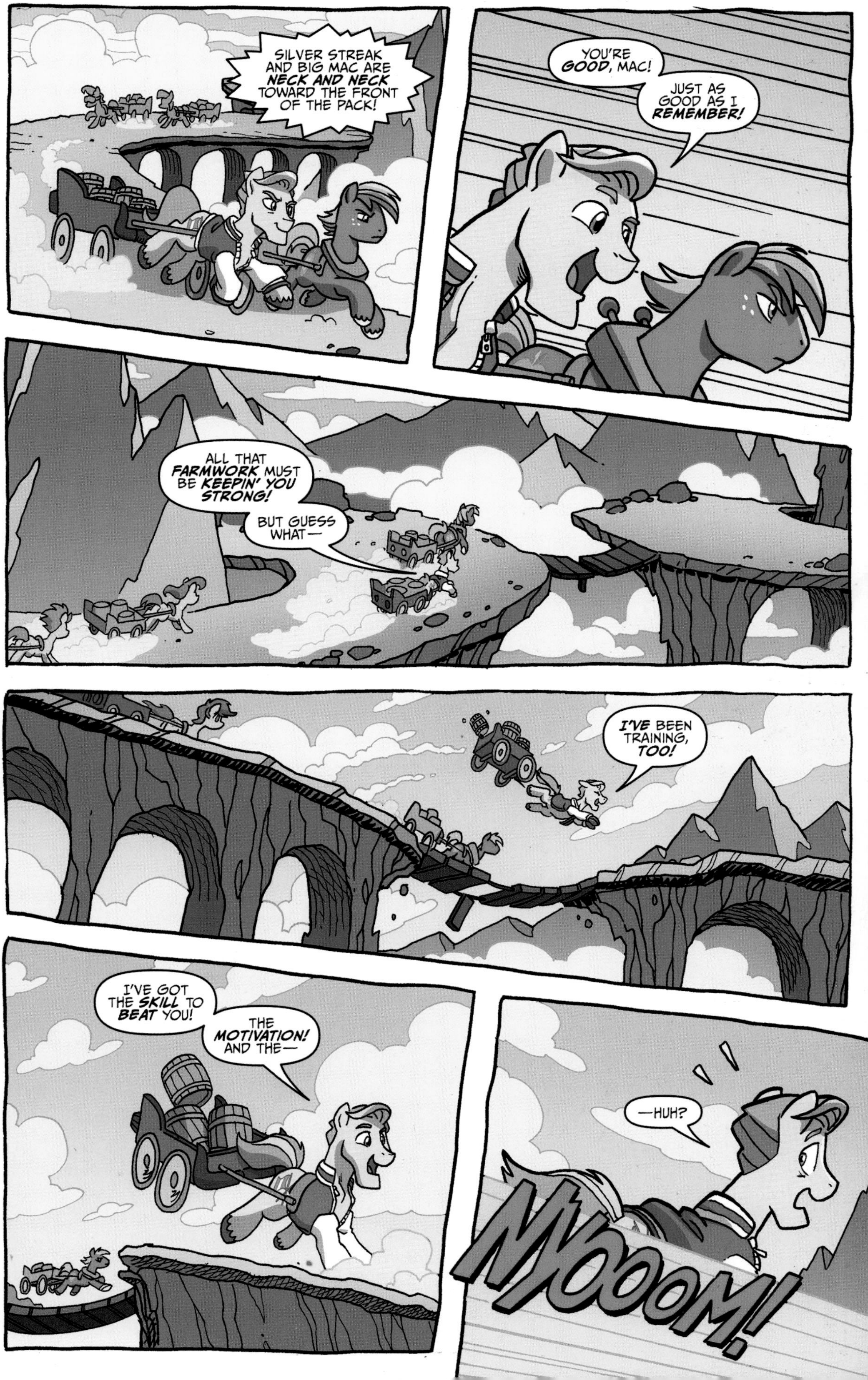

SILVER STREAK AND BIG MAC ARE **NECK AND NECK** TOWARD THE FRONT OF THE PACK!

YOU'RE ***GOOD***, MAC!

JUST AS GOOD AS I ***REMEMBER!***

ALL THAT ***FARMWORK*** MUST BE ***KEEPIN' YOU STRONG!***

BUT GUESS WHAT—

I'VE BEEN TRAINING, ***TOO!***

I'VE GOT THE ***SKILL*** TO ***BEAT*** YOU!

THE ***MOTIVATION!*** AND THE—

—HUH?

NYOOOM!

HA! GOT MY SECOND WIND!
DASH, YOU'RE MAKIN' THIS EMOTIONAL CATHARSIS AWFUL HARD TO ACHIEVE!
RRGH! IT DOESN'T MATTER!
ALL THAT MATTERS IS YOU AND ME, MAC!
THIS IS A BATTLE BETWEEN OLD FRIENDS! IT'LL DECIDE EVERYTHING!
I DON'T CARE ABOUT ANYPONY ELSE!
Pant PANT Pant PANT
OH, COME ON!
16

OH MY! A LARGE, SWEATY BLUR IS ZOOMING UP THE TRACK!
PANT PANT
ALMOST— THERE—
FINISH
FINISH
I CAN SEE THE FINISH LINE! I'M ALMOST THERE!
MINE!
WHAT TH—
KTONK!
WHOA! HEY!
WE'RE GONNA—

WHUMP!!!
OH NO! THERE'S BEEN A CRASH ON THE TRACK!
LEAP
FINISH
CLEAR TH' TRACK, SLOWPOKE!
S-S-S-SURE!
I'M AHEAD! I'M AHEAD!
THE RACE IS MINE!
THUMPITA
AND THE WINNER OF THIS YEAR'S DRAYTONA BREACH IS—
THUMPITA
THUMPITA

SILVER STREAK!
I WIN!
YOU SEE THAT, MAC?
I'M—

WHAT THE HAY WAS THAT?!
I GOT KNOCKED OVER BY—

HEY! YOU!
YOU HIJACKED MY CART!

PANT— DANGEROUS THIEF—
GASP STOLEN STATUE IN—PANT—DASH'S CART—
—CATCH HIM—
WHAT?

YEEP!

FINISH

RMBL
RMBL
RMBL

JUST— NEED—TO GET— ACROSS—THE FINISH—
I CAN MAKE IT—

FINISH
I'M GOING TO ***MAKE IT!***
I'LL VANISH INTO THE CROWD AND ESCAPE WITH THE ***LOOT!***
I'M GOING TO—

FINI
YONA ***WINS!***
WHOMP

S-S-SACKS ROAMER, YOU'RE UNDER ARREST FOR M-M-**MULTIPLE** COUNTS OF ANTIQUITIES TH-TH-**THEFT!**
NUTS!
HOORAY! DRAGONS GOT **STATUE** BACK!
N-N-NOW WE CAN HEAD **HOME** AND GET W-W-**WARM!**
YOU S-S-**SAID** IT.

FINISH
RAINBOW DASH OKAY?
YEAH, I JUST GOT THE **WIND** KNOCKED OUTTA ME.
I'VE TAKEN WORSE HITS IN WONDERBOLTS PRACTICE.

I'M JUST SORRY YOU DIDN'T GET TO FINISH YOUR **RACE,** BIG MAC.
MAYBE IT WOULD'VE HELPED CLEAR THINGS UP WITH SILVER STREAK...
WELL, MAYBE IT'S NOT TOO **LATE.**

FINISH
BIG MAC, I...
WHEN I CROSSED THAT FINISH LINE, I LOOKED BACK, AND...

I SAW YOU BACK THERE, HELPING YOUR **FRIEND...**
...AND I REALIZED I DON'T KNOW **ANYPONY** WHO'D DO THAT FOR **ME.**

I GOT SO OBSESSED WITH **RACING** THAT, WELL...
...I NEVER BOTHERED TO MAKE ANY **FRIENDS.**

I SPENT SO MUCH TIME CHASING **GLORY,** I MISSED WHAT I **ALREADY HAD.**
I'M **SORRY,** BIG MAC.
CAN YOU EVER FORGIVE ME?

AYUP.

I'LL WRITE TO YOU IN PONYVILLE, **OLD FRIEND!**
WE'VE GOT A **LOT** TO **CATCH UP** ON!

WELL, THAT WAS ONE OF THE *WEIRDER* RACES I'VE EVER SEEN—
—BUT AT LEAST BIG MAC GOT HIS OLD FRIEND BACK!
EE-YUP.
FINISH
WAITAMINUTE! THE *RACE!*
THAT MIGHT BE THE FIRST RACE I'VE EVER *RUN* BUT DIDN'T *FINISH!*
IS THAT *TRUE?*
WITH THE SHENANIGANS *WE* GET INTO, WHO CAN TELL?
NO, SERIOUSLY! THIS IS *MAJOR!*
IT'S THE *END* OF AN *ERA!*
EH, THERE'S ALWAYS *NEXT SEASON.*
THE END!

art by Sara Richard

art by Tony Fleecs

art by **Sara Richard**

art by Lanna Souvanny

art by Christina-Antoinette Neofotistou

art by Beth Hughes

art by Muffy Levy

art by Yancey Labat

art by Tony Fleecs

FALLEN ANGELS

WRITER
JO DUFFY

PENCILERS
KERRY GAMMILL,
MARIE SEVERIN
& JOE STATON

INKERS
TOM PALMER,
VAL MAYERIK
& TONY DEZUNIGA

COLORIST
PETRA SCOTESE

LETTERERS
JIM NOVAK,
BILL OAKLEY
& L.P. GREGORY

EDITOR
ANN NOCENTI

FRONT COVER ART
KERRY GAMMILL

FRONT COVER COLORS
THOMAS MASON

BACK COVER ART
MIKE MIGNOLA & AL WILLIAMSON

BACK COVER COLORS
TOM SMITH

Collection Editor
John Barber

Assistant Editors
Nelson Ribeiro
& Alex Starbuck

Editors, Special Projects
Mark D. Beazley
& Jennifer Grünwald

Senior Editor, Special Projects
Jeff Youngquist

Color Reconstruction & Production
ColorTek

Research
Jeph York

SVP of Print & Digital Publishing Sales
David Gabriel

Editor in Chief
Axel Alonso

Chief Creative Officer
Joe Quesada

Publisher
Dan Buckley

Executive Producer
Alan Fine

FALLEN ANGELS

X-MEN: FALLEN ANGELS. Contains material originally published in magazine form as FALLEN ANGELS #1-8. First printing 2013. ISBN# 978-0-7851-8453-9. Published by MARVEL WORLDWIDE, INC., a subsidiary of MARVEL ENTERTAINMENT, LLC. OFFICE OF PUBLICATION: 135 West 50th Street, New York, NY 10020. **Printed in the U.S.A.** ALAN FINE, EVP - Office of the President, Marvel Worldwide, Inc. and EVP & CMO Marvel Characters B.V.; DAN BUCKLEY, Publisher & President - Print, Animation & Digital Divisions; JOE QUESADA, Chief Creative Officer; TOM BREVOORT, SVP of Publishing; DAVID BOGART, SVP of Operations & Procurement, Publishing; C.B. CEBULSKI, SVP of Creator & Content Development; DAVID GABRIEL, SVP of Print & Digital Publishing Sales; JIM O'KEEFE, VP of Operations & Logistics; DAN CARR, Executive Director of Publishing Technology; SUSAN CRESPI, Editorial Operations Manager; ALEX MORALES, Publishing Operations Manager; STAN LEE, Chairman Emeritus. For information regarding advertising in Marvel Comics or on Marvel.com, please contact Niza Disla, Director of Marvel Partnerships, at ndisla@marvel.com. For Marvel subscription inquiries, please call 800-217-9158. **Manufactured between 6/7/2013 and 7/15/2013 by R.R. DONNELLEY, INC., SALEM, VA, USA.**

10 9 8 7 6 5 4 3 2 1

MARVEL
© 1987 MARVEL COMICS GROUP
75¢ US
95¢ CAN
1 APR
02409
APPROVED BY THE COMICS CODE AUTHORITY
#1 IN AN EIGHT-ISSUE LIMITED SERIES
FALLEN ANGELS
ONE MOMENT OF ANGER...
AND THEIR LIVES ARE CHANGED FOREVER!

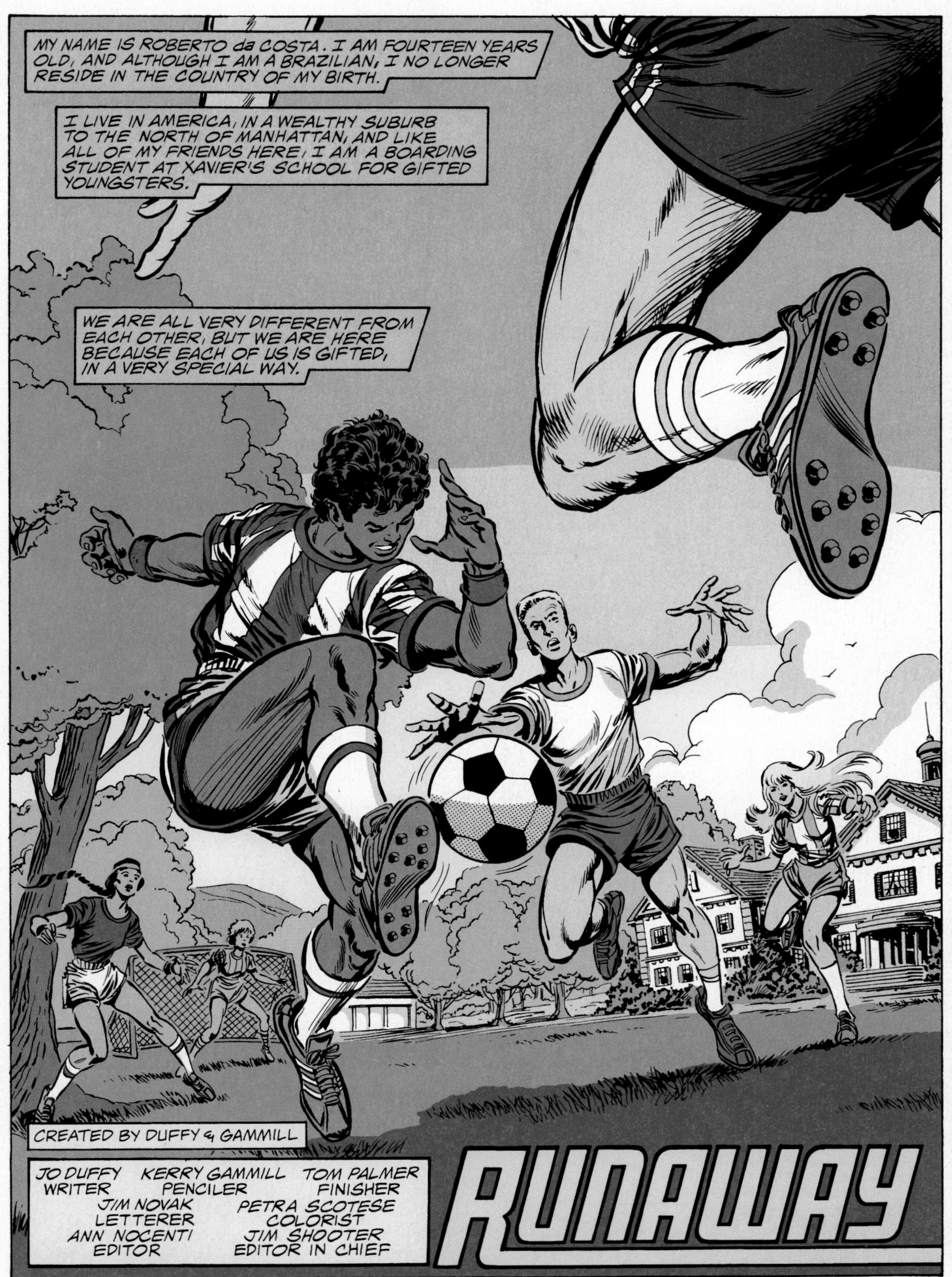
MY NAME IS ROBERTO da COSTA. I AM FOURTEEN YEARS OLD, AND ALTHOUGH I AM A BRAZILIAN, I NO LONGER RESIDE IN THE COUNTRY OF MY BIRTH.
I LIVE IN AMERICA, IN A WEALTHY SUBURB TO THE NORTH OF MANHATTAN, AND LIKE ALL OF MY FRIENDS HERE, I AM A BOARDING STUDENT AT XAVIER'S SCHOOL FOR GIFTED YOUNGSTERS.
WE ARE ALL VERY DIFFERENT FROM EACH OTHER, BUT WE ARE HERE BECAUSE EACH OF US IS GIFTED, IN A VERY SPECIAL WAY.
CREATED BY DUFFY & GAMMILL
JO DUFFY WRITER
KERRY GAMMILL PENCILER
TOM PALMER FINISHER
JIM NOVAK LETTERER
PETRA SCOTESE COLORIST
ANN NOCENTI EDITOR
JIM SHOOTER EDITOR IN CHIEF
RUNAWAY

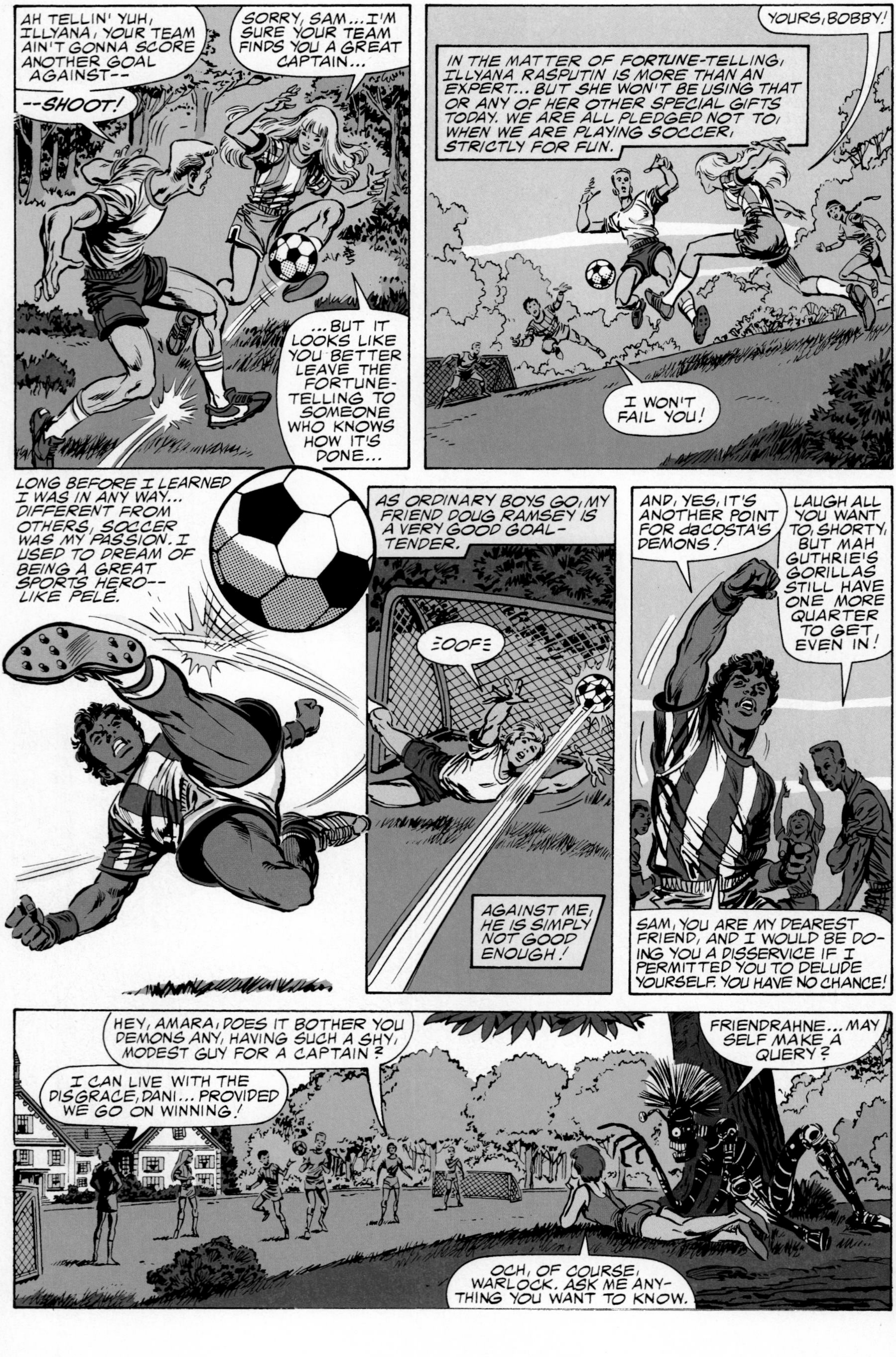

AH TELLIN' YUH, ILLYANA, YOUR TEAM AIN'T GONNA SCORE ANOTHER GOAL AGAINST--

SORRY, SAM... I'M SURE YOUR TEAM FINDS YOU A GREAT CAPTAIN...

--SHOOT!

...BUT IT LOOKS LIKE YOU BETTER LEAVE THE FORTUNE-TELLING TO SOMEONE WHO KNOWS HOW IT'S DONE...

YOURS, BOBBY!

IN THE MATTER OF FORTUNE-TELLING, ILLYANA RASPUTIN IS MORE THAN AN EXPERT... BUT SHE WON'T BE USING THAT OR ANY OF HER OTHER SPECIAL GIFTS TODAY. WE ARE ALL PLEDGED NOT TO, WHEN WE ARE PLAYING SOCCER, STRICTLY FOR FUN.

I WON'T FAIL YOU!

LONG BEFORE I LEARNED I WAS IN ANY WAY... DIFFERENT FROM OTHERS, SOCCER WAS MY PASSION. I USED TO DREAM OF BEING A GREAT SPORTS HERO--LIKE PELE.

AS ORDINARY BOYS GO, MY FRIEND DOUG RAMSEY IS A VERY GOOD GOAL-TENDER.

OOF

AGAINST ME, HE IS SIMPLY NOT GOOD ENOUGH!

AND, YES, IT'S ANOTHER POINT FOR daCOSTA'S DEMONS!

LAUGH ALL YOU WANT TO, SHORTY, BUT MAH GUTHRIE'S GORILLAS STILL HAVE ONE MORE QUARTER TO GET EVEN IN!

SAM, YOU ARE MY DEAREST FRIEND, AND I WOULD BE DOING YOU A DISSERVICE IF I PERMITTED YOU TO DELUDE YOURSELF. YOU HAVE NO CHANCE!

"GIFTED" IS A EUPHEMISM FOR WHAT WE REALLY ARE. MY FRIENDS AND I ARE KNOWN AS THE NEW MUTANTS--

EVEN WARLOCK, WHO CAME FROM ANOTHER PLANET AND ISN'T EVEN HUMAN IS A MUTANT OF SORTS. AMONG A RACE BORN ALWAYS TO BE SAVAGE, KILL OR BE KILLED, HE ALONE WAS BORN WITH THE CAPACITY TO CARE ABOUT OTHERS...
QUERY: PUFFPLANTS ARE NOT SENTIENT BEINGS?
THE DANDELIONS? NO, THEY HAVE NO HEARTS OR MINDS, IF THAT'S WHAT YOU MEAN.
IS IT ACCEPTABLE TO CONSUME LIFEGLOW?

--EACH OF US MARKED BY SOME GENETIC ANOMOLY WHICH GIVES US EXTRA TALENTS OR ABILITIES AND SEPARATES US FROM THE REST OF THE HUMAN RACE.
WHY DOES FRIENDRAHNE NOT PARTICIPATE IN GAME WITH OTHERFRIENDS?
WHEN I'M NOT IN MY WOLF FORM, I'VE NO TURN FOR SPORTING PASTIMES ...AND THIS WAY THE SIDES STAY EVEN.
BESIDES, IT'S SO LOVELY AND PEACE-FUL HERE WITH YOU.

YOU MEAN, CAN YOU EAT ONE? I DINNA SEE WHY NOT? FOR ALL THEY'RE PRETTY, AND FUN TO BLOW AROUND, THEY CAN BECOME DREADFUL NUISANCES, IF THEY GROW UNCHECKED.

EVEN IF WARLOCK WEREN'T A MUTANT AMONG HIS OWN KIND, THOUGH, HIS NATIVE ABILITIES WOULD COUNT AS POWERFUL GIFTS. FOR NOT ONLY CAN HE ALTER THE ORGANIC CIRCUITRY OF HIS BODY INTO ALMOST ANY FORM...

BUT, WHEN HE WISHES TO "EAT", HE FIRST INFECTS HIS FOOD WITH A VIRUS THAT CONVERTS IT INTO THE SAME KIND OF CIRCUITRY, AND THEN CONSUMES ITS ENERGY, LEAVING A HUSK BEHIND.

PROFESSOR CHARLES XAVIER, WHO COULD READ MINDS AND WHO BROUGHT US ALL TOGETHER, ISN'T IN CHARGE OF OUR SCHOOL ANY MORE... HE HAD TO LEAVE, AND WHEN HE WENT, LEFT US IN THE CHARGE OF A SURPRISING SUBSTITUTE--
--A MAN WHO WAS BAPTIZED MAGNUS, AND WHO CURRENTLY CALLS HIMSELF MICHAEL XAVIER, BUT WHO MOST OF THE WORLD KNOWS AS MAGNETO, MASTER OF MAGNETISM.
IT IS VERY STRANGE TO BE HIS STUDENT, AND TO SEE HOW HARD HE TRIES TO LIVE UP TO PROFESSOR XAVIER'S DREAM OF BETTERING THE PLACE OF MUTANTS IN THE WORLD OF ORDINARY HUMANS.
BECAUSE MAGNETO'S GREATEST ENEMIES WERE THE X-MEN-- THE ORIGINAL STUDENTS AT THIS SCHOOL...
...BACK WHEN HE WAS A VILLAIN, AND LED THE BLOB, THE TOAD, AND THE VANISHER, ALL EVIL MUTANTS WHO WANTED TO CONQUER AND SUPPLANT HUMANITY.
NOW I HAVE A BETTER AMBITION THAN TO BE A SOCCER STAR. ONE DAY I WANT TO BE AS GREAT A HERO AS THE X-MEN...OR CAPTAIN AMERICA... OR THOR... OR EVEN MAGNUM, P.I.
FOR A daCOSTA, NOTHING IS IMPOSSIBLE!
IMPOSSIBLE... CHARLES, IT IS SIMPLY IMPOSSIBLE...
I TRY MY BEST TO TEACH YOUR STUDENTS AS YOU WOULD HAVE WISHED AND TO RUN YOUR SCHOOL... BUT I HAVE NO HAND FOR ADMINISTRATION.
THERE IS, HOWEVER, IN SCOTLAND, A WOMAN WITH A GREAT GIFT FOR IT, AND FOR DEALING WITH YOUNG MUTANTS AS WELL.
I SHALL PLACE A CALL TO MUIR ISLE AND TRUST THAT, OUT OF HER FEELINGS OF KINDNESS FOR YOU, DR. MOIRA MACTAGGART WILL AGREE TO COME AND HELP ME.

REEEEEEEEEEEEEEEEE
SIRYN IS DOIN' WONDERFULLY WELL, JAMIE, IS SHE NOT? SHE'S BEEN HOLDIN' HERSELF ALOFT ON THE STRENGTH OF THAT ONE NOTE FOR FIVE MINUTES NOW...
...WITH NO SIGNS OF STRAIN.

IT'S HARD FOR ME TO JUDGE, MOIRA, BUT IF YOU SAY SO--!
WAIT, THERE'S THE PHONE LIGHT BLINKIN', AN' I NEVER EVEN HEARD IT RING. GO ASK THE LASS TO QUIET DOWN, OR I'LL NEVER BE ABLE TO TAKE THIS CALL.

SIRYN? HEY, SIRYN!
NUTS, SHE CAN'T HEAR ME OVER HER OWN RACKET.
THIS CALLS FOR A DOSE OF MY OWN POWER.

HEY, SIRYN!!!
WHO IN--?

OH, IT'S YOU IS IT, JAMIE MADROX? NOW THAT YOU HAVE MY ATTENTION, WHAT WOULD THE LOT OF YOU BE WANTIN'?
A LITTLE QUIET...MOIRA'S ON THE PHONE!

THERE NOW. THAT'S BETTER.
THIS IS DR. MACTAGGART. WHO IS THIS, PLEASE?

IT IS I, DOCTOR--
MAGNETO... I'M CALLING TO ASK OF YOU A FAVOR.
IF THERE'S SOMETHING I CAN DO TO HELP YOU WITH CHARLES' SCHOOL, OR HIS STUDENTS, YOU HAVE ONLY TO ASK.
IT'S GOOD OF YOU TO SAY THAT... YOU SEE A MARKING PERIOD IS UPON US... AND HAVING AGREED TO TAKE CHARGE OF THE PLACE, I MEAN TO DO SO WHOLLY...

BUT I HAVE LITTLE TASTE FOR FORMAL ACADEMICS, AND A MOST INCOMPLETE UNDERSTANDING OF THE CRITERIA USED BY CHARLES IN DRAWING UP WHAT HE TERMED "REPORT CARDS."

MOREOVER... MOST OF THE NEW MUTANTS HAVE UNDERGONE SOME SHATTERING EMOTIONAL EXPERIENCES LATELY... THEY SEEM WELL ENOUGH, BUT I KNOW THERE IS DEEP TRAUMA...

SO, IF YOU WOULD, HOWEVER BRIEFLY, CONSENT...

READY OR NOT, BOBBY, HERE AH COME, AND AH'M GONNA POP THIS LITTLE BEAUTY RIGHT INTO THE GOAL BEHIND YOU!
YOU ARE WELCOME TO TRY, MY FRIEND.

THEN LOOK OUT!

HAH! AN EASY--
WHOOAA!
--UGKH
OOMPH
GET--
--OFF!!!
MY NAME IS ROBERTO daCOSTA. I AM FOURTEEN YEARS OLD, AND MY BODY IS A LIVING SOLAR POWER CELL.

ALARMCONFUSIONDISMAY CONFUSIONALARMEXPLANATION? EXPLANATION?
SAM...

ALMOST FROM THE DAY THE NEW MUTANTS WERE FORMED, SAM GUTHRIE HAS BEEN MY DEAREST FRIEND. HOLY MADONNA, WHAT HAVE I DONE?
HE'S NOT MOVING!
IS HE EVEN BREATHING?
IT LOOKS LIKE HE'S BADLY HURT...

IS SAM ALL RIGHT? IS HE BREATHING?
HOW BADLY DID I HURT HIM?
PLEASE, DANI, SOMEBODY... FOR THE LOVE OF HEAVEN, ANSWER ME!!

IF YOU WANT TO KNOW IF YOU KILLED HIM, BOBBY, THEN THE ANSWER IS NO...
WE HOPE THAT DOESN'T DISAPPOINT YOU.

I...
I THOUGHT YOU WERE MY FRIENDS!! HOW CAN YOU TALK LIKE SUCH IDIOTS?!

ARE WE SUCH IDIOTS? WE ALL JUST SAW WHAT YOU DID TO SAM, BOBBY. IF THAT'S HOW YOU TREAT YOUR FRIENDS, THEN NO ONE HERE WANTS ANY PART OF IT.
BUT I-I DIDN'T MEAN TO. WHEN HE HURT ME LIKE THAT... I PANICKED...
I LOST MY HEAD...

YOU LOST YOUR TEMPER.
WE DON'T WANT TO HEAR YOUR EXCUSES, BOBBY. MAYBE SAM'S MOTHER AND LITTLE BROTHERS WILL... IF IT COMES TO THAT.

YOU CANNA MEAN... A FUNERAL?
IS FRIENDSAM'S LIFEGLOW FADING?
PLEASE, FRIEND-DANI, EXPLAIN!!

GET BOBBY TO EXPLAIN IT TO YOU, WARLOCK. HE'S THE ONE WHO DID IT.

THEY WON'T LET ME NEAR SAM, NOT EVEN TO SEE IF HE'S ALL RIGHT AND HELP HIM IF I CAN. THEY DO NOT TRUST ME TO...

MY FRIENDS... NO LONGER WANT ME AMONG THEM.

THEY ARE...

...RIGHT.

ATTENTION! ALERT! FRIENDSHAN AND MAGNETO ENTITY ARE APPROACHING!
SURELY MAGNETO'LL KNOW WHAT'S TO BE DONE!
WHAT HAPPENED HERE?

IT WAS BOBBY, SIR. HE USED HIS SUN-SPOT POWER TO HURL SAM HEAD-LONG INTO A TREE!
WHAT IS CURRENT STATUS OF FRIENDSAM'S LIFEGLOW?!
HE'S MOVING, WARLOCK! THAT'S A GOOD SIGN!

BOBBY, ARE YOU OKAY? DID WE GET THE GOAL?

WHAT A RELIEF!
JUBILATION! JUBILATION!
TAKE IT EASY, SAM. YOU'VE HAD A NASTY SHOCK.

I'LL USE THE LIMOUSINE TO DRIVE YOU INTO SALEM CENTER, SO THAT A DOCTOR MAY X-RAY YOU...
AND, I SUSPECT, WHEN I COME HOME, I SHALL FACE AN EQUALLY GRAVE, ALBEIT LESS LIFE-THREATENING PROBLEM.

WHAT I HAVE DONE... WAS NOT THE ACT OF A HERO...
I HAVE NEVER HEARD OF CAPTAIN AMERICA LOSING HIS TEMPER... OR THE MIGHTY THOR HURTING SOMEONE HE CARES ABOUT, SIMPLY BECAUSE HE COULD NOT CONTROL HIMSELF...
IF I MET THE GREAT THOMAS MAGNUM, OF MAGNUM PI, TODAY, I WOULD NOT BE ABLE TO LOOK HIM IN THE FACE...
I WISH I COULD GO HOME...
BUT...

MY PARENTS ARE NO LONGER TOGETHER... MY FATHER, MORE CONCERNED WITH HIS WEALTH AND THE POWER THAT HIS BUSINESS BRINGS HIM THAN WITH HIS FAMILY...
HE HAS JOINED THE HELLFIRE CLUB... AND THEY ARE EVIL PEOPLE, AND AMONG MY GREATEST SWORN ENEMIES.

MY MOTHER... IS A BRAVE WOMAN, AND TALENTED. SHE IS AN ARCHEOLOGIST...
AND SOMETIMES I AM AFRAID... THAT SHE LOVES HER MUSTY OLD DIGS-- THE RELICS OF PEOPLE WHO HAVE BEEN DEAD FOR MILLENNIA-- MORE THAN SHE DOES HER OWN LIVING SON.

THIS IS MY HOME NOW. MY FRIENDS ARE HERE.

AND ALTHOUGH THEY HAVE BEEN UNFAIR TO ME... ALTHOUGH THEY NEVER UNDERSTAND ME... THEY ARE MY FAMILY NOW.

I WISH PROFESSOR XAVIER WERE HERE. HE ALWAYS UNDERSTOOD.

MAGNETO? MAY I TALK TO YOU, SIR... ABOUT WHAT HAPPENED?
SHALL I WAIT UNTIL HE RETURNS, OR...
PERSONAL REPORT
Da COSTA, R.
CONFIDENTIAL
MY REPORT...? I WONDER WHAT PROFESSOR XAVIER WROTE OF ME ...SURELY IF NO ONE EVER FINDS OUT I LOOKED, THERE CAN BE NO HARM IN...
A MOST PRECOCIOUS LAD. BUT ALSO, I SUSPECT, DEEPLY TROUBLED. HIS FATHER—WHOM ROBERTO IDOLIZED—JOINED THE RANKS OF THE HELLFIRE CLUB, THE VERY PEOPLE RESPONSIBLE FOR THE DEATH OF ROBERTO'S GIRLFRIEND.
ROBERTO AND SAM HAVE GROWN ESPECIALLY CLOSE—MY HOPE IS THAT SAM PROVIDES A STEADYING INFLUENCE. ROBERTO'S BRASH SELF-CONFIDENCE COULD SO EASILY BECOME ARROGANCE...
...AND FROM THERE LEAD HIM INEVITABLY DOWN THE ROAD CHOSEN BY HIS FATHER.

WELL, SAM, I'VE CHECKED YOUR X-RAYS, AND I DON'T THINK THERE'S ANYTHING TO WORRY ABOUT...
WHAT YOU HAVE IS A CONCUSSION AND NOT A SKULL FRACTURE.

A FEW DAYS' BED REST-- NO STUDYING AND NO SPORTS, MIND YOU-- AND YOU'LL BE AS GOOD AS NEW.
THAT'S A RELIEF, DOCTOR. THANK YOU FOR SEEING HIM SO PROMPTLY.
NOT AT ALL, MR. XAVIER. IT IS PART OF YOUR SCHOOL'S HEALTH COVERAGE AFTER ALL... NOW, IF YOU'D COME ALONG AND FILL OUT THE FORMS...?

OF COURSE.
AH'M MUCH OBLIGED TO YOU, SIR.
Y'KNOW, I AIN'T GONNA BE EASY IN MAH MIND UNTIL WE GET HOME AN' I CAN SET THINGS RIGHT WITH BOBBY. AH OWE HIM ONE BIG APOLOGY.
WHAT FOR? SURVIVING?

SAM, WE ALL SAW WHAT HE DID. HIS LOSS OF TEMPER COULD HAVE CAUSED YOUR DEATH.
BUT, LAHK AH TOLD YOU-ALL IN THE CAR, IT AIN'T WHAT IT LOOKED LAHK. I HIT HIM HARD FIRST. I DANG NEAR BROKE HIS NECK.
FRIENDBOBBY SHOWED GREAT ALARM AND CONCERN. SURELY WHEN HE HEARS FRIENDSAM'S WELL-BEING IS ESTABLISHED, HE WILL EXPRESS REGRET...?
I WOULDN'T COUNT ON IT, PAL-- AND YOU'D BETTER CONCENTRATE ON MAINTAINING YOUR HUMAN SHAPE UNTIL WE'RE OUT OF HERE...
OR IT WILL BE THE DOCTOR WHO EXPRESSES GREAT ALARM AND CONCERN.

SIRYN, GIRL, YOU SEEM T'BE WORKIN' YUIRSELF INTO A FINE STATE O'EXCITEMENT.

AYE, LADY MOIRA, AN' WHY SHOULD I NOT? IT'S T' AMERICA WE'RE GOIN' AFTER ALL--NEW YORK ITSELF--AN' AFTER MONTHS O'SECLUSION ON THIS ISLAND O'YUIRS, IT'LL BE A FINE CHANGE...
MEANIN' NO OFFENSE, MA'AM.

AND I'VE TAKEN NONE. I LIKE A BIT OF A CHANGE MESELF EVERY NOW AND AGAIN.
HAVE WE FORGOTTEN ANYTHIN'?

I DON'T THINK SO. HERE'S THE LAST OF OUR LUGGAGE...

...AND I HAVE OUR PLANE TICKETS...

...AND I PICKED UP A FEW THINGS WE MIGHT NEED FOR THE TRIP.

VERY CLEVER, LAD. NOW PULL YUIR-SELF TOGETHER AND LET'S BE OFF... UNLESS YOU BOOKED YUIRSELF THREE SEATS ON THAT FLIGHT.

DEAR EVERYONE—

YOU WERE ALL RIGHT AND I WAS WRONG. IT WAS TERRIBLE OF ME TO HURT SAM, WHO IS THE BEST FRIEND I EVER HAD. YOU ARE ALL GOOD FRIENDS, AND I HAVE BEEN PROUD TO KNOW YOU ALL AND BE ONE OF YOU ... BUT I DO NOT BELONG HERE. I KNOW THAT NOW. I AM AN EVIL PERSON, AND IF I STAY I WILL ONLY END UP HURTING SOMEONE OR DISGRACING YOU. I SAW MY REPORT CARD, SO I KNOW PROFESSOR XAVIER KNEW THIS, TOO. FAREW... PLEASE FORGIVE ME. AND TELL SAM I HOPE HIS HEAD IS BETTER SOON.

Roberto

QUERY: REPAIR?
MAGNETOENTITY GOES TO ENACT REPARATION OF HARM... OTHERFRIENDS GO TO CONTEMPLATE...
QUERY: IS FRIENDBOBBY PERMITTED TO LEAVE WHILE MISUNDERSTOOD AND UNFORGIVEN?

ALARM...DISMAY... UNACCEPTABLE! UNACCEPTABLE!
ALLFRIENDS MUST REMAIN TOGETHER TO FORM A HARMONIOUS UNIT DESPITE DIFFERENCES...

IS THIS NOT THE NATURE OF FRIENDSHIP-STATE?
FRIENDBOBBY MUST BE FOUND, REASSURANCES GIVEN, AND HARMONY RESTORED.

STATEMENT: ENTITIES SEEKING LOSS OF SELF DO SO WITH GREAT FREQUENCY IN LOCATION KNOWN AS MANHATTAN.

FRIENDBOBBY CANNOT HAVE BEEN GONE FOR LONG.
SELF WILL SEEK HIM IN MANHATTAN...

...USING GREATEST POSSIBLE SPEED!

BBBBZZZZZZ

I SLEPT LAST NIGHT ON A BENCH IN THE PORT AUTHORITY BUS STATION. IT WAS UNCOMFORTABLE AND SMELLED BAD, AND I WAS AWAKENED AT DAWN BY AN EVIL FELLOW WHO OFFERED ME A CHANCE TO MAKE MONEY...
...BY BEING FRIENDLY TO LONELY OLD WOMEN AND MEN WITH STRANGE APPETITES ...I CURSED HIM AWAY...

BUT TO THINK THE DAY WOULD COME WHEN I, A daCOSTA, SHOULD HAVE TO LISTEN TO SUCH THINGS.

THE BUS FARE TOOK ALL THE MONEY I HAD... AND ALTHOUGH I KNOW I AM NOT A GOOD MAN... WHAT I REMEMBER OF HONOR WOULD NOT LET ME CONTEMPLATE STEALING FROM MY FRIENDS BEFORE I LEFT OUR SCHOOL FOREVER...

NOW I AM SO HUNGRY...
...I THINK I SHALL STARVE.
?
AL'S

HMMM... NEW BLOOD IN TOWN. DOESN'T LOOK LIKE HE'S WORTH HUSTLIN'. THE CLOTHES ARE EXPENSIVE, BUT THEY ONLY LOOK THAT MISERABLE WHEN THEY DON'T HAVE ANY MONEY.
NOT MY PROBLEM. SOMEONE WILL TAKE CARE OF HIM-- ONE WAY OR ANOTHER-- OR HE'LL TOUGHEN UP FAST, THE FIRST TIME THEY TRY.

HEY, MISTER...
WANT TO BUY A CALENDAR? VERY PRETTY, VERY CHEAP. ORIENTAL BEAUTIES, ALL THE MONTHS OF THE YEAR.

"ORIENTAL BEAUTIES", HUNH? LET'S SEE.

SEE? THIS IS WHAT I THINK OF YOUR BEAUTIES AND YOUR CALENDARS!
D-DON'T DO THAT... IF YOU DON'T WANT IT, JUST GIVE ME YOUR MONEY AS A DONATION, AND I'LL SELL THE CALENDAR TO SOMEONE ELSE!

YOU CAN'T BE MORE THAN TEN YEARS OLD ...YOU SHOULDN'T EVEN BE OUT OF BED YET, AND HERE YOU ARE HAWKING IMPORTED GOODS ON THE STREET...DID YOUR PARENTS SEND YOU OUT HERE? DID THEY?!
DID THEY TELL YOU NOT TO COME HOME UNTIL YOU'D SOLD EVERY CALENDAR... AND MADE A LOT OF MONEY FOR REVEREND YUNE KIM PARK AND THE GLORIFICATION CHURCH?

THAT'S WHAT MY FAMILY USED TO DO TO ME. THE GLORIFICATION CHURCH BROUGHT US TO THIS COUNTRY, PROMISED THEY'D MAKE US CITIZENS ...AND MADE US WORK LIKE SLAVES AN' THANK THEM FOR THE PRIVILEGE.
THAT'S WHY I RAN AWAY. MAYBE THERE IS A GOD AND A HEAVEN, BUT THEY'VE GOT NOTHIN' TO DO WITH PARK AN' HIS GLORIES!

I'M GONNA TAKE YOUR MONEY, AN' YOUR CALENDARS. NOW YOUR FAMILY HAS TO LET YOU COME HOME AN' GO TO BED... OR TO SCHOOL!
YOU... YOU'RE NOT A BOY AT ALL!
PAWN

YOU'RE A GIRL... YOU'RE THE ONE THEY CALL CHANCE, THE RENEGADE.
I'M GONNA TELL THE REVEREND PARK.
SURE. YOU TELL HIM THERE'S NO CHANCE FOR HIM IN THIS TOWN!
NOT AS LONG AS I'M ON THE STREET!

NOT BAD...NOT BAD. AT ALL...
LOOK WHAT'S COMIN'.
LOOK WHAT SHE GOT.

HEY, LITTLE SWEET-HEART, IT'S NOT SAFE TO WALK AROUND A NEIGHBORHOOD LIKE THIS WITH ALL THAT CASH IN PLAIN SIGHT.
WE'LL TAKE IT FOR YOU.

YOU WANT IT?

YOU GOT IT!
OOH!
OW!!
ALL YOU HAVE TO DO IS COME AND GET IT!

THAT KID IS CRAZY!
GET AFTER HER!

YIPE!

AND NOW...
CHA-KLIK
H-H-HERE...DON'T BE MAD. I JUST THOUGHT YOU'D ENJOY THE MONEY MORE... IF YOU HAD TO WORK FOR IT. A LITTLE.
DON'T WORRY. WE'RE GONNA ENJOY OURSELVES.
DO NOT BE AFRAID, MISS, AND DON'T DEMEAN YOURSELF BY TRYING TO APPEASE THESE JACKALS. I ASSURE YOU, THERE IS NO NEED.
IF THEY TRY TO HARM YOU, I SHALL STOP THEM!
IT'S A JOKE, RIGHT?
THE NEW KID... HE CAME BACK!
HEY, AFTER WE TAKE HER MONEY, WE'LL CUT YOU OPEN AN' SEE WHAT YOU'RE CARRYIN'!
WILL YOU?

HE'S SOME KIND OF FREAK!
WELL, LET'S GET HIM ANYWAY! I AIN'T AFRAID OF NO FREAKS!
NO? YOU SHOULD BE!
SNEK
WELL, ALL RIGHT!
AND NOW, DOG, YOU WILL APOLOGIZE TO THIS CHILD, OR FEEL THE WRATH OF ONE WHOSE POWER IS AS LIMITLESS AS THE SUN ITSELF!
YEAH! HIT HIM AGAIN!
I...
WHY DO I FEEL SO STRANGE?

SURELY THIS CUR IS NOT THAT HEAVY...?
MY POWER... IT IS DRAINING AWAY...
NOT GOOD ENOUGH, WERE YOU, FREAK-O?
LET'S SEE WHAT GOOD A LEAD PIPE IS AGAINST A FREAK.
TO BE CONTINUED...

MARVEL®
#2 IN AN EIGHT-ISSUE LIMITED SERIES
FALLEN ANGELS™
© 1987 MARVEL COMICS GROUP
75¢ US
95¢ CAN
2
MAY
CC 02409
APPROVED BY THE COMICS CODE AUTHORITY

I'LL TAKE THE HIGH ROAD AND I'LL TAKE THE LOW ROAD
AND I'LL GET TO SUNSPOT BEFORE ME
MY NAME IS ROBERTO daCOSTA. I AM FOURTEEN YEARS OLD...
...AND I THINK TODAY I AM GOING TO DIE.
CREATED BY DUFFY AND GAMMILL.
JO DUFFY WRITER
KERRY GAMMILL PENCILER
TOM PALMER- FINISHER
JIM NOVAK LETTERER
PETRA SCOTESE COLORIST
ANN NOCENTI EDITOR
JIM SHOOTER EDITOR IN CHIEF

THE LITTLE KOREAN GIRL WHOM I SAVED FROM THESE CURS MAY WELL SHARE MY FATE... AND FOR THAT, I AM SORRY...
HEY...BRACE UP, MAN! YOU WERE DOING SO WELL AGAINST THEM!
WHAT HAPPENED?
I-I'M SORRY... FORGIVE ME...
I...AM A MUTANT, A LIVING SOLAR BATTERY KNOWN AS SUNSPOT.
ONE MOMENT, I HELD ONE OF THESE MONSTERS ALOFT... AND THEN, FOR THE FIRST TIME IN MY LIFE, FOR REASONS I DO NOT UNDERSTAND...
...I FELT MY POWER DRAINING AWAY... AND MY NORMAL HUMAN STRENGTH WAS NOT ENOUGH TO SUPPORT THE WEIGHT OF THE LOUT...
CUT THE LITTLE FREAK OPEN, SEE WHAT HE'S MADE OF...
SORRY, MAN... BUT IF YOU'RE GOING TO STICK AROUND AND WAIT FOR THEM TO SLIT YOUR THROAT...
I BETTER TAKE MY CHANCES ALONE!
HEY! DIVIDE AND CONQUER! ALL RIGHT!
LITTLE DARLIN' YOUR CHANCE IS NO CHANCE AT ALL!
NO...THEY'RE BEATING HER. SHE'S JUST A BABY!
COWARDS! ANIMALS! LET HER ALONE!

OKAY... WE'LL FINISH YOUR BUSINESS FIRST!
GO AHEAD... CUT 'IM...
LATER FOR THAT... YOU JUST HOLD HIM. THIS CAT HAS SOME DUES TO PAY.

THEY'LL KILL HIM, UNLESS--
--?

CHANCE! CHANCE, ARE YOU OUT THERE?
ARIEL? IS THAT YOU?

NO ONE ELSE! NOW HURRY AND GET IN HERE...
...UNLESS YOU LIKE SEEING DEAD TEEN-AGER MOVIES WITH-OUT GOING TO THE MOVIES.
BUT... BUT THEY'RE ATTACKING HIM BECAUSE HE DEFENDED ME.

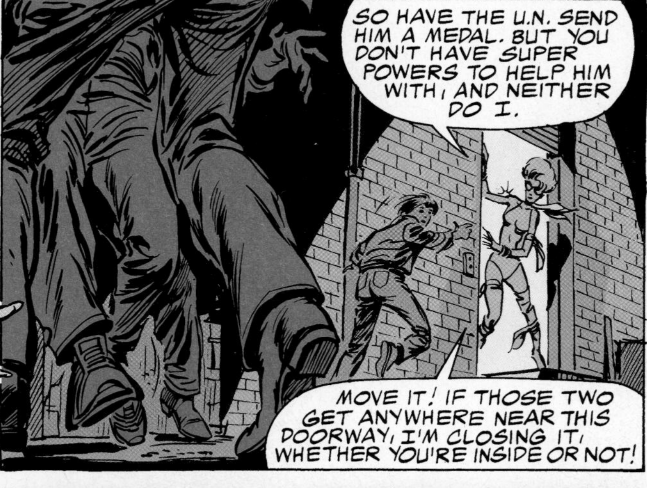
SO HAVE THE U.N. SEND HIM A MEDAL. BUT YOU DON'T HAVE SUPER POWERS TO HELP HIM WITH, AND NEITHER DO I.
MOVE IT! IF THOSE TWO GET ANYWHERE NEAR THIS DOORWAY, I'M CLOSING IT, WHETHER YOU'RE INSIDE OR NOT!

I'M COMING! I'M COMING!
AT LEAST I HAVE SAVED A LIFE...
NOT SO TOUGH NOW, IS HE?

PERHAPS... DYING WILL NOT BE TOO BAD...

H-HEY...

NOOOO

NOOO

NOOO

NOOOOOOOOOOOO

YESTERDAY I BEHAVED BADLY. IN A MOMENT OF ANGER, I NEARLY SLEW ONE OF MY FELLOW NEW MUTANTS --MEMBERS OF THE TEAM TO WHICH WARLOCK AND I BOTH BELONG.
CAIN, WHO STRUCK DOWN HIS BROTHER, IS NO MORE EVIL THAN I. I CANNOT BE PART OF ANY HONORABLE TEAM... OF ANY FAMILY...
WARLOCK, LEAVE ME.
QUERY: WHY? DOES FRIENDBOBBY NO LONGER LIKE SELF?

YOU... HAVE NEVER BEEN MORE DEAR TO ME, MY FRIEND. BUT I...
I AM NOT FIT TO TOUCH YOU. LEAVE ME TO MY LIFE AS AN OUTCAST-- A PARIAH!
NEGATIVE. FRIENDBOBBY MEANT NO HARM. SELF WILL REMAIN. BOTH UNITS SHALL BE OUTCASTS, TOGETHER.

YOU KNOW, MY FRIEND... IT HAS JUST OCCURRED TO ME... I STILL HAVE A LITTLE UNFINISHED BUSINESS, CONNECTED TO THAT BEATING I JUST RECEIVED.

I SAW THAT GIRL I HELPED-- AND HER FRIEND-- DISAPPEAR INTO A BRIGHTLY LIT ROOM BEHIND THIS DOOR, SO THEY MUST BE...

GONE!
THEY AND THE ROOM THEY BOTH RAN INTO ARE GONE WITHOUT A TRACE!

WHAT DO YOU MEAN, GONE? THEY CAN'T BE GONE!
WHERE DID THEY GO?

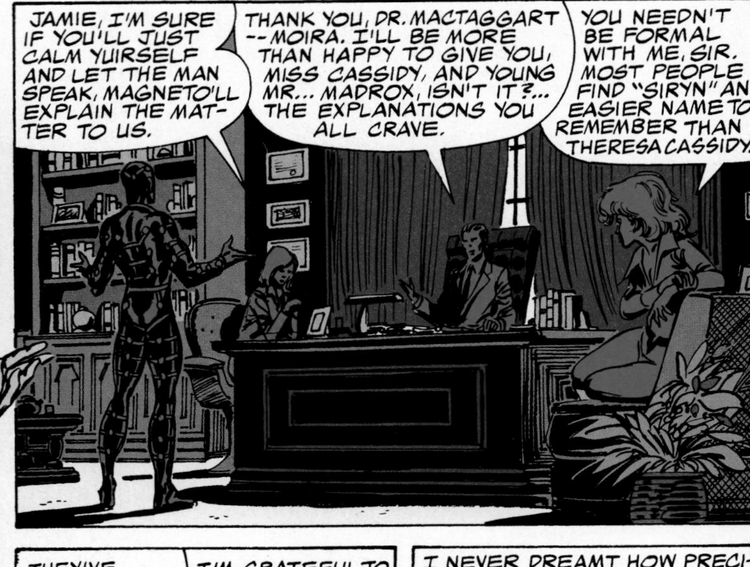
JAMIE, I'M SURE IF YOU'LL JUST CALM YUIRSELF AND LET THE MAN SPEAK, MAGNETO'LL EXPLAIN THE MATTER TO US.
THANK YOU, DR. MACTAGGART --MOIRA. I'LL BE MORE THAN HAPPY TO GIVE YOU, MISS CASSIDY, AND YOUNG MR... MADROX, ISN'T IT?... THE EXPLANATIONS YOU ALL CRAVE.
YOU NEEDN'T BE FORMAL WITH ME, SIR. MOST PEOPLE FIND "SIRYN" AN EASIER NAME TO REMEMBER THAN THERESA CASSIDY.

MAGNETO, WHEN YOU CALLED ME, YOU SAID THAT THERE WAS SOME KIND OF EMOTIONAL TROUBLE BREWING AMONG YOUR STUDENTS...
...AND THAT YOU HOPED THAT I, AS AN EXPERT ON ALL SORTS OF MUTATIONS, MIGHT BE ABLE TO HELP THEM AND YOU TO DEAL WITH THEM.
I ASKED SIRYN AND JAMIE TO COME WITH ME BECAUSE THEY'RE MUTANTS THEMSELVES, AND BOTH ARE STILL IN THEIR TEENS.

THEY'VE ALWAYS BEEN A GREAT HELP TO ME IN MY RESEARCHES, AND THEY CAN RELATE TO YOUR YOUNGSTERS IN WAYS THAT NEITHER YOU NOR I COULD EVER HOPE TO.
I'M GRATEFUL TO ALL THREE OF YOU FOR COMING, ALTHOUGH I'LL ADMIT THAT YESTERDAY ALL I HAD WERE CERTAIN VAGUE PREMONITIONS OF TROUBLE ON THE HORIZON.

I NEVER DREAMT HOW PRECIPITOUSLY MY FEARS FOR MY STUDENTS WOULD BE REALIZED...
...BUT OUT ON THE ATHLETIC FIELD WHERE THE REMAINING NEW MUTANTS ARE NOW ENJOYING THE FRESH AIR, SOMETHING CATASTROPHIC OCCURRED.

ROBERTO daCOSTA, IN RESPONSE TO SOME INJURY HE'D RECEIVED, LASHED OUT AT HIS BEST FRIEND, SAM GUTHRIE, AND VERY NEARLY CAUSED SAM'S DEATH.
12

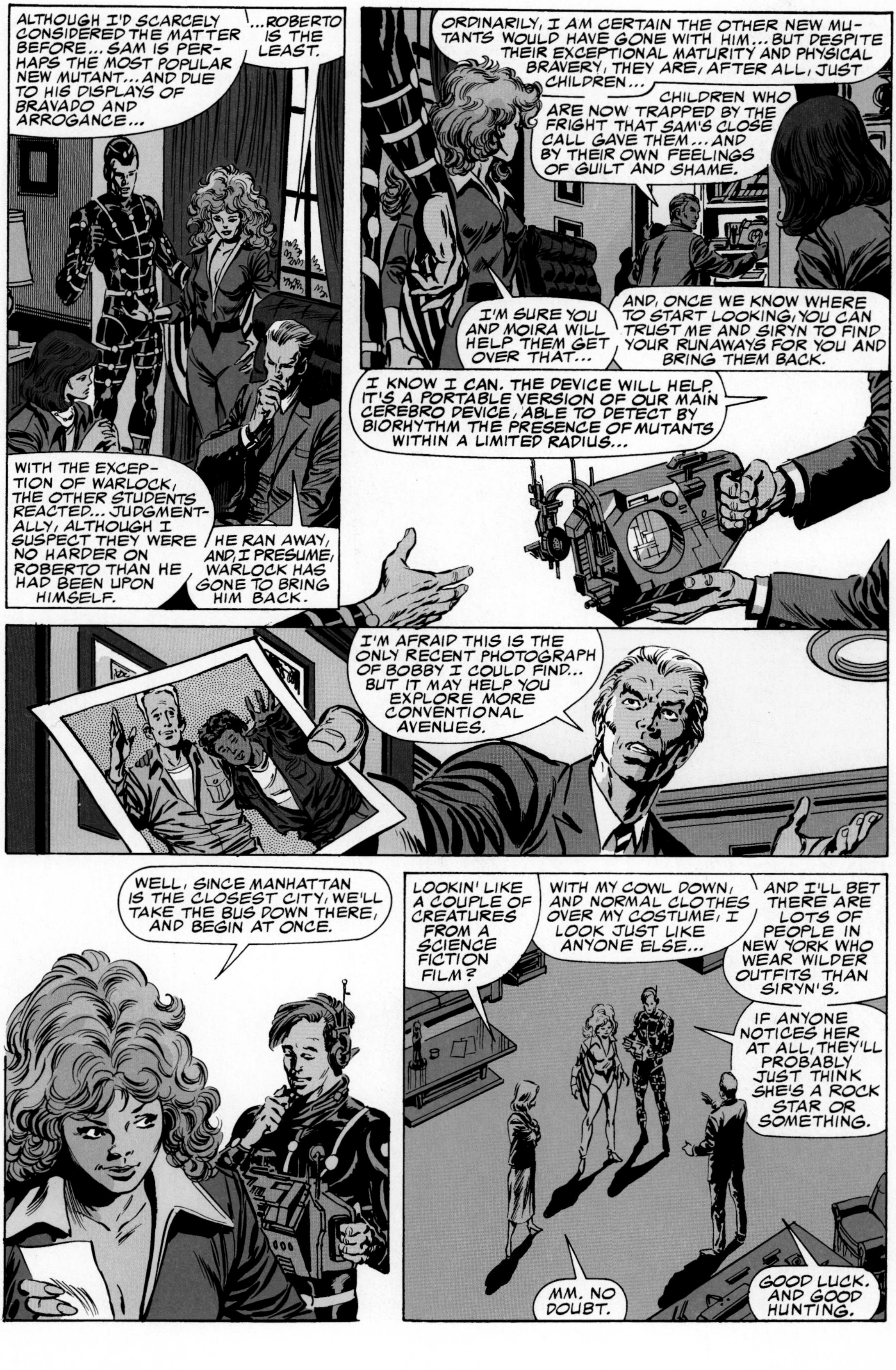

ALTHOUGH I'D SCARCELY CONSIDERED THE MATTER BEFORE... SAM IS PERHAPS THE MOST POPULAR NEW MUTANT... AND DUE TO HIS DISPLAYS OF BRAVADO AND ARROGANCE...

...ROBERTO IS THE LEAST.

WITH THE EXCEPTION OF WARLOCK, THE OTHER STUDENTS REACTED... JUDGMENTALLY, ALTHOUGH I SUSPECT THEY WERE NO HARDER ON ROBERTO THAN HE HAD BEEN UPON HIMSELF.

HE RAN AWAY, AND, I PRESUME, WARLOCK HAS GONE TO BRING HIM BACK.

ORDINARILY, I AM CERTAIN THE OTHER NEW MUTANTS WOULD HAVE GONE WITH HIM... BUT DESPITE THEIR EXCEPTIONAL MATURITY AND PHYSICAL BRAVERY, THEY ARE, AFTER ALL, JUST CHILDREN...

CHILDREN WHO ARE NOW TRAPPED BY THE FRIGHT THAT SAM'S CLOSE CALL GAVE THEM... AND BY THEIR OWN FEELINGS OF GUILT AND SHAME.

I'M SURE YOU AND MOIRA WILL HELP THEM GET OVER THAT...

AND, ONCE WE KNOW WHERE TO START LOOKING, YOU CAN TRUST ME AND SIRYN TO FIND YOUR RUNAWAYS FOR YOU AND BRING THEM BACK.

I KNOW I CAN. THE DEVICE WILL HELP. IT'S A PORTABLE VERSION OF OUR MAIN CEREBRO DEVICE, ABLE TO DETECT BY BIORHYTHM THE PRESENCE OF MUTANTS WITHIN A LIMITED RADIUS...

I'M AFRAID THIS IS THE ONLY RECENT PHOTOGRAPH OF BOBBY I COULD FIND... BUT IT MAY HELP YOU EXPLORE MORE CONVENTIONAL AVENUES.

WELL, SINCE MANHATTAN IS THE CLOSEST CITY, WE'LL TAKE THE BUS DOWN THERE, AND BEGIN AT ONCE.

LOOKIN' LIKE A COUPLE OF CREATURES FROM A SCIENCE FICTION FILM?
WITH MY COWL DOWN, AND NORMAL CLOTHES OVER MY COSTUME, I LOOK JUST LIKE ANYONE ELSE...
AND I'LL BET THERE ARE LOTS OF PEOPLE IN NEW YORK WHO WEAR WILDER OUTFITS THAN SIRYN'S.
IF ANYONE NOTICES HER AT ALL, THEY'LL PROBABLY JUST THINK SHE'S A ROCK STAR OR SOMETHING.
MM. NO DOUBT.
GOOD LUCK. AND GOOD HUNTING.

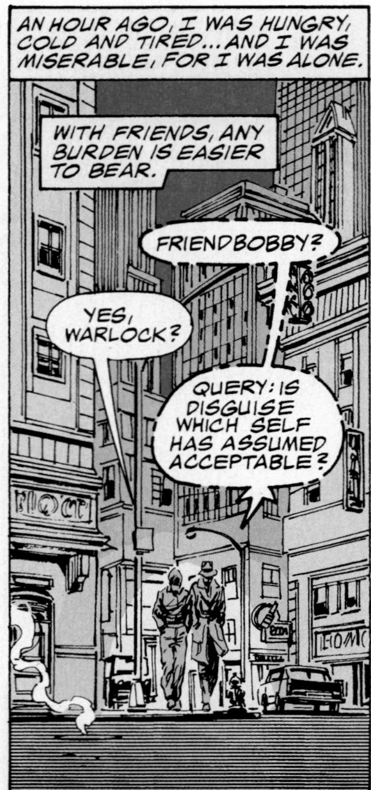
AN HOUR AGO, I WAS HUNGRY, COLD AND TIRED... AND I WAS MISERABLE, FOR I WAS ALONE.
WITH FRIENDS, ANY BURDEN IS EASIER TO BEAR.
FRIENDBOBBY?
YES, WARLOCK?
QUERY: IS DISGUISE WHICH SELF HAS ASSUMED ACCEPTABLE?

SO LONG AS WE WISH TO REMAIN INCONSPICUOUS, ANY FORM IS PREFERABLE TO YOUR NATURAL STATE.
BESIDES... I LIKE BEING SEEN WITH SAM SPADE. HE WAS ONE OF THE GREATEST FICTITIOUS DETECTIVES THE WORLD HAS EVER KNOWN--
--ALMOST AS GREAT AS THOMAS MAGNUM, OF MAGNUM, P.I.

SELF IS AWARE THAT DISGUISE WOULD BE MORE EFFICIENT IF PHYSICAL UNIT MAINTAINED AN UNBROKEN FACADE, BUT CONCENTRATION IS DIFFICULT...
FRIENDBOBBY ... SELF IS HUNGRY.

OBSERVE, SENHOR SPADE! THERE IS A GREAT DEAL OF ORGANIC MATTER IN THAT TRASH CAN.
QUERY: MAY SELF CONSUME LIFEGLOW OF GARBAGE?
YOU ARE WELCOME TO WHATEVER SUSTENANCE IT CAN PROVIDE, ONCE YOU'VE CONVERTED IT INTO DIGESTIBLE ORGANIC MACHINERY.

ANTICIPATION!

JOY!

CONTENTMENT!

?
BURP

NOW, I AM HUNGRIER THAN EVER.
AND I FIND IT HARD NOT TO ENVY WARLOCK THE PHYSIOLOGY THAT ENABLES HIM TO SUSTAIN HIMSELF ON WHATEVER ORGANIC MATTER IS AT HAND, HOWEVER UNPALATABLE.
FOOD
BUT, EVEN IF SUCH A COURSE WERE OPEN TO ME, I, A daCOSTA, COULD NOT TAKE IT. I...HAVE ACCEPTED THAT A LIFE OF EVIL LIES BEFORE ME...

...BUT I SHALL STARVE SOONER THAN EMBRACE DEGRADATION.

QUERY: WHY IS FRIEND-BOBBY SO SILENT?
I, LIKE YOU, MUST CONSUME SOMETHING IF I AM TO SURVIVE... AND I DO NOT HAVE THE MONEY WITH WHICH TO PURCHASE SUITABLE FOOD.
QUERY: IF FRIENDBOBBY HAS EMBRACED CONCEPT OF EVIL AS LIFEPATTERN...THEN IS PURCHASE NOT RENDERED UNNECESSARY AS MEANS OF ACQUISITION OF GOODS AND SERVICES?

OF COURSE! MY NAIVE, CHANGELING COMRADE HAS DETECTED THE FLAW IN MY OWN THINKING THAT I WAS TOO CLOSE TO SEE.
DISCOUNT
HEROES, LIKE THOMAS MAGNUM OR THE NEW MUTANTS, MAY WORRY ABOUT RIGHT AND WRONG.

COME ALONG, MY FRIEND, WHILE I PUT MY MUTANT STRENGTH TO GOOD USE!
SUNSPOT IS A VILLAIN--

--AND HE TAKES WHATEVER HE NEEDS!!

FORGIVE ME...

QUERY: WHY DOES FRIENDBOBBY HESITATE...
I-I CAN'T...

IS THERE SOMEONE OUT THERE? WHAT WAS THAT SOUND?
OH, NO...

I...I CAME TO ROB THE HOUSE OF GOD!
WHY DOES THIS HOLY MAN NOT SHOUT CURSES AND CONDEMNATION AT ME?
YOU'RE JUST CHILDREN, AREN'T YOU?

I'M SORRY I SPOKE SHARPLY, BUT I THOUGHT I'D LOCKED THE DOORS!
ARE YOU IN SOME KIND OF TROUBLE?

CAN I HELP YOU SOMEHOW?
NO! NO ONE CAN!!
NOT ONLY AM I EVIL... I AM WEAK!

THERE WAS SOMETHING UNUSUAL ABOUT THOSE BOYS. IF ONLY THEY'D STAYED AND UNBURDENED THEMSELVES TO ME.
I WONDER WHAT EXACTLY DID HAPPEN TO THESE DOORS...

HEY, THA'S NOT SAFE, YUKNOW.
I CAN MANAGE, THANK YOU... UNLESS THERE'S SOMETHING I CAN DO TO HELP YOU MEN?

NAW, THANKS. WE'LL JUST HELP OURSELVES.
OOOF!
SEE, WAY I FIGURE IT, YOU'RE GONNA BE ATTRACTIN' TROUBLE, LONG'S THE DOOR'S BROKE...

PEOPLE CAN SEE ALL THE GOOD STUFF YOU GOT IN HERE, FANCY HARDWARE, GOLD...
WE'LL SPARE YOU THE WORRY. TAKE IT AWAY, WHERE OTHER PEOPLE WON'T BE SO TEMPTED...

MUCH AS I HATE TO INTERFERE IN MATTERS THAT ARE NONE OF MY BUSINESS...
MY COMPANIONS HAVE POINTED OUT TO ME THAT YOUR INTENTIONS ARE CLEARLY FELONIOUS, AND DO NOT TAKE INTO ACCOUNT THE WISHES OF THAT PRIEST YOU ASSAULTED.
DESIST AND GO ABOUT YOUR BUSINESS...
OR DON, BILL AND I WILL SEND YOU ON YOUR WAY. BY FORCE.

HAW HAW HAW
HAW HAW HAW
HEY, LOOKIT WHUT HE'S GOT WIT'EM! WHAT ARE THOSE THINGS ?!

HEY! OW!!
YIPE!!
AIEEE!!

BAM
GET'EM, DON!!
SMASH
BASH
NICE, GOING, BILL!!

CLICK

WHAT IN HEAVEN'S NAME HAPPENED HERE?

I AGREE WITH YOU THAT AN ACT OF ALTRUISM NEVER REQUIRES AN APOLOGY... BUT WE WERE INSTRUCTED TO FIND SUNSPOT AND HIS STRANGE FRIEND...
AND CONVINCE THEM TO COME WITH US.
KEEP NEW YORK CLEAN
THANKS TO THAT DELAY, WE MAY HAVE LOST THEM!

I AM MAKING HASTE AS I MAKE CONVERSATION!
I SUGGEST YOU TWO DO THE SAME!

LOOK, SIRYN... I KNOW THIS ISN'T THE BEST PLACE IN TOWN... BUT SUNSPOT MUST HAVE TAKEN THE BUS HERE FROM XAVIER'S SCHOOL...
SO THE PORT AUTHORITY BUS TERMINAL IS THE MOST LOGICAL PLACE IN MANHATTAN FOR US TO START LOOKING FOR HIM.

BUT, THE CITY'S SO BIG, AND THIS GREAT PLACE SO CROWDED... HOW CAN WE EVER FIND TWO LOST BOYS HERE?
THAT'S PART OF WHAT YOU HAVE *ME* FOR, REMEMBER?
YOU HAVE NO IDEA HOW HANDY A POWER LIKE MINE COMES IN, WHEN YOU'RE LOOKING FOR A NEEDLE IN A HAYSTACK --AS WE USED TO SAY WHEN I LIVED ON THE FARM.

DID YOU REALLY SAY THAT, LADDIE?
WELL... I SAID IT TO MYSELF, AFTER MY PARENTS DIED, AND I LIVED THERE ALONE.

BUMP
OH, PLEASE EXCUSE...

ME...?
PARDON ME FOR STARING. FOR A MOMENT, I THOUGHT I WAS SEEING DOUBLE. YOU MUST BE TWINS!

YES, I SUPPOSE WE MUST.
YOUR BAG FELT... UH, LOOKS KIND OF HEAVY. LET ME CARRY IT FOR YOU.

GO AHEAD. MEET US AND THE REST OF THE, ER, FAMILY DOWNSTAIRS AT THE TAXI STAND.
TAXI STAND

HOW YOU COMIN' LADDIE ?

JUST FINE, THANKS! AND YOU ?

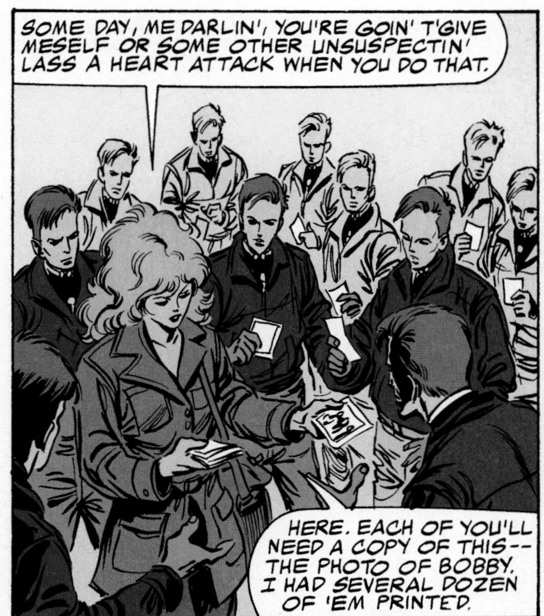
SOME DAY, ME DARLIN', YOU'RE GOIN' T'GIVE MESELF OR SOME OTHER UNSUSPECTIN' LASS A HEART ATTACK WHEN YOU DO THAT.
HERE. EACH OF YOU'LL NEED A COPY OF THIS-- THE PHOTO OF BOBBY. I HAD SEVERAL DOZEN OF 'EM PRINTED.

8E
FINE. WE CAN SHOW THIS AROUND ALL OVER TOWN.
AND I'LL STAY WITH YOU. WE CAN USE THE SMALL DETECTOR UNIT.
JUST BE SURE NO TWO OF YOU LEAVE THE STATION TOO CLOSE TOGETHER.
RIGHT... AND ONE OF US HAS TO HOOK UP WITH THE GUY WHO TOOK THAT LADY'S BAGS.

MY GOODNESS! DON'T THOSE BOYS OVER THERE LOOK...

...ALIKE?!
GEE, I DON'T THINK SO..

PICKING ANYTHING UP YET?
I'M PICKIN' UP PLENTY... BUT THAT'S HARDLY SURPRISING, CONSIDERIN' HOW MANY MUTANTS THERE MUST BE IN A CITY THIS SIZE.
IT'LL TAKE US A LOT OF LEG WORK, TILL WE FIND THE PAIR WE'RE LOOKIN' FOR...

BUT, T'SAVE US A BIT OF TIME, I CALI-BRATED THIS SO IT WON'T REGISTER ANY OF THE KNOWN WORKIN' HEROES IN THIS TOWN...
...OR ANY OF THE REST OF YOU!
GOOD.

DON'T LET THIS GET YOU DOWN! I'M SURE THEY'RE ONLY A LITTLE WAY AHEAD OF US! COME ON, NEVER SAY DIE!
SHOW THAT PIONEER SPIRIT YOUR KIND IS RENOWNED FOR!
SHOW SOME APPRECIATION FOR THE THRILL OF THE CHASE, FELLOWS!

NO...NO STOPPING FOR LUNCH. OUR ORDERS AS REGARDED FOOD BEFORE WE FOUND OUR QUARRY WERE, AFTER ALL, MOST SPECIFIC!
ALTHOUGH, I DO SEE THE MERIT IN YOUR POINT ABOUT FEEDING YOUR INNER BEING, SO THAT SPIRIT DOES NOT FAIL ONE, BILL.
RESTAURANT
TODAY'S SPECIAL
PERHAPS WE COULD--

--DON! DON'T GO IN THERE!!
--ARE YOU BLIND? READ THE SIGN!!

THAT'S A SEAFOOD RESTAURANT!
Seafood

NOW, WHAT HAVE BILL AND I TOLD YOU ABOUT NOT TAKING FOOLISH CHANCES...?
TODAY'S SPECIAL

RATS! STILL NO SIGN OF THEM.
I WONDER HOW THE REST OF ME ARE DOING...
TODAY'S SPECIAL
Stuffed Lobster

THOSE KIDS LOOK ABOUT THE RIGHT AGE. I WONDER IF THEY'VE SEEN THEM.

EXCUSE ME, GUYS. SORRY TO BOTHER YOU, BUT WOULD EITHER OF YOU HAPPEN TO HAVE SEEN--

--GLEEPS!!
WARLOCK!! BOBBY!!
QUERY: WAS FRIENDMADROX FOOLED BY SELF'S CLEVER DISGUISE?
?
WH-WHAT DO YOU WANT HERE, MADROX?

TO FIND YOU TWO AND BRING YOU BOTH HOME, YOU NUT! DON'T YOU KNOW HOW WORRIED ABOUT YOU EVERYONE'S BEEN?
SELF WOULD LIKE TO EXPRESS RELIEF AND APPROVAL AT FRIENDMADROX'S REPRESENTATION OF EMOTIONAL STATE OF OTHER-FRIENDS!
B-BUT...
HEY! LOOK OVER THERE! IT'S THEM!

FOUND THEM! NICE GOING!!
EH...? A COMMOTION...
EUREKA!

WAIT! YOU! SUNSPOT! DON'T GO ANYWHERE WITH THAT... ER, MEN!
FIRST YOU MUST HEAR ME OUT!
WHO ARE YOU?

MY NAME IS NOT IMPORTANT... (IT'S GOMI)...
...BUT MY MESSAGE TO YOU IS!!

FORSAKE YOUR DESTINY AND COME WITH US TO BEAT STREET! THE FALLEN ANGELS WANT YOU!
BUT, I--!
AND WATCH YOUR STEP! YOU ALMOST STEPPED ON BILL!

BILL...?

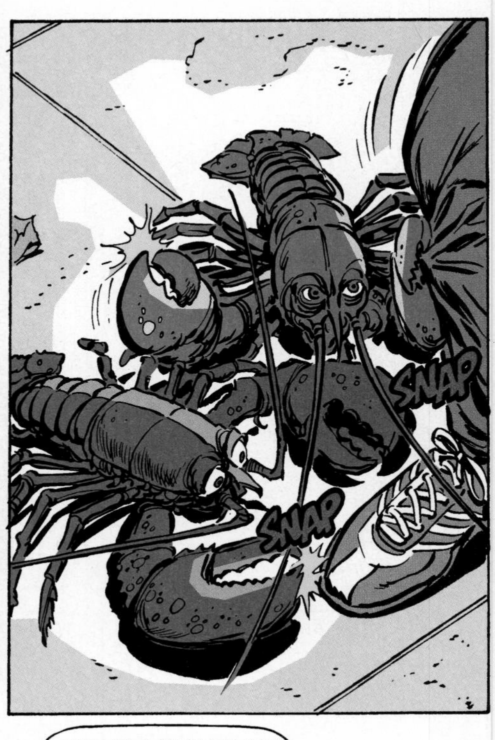
SNAP
SNAP

BUT...THEY'RE LOBSTERS!
MARINE CRUSTACEANS, GENUS HOMARUS, YES.
THE GREEN ONE IS BILL, AND DON IS BLUE.
QUERY: MAY SELF EXPRESS SELF'S EXTREME GRATIFICATION AT MAKING THE ACQUAINTANCE OF ENTITIES SO ELEGANTLY SUITED TO--
NEVER MIND, WARLOCK. THEY CAN'T UNDERSTAND. THEY'RE JUST ANIMALS...
...I THINK.

AREN'T WE ALL?
NOW, THE BEAT STREET CLUBHOUSE IS THIS WAY, AND...
BUT I CAN'T LEAVE MY FRIENDS...
THEN BRING THEM.
QUERY: WOULD SELF TRULY BE WELCOME?
IT DOESN'T MATTER, WARLOCK. NEITHER OF OF YOU IS GOING ANYWHERE!
BOBBY, WEREN'T YOU LISTENING TO ME?!
YES...AND I KNOW THE NEW MUTANTS, TOO! HAD ANY OF THEM TRULY CARED ABOUT MY WELL-BEING OR WANTED WARLOCK AND ME BACK...
...NOT EVEN THE FIRES OF HELL COULD HAVE KEPT THEM FROM COMING AFTER US, IN PERSON!
RATS!

HE'S RIGHT, YOU KNOW.
THAT'S HOW TEAMS ARE ...LET YOU DOWN IN A PINCH, RIGHT WHEN YOU NEED THEM THE MOST!
THAT'S ALL ANY OF MY TEAMS EVER DID FOR ME. AND THE ONES LED BY MAGNETO WERE THE WORST...
BUT, THOUGH I HAVE OFTEN QUARRELED WITH MAGNETO IN THE PAST, THOUGH THE NEW MUTANTS ARE BEHIND ME, THIS ROGUE SHALL NOT SPEAK ILL OF THEM!

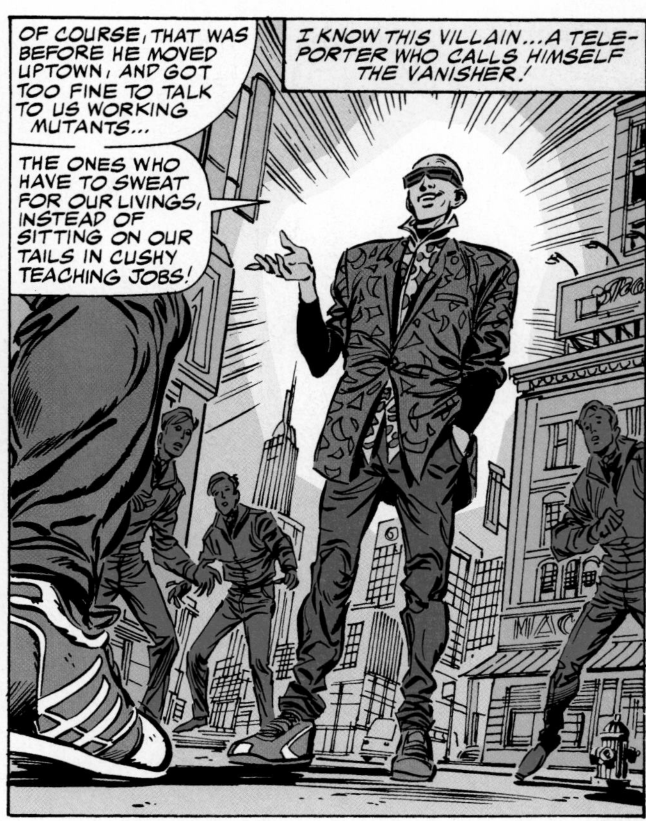
OF COURSE, THAT WAS BEFORE HE MOVED UPTOWN, AND GOT TOO FINE TO TALK TO US WORKING MUTANTS...
I KNOW THIS VILLAIN...A TELEPORTER WHO CALLS HIMSELF THE VANISHER!
THE ONES WHO HAVE TO SWEAT FOR OUR LIVINGS, INSTEAD OF SITTING ON OUR TAILS IN CUSHY TEACHING JOBS!

MAKE A MOVE TO HARM ANY OF MY FRIENDS, VANISHER, OR BREATHE ANOTHER WORD OF SLANDER AGAINST THEM...

...AND I SHALL--!
MY, MY, MY, YOU DO HAVE A TEMPER, DON'T YOU! CALM DOWN, SUNSPOT. PLEASE, CALM DOWN.!!
I DIDN'T MEAN ANY HARM. HONEST! WORD OF HONOR...
IT'S JUST THAT...WELL, I KNOW HOW IT FEELS TO BE A MISUNDERSTOOD OUTCAST. I WANTED TO LET YOU KNOW SOMEONE CARES, THAT'S ALL...

CAN I, WHO HAVE BEEN JUDGED SO HARSHLY BY THOSE I LOVED, BE SO QUICK TO CONDEMN A MAN...ONLY ON THE WORDS OF OTHERS...?
DO YOU REALLY CARE?

WHEEEEEEEEEEE

I HAVE NEVER MET SIRYN'S FATHER, SEAN CASSIDY, THE LEGENDARY BANSHEE... BUT THEY SAY HIS DAUGHTER HAS INHERITED MOST OF HER SIRE'S SKILL...

...AND ALL OF THE POWER OF HIS TERRIBLE SONIC BLASTS!

OH, NO! SHE'S ATTACKING!

SHE MUST THINK THE VANISHER IS UP TO NO GOOD!

YIPES!

WHEEEP

SHE'S PROTECTING US!

QUERY: DID SONIC BLASTS ELIMINATE VANISHER-ENTITY?
PLINK
NO, WARLOCK. HE'S A MUTANT, SAME AS WE ARE. HE TELE-PORTED AWAY FROM SIRYN'S ATTACK.
I CONCUR, DON. A DISTRESSING, BUT PRE-DICTABLE, DEVELOPMENT.

SO, WHY DON'T YOU WANT TO COME TO BEAT STREET, SUNSPOT?

DON'T YOU HAVE THE COURAGE TO TAKE A CHANCE?
CHANCE! YOU!!

OF COURSE IT'S HER, AND SHE'S VERY GLAD TO SEE YOU! AS GLAD AS YOU ARE TO SEE HER!
I-I *WAS* CONCERNED...
THEN COME IN HERE, AND TELL HER SO.
BUT MY FRIENDS... I...
THEY WANT TO COME, TOO. DON'T YOU, BOYS?

AFFIRMATIVE!
I GUESS SO, BUT ... BOBBY SHOULD GO BACK TO--!
I AM MY OWN MAN, MADROX, AND SHALL DO AS I PLEASE, BUT I WEL-COME YOU TO FOLLOW ME!
OH, HECK! OKAY!
COME OUT OF THERE, ALL OF YOU!
JAMIE, WHERE D'YOU THINK YOU'RE GOIN'?

--WAIT!!

?

OH, THERE'S NO WAITING! IF MISS IS READY TO BE SEATED RIGHT NOW, SHE CAN HAVE A TABLE IMMEDIATELY.

CONTINUED

MARVEL
#3 IN AN EIGHT-ISSUE LIMITED SERIES
FALLEN ANGELS
© 1987 MARVEL ENT. GROUP, INC.
75¢ US
95¢ CAN
3
JUNE
02409
APPROVED BY THE COMICS CODE AUTHORITY
GAMMILL

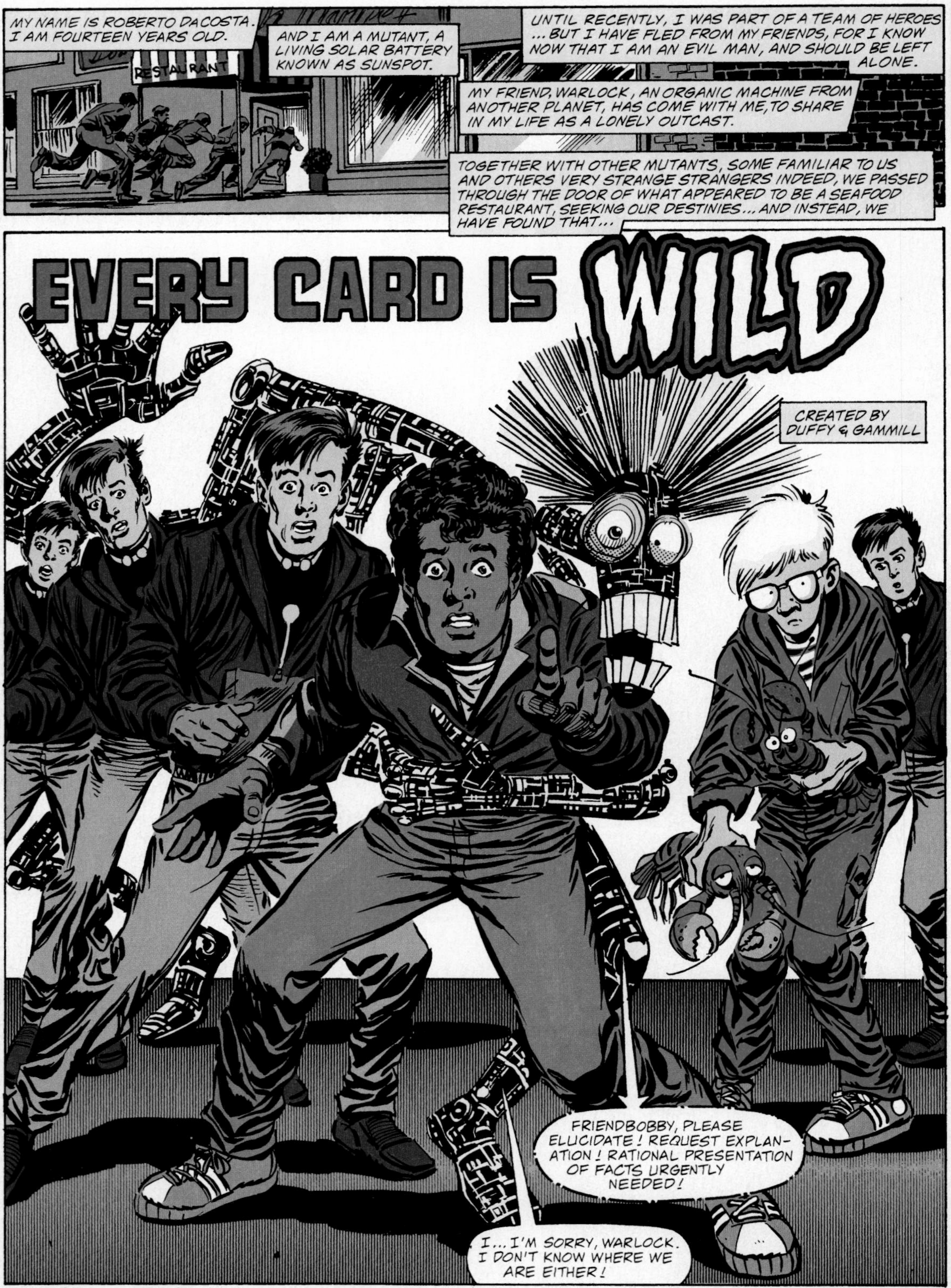

EVERY CARD IS WILD

CREATED BY DUFFY & GAMMILL

FRIENDBOBBY, PLEASE ELUCIDATE! REQUEST EXPLANATION! RATIONAL PRESENTATION OF FACTS URGENTLY NEEDED!

I... I'M SORRY, WARLOCK. I DON'T KNOW WHERE WE ARE EITHER!

JO DUFFY WRITER · MARIE SEVERIN GUEST PENCILER · TOM PALMER FINISHER · BILL OAKLEY LETTERER · PETRA SCOTESE COLORIST · ANN NOCENTI EDITOR · JAMES SHOOTER EDITOR IN CHIEF

WELCOME, WELCOME ALL OF YOU... YOU ALL KNOW WHO I AM, OF COURSE-- YOUR LEADER AND YOUR HOST, THE VANISHER!
AND I'D JUST LIKE TO SAY, TO ALL OF MY LOYAL FOLLOWERS, AS WELL AS YOU NEW RECRUITS, WELCOME TO THE BEAT STREET CLUB! WELCOME HOME!!
THE BEAT ST. CLUB
BONGO VIDEO GAME
WHAT DO YOU MEAN "HOME"?! WHERE IS THIS PLACE?
IT'S WHERE WE ARE, STUPID.
YEAH. AFTER ALL, EVERYONE HAS GOT TO BE SOMEWHERE.
BEAT STREET IS THE HOME FOR THE FALLEN ANGELS, ALL OF US MISFITS WHO KNEW WE WEREN'T GOING TO MAKE IT AS HEROES... OR MAYBE DIDN'T THINK IT WAS WORTH IT TO EVEN TRY...
AND WE CAN TELL JUST BY LOOKIN', THAT DESCRIPTION FITS ALL OF YOU!

IT WAS WHY WE SENT THE REST OF THE ANGELS OUT TO FIND YOU AND MAKE SURE YOU AND YOUR FRIENDS WERE ALL RIGHT.
AND IT'S WHY WE BROUGHT YOU AND WARLOCK AND THAT CHORUS LINE OF REALLY HANDSOME GUYS BACK TO BEAT STREET WHERE YOU'D BE SAFE.
SAFE AND APPRECIATED!
REALLY?

WHY ELSE?
AND... IF I STAY FOR AWHILE... WARLOCK IS WELCOME, TOO?

WE WOULDN'T DREAM OF SEPARATING YOU. AFTER ALL, ONCE AN ANGEL HAS FALLEN, WHAT'S HE GOT LEFT BUT HIS FRIENDS?
THIS GIRL--THIS ARIEL--SHE SOUNDS SO... WISE.

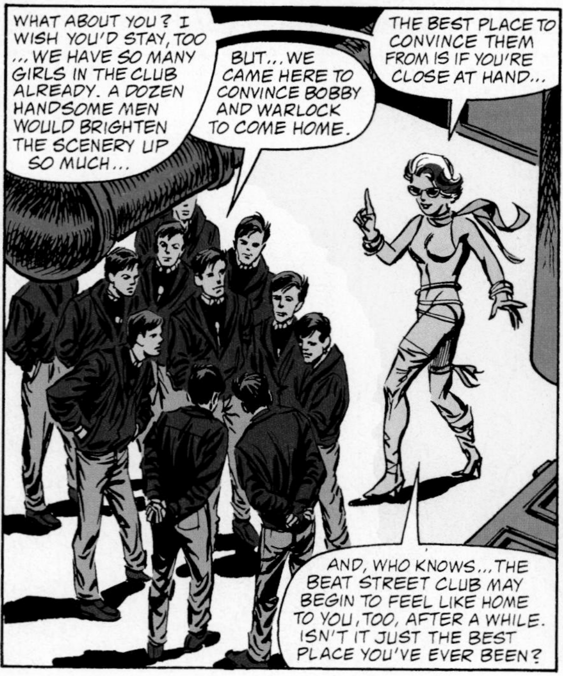
WHAT ABOUT YOU? I WISH YOU'D STAY, TOO ... WE HAVE SO MANY GIRLS IN THE CLUB ALREADY. A DOZEN HANDSOME MEN WOULD BRIGHTEN THE SCENERY UP SO MUCH...
BUT... WE CAME HERE TO CONVINCE BOBBY AND WARLOCK TO COME HOME.
THE BEST PLACE TO CONVINCE THEM FROM IS IF YOU'RE CLOSE AT HAND...
AND, WHO KNOWS... THE BEAT STREET CLUB MAY BEGIN TO FEEL LIKE HOME TO YOU, TOO, AFTER A WHILE. ISN'T IT JUST THE BEST PLACE YOU'VE EVER BEEN?

IT IS NICE...
COZY...
NICE AMBIANCE.
GOOD. AS LONG AS IT'S SETTLED, MAKE ALL OF YOURSELVES COMFORTABLE ... I'M GOING TO DO THE SAME FOR DON AND BILL.

OKAY, DON... WHAT DO YOU WANT TO HEAR?
BONGO VIDEO GAME
HMMM... EITHER "TALKING HEADS"...OR "THE ALBUQUERQUE FAT BOYS' GREATEST POLKA HITS"...

!
I'M SORRY, BILL! I SHOULD HAVE NOTICED! BUT IF YOU WERE THAT HUNGRY, I WISH YOU'D SAID SOMETHING SOONER, 'STEAD OF JUST SUFFERING!

DID YOU HEAR WHAT GOMI SAID, CHANCE? POOR DON AND BILL ARE STARVING!
LIFE IS TOUGH.
YOURS IS GOING TO GET A LOT TOUGHER IN ABOUT FIVE SECONDS, UNLESS YOU...
OH, DON'T MAKE ME SAY IT. YOU KNOW THE RULES, CHANCE.
YEAH...ONLY I NOTICED THEY ONLY APPLY TO SOME OF US...

C'MON, ARIEL... LET'S GO GET SOME FOOD.

QUERY: ARE DON-- AND BILL-- CRUSTACEANS... SENTIENT BEINGS?
IT WOULD APPEAR GOMI THINKS SO...
I'VE NEVER HEARD OF SMART LOBSTERS BEFORE...
THIS IS SO ANNOYING! SOMEONE LEFT "THE BESTIYRI OF FLANDERS AND SWANN" OUT OF THE DUST JACKET... AND NOW IT'S SCRATCHED-- RIGHT ACROSS "THE HIPPOPOTAMUS"!

WHATDOYOUMEANTHEY'RE NOTHERETHEYHAVETOBEHERE ISAWTHEMCOMEINHEREAND THERE'SNOWHEREELSETHEY COULDBE!!!
RESTAURANT
NOW, SIRYN...
DON'T, "NOW, SIRYN..." ME, JAMIE. I'M ANGRY AND FRUSTRATED, AND I HAVE A RIGHT TO BE...
I MEAN, JUST LOOK AT THIS PLACE! LOOK AT IT!!!

IT LOOKS LIKE A SEAFOOD RESTAURANT TO ME.
I KNOW! THAT'S WHAT'S WRONG WITH IT!!
WOULD THE YOUNG LADY LIKE A TABLE FOR TWO, PERHAPS?

SIRYN, IT SAYS OUTSIDE IT'S A SEAFOOD RESTAURANT... SO WHAT'S WRONG WITH IT BEING ONE?
YOU SAW! YOU AND I AND ALL THOSE DUPLICATES OF YOURSELF HAVE BEEN LOOKING FOR SUNSPOT AND WARLOCK ALL DAY... AND JUST WHEN WE ALMOST CAUGHT UP WITH THEM...
THEY ALL RAN THROUGH THIS VERY DOORWAY, AND INTO A ROOM THAT LOOKED NOTHING LIKE THIS ONE... AND SLAMMED THE DOOR IN MY FACE...
I'M SURE WHATEVER IT IS, IT WILL ALL SEEM BETTER AFTER A PLATE OF SCAMPI...
AND NOW THEY'RE GONE! THE WHOLE ROOM IS GONE!!!
AND WE HAVE TO START LOOKING FOR THEM ALL OVER AGAIN!!

SIRYN, PLEASE DON'T RAISE YOUR VOICE... YOU'RE FORGETTING YOUR SONIC POWERS...

RRRIIIINHH

NOW YOU'VE DONE IT!
BINK
PLIK
PLINK

GEEE, AH... I GUESS A... A LOW FLYING PLANE... OR AN SST OR SOMETHING... WENT BY... HEH.
Y'KNOW, SIR, SCAMPI DOES SOUND LIKE A GOOD IDEA!
RIGHT THIS WAY, SIR.
I SUPPOSE YOU THINK YOU'RE QUITE THE CLEVER LAD, THEN, FOR AVERTING THE SCENE I WAS ABOUT TO CAUSE.

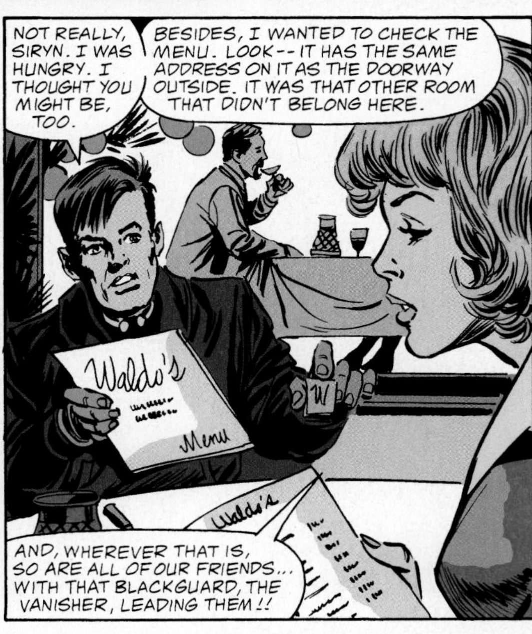
NOT REALLY, SIRYN. I WAS HUNGRY. I THOUGHT YOU MIGHT BE, TOO.
BESIDES, I WANTED TO CHECK THE MENU. LOOK-- IT HAS THE SAME ADDRESS ON IT AS THE DOORWAY OUTSIDE. IT WAS THAT OTHER ROOM THAT DIDN'T BELONG HERE.
Waldo's
Menu
AND, WHEREVER THAT IS, SO ARE ALL OF OUR FRIENDS... WITH THAT BLACKGUARD, THE VANISHER, LEADING THEM!!

LUV, I'M SORRY TO BE TAKIN' THIS SO BADLY, WHEN YOU'RE TAKIN' IT SO WELL. YOU MUST BE WORRIED SICK, WITH ALL YOUR DUPLICATES DISAPPEARING.

THAT'S EXACTLY WHY I'M NOT WORRIED. BOBBY HAS A TEMPER... AND WARLOCK IS SO INNOCENT, HE'S LIKE A BABY, BUT JAMIE MADROX THE MULTIPLE MAN IS A REALLY LEVEL-HEADED GUY.
WHEREVER THEY ARE, SO AM I, KEEPING THEM BOTH IN LINE AND OUT OF TROUBLE. THE ONLY PROBLEM IS, I DON'T KNOW WHERE I AM.
BUT YOUR COPIES...
I'VE TOLD YOU BEFORE, SWEET-HEART, THERE ARE NO COPIES. EACH AND EVERY ONE OF ME IS GENUINE, WITH HIS OWN LIFE AND MEMORIES FOR AS LONG AS HE'S APART FROM THE REST OF ME...

BUT EACH MADROX IS COMPLETE UNTO HIMSELF... LIKE THE INDIVID-UAL PACKETS OF SUGAR IN THIS BOWL HERE, OR CARDS TAKEN FROM A DECK.
I'M NO REALER OR BETTER THAN ANY OF THE REST OF ME. I'M JUST LUCKIER. I'M THE ONLY ONE WITH YOU.

THIS IS WHERE YOU LIVE, MA'AM? REALLY? WOW!
I STILL CAN'T GET OVER HOW CONSIDERATE YOU'VE BEEN, HELPING ME BRING ALL MY LUGGAGE FROM THE BUS TERMINAL TO MY HOME.
JUST CARRYING IT TO THE TAXI WAS MORE CHIVALRY THAN I'D HAVE EXPECTED IN THIS TOWN AND THIS DECADE.
BUT YOUR TWIN BROTHER, THE ONE I SAW YOU WITH... WON'T HE BE WORRYING ABOUT YOU?

LET HIM WORRY. I'LL BET HE HASN'T EVEN NOTICED I'M GONE YET. BESIDES, THIS IS SO GREAT. I WAS ONLY IN MANHATTAN ONCE BEFORE...

AND I GOT HASSLED SO MUCH, I NEVER REALLY GOT TO SEE THE SIGHTS.
Hall RADIO CITY
NEW SHOW THE ROCKETTES CEL
SABRETT
SABRETTS
FRANKFURTERS & ROLLS
AND WHEN I THINK OF THOSE LONG, LONELY, MISERABLE YEARS ON THE FARM, AFTER MA AND PA DIED...
THEY LEFT YOU AND YOUR BROTHER ALL ALONE?
AH, NO... THERE WERE A LOT OF US ...TOO MANY...

AND... WHEN I REJOIN THE OTHERS... ALL I'LL HAVE IS MY MEMORIES, CONFLICTING WITH OTHER MEMORIES OF HOW THEY'VE ALL SPENT THIS TIME!
IT'LL BE LIKE DYING... LIKE LOSING MYSELF!!

Y'KNOW... WHEN THE GIRLS GET BACK, I DOUBT THEY'LL HAVE BROUGHT ENOUGH FOOD FOR EVERYBODY... AND I'M STARVING.
ME, TOO!
THAT FIGURES, DUMMY- WE ALL ARE.
AND THERE AREN'T ENOUGH CHAIRS. BESIDES, I THINK ONE OF ME IS ALL THAT'S NEEDED AT THE MOMENT. WANT TO PULL MYSELF TOGETHER?
WHY NOT?
BONGO

LIKE SLAM DANCING, WITH A DIFFER- ENCE!
LAST ONE LEFT HAS TO EAT JUNK FOOD!
ABSORB YOUR PARTNERS AND DANCE!!

EIGHT GOES INTO FOUR...
...FOUR GOES INTO TWO...

...AND IT LOOKS LIKE IT'S JUST THEE AND ME, PAL.

WE'RE BACK! WITH MCNUTLEY'S SPECIALS FOR EVERYONE!!! AND DON'T INSULT US BY ASKING IF WE PAID FOR IT.
BUT DON'T EXPECT ME TO CLEAR THE TABLE FOR THIS, BECAUSE I AIN'T GONNA.
McNUTLY'S
McNUTLYS

FAIR ENOUGH. DIVISION OF LABOR ISN'T TOO MUCH TO ASK FOR... AFTER ALL, WE ARE A TEAM. A VERITABLE FAMILY.
GOMI, YOU CLEAR THE TABLE.
OKAY.

I'LL JUST CONCENTRATE MY POWERS OF MIND OVER MATTER, AND...

BAMMO

EEK!
WHOOPS!
LOOK OUT, EVERYONE!
NO! NO! NO! NO!
NOT LIKE THAT, YOU FOOL! BLITHERING INCOMPETENT! IMBECILE! NINCOM--

--POOP!!
OW! OW! OW! OW!!

GRRR...

YOUR OWN FAULT, VANISHER. YOU KNOW THE LOBSTERS DON'T LIKE IT IF ANYONE PICKS ON GOMI MORE THAN USUAL.
EVEN AMONG CRUSTACEANS, SUCH LOYALTY TO ONE'S FRIENDS!!
ONCE, I ENJOYED THAT SAME GIFT, BEFORE I WANTONLY TOSSED IT ASIDE.

FRIENDBOBBY'S ATTITUDE IS ONE OF DEJECTION. QUERY: IS SELF'S FRIENDSHIP NOT SATISFACTORY?
WARLOCK... I DO NOT KNOW WHAT GOOD ACT I HAVE PERFORMED IN THIS WASTED LIFE OF MINE... TO DESERVE AS TRUE A FRIEND AS YOU.
QUERY: LIKEWISE, MAY FRIEND-MADROX BE COUNTED AS A STILL-SATISFACTORY COMPANION? HE, TOO, FOLLOWED, WHEN OTHER-FRIENDS APPROVED POLICY OF PERSONAL ISOLATION AND OSTRACISM...
IF JAMES MADROX DOES NOT CONSIDER HIMSELF SULLIED BY THE COMPANY OF SUCH PARIAHS AS WE... I SHALL CONSIDER MYSELF HONORED.
I SUPPOSE... EVEN OUTLAWS MUST HAVE GANGS.

EXTRA FRENCH FRIES?
NATURALLY.
AND FISH McNUGGETS FOR DON AND BILL?
NAH... THERE WAS A SPECIAL ON PENGUIN McBURGERS. I FIGURED THEY'D LIKE THAT BETTER.

ARIEL... YOU TOOK MY SEAT.
THAT'S BECAUSE I KNEW YOU KNEW I'D BE TIRED AFTER STEALING THE FOOD, AND YOU'D WANT TO BE NICE AND GIVE ME YOUR COMFORTABLE CHAIR...
AND SIT ON A BOX.
OH. OH, YEAH. I GUESS YOU'RE RIGHT.
THAT MAKES SENSE.

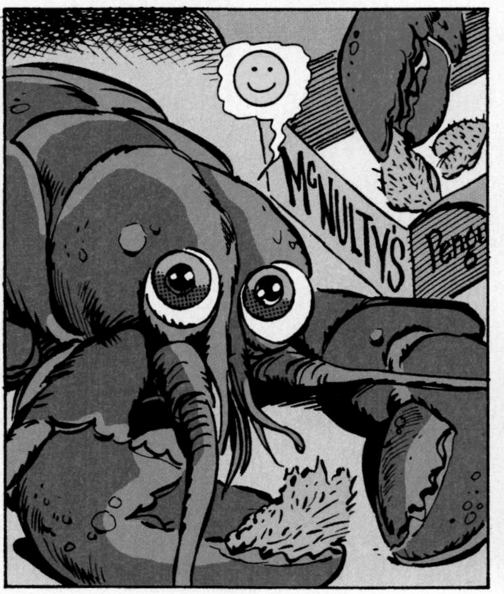
McNULTY'S
Peng

GOMI, I HAVE TO ADMIT, YOU AND YOUR PALS HAVE ME CURIOUS... EXCEPT FOR DON'S COLOR, THEY LOOK LIKE ORDINARY LOBSTERS... BUT THEY'RE OBVIOUSLY NOT...
WHERE DID THEY COME FROM? ARE THEY MUTANTS? ARE YOU?

WELL, I WOULDN'T INSULT ANYONE'S INTELLIGENCE BY POINTING OUT THAT DON'S COLOR MARKS HIM AS A RARE MUTANT LOBSTER... BUT MUTATIONS AREN'T WHAT GAVE ANY OF US OUR EXTRAORDINARY ABILITIES.
WE ARE ALL THREE CYBORGS --CYBERNETIC ORGANISMS, PART OF WHOSE FLESH AND BLOOD HAS BEEN REPLACED BY MACHINE PARTS AND CIRCUITRY.
I EVEN HAD A SMALL HAND IN THEIR CREATION.

"YOU SEE, MY COUSIN, RAMON LIPSCHITZ, AND HIS BEST FRIEND, TADASHI FUJITA ARE, DESPITE ONLY BEING COLLEGE SENIORS, TWO OF THE MOST BRILLIANT SCIENTISTS OF OUR AGE.
"IN FACT, SOME OF THEIR PROFESSORS AT THE UNIVERSITY HAVE ALREADY COMPARED THEM TO TONY STARK... OR REED RICHARDS... OR EVEN VICTOR VON DOOM...

"AND, WHEN THEY WERE GIVEN A RESEARCH GRANT AND FACILITIES NEAR CONEY ISLAND, AND NEEDED A LAB ASSISTANT, THEY CALLED ON ME. I LIKE TO THINK IT'S BECAUSE I AM NEITHER COMPLETELY UNINTELLIGENT NOR AM I UNFAMILIAR WITH SCIENTIFIC METHODS."
HE'LL WORK CHEAP?
FOR FREE. HE'S ALWAYS DONE WHATEVER I TELL HIM, AND HE DOESN'T EAT MUCH, EITHER.

"RAMON AND HIS PARTNER HAVE ALWAYS BEEN GOOD TO ME. WHEN THEY FOUND OUT HOW MUCH I HATE MY REAL NAME-- AND I'M NOT GOING TO TELL YOU WHAT IT IS, SO DON'T ASK ME--
"--FUJITA SAID HE UNDERSTOOD COMPLETELY, AND GAVE ME MY NEW JAPANESE NAME, GOMI*, AND NOW THAT'S ALL ANYONE CALLS ME.
* IT'S JAPANESE FOR "GARBAGE"-- ANN.

"THEIR PROJECT WAS ON SUPERBEINGS, THE WAVE OF THE FUTURE. THEY WANTED TO USE CYBERNETICS TO TRY AND ENHANCE NORMAL CREATURES' ABILITIES...
"...AND WERE USING LOBSTERS FOR THEIR SUBJECTS, ONE PERFECTLY ORDINARY, AND ONE A BLUE MUTANT, AS A CONTROL, SINCE MUTATIONS ARE BECOMING MORE COMMON EVERY DAY...
"...AND CAN BE A MAJOR SOURCE OF ENHANCED CAPABILITIES.

BELIEVE ME, YOU TWO ARE GOING TO ENJOY LIFE AS SENTIENT BEINGS. NEITHER OF YOU SHOWS ANY SIGNS OF REJECTING YOUR PARTS...
SO, SOON YOU'LL BE ABLE TO THINK, AND TO COMMUNICATE. YOU'LL BE ABLE TO LIVE OUTSIDE OF THE WATER FOR LONG PERIODS OF TIME... YOU'LL HAVE SUPERIOR STRENGTH...
TUNA
TUNA

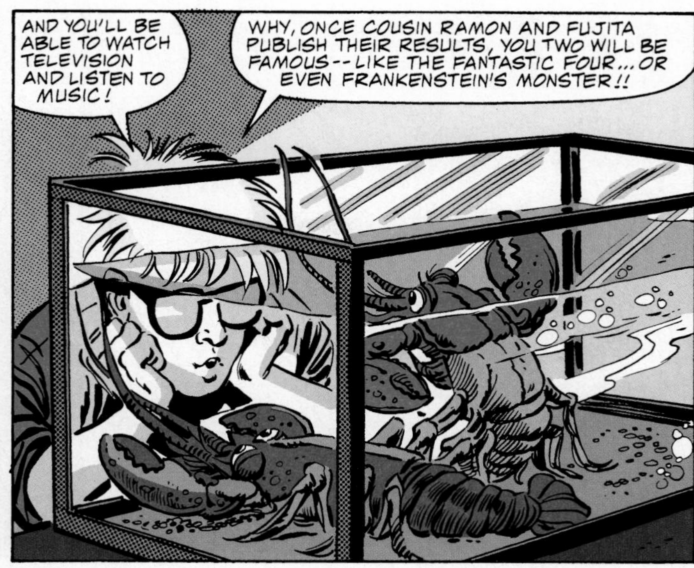
AND YOU'LL BE ABLE TO WATCH TELEVISION AND LISTEN TO MUSIC!
WHY, ONCE COUSIN RAMON AND FUJITA PUBLISH THEIR RESULTS, YOU TWO WILL BE FAMOUS--LIKE THE FANTASTIC FOUR... OR EVEN FRANKENSTEIN'S MONSTER!!

"HOWEVER, OVER THE COURSE OF THEIR RESEARCH, OUR BOSSES HAD DEVELOPED A MORE-THAN-ACADEMIC INTEREST IN ONE PARTICULAR SUPERBEING."
HERE'S TO MARVEL GIRL, OF THE X-MEN, WHOEVER SHE MAY REALLY BE.
MARVEL GIRL
WHO CARES WHO SHE REALLY IS? SHE'S PERFECT JUST THE WAY SHE IS. TELEKINESIS--MIND OVER MATTER--IS SUCH AN ELEGANT POWER.
Best wishes, Marvel Girl
DELICATE!
FEMININE!

DO YOU SUPPOSE... WE'LL EVER GET TO MEET HER... IN THE FLESH?

MY DEAR FUJITA! ONCE WE PUBLISH, SUPERBEINGS WILL FLOCK TO US, AND OF COURSE, SHE WILL BE AMONG THEM!!

AH, LOOK AT HIM! HE CAN DO IT!
SUCCESS!
SUCCESS!
SUCCESS!
RIP
PHONE
COUNTY

BUT, MY DEAR FUJITI, DID YOU EVER DOUBT US?
NEVER FOR AN INSTANT, LIPSCHITZ. NOT THAT IT WOULD HAVE MATTERED IF WE HAD FAILED. LOBSTERS MAKE SUCH GOOD EATING, AFTER ALL.
"OF COURSE, THEY WERE AS PROUD OF DON AND BILL AS I WAS... BUT THEY HAD TO MAINTAIN THEIR SCIENTIFIC DETACHMENT...

"...SO, THEY LEFT ME TO PERSONALIZE THE LOBSTERS' LIVING CONDITIONS."
GOMI, I'M NOT GOING TO WARN YOU AGAIN ABOUT WASTING OUR MONEY ON GOURMET FOOD FOR THOSE THINGS. THEY'RE EATING BETTER THAN WE ARE AS IT IS.
AND TURN DOWN THAT STUPID STEREO OR WE'LL TAKE IT AWAY.
TUNA
SALMON
BUT DON AND BILL LIKE MENUDO.

"THEN, ONE DAY, AFTER THE STARCORE SPACEFLIGHT DISASTER, AND THE APPEARANCE OF A NEW SUPER-BEING, PHOENIX--DISASTER STRUCK!"
FUJITA--IT'S TERRIBLE! THE WORST THING IMAGINABLE!
WHERE, LIPSCHITZ? WHERE?
TIME
HERE, IN TIME MAGAZINE! THIS NEW SUPERWOMAN WHO APPEARED WITH THE X-MEN--THE ONE WHO FOUGHT FIRELORD!
JUST LOOK AT HER!!

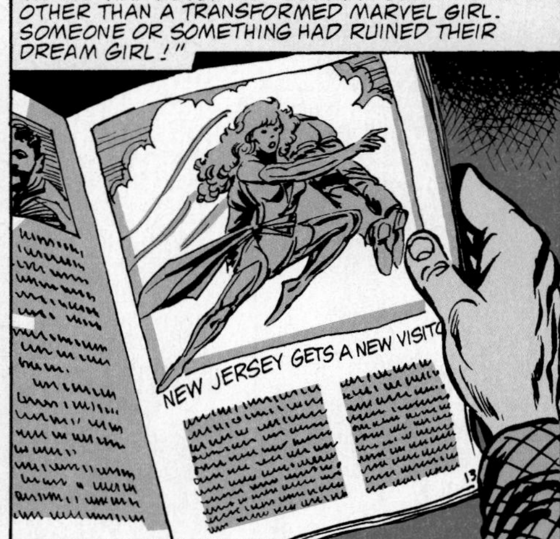
"YES, COUSIN RAMON AND HIS PARTNER HAD DISCERNED SOMETHING THAT MOST OF THE WORLD HAD NEVER NOTICED. PHOENIX WAS NONE OTHER THAN A TRANSFORMED MARVEL GIRL. SOMEONE OR SOMETHING HAD RUINED THEIR DREAM GIRL!"
NEW JERSEY GETS A NEW VISITO
13

"AND SO, A NEW PHASE OF OUR RESEARCH WAS IMMEDIATELY UNDERTAKEN, AS COUSIN RAMON AND TADASHI FUJITA WORKED FEVERISHLY TO DEVELOP CYBERNETICS THAT WOULD RECREATE THE ORIGINAL MARVEL GIRL!"

CAN WE DO IT?
DO YOU DOUBT US?
NEVER!

IT WORKS! IT WORKS!
SO IT WOULD APPEAR... AND YET...
FUJITA... WHAT IF THIS DEVICE IS NOT YET THE UNPARALLELED SUCCESS WE REQUIRE?

WE GO IMPLANTING IT IN SOME OTHERWISE LOVELY, DELICATE, FEMININE CREATURE... AND THEN, IF OUR CALIBRATIONS HAVE BEEN EVEN MINUTELY AWRY...
WELL, THERE YOU HAVE IT! WE'LL HAVE RUINED A PERFECTLY GOOD GIRL FOR NOTHING!!

AHA! BUT... WHAT DO WE HAVE LAB ANIMALS FOR, IF NOT TO EXPERIMENT UPON?
MY SENTIMENTS EXACTLY!
CHLOROFORM

"OF COURSE, IN THE NAME OF SCIENCE AND TRUE LOVE, WHAT COULD I DO BUT VOLUNTEER?"
MMMPH!!

I ALWAYS KNEW SOME DAY THE LITTLE NERD WOULD BE GOOD FOR SOMETHING!
ZZZZZZZZZ
B-BUT... IF THIS DOESN'T WORK... WHO WILL WE GET TO DO THE SWEEPING UP?

"OF COURSE, I WAS PROUD OF MAKING ANY SACRIFICE FOR SO NOBLE A CAUSE..."
I DON'T KNOW WHY YOU HAD TO GO AND PICK ON ME FOR. I'M NOT IN LOVE WITH HER.
BUT, GOMI, MY DEAR, YOU ARE SIMPLY GOING TO LOVE HAVING SUPER POWERS.
TRUST US!

"HOWEVER, IT SOON BECAME CLEAR THAT SOMETHING HAD GONE SERIOUSLY WRONG WITH THEIR INVENTION. IT MANIPULATED A FORM OF TELEKINESIS, TRUE...
"BUT IT WAS CAPABLE ONLY OF CREATING A PILLAR OF PURE BRUTE FORCE. THERE WAS NO FINE MOTOR CONTROL WHATSOEVER.

"AND, AN EVEN BIGGER DISASTER LURKED AROUND THE CORNER. THE NEW ADMINISTRATION HAD CUT GRANTS TO THE SCIENCES... AND WE HEARD THEY WERE SENDING AN INSPECTOR TO EXAMINE OUR RESULTS!"
WHAT RESULTS?!
UNA

WE'LL HAVE TO EAT THEM!
THE LOBSTERS, MAYBE, BUT WE CAN'T EAT GOMI!!
WHY NOT?
OUR MOTHERS PLAY MAH-JOHNNG TOGETHER!

SO, DON AND BILL AND I TOGETHER AWAITED AN INSPECTION THAT, IRONICALLY ENOUGH, THANKS TO A BUREAUCRATIC SNAFU, NEVER OCCURED.
INSTEAD, ALONG CAME THE FALLEN ANGELS, ON A MEMBERSHIP DRIVE.
HOME REPAIRS
AND WE VOTED, TWO TO ONE, THAT WE WERE SICK OF LIVING ALONE, SO WE JOINED UP.
WHEW

QUERY: MAY SELF CONSUME LIFE-GLOW OF REMAINING ORGANIC MATTER?
YOU MEAN TURN THE GARBAGE INTO LIVING CIRCUITRY LIKE YOU'RE MADE OF AND THEN EAT IT?

SURE, WHY NOT?

URP

WHAT ABOUT YOU, ARIEL? I STILL DON'T UNDERSTAND HOW YOU PULL THAT LITTLE TELEPORTATION STUNT OF YOURS. ARE YOU A MUTANT, TOO?
NO, NOT ME. THAT'S JUST A LITTLE TRICK SOME OF THE FOLKS AT HOME TAUGHT ME. SEE, IT ALL HAS TO DO WITH DOORWAYS... I CONCENTRATE ON A CLOSED DOOR, AND MENTALLY JUXTAPOSE IT WITH ANOTHER CLOSED DOOR...
AND WHEN I OPEN THE DOOR IN FRONT OF ME, THE OTHER SIDE IS THE OTHER SIDE OF THE OTHER DOOR I WAS THINKING OF. I'M NOT SURE HOW IT WORKS SCIENTIFICALLY. I THINK IT INVOLVES BENDING SPACE.
THE IMPORTANT THING IS THAT IT ALWAYS WORKS.

NOW, ARIEL, IT'S NOT LIKE YOU TO BE SO MODEST. I'M SURE MADROX, SUNSPOT AND WARLOCK WOULD BE MUCH MORE IMPRESSED BY A DEMONSTRATION, NOW THAT THEY UNDERSTAND A LITTLE ABOUT YOUR SPACE-BENDING TRICK.
WHAT ARE YOU DRIVING AT?
BOOM BOOM, YOU AIRHEAD! HAVE YOU FORGOTTEN SHE IS IN THE CLUTCHES OF THOSE NOTORIOUS MUTANT HUNTERS, X-FACTOR?!
SO, LET THEM HAVE HER! GOOD OLD "TIME BOMB" TURNED THE REST OF US IN, OF HER OWN FREE WILL. IF SHE'S STUCK NOW, TOO BAD!

DON'T BE SO HASTY AND UNFORGIVING, CHANCE! I UNDERSTAND HOW YOU FEEL, BUT THERE ARE MORE IMPORTANT THINGS AT STAKE HERE THAN INDIVIDUAL EMOTIONS.

MUCH MORE IMPORTANT... OR DO I HAVE TO PAINT YOU A PICTURE?

OH, YEAH. THAT'S RIGHT. SORRY, ARIEL. I FORGOT.
GO AHEAD AND BRING HER HOME.

I THINK WE'RE ONTO SOMETHING, SIRYN. THE DETECTORS ARE GOING CRAZY. THIS BUILDING WE'RE PASSING MUST BE FULL OF MUTANTS.
IT WOULD BE, LADDIE. THIS IS THE HEAD-QUARTERS OF X-FACTOR.
I SUGGEST WE MOVE ALONG QUICKLY. IT WOULDN'T DO TO HAVE ANYONE INSIDE TAKIN' NOTICE OF US!
ER WAREHOU

RIGHT. OKAY, WELL, WE'VE GOT ANOTHER CONCENTRATION WE HAVEN'T CHECKED OUT YET, NEAR THE MIDTOWN AREA.

C STORAGE
THIS WOULD ALL BE SO MUCH EASIER IF ONLY WE HADN'T GIVEN OUR WORD TO BE DISCREET AND ANONYMOUS WHILE WE WERE SEARCHIN'!

AND, IN THE LAB INSIDE X-FACTOR HEADQUARTERS WE FIND HANK McCOY AND BOBBY DRAKE--
--TWO OF THE MUTANT HUNTERS WHO, LIKE THEIR FELLOWS IN X-FACTOR, ARE ACTUALLY MUTANTS THEMSELVES, IN THIS CASE THE BEAST AND THE ICEMAN.

HOW'S IT GOING, HANK?
NOT WELL, BOBBY. NOT AT ALL WELL. I CAN'T GET OVER THE FEELING THAT I SHOULDN'T BE FINDING THESE CALCULATIONS SO DIFFICULT!

I BEEN LOOKIN' FOR YOU GUYS. WHY AREN'T YOU UPSTAIRS? THERE'S SOMETHIN' GOIN' ON UP THERE! SOMETHIN' IMPORTANT.*
OH, HI, BOOM BOOM.
*TO FIND OUT WHAT, SEE X-FACTOR #17--ANN.

WE'RE IN THE MIDDLE OF SOMETHING HERE, SO IF YOU'LL JUST MOVE ALONG...
WE ARE SORT OF BUSY...
BUT I NEED YOU!

HANK, THERE MIGHT REALLY BE SOMETHING.
OH, SURE. SHE PROBABLY WANTS TO LURE US INTO A DEADFALL SHE'S GOT SET IN THE HALLWAY OR SOMETHING.
THEY NEVER LISTEN OR TAKE ME SERIOUSLY! BUT I'LL SHOW THEM WHAT HAPPENS...

...WHEN THEY UNDERESTIMATE A GIRL...
...WHO CAN CREATE HER OWN LITTLE TIME BOMBS.

HANK, I THINK WE REALLY UPSET HER.
GOOD.
<SIGH> NEVER MIND. IF IT DOESN'T MATTER TO YOU, THEN I GUESS IT DOESN'T MATTER TO ME EITHER.

BOOM

YAAY! CATCH ME IF YOU CAN, SUCKERS!!
WELL, YOU HEARD HER, BOBBY!

BEA
NOW, I'VE NEVER BEEN INSIDE X-FACTOR HEADQUARTERS, THANK GOODNESS... BUT I THINK WE CAN ASSUME THAT A BUILDING THAT SIZE HAS AT LEAST ONE BROOM CLOSET IN IT, AND THAT THEY DON'T LEAVE THE DOOR OPEN.

SO, I OPEN OUR DOOR, CONCENTRATING ON **THEIR** DOOR, AND INSTEAD OF THE ALLEY OUTSIDE...

PRESTO! HEY, NICE PLACE THEY HAVE!
BOOM BOOM! HEY, TABITHA, TIME BOMB, OR WHATEVER YOU'RE CALLING YOURSELF!
ALL ABOARD FOR BEAT STREET!!

OBOY! THAT SOUNDS LIKE MY RIDE HOME!
HEY, NO FAIR ICING UP THE STAIRS! YOU WANT ME TO BREAK MY ANKLE?
YES!!

IN HERE! HURRY!
WHOOPS! HERE I COME!!

HOME FREE!

BOTH OF YOU COME OUT OF THERE!
SLAM

I DON'T GET IT! WHERE DID THEY GO?!!

WHO CARES? THE IMPORTANT THING IS THAT LITTLE WALKING DISASTER AREA IS BACK OUT OF OUR LIVES!!
UTILITY C4

GREAT GOING! YOU COULDN'T HAVE TIMED IT BETTER!
I'M GLAD YOU...
NOW, BOOM BOOM, SURELY OUR LONG ASSOCIATION HAS TAUGHT YOU TO COUNT ON THE VANISHER. I DON'T WANT TO BRAG...
...BUT IT WAS, AFTER ALL, I WHO SELECTED BOTH THE MEANS AND THE TIMING OF YOUR RESCUE FROM THE CLUTCHES OF THOSE FIENDS.

OH, THEY WEREN'T SUCH FIENDS. ONE OR TWO OF THEM WERE KIND OF CUTE...
BUT, NOW THAT I MENTION IT, I NOTICE THE SCENERY AROUND BEAT STREET HAS REALLY IMPROVED.
HI. I'M TABITHA... BUT EVERYBODY CALLS ME BOOM BOOM. WHO'RE YOU?
JAMIE MADROX.

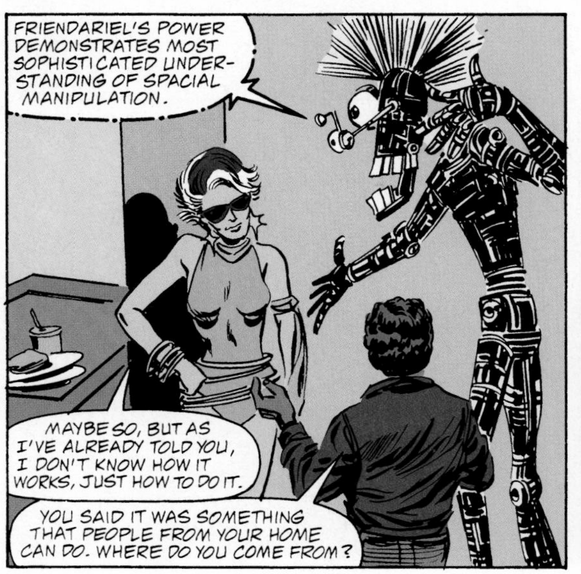
FRIENDARIEL'S POWER DEMONSTRATES MOST SOPHISTICATED UNDERSTANDING OF SPACIAL MANIPULATION.
MAYBE SO, BUT AS I'VE ALREADY TOLD YOU, I DON'T KNOW HOW IT WORKS, JUST HOW TO DO IT.
YOU SAID IT WAS SOMETHING THAT PEOPLE FROM YOUR HOME CAN DO. WHERE DO YOU COME FROM?

OH, I'LL TELL YOU ALL ABOUT IT, SOMEDAY. MAYBE WE'LL EVEN GO THERE... BUT YOU'RE NOT INTERESTED IN THAT RIGHT NOW, ARE YOU?
I... SUPPOSE NOT.
SELF... CAN FORMULATE NO FURTHER QUESTIONS AT THIS TIME.

AND... YOU REALLY HAVE COMPLETE CONTROL OVER YOUR POWER.
OF COURSE. FOR EXAMPLE, I'M GOING TO OPEN THE DOOR WITHOUT DOING ANYTHING...
AND ALL THAT WILL BE OUT THERE IS WHAT-EVER IS REALLY IN THE ALLEY OUTSIDE.

SEE?
WHOOPS!
AHA!
FOUND YOU AT LAST!

ABOUT TIME, TOO. WE WERE BEGINNING TO THINK YOU'D NEVER GET HERE.
WE'VE BEEN JUST DYING FOR YOU TO SHOW UP. IN FACT, I WAS JUST SAYING...
UH... THANKS. THAT'S VERY NICE OF YOU.

ALL RIGHT, MR. ROBERTO da COSTA, I'VE HAD A LONG AND TIRING DAY, AND I'M NOT IN THE MOOD FOR ANY...

OF COURSE YOU'RE TIRED. WE'RE ALL TIRED. NO REASON TO BE UPSET. CALM DOWN AND START OVER. YOU JUST GOT HERE, AFTER ALL.
IF MISS CASSIDY INTENDS TO GO ON AS SHE BEGAN, THEN LET HER SPARE HERSELF THE TROUBLE OF ANY FURTHER WORDS!

YEAH! WHAT HE SAID! WHO DO YOU THINK YOU ARE, ANYWAY?

SO, HOW'VE YOU BEEN?
CAN'T COMPLAIN ... ROOM FOR ONE MORE, IF YOU'D CARE TO COME ABOARD.

SO THAT'S HIS POWER. TOO BAD. I LIKED HIM BETTER WHEN I THOUGHT HE WAS TWINS.

I DON'T BLAME YOU FOR BEING UPSET...

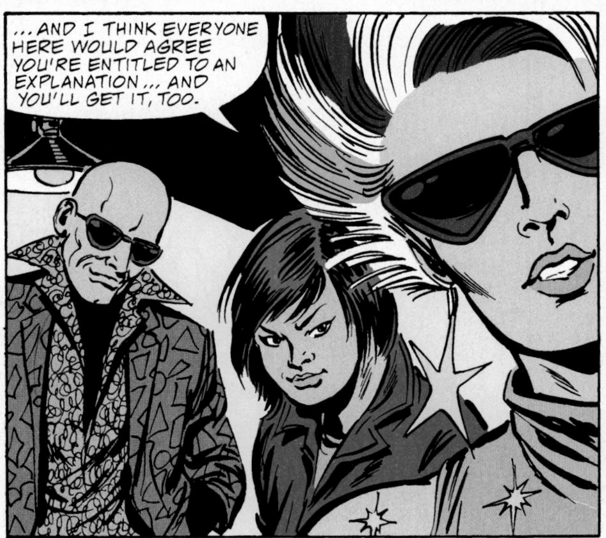
...AND I THINK EVERYONE HERE WOULD AGREE YOU'RE ENTITLED TO AN EXPLANATION... AND YOU'LL GET IT, TOO.

BUT IT'S SO HOT AND CROWDED IN HERE. WE CAN ALL BE A LOT MORE COMFORTABLE, IF EVERY-ONE WILL JUST STEP OUTSIDE...
OKAY.

?
SO, I SUPPOSE YOU'RE ALL WONDERING WHY I'VE CALLED YOU HERE...

TO BE CONTINUED...

#4 IN AN EIGHT-ISSUE LIMITED SERIES
MARVEL®
© 1987 MARVEL
TM
FALLEN ANGELS
75¢ US
95¢ CAN
4
JULY
CC 02409
APPROVED BY THE COMICS CODE
AUTHORITY
GAMMILL - PALMER

A DEVIL AMONG THE ANGELS!
Created by DUFFY and GAMMILL
JO DUFFY WRITER ○ KERRY GAMMILL PENCILER ○ VAL MAYERIK INKER
L.P. GREGORY LETTERER ○ PETRA SCOTESE COLORIST
ANN NOCENTI EDITOR
JIM SHOOTER EDITOR IN CHIEF
EVERYONE, RUN FOR YOUR LIVES!
MY NAME IS ROBERTO DA COSTA.
I AM FOURTEEN YEARS OLD...
1

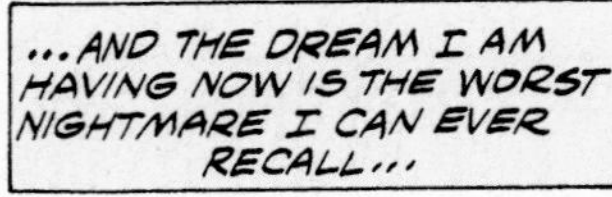

...AND THE DREAM I AM HAVING NOW IS THE WORST NIGHTMARE I CAN EVER RECALL...

...ALL THE MORE FRIGHTENING FOR MY INABILITY TO REMEMBER...

...JUST WHEN I WENT TO SLEEP.

I WAS IN OUR HEADQUARTERS, THE BEAT STREET CLUB, WITH MY FELLOW FALLEN ANGELS--
--MOST OF US TEENAGERS, ALL BUT ONE OF US MARKED BY SOME SUPERHUMAN ABILITY--
--WHEN AN ARGUMENT SPRANG UP.
SIRYN--A MUTANT WITH POWERFUL SONIC ABILITIES--AND MADROX, THE MULTIPLE MAN, WERE INSISTING ON EXPLANATIONS OF WHO AND WHAT THE REST OF THE GROUP WERE.

AND ARIEL SUGGESTED WE ALL STEP OUTSIDE TO CALM DOWN.

SHE SOUNDED SO REASONABLE AND PERSUASIVE THAT NONE OF US CONSIDERED THAT ARIEL HAS THE POWER TO ACTUALLY BEND SPACE...

SO THAT ANY DOOR SHE OPENS MAY COMMUNICATE ONTO ANY OTHER DOORWAY SHE CHOOSES, HOWEVER FAR AWAY...

AND SO WE FOUND OURSELVES IN A PLACE THAT RESEMBLES OUR OWN EARTH OF MILLIONS OF YEARS AGO...

HEY, TAKE US BACK NOW, OR I'LL BLOW YOU TO KINGDOM COME.

THEY DON'T CALL ME BOOM BOOM FOR NOTHING, YOU KNOW!!

BUT I THOUGHT YOU'D ENJOY THE FRESH AIR!

NOW, GIRLS...

sh...?

THAT WAS WHEN WE HEARD THE DREADFUL ROAR...

2

AND I KNEW THAT THIS COULD ONLY BE A BAD DREAM!
WHAT WILL WE DO IF IT COMES OUR WAY?
THE ADULT WHO LEADS US IS CALLED THE VANISHER...

...FOR EXCELLENT REASONS.
PLINK!
OH, GREAT!

STAND YOUR GROUND, ARIEL. IF YOU ACT BRAVE AND KEEP STILL, IT MAY NOT ATTACK YOU!
B-BUT...BUT, CHANCE, I...

DOES FRIENDSIRYN HAVE PLANNED A COURSE OF ACTION IN WHICH ALL MAY PARTICIPATE? FRIEND-GOMI, PLEASE ENLIGHTEN SELF!
MY APOLOGIES, WARLOCK, BUT AT THE MOMENT, MY KNOWLEDGE IS AS LIMITED AS YOUR OWN.
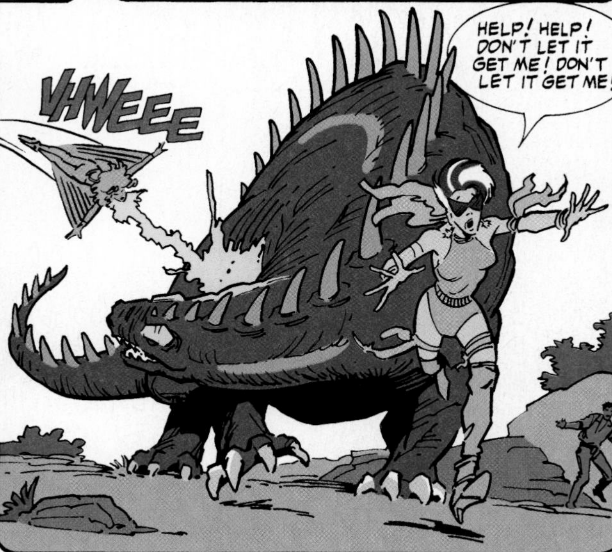
VHWEEE
HELP! HELP! DON'T LET IT GET ME! DON'T LET IT GET ME!

EAT HOT TIME BOMB, BIG AND SCALY! AND THE NEXT ONE'S GONNA BE SET TO GO OFF TWICE AS HARD!
OOF!

BOOM BOOM, WE'RE GOING TO NEED MORE PEOPLE THAN WE HAVE HERE TO GET GOMI AND THE OTHERS CLEAR! HIT ME!
WHAT?
YOU HEARD ME. HIT ME!!
3

DON'T STAND THERE GAPING. SNAP OUT OF IT!
NOW!!
YOU HIT ME!! YOU DIRTY, ROTTEN... NO ONE HITS ME!!
TAKE THAT!!
BOTH OF YOU!
HEY! NOW THERE'S TWO OF YOU!
WHAM!
RIGHT. I'M THE MULTIPLE MAN, REMEMBER? NOW HIT ME A FEW MORE TIMES 'CAUSE TWO ISN'T ENOUGH.
MY PLEASURE.
HER PLEASURE. SURE. NO ONE HITS HER. EVERYONE HITS ME.
OKAY, EVERYONE. WHILE SIRYN'S DISTRACTING THE DINOSAUR, GET TO SAFETY.
WARLOCK, YOU GET GOMI AND THE LOBSTERS TO SAFETY!
AFFIRMATIVE!
MY GLASSES!
GIVE THEM TO YOU LATER!
BUT I'M NOT AFRAID!!
YOU'LL BE BRAVE AND DEAD, UNLESS...
...WHOA!!
CHANCE... MADROX!
4

I AM A MUTANT, ALSO KNOWN AS SUNSPOT, AND MY BODY IS A LIVING SOLAR BATTERY.

AT FULL POWER, MY STRENGTH IS PRODIGIOUS, AND TODAY THE SUN IS STRONG...

BUT I KNOW MY LIMITATIONS...

AND THE STRENGTH OF THIS BEAST FAR EXCEEDS THEM... AND I AM AS VULNERABLE AS ANY OTHER MAN.

5

HEY, HOW DID YOU DO THAT ?!
I THOUGHT YOU WEREN'T THAT STRONG.
I... I'M NOT.
WELL, WHATEVER YOU DID, YOU BETTER GET READY TO DO IT AGAIN, 'CAUSE HERE COMES YOUR FRIEND!
BE READY TO RUN!
6

RIGHT.

UHN!

AT LEAST I CAN HOPE THAT WHEN I AWAKEN...
...MY NIGHT-MARE WILL HAVE ENDED.

HEY, DA COSTA! DA COSTA!
BOBBY!
HE KNOCKED HIMSELF OUT. CLOWN.
LUCKY HE WAITED TILL THE MONSTER WAS GONE TO BE SO STUPID!

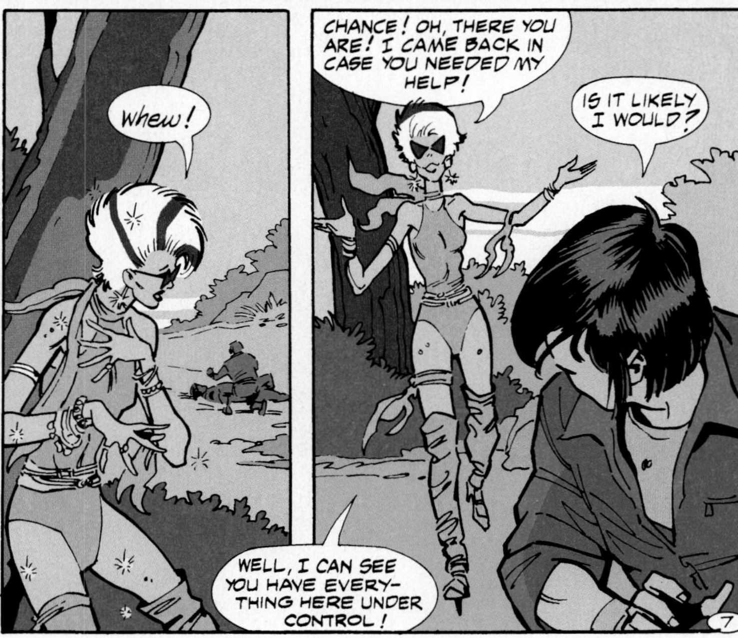
Whew!
CHANCE! OH, THERE YOU ARE! I CAME BACK IN CASE YOU NEEDED MY HELP!
IS IT LIKELY I WOULD?
WELL, I CAN SEE YOU HAVE EVERY-THING HERE UNDER CONTROL!
7

THERE, YOU SEE, MY BROTHER? TRULY, THESE STRANGERS ARE OF GREAT STRENGTH AND COURAGE, AND STAND IN NO NEED OF OUR AID...
ALTHOUGH, HAD YOU CHOSEN TO AID THEM, I KNOW FROM THE ACTIONS I HAVE SEEN THAT THEY WOULD BE WORTHY ALLIES...OR WORTHY FOES, IF THEY CHOSE TO STAND AGAINST US...
I WONDER WHAT HAS BROUGHT SUCH STRANGE AND MIGHTY BEINGS TO THE VALLEY OF THE FLAME.
GGRPH!

WHAT MADE YOU TAKE US TO SUCH A STUPID DANGEROUS PLACE ANYWAY, ARIEL? DON'T YOU CARE THAT YOU ALMOST GOT US...uh, BOBBY...KILLED?
I THOUGHT MUTANTS WERE SO IMPORTANT TO YOU...SO WHAT ARE YOU DOING TAKING HIM SOMEPLACE WHERE HE HAS TO RISK HIS LIFE?

I CHECKED OUT THIS PLANET PRETTY CAREFULLY BEFORE WE CAME HERE. IT'S IN A REALLY POTENT EVOLUTIONARY PHASE...A LOT LIKE EARTH WAS BEFORE HUMANS BECAME THE DOMINANT SPECIES.

THERE ARE AT LEAST TWO REALLY SIGNIFICANT NATIVE MUTANTS RIGHT HERE IN THIS REGION...IMPORTANT ENOUGH TO JUSTIFY THE LOSS OF A LESSER ONE...

EXCEPT OF COURSE, THAT I KNEW NONE OF THEM WOULD REALLY GET KILLED.
8

BY THE WAY... I HOPE YOU'RE NOT GOING SOFT ON SUNSPOT. THE JOB WE HAVE TO DO WON'T BE ANY EASIER IF YOU START FORMING EMOTIONAL ATTACHMENTS.
YOU THINK I CARE WHAT HAPPENS TO HIM? I CARE ABOUT NO ONE BUT MYSELF... ESPECIALLY NOT A LITTLE MACHO LIKE THIS ONE.
Mmmmm
THUMP!

IS MY NIGHTMARE OVER?

NO, YOU'RE STUCK RIGHT IN THE MIDDLE OF THE WORST PART OF IT--
--ALONE.

`BYE.
WAIT... PLEASE...

?

9

HUFF
PUFF
PUFF
PUFF
AM I SAFE? I THINK SO.

BUT WHAT ABOUT THE KIDS... MY CHILDREN, MY FALLEN ANGELS, MY DARLINGS?
THEY WERE RIGHT IN THE PATH OF THAT FEROCIOUS BEAST... MAYBE I SHOULD GO BACK...

NAW! THEY'RE CAPABLE.
THEY'LL PROBABLY BE ALL RIGHT.

?

YAAAHH!

PLINK!
10

I'M SORRY, DON, BUT I MUST CONTRADICT YOU. TRUE, YOU BILL AND I HAVE INTELLIGENCE FAR IN EXCESS OF THAT OF THE DINOSAURS WE'VE ENCOUNTERED THUS FAR...
AND WHILE I DO ACKNOWLEDGE THAT LIKE MINE, YOUR CYBERNETICALLY AUGMENTED STRENGTH PLACES YOU IN A CLASS FAR ABOVE THE REST OF YOUR SPECIES...
...STILL I MUST CONTEND THAT IN THE CLASSIC STRUGGLE OF DINOSAUR AGAINST LOBSTER, THE SHEER PHYSICAL MASS OF THE DINOSAUR IS BOUND TO PREVAIL.
PUT ME DOWN!!!

QUERY: FRIENDSIRYN, IS IT NOW SAFE TO LAND?
AYE, I THINK SO, WARLOCK. WE'VE PUT SOME DISTANCE BETWEEN OURSELVES AND THE BEASTIE, ANYWAY!

LEMME GO, LEMME GO! I CAN RUN FASTER WITHOUT YOUR HELP, YOU BIG LUMMOX!
SWEETHEART, IT WILL BE MY PLEASURE...
...TO DROP YOU RIGHT ON YOUR HEAD, IF YOU DON'T COOL OFF!

SWEETHEART?
MAY AS WELL PULL MYSELF TOGETHER...
A LITTLE IMPACT... AND ONE OF ME'S ALL THAT'S LEFT!
ENOUGH FOR ME, LOVE.
THANKS. AND THANKS FOR SAVING MY LIFE BACK THERE, TOO.
FOOEY.
11

SELF IS ANXIOUS ABOUT WELLBEING OF FRIENDBOBBY AND FRIENDCHANCE'S PHYSICAL UNITS!
QUERY: MAY SELF SEEK THEM AND DETERMINE IF EITHER UNIT REQUIRES AID.
GOOD IDEA. YOU MIGHT LOOK FOR ARIEL, TOO, SINCE WE SEEM TO HAVE MISLAID HER AGAIN.
JUST BE CAREFUL.

SELF WILL USE MALLEABILITY OF SELF'S ORGANIC CIRCUITRY TO MIMIC NATIVE LIFE FORM...
...AND SO ACHIEVE MAXIMUM DISCRETION.

PARDON THE INTERRUPTION, BUT I'VE BEEN CONFERRING WITH DON AND BILL, AND WE HAVE REACHED THE CONSENSUS THAT OUR FIRST PRIORITIES, AS A GROUP, MUST BE THE BUILDING OF A FIRE FOR WARMTH AND PROTECTION...
AND, OF COURSE, THE ACQUISITION AND PREPARATION OF SUSTENANCE IN SUFFICIENT QUANTITIES FOR ALL.

GREAT PLAN, GOMI. JUST WHAT DO YOU EXPECT TO USE TO BUILD THIS FIRE OF YOURS?

ONE GENERALLY BEGINS...

...WITH KINDLING.
YIPE!!

GOMI, YOU MORON! YOU KNOW YOU DON'T HAVE ANY CONTROL OVER THAT MAN-MADE FORCE BEAM OF YOURS.
YOU COULD HAVE KILLED ME!!
12

BUT TWO CAN PLAY AT THAT GAME!
BOOM BOOM, DON'T! A FORCE PELLET OF THAT SIZE REALLY COULD KILL HIM!

I DON'T CARE, I--
--HEY!!!
OOF!
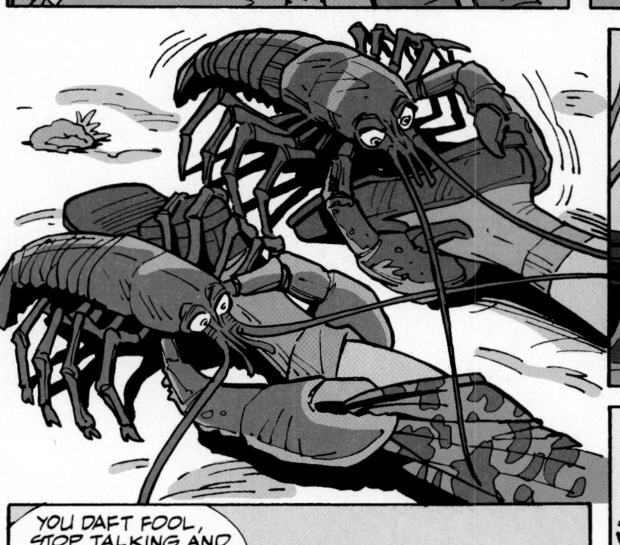

DEFTLY DONE, FELLOWS. THE PELLET HAS ROLLED RIGHT INTO THE THICKET, WHERE--!

YOU DAFT FOOL, STOP TALKING AND START DUCKING OR YOU'LL WIND UP AS KINDLING YOURSELF!

13

I JUST DON'T KNOW WHAT TO DO WHEN A MAN USES HIS STRENGTH ON ME LIKE THAT.
BUT I WAS JUST... I MEAN I...
I TRIPPED, THAT'S ALL.

YOU KNOW, THERE ARE OTHER WAYS OF STARTIN' A FIRE MORE EFFICIENT THAN THE ONE YOU'RE USING...
...EVEN IF THEY'RE NOT AS MUCH FUN.

SELF'S HOSTILE EXTRUSIONS WILL HOLD PREDATORS AT BAY... BUT SELF'S CONCERN FOR FRIENDBOBBY INCREASES GEOMETRICALLY...
...WITH EACH ENCOUNTER WITH INIMICAL LIFEFORMS!

SHEEARGHCK!
IDENTIFICATION: DEATHSOUND!

FRIENDBOBBY! IF YOU ARE PRESENT IN IMMEDIATE AREA, PLEASE RESPOND AT ONCE!
REQUEST URGENT!!
14

!

JUBILATION! SELF IS DELIGHTED TO SEE SELF'S TRUEFRIEND IN SUCH GOOD WORKING ORDER!
THANK YOU. I'M... HAPPY TO SEE YOU, TOO.
ARE THE OTHERS WELL?
VANISHERENTITY PRESUMED TO BE IN GOOD CONDITION, AS HE HAS NOT YET REAPPEARED. FRIENDSCHANCE AND ARIEL HAVE LIKEWISE VANISHED.
ALL OTHERS ACCOUNTED FOR AND OPERABLE.
CHANCE AND ARIEL ARE BOTH WELL. THEY DIDN'T LEAVE HERE TILL THE FIRST DANGER WAS PAST.
FRIENDBOBBY...?
YES?

SELF THOUGHT WHEN FRIEND-BOBBY JOINED FALLEN ANGELS, HE REPUDIATED HEROIC IDEALS. QUERY: WAS NOT RESCUE OF FRIENDCHANCE AN ACT OF HEROISM?
TEAMMATES ARE DIFFERENT. EVEN VILLAINS SHOULD STAND BY THEIR OWN!

QUERY: HAS VISIT TO THIS WORLD INCREASED FRIENDBOBBY'S POWER?
I DON'T THINK SO. WHATEVER THAT POWER BURST I HAD WAS, IT DIDN'T OUTLAST A BUMP ON THE HEAD.
WITHOUT AUGMEN-TATION HOW DID FRIENDBOBBY DEFEAT SECOND ATTACKING PREDATOR.

TO TELL YOU THE TRUTH, MY FRIEND, I DID NOT.
15

THEY DID!
16

I FIRST LEARNED ABOUT THESE MUTANTS... WELL, ABOUT ONE OF THEM REALLY, THROUGH THE AMERICAN ENTERTAINMENT MEDIA. SEE, HE CAME TO EARTH ONCE OR TWICE...
...THROUGH MAGIC, OR SPACE WARPS, I IMAGINE, AND PEOPLE JUST ASSUMED HE'D COME FORWARD IN TIME FROM EARTH'S PAST...
YOU KEEP MAKING THAT RACKET YOU'LL ATTRACT MORE HUNGRY PREDATORS.

I'M SORRY. I'LL KEEP IT DOWN. THE THING IS, AS SOON AS WE FIND THESE TWO, WE CAN HEAD BACK TO BEAT STREET, AND--!

QUIET!

THERE'S SOMETHING MOVING OVER THERE!

WE CAN CATCH IT OFF GUARD!
CHANCE, ARE YOU CRAZY? THAT'S DANGEROUS!

HAH!
NO! HELP! MOTHER!
17

HEY, BOSS! IT'S US!
DON'T BE AFRAID!
AND DON'T VANISH! WE AREN'T GOING TO HURT YOU!
PLEASE LET ME GO! I TASTE TERRIBLE AND IT'S AGAINST MY RELIGION TO BE EATEN AND ANYWAY...
?
whew!
I WAS ONLY FOOLING! YOU DIDN'T THINK I WAS AFRAID, DID YOU? ME? NOT REALLY!
I KNEW IT WAS YOU ALL THE TIME!
IN FACT, I WAS JUST ON MY WAY TO FIND YOU AND THE OTHERS, SO IF YOU'LL JUST FOLLOW ME...
THAT'S THE DIRECTION WE JUST CAME FROM. THE OTHERS WENT THIS WAY.
OH. I KNEW THAT.
BY THE WAY, HOW DID THE DINOSAUR ATTACK GO?
DID ANYONE GET KILLED?
18

THANK YOU VERY MUCH, BILL. I THINK WE HAVE ENOUGH FUEL FOR THE FIRE NOW.
WHATCHA GOT?
ITS INVENTOR CALLED THE ORIGINAL VERSION OF IT *CEREBRO.*

YES, DON, YOU CAN HAVE THE DARK MEAT... ASSUMING THIS CREATURE HAS ANY DARK MEAT.

THIS IS A PORTABLE VERSION. IT DETECTS MUTANTS BY TRACKING THEIR BIOENERGIES, WHICH ARE DISTINCT FROM THOSE OF NORMAL CREATURES, BOTH WHEN THEY ARE USING THEIR ABILITIES AND WHEN IN REPOSE.
I WISH SHE'D STOP STARING AT ME.

THAT SMELLS DELICIOUS, GOMI. YOU MUST BE QUITE A COOK. WHAT IS IT?
I HAVE NO IDEA. DON AND BILL TRACKED AND KILLED IT.

TAKE THE LOBSTERS, FOR EXAMPLE.
I CAN THINK OF SOMEONE ELSE I'D RATHER TAKE.
UH...

WHAT JAMIE MEANS IS THAT YOU MIGHT THINK, FROM THEIR ABILITIES, THAT BOTH DON AND BILL ARE MUTANTS. HOWEVER, THEIR POWERS COME FROM THEIR ROBOT PARTS.
DON, HOWEVER, DOES REGISTER AS MUTANT BECAUSE OF HIS RARE AZURE COLORATION.
KLAK
KLAK
OF COURSE, GREEN IS NICE, TOO.
19

HEY, THIS IS ODD! I'M GETTING SOME KIND OF READING FROM BOTH OF YOU GIRLS... LIKE YOU WERE LATENT MUTANTS, OR SOMETHING.

YOU'RE PROBABLY HOLDING THE STUPID THING UPSIDE-DOWN, OR SOMETHING.

I COULDN'T BE A MUTANT, JAMIE. IT'S JUST NOT POSSIBLE. AND NEITHER IS CHANCE.

WELL, I SUPPOSE WE CAN TAKE TIME OUT FOR FOOD, FIRST!
I GET THE FIRST HELPING, GOMI... AFTER YOU TASTE IT TO SEE IF IT'S POISONED, OF COURSE.
BUT DON AND BILL... sigh

YOU WEREN'T SERIOUSLY THINKIN' OF LEAVIN' WITHOUT WARLOCK AND BOBBY, WERE YOU?
UUMMM
TELL YOU WHAT. THE REST OF US CAN GO HOME... AND ARIEL CAN WAIT HERE FOR THEM TO SHOW UP.

SHOW UP?! YOU MISERABLE COWARD, WE DON'T EVEN KNOWN IF THEY'RE...
RELAX, SIRYN, ACCORDING TO MY READINGS, THEY'VE JUST SHOWN...

WARLOCK! BOBBY!
GREETINGS, HELLO, AND OTHER EXPRESSIONS OF SALUTATION AND FELICITATION.
DID YOU SAVE US SOME FOOD?
YOU SEE? I KNEW THEY COULD BE DEPENDED ON TO REJOIN US WITHOUT A LOT OF INSULTING NURSEMAIDING.

RUSTLE
CRUNCH
KRAK
NEWFRIENDS ENSURED SAFE RETURN OF BOTH FRIENDBOBBY AND SELF.
WHICH "NEWFRIENDS", WARLOCK?
WHOEVER THEY ARE, THEY'LL HAVE TO BRING THEIR OWN FOOD, BECAUSE I'M NOT SHARING.

HEY... THE CEREBRO UNIT IS READING OFF THE SCALE! EITHER THERE ARE A HUNDRED MUTANTS COMING, OR ELSE...
21

HELLO! THIS IS DEVIL DINOSAUR, AND I AM **MOON BOY**!

WELCOME TO THE GROUP. WANT SOME DINNER?

CONTINUED...

NEXT ISSUE: LOST AND FOUND!

22

MARVEL®
#5 IN AN EIGHT-ISSUE LIMITED SERIES
FALLEN ANGELS
© 1987 MARVEL ENT. GROUP INC.
75¢ US
95¢ CAN
5
AUG
CC 02409
APPROVED BY THE COMICS CODE AUTHORITY
THIS ISSUE--
AN ANGEL
DIES!
GAMMILL-PALMER

LOST AND FOUND
BOOM BOOM!!!
CREATED BY DUFFY & GAMMILL
JO DUFFY WRITER
JOE STATON PENCILER
VAL MAYERIK INKER
BILL OAKLEY LETTERER
PETRA SCOTESE COLORIST
ANN NOCENTI EDITOR
JIM SHOOTER -- EDITOR IN CHIEF

WHAT ARE YOU TRYING TO DO? I ONLY ASKED FOR A SMALL DEMONSTRATION. YOU NEARLY BLEW THE BUILDING DOWN.
THE BEAT ST. CLUB
I'M SORRY, JAMIE... I DIDN'T MEAN...

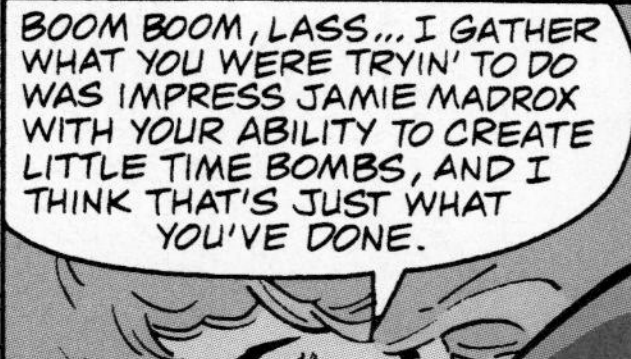
BOOM BOOM, LASS... I GATHER WHAT YOU WERE TRYIN' TO DO WAS IMPRESS JAMIE MADROX WITH YOUR ABILITY TO CREATE LITTLE TIME BOMBS, AND I THINK THAT'S JUST WHAT YOU'VE DONE.

I THINK YOU'RE TOO KIND TO HER, SIRYN. HER FLIRTATION PUT ALL OF OUR LIVES AT RISK...
BUT, BOBBY, SHE SAID SHE DIDN'T MEAN...

TRULY, THE WRATH AND POWER OF SHE-WHO-IS-LIKE-A-LIVING-FIRE-MOUNTAIN ARE BEYOND BELIEF. WHAT HAPPENED TO DISPLEASE HER?
SORRY, KID, BUT ALL I'M GETTING FROM YOU IS "OOP-ACK."
HEY, CHANCE, WHAT'S MOON BOY SAYING?

WELL, I CAN'T EXACTLY GIVE YOU AN EXACT TRANSLATION, VANISHER...
BUT IT'S PROBABLY SOMETHING TO DO WITH HOW MUCH BETTER OFF ALL THE FALLEN ANGELS WOULD BE IF BOOM BOOM WOULD STOP SHOWING OFF AND LEARN A LITTLE SELF-CONTROL.

BUT... IT WASN'T MY FAULT!
I ONLY SET OFF A LITTLE TIME BOMB, BECAUSE JAMIE WANTED TO SEE IT...
I WOULDN'T DO ANYTHING TO HURT HIM! YOU KNOW I WOULDN'T!
BUT IT WAS TWICE AS POWERFUL AS I INTENDED!

WHO ARE YOU LYING TO? I'VE BEEN PART OF THIS TEAM AS LONG AS YOU, AND I KNOW JUST HOW WELL YOU CAN CONTROL YOUR POWERS!
YOU MAKE THOSE LITTLE ENERGY PELLETS, YOU GIVE THEM A COMMAND, AND THEY GO OFF WHEN AND HOW HARD YOU SAY!
WELL, THIS ONE DIDN'T FOLLOW ORDERS, CHANCE.

AND SINCE WHEN HAVE YOU BEEN THE BIG EXPERT ON SUPER POWERS, ANY-WAY? IT'S NOT AS THOUGH YOU HAVE ANY, LIKE THE REST OF US.

WELL, EXCUSE ME FOR NOT BEING A MUTANT!
I NOTICE THAT WHEN THE FAMOUS MUTANT HUNTERS, X-FACTOR, CAUGHT YOU, THEY DECIDED NOT TO KILL YOU, SO HOW COME...
SEE WHAT'S COME OF YOUR FLIRTIN' WITH BOOM BOOM, MY JAMIE?
SIRYN, I DID NOTHING TO ENCOURAGE THAT LITTLE MENACE, YOU KNOW I...
BOB-BEE...

PLEASE, YOU MUST EXPLAIN TO ME WHY EVERYONE IS SO DISMAYED!
BUT I DON'T... I WISH I KNEW YOUR LANGUAGE...
MY NAME IS ROBERTO da COSTA. I AM FOURTEEN YEARS OLD... AND I AM A MUTANT, A LIVING POWER BATTERY, ALSO KNOWN AS SUNSPOT.
ALTHOUGH I AM BRAZILIAN, I LIVE IN THE UNITED STATES. ONCE, I WAS PART OF THE NEW MUTANTS, A TEAM OF HEROES, UNTIL, IN A MOMENT OF ANGER I USED MY STRENGTH AGAINST A DEAR FRIEND, AND NEARLY KILLED HIM.
AND SO, PURSUED BY SEVERAL OF MY FRIENDS, I FLED FROM MY OLD LIFE AND JOINED THE FALLEN ANGELS, A BAND OF VAGRANTS, MISFITS AND PETTY CRIMINALS WHO LIVE IN MANHATTAN IN WHAT WE CALL THE BEAT STREET CLUB.

OH, YEAH? WELL, MAYBE X-FACTOR LET YOU GO BECAUSE YOU MADE A DEAL WITH THEM... MAYBE YOU'RE DELIBERATELY TRYING TO KILL OTHER MUTANTS!
BUT I WASN'T...
SIRYN, CHANCE IS CAPABLE OF USING THAT KNIFE...

WELL, A LITTLE SONIC VIBRATION, AND SHE WON'T EVEN BE CAPABLE OF HOLDING IT!

OW!
VRIIINH
SKREENK
NOW, HOW IN THE NAME OF HEAVEN...?
I THOUGHT YOU WERE JUST GOING TO VIBRATE IT... NOT DESTROY IT!
THAT WAS MY INTENT...BUT THE BLAST WAS MUCH MORE POWERFUL THAN THE EFFORT I PUT INTO IT.
ALL RIGHT, NOW I DON'T CARE WHY EVERYONE'S SCREWING UP ALL OF A SUDDEN ... BUT I WANT IT TO STOP!
THIS CLUBHOUSE IS A PIGSTY. IN FACT, PIGS WOULD BE ASHAMED TO BE SEEN IN IT. I WANT SOMEONE TO CLEAN UP ALL THIS RUBBLE AND DEBRIS!
RIGHT! JAMES MADROX, THE MULTIPLE MAN, VOLUNTEER-ING FOR TRASH DETAIL, SIR. JUST GIVE ME A MOMENT TO DUPLICATE MYSELF INTO A COMMITTEE.

BOBBY, WOULD YOU CARE TO HELP ME OUT WITH IT... JUST A SMALL, SHARP IMPACT OUGHT TO DO IT... BUT PLEASE, STICK TO YOUR HUMAN FORM...

IF WHATEVER IS INCREASING OUR POWERS SENT YOUR SUNSPOT STRENGTH HAYWIRE, YOU COULD EASILY KILL ME.
BUT DON'T BE TOO GENTLE WITH HIM, LAD. HIT HIM HARD ENOUGH TO CAUSE HIM TO REPLICATE!

BUT... I THOUGHT I DID.
YOU DID, ALL RIGHT. NOW MY POWER SEEMS TO BE ON THE FRITZ.
TRY IT AGAIN, BOBBY.

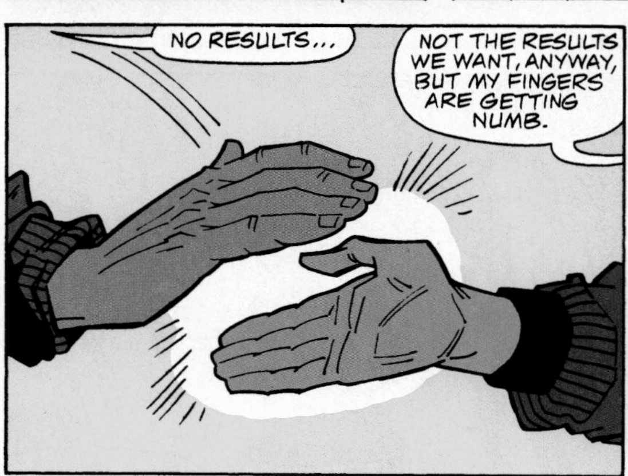
NO RESULTS...
NOT THE RESULTS WE WANT, ANYWAY, BUT MY FINGERS ARE GETTING NUMB.

I DON'T BELIEVE THAT THIS SISSY COULD HIT ANYONE THAT HARD WHEN HE'S NOT POWERED UP.
LET ME TRY.

NICE WORK, CHANCE.
I'M GLAD YOU THINK SO...
...BUT DO YOU REALIZE THERE ARE FOUR OF ME... FROM AN IMPACT THAT WOULD ONLY HAVE PRODUCED TWO.
TRY AGAIN, LOVE.

RIGHT. IF WE DO THIS RIGHT, WE TWO WILL BECOME FOUR...
...MAKING A TOTAL OF SIX OF US.

FOUR TOO MANY! AGAIN.

QUERY: WHAT CHARACTERISTICS HAS THIS LOCATION TO MAKE IT PREFERABLE TO BEAT STREET CLUBHOUSE? FRIEND-GOMI, FRIENDARIEL, PLEASE EXPLAIN.

NOW, WARLOCK, AS ARIEL AND I HAVE TOLD YOU, WE'RE NOT LOOKING FOR A PLACE THAT'S BETTER THAN OUR CLUB, JUST LARGER. IN FACT, CLOSE PROXIMITY MAKES THIS PARTICULAR ROOM THE MOST DESIRABLE WE'VE EXAMINED SO FAR.
AFTER ALL, THE BEAT STREET CLUB JUST ISN'T BIG ENOUGH TO HOUSE ALL OF OUR MEMBERS ANY MORE, BUT WITH A SPACE LIKE THIS...

WELL, LOOK AROUND YOU, WARLOCK, MAKE SURE THE DOORS ARE LARGE ENOUGH FOR WHAT WE NEED... AND TRY TO PICTURE THINGS WE COULD DO TO MAKE IT MORE HOMELIKE.
I MEAN, HOMELIKE BY EARTH STANDARDS. YOU AND I -- AND OUR NEWEST MEMBERS, FOR THAT MATTER --ARE BOTH ALIENS... BUT YOU KNOW WHAT I MEAN. COZY. HOSPITABLE.
AFFIRMATIVE.
HEY, GOMI, WEREN'T DON AND BILL WITH US WHEN WE CAME IN? WHERE HAVE THEY GOTTEN TO?

BILL IS SURVEYING THINGS FROM THE VANTAGE OF A PACKING CRATE AND DON IS...

DON! THERE YOU ARE!
HOW OFTEN DO BILL AND I HAVE TO WARN YOU ABOUT NOT WANDERING AROUND UNDERFOOT WHEN YOU COULD GET STEPPED ON?
YES, I KNOW THAT BEING BIONIC MAKES YOU TOUGHER THAN MOST LOBSTERS, BUT I MUST INSIST THAT YOU BE MORE CAREFUL IN THE FUTURE.

NOW, DON'T BE CARELESS AND MISS ANY DIRT. A TEAM'S CLUB IS THEIR LEADER'S CASTLE, AFTER ALL.
YES, VANISHER.
DON'T WEAR YOUR FEET OUT, STANDING AROUND GIVING ORDERS, BOSS.

SAY... DO YOU HEAR ANYTHING COMING FROM THE WALL...
SORT OF LIKE A THUMP, CREAK, THUMP, CREAK?

OH, NO! THE WALL IS MOVING! IT'S THE POLICE, OR THE MAFIA! OR X-FACTOR!
WELL, DON'T VANISH YET. WHOEVER THEY ARE, IF THEY'RE HERE TO MAKE TROUBLE, THEY'RE IN FOR A FIGHT!

ST. CLUB
YEAH! THE FIRST ONE IN WILL GET BLOWN SKY HIGH IF...
GREETINGS! SELF HOPES ALL SELF-FRIENDS ARE IN GOOD WORKING ORDER ON THIS SALUBRIOUS DAY!

WARLOCK! BUT HOW DID YOU MOVE THE WALL, MY FRIEND... AND WHAT ARE YOU DOING HERE?
SELF HAS HELPED OTHERFRIENDS WITH SOLUTION OF FALLEN-ANGEL'S GREATEST PROBLEM. PLEASE OBSERVE.

WE WERE IN THE LOADING BAY THAT ADJOINS THIS BUILDING, AND GOMI WORKED OUT A RATHER NIFTY SOLUTION TO OUR LITTLE PROBLEM...
BUT I'D REALLY RATHER SHOW YOU THAN TELL YOU, SO...

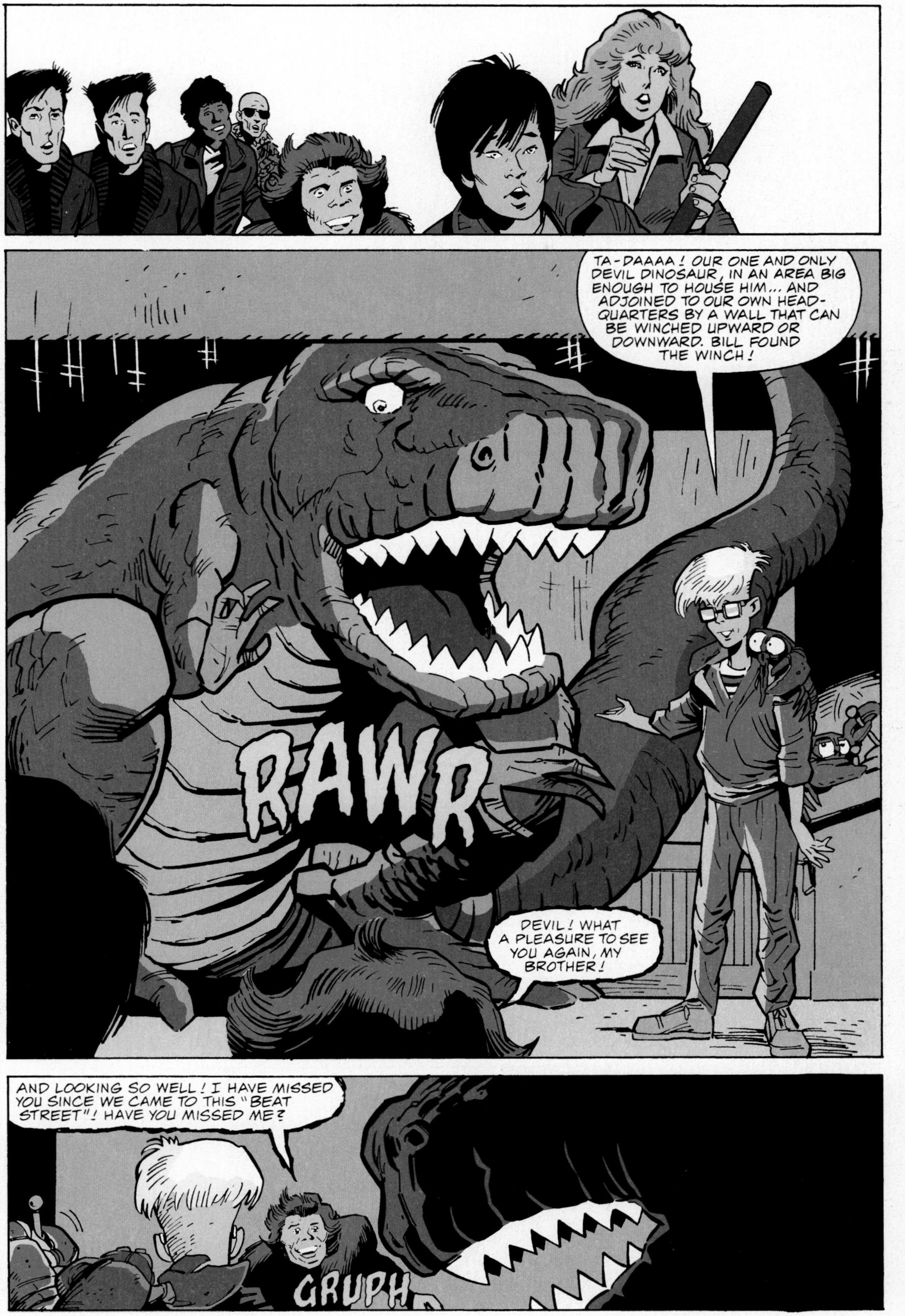

TA-DAAAA! OUR ONE AND ONLY DEVIL DINOSAUR, IN AN AREA BIG ENOUGH TO HOUSE HIM... AND ADJOINED TO OUR OWN HEAD-QUARTERS BY A WALL THAT CAN BE WINCHED UPWARD OR DOWNWARD. BILL FOUND THE WINCH!
RAWR
DEVIL! WHAT A PLEASURE TO SEE YOU AGAIN, MY BROTHER!

AND LOOKING SO WELL! I HAVE MISSED YOU SINCE WE CAME TO THIS "BEAT STREET"! HAVE YOU MISSED ME?
GRUPH

WHAT A WONDROUS CAVE OUR NEW COMRADES HAVE FOUND FOR YOU! IT LOOKS TO BE WARM AND DRY!
SURELY WE SHALL BOTH BE COMFORTABLE NOW THAT WE HAVE JOINED THEM! THANK YOU FOR SIGNIFYING THAT YOU WISHED TO DO SO!!

BOB-BEE, YOU MUST COME AND SEE DEVIL'S FINE NEW CAVE!
AND IF YOU WISH, BRING ALONG HE-WHOSE-SHAPE-CHANGES-LIKE-A-FERN-IN-THE-WIND!

NICE SPEECH OF THANKS MOON-BOY JUST MADE, DON'T YOU THINK, SIRYN?
WELL, I BELIEVE DEVIL DINOSAUR SAID IT JUST AS GRACEFULLY, IF A BIT MORE BRIEFLY.
SERIOUSLY, DID YOU UNDERSTAND ONE WORD HE SAID?

CERTAINLY. HE SAID, "OOGA, OOGA."
I THOUGHT HE SAID, "ICK-ICK-ICK."
VERY FU- UHN...
JAMIE, WHAT'S WRONG?
NOTHING...WHEN I PULLED MYSELVES TOGETHER, I...GOT JUST A LITTLE DIZZY FOR A MOMENT.

I THINK WHAT HE NEEDS IS A LITTLE FRESH CITY AIR. IN FACT, I THINK IT'S ABOUT TIME ALL OF YOU GOT OUT AND EARNED YOUR KEEP.
NOW, I'M NOT SAYING THAT ADDING A TYRANNOSAUROUS REX TO THE TEAM WAS A BAD IDEA-- I'M SURE HE CAN BE USEFUL TO ME IN ALL SORTS OF WAYS WE HAVEN'T THOUGHT OF YET...
...BUT SINCE WE DON'T KNOW YET WHAT HE EATS OR HOW OFTEN HE GETS HUNGRY, I THINK IT OUGHT TO BE EVERYBODY'S BUSINESS TO STEAL ENOUGH FOOD SO THAT WE NEVER FIND OUT THE HARD WAY.

MOON BOY, SINCE HE'S NOT EXACTLY MR. INCONSPICUOUS, IS EXCUSED FROM FORAGE DUTY... ESPECIALLY SINCE I WANT HIM TO STAY HERE AND KEEP HIS FRIEND HAPPY.
BUT THE REST OF YOU SPLIT UP AND GET CRACKING. TEAMS OF TWO.

WELL, I KNOW HOW HIGHLY YOU THINK OF THE WORK CHANCE AND I HAVE ALWAYS DONE TOGETHER, SO I WON'T UPSET YOU BY SUGGESTING WE SPLIT UP.
GOOD! SEE THAT YOU DON'T!
I WOULDN'T WORK WITH ANY OF THE REST OF THESE LOSERS, ANYWAY.

QUERY: MAY SELF ACCOMPANY FRIEND-BOBBY?
WARLOCK, THERE IS NO ONE I WOULD RATHER HAVE.

AND I'LL TAKE MADROX.
I'M SORRY, M'DEAR, BUT THE LAD HAS A PREVIOUS ENGAGEMENT-- ALL OF HIM.

OH, GREAT. THEN I GET STUCK WITH GOMI!
IT'S MUTUAL, I'M SURE.
SNAP!
SNAP!
SNAP! SNAP!

WHERE IS EVERYONE GOING, MY BROTHER? I WISH I KNEW, SO THAT WE COULD GO WITH THEM! I HOPE THEY ARE NOT GONE FOR LONG.

THIS CAVE IS WARM... BUT IF WE MUST STAY FOR LONG ALONE IN THE COMPANY OF HIM-WHO-LACKS-HAIR-BUT-YELLS-MUCH-AND-HIDES-OFTEN, I SHALL BE SORRY WE EVER LEFT THE VALLEY OF THE FLAME.

JAMIE, LAD...DOES IT TROUBLE YOU ANY THAT WE'RE NO CLOSER TO ACCOMPLISHING OUR GOAL THAN WE WERE WHEN WE SET OUT?
WHAT DO YOU MEAN, SIRYN?
WE CAME HERE BECAUSE THE NEW MUTANTS TRUSTED US TO FIND BOBBY AND WARLOCK, WHICH WE'VE DONE... AND BRING THEM HOME, WHICH WE HAVEN'T EVEN ATTEMPTED.

I ATTEMPTED IT... AND VERY NEARLY LOST BOBBY'S TRUST AS A RESULT.
AT LEAST WHILE WE'RE IN THE FALLEN ANGELS WITH THEM, WE'RE HELPING TO KEEP THEM OUT OF TROUBLE...

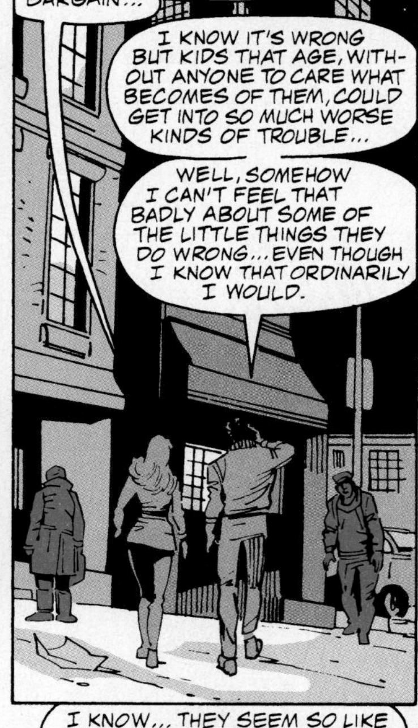
AYE... AND BECOMIN' PETTY THIEVES OURSELVES IN THE BARGAIN...
I KNOW IT'S WRONG BUT KIDS THAT AGE, WITHOUT ANYONE TO CARE WHAT BECOMES OF THEM, COULD GET INTO SO MUCH WORSE KINDS OF TROUBLE...
WELL, SOMEHOW I CAN'T FEEL THAT BADLY ABOUT SOME OF THE LITTLE THINGS THEY DO WRONG... EVEN THOUGH I KNOW THAT ORDINARILY I WOULD.

I KNOW... THEY SEEM SO LIKE FAMILY... IT'S EASY TO FORGIVE THE GROUP FOR ITS FLAWS.
REALLY EASY.
HOW'S YOUR HEAD...? I'M REALLY BEGINNIN' T'WORRY ABOUT THESE SICKLY TURNS YOU'VE BEEN HAVING.
ME, TOO... THEY'RE THE ONE NEW THING IN MY LIFE I HAVEN'T ENJOYED LATELY.

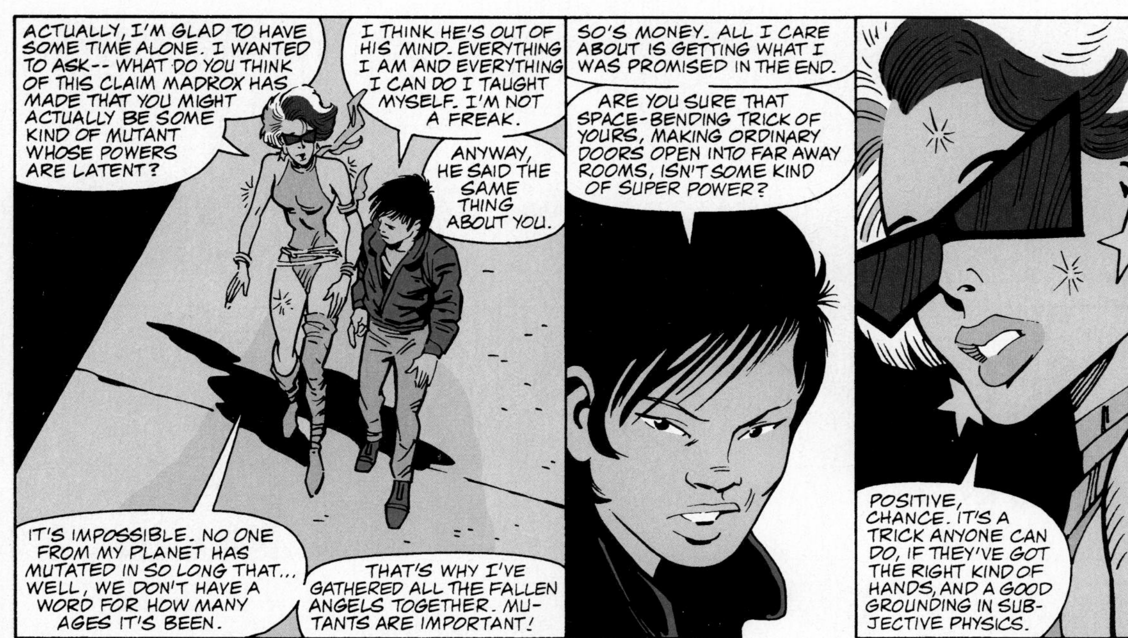
ACTUALLY, I'M GLAD TO HAVE SOME TIME ALONE. I WANTED TO ASK-- WHAT DO YOU THINK OF THIS CLAIM MADROX HAS MADE THAT YOU MIGHT ACTUALLY BE SOME KIND OF MUTANT WHOSE POWERS ARE LATENT?
I THINK HE'S OUT OF HIS MIND. EVERYTHING I AM AND EVERYTHING I CAN DO I TAUGHT MYSELF. I'M NOT A FREAK.
ANYWAY, HE SAID THE SAME THING ABOUT YOU.
IT'S IMPOSSIBLE. NO ONE FROM MY PLANET HAS MUTATED IN SO LONG THAT... WELL, WE DON'T HAVE A WORD FOR HOW MANY AGES IT'S BEEN.
THAT'S WHY I'VE GATHERED ALL THE FALLEN ANGELS TOGETHER. MUTANTS ARE IMPORTANT!
SO'S MONEY. ALL I CARE ABOUT IS GETTING WHAT I WAS PROMISED IN THE END.
ARE YOU SURE THAT SPACE-BENDING TRICK OF YOURS, MAKING ORDINARY DOORS OPEN INTO FAR AWAY ROOMS, ISN'T SOME KIND OF SUPER POWER?
POSITIVE, CHANCE. IT'S A TRICK ANYONE CAN DO, IF THEY'VE GOT THE RIGHT KIND OF HANDS, AND A GOOD GROUNDING IN SUB-JECTIVE PHYSICS.

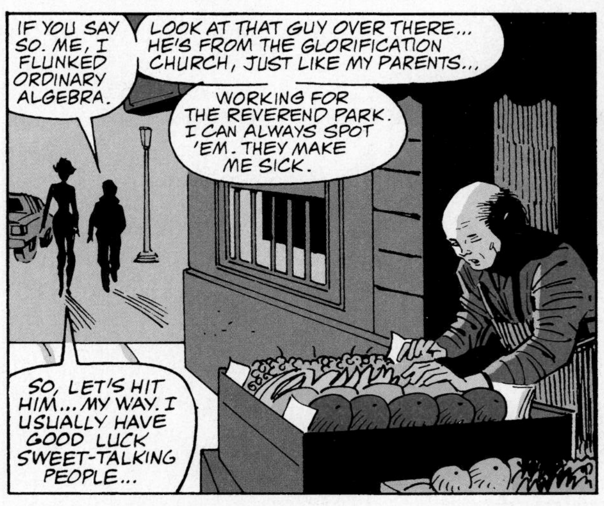
IF YOU SAY SO. ME, I FLUNKED ORDINARY ALGEBRA.
LOOK AT THAT GUY OVER THERE... HE'S FROM THE GLORIFICATION CHURCH, JUST LIKE MY PARENTS...
WORKING FOR THE REVEREND PARK. I CAN ALWAYS SPOT 'EM. THEY MAKE ME SICK.
SO, LET'S HIT HIM... MY WAY. I USUALLY HAVE GOOD LUCK SWEET-TALKING PEOPLE...

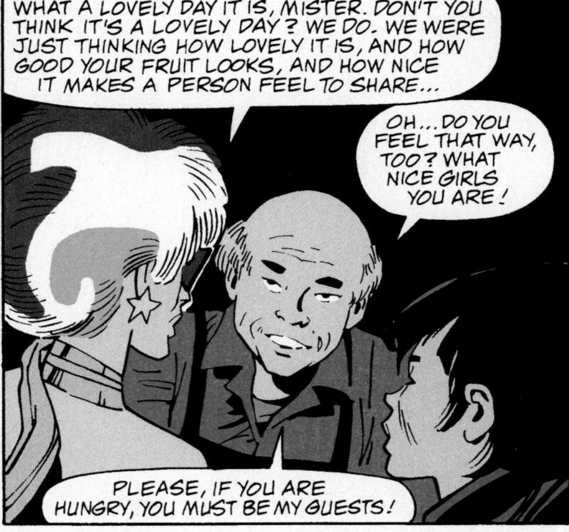
WHAT A LOVELY DAY IT IS, MISTER. DON'T YOU THINK IT'S A LOVELY DAY? WE DO. WE WERE JUST THINKING HOW LOVELY IT IS, AND HOW GOOD YOUR FRUIT LOOKS, AND HOW NICE IT MAKES A PERSON FEEL TO SHARE...
OH... DO YOU FEEL THAT WAY, TOO? WHAT NICE GIRLS YOU ARE!
PLEASE, IF YOU ARE HUNGRY, YOU MUST BE MY GUESTS!

THANK YOU. HAVE A NICE DAY.
OH, BROTHER.

WELL, LOOK WHO ELSE IS WORKING THIS SIDE OF THE STREET.
CHANCE... YOU HAVEN'T GOTTEN ...FOND OF da COSTA, HAVE YOU? I'D HATE FOR YOU TO HAVE A PROBLEM WITH WHAT WE HAVE TO DO LATER.
I'LL SHOW YOU HOW FOND I AM OF HIM!

¡GASP!¡
THANKS, LADY, DON'T MIND IF I DO!
HEY, BOBBY, HEADS UP!

STOP, THIEVES!!
HEY, da COSTA, YOU EVER BEEN IN JAIL?
OF COURSE NOT!

WELL, YOU AND WARLOCK BETTER RUN FOR IT WITH US, 'CAUSE THERE'S A FIRST TIME FOR EVERY-THING!
B-BUT...

ARIEL! YOU DIDN'T TELL ME YOU WERE GOING TO WARP US INTO ANOTHER LOCATION!
YOU DIDN'T ASK!
WHERE ARE WE?

Y.W.C.A., DON'T YOU RECOGNIZE IT?
ENJOY THE VIEW, MACHO!

CHANCE AND I ARE CUTTING OUT!!

WELL, WELCOME BACK. WHERE DID YOU TWO POP IN FROM?
A TRIUMPH!

I DON'T KNOW WHO WAS MORE SURPRISED-- BOBBY, WARLOCK, OR ALL THOSE WOMEN!
WHAT ARE YOU TALKING ABOUT?
NOTHING THAT MATTERS, BOSS. WANT TO SEE THE PRESENTS WE BROUGHT YOU?

FRESH FRUIT...
...AND SOME NICE, CRISP GREENS!

HMMM, NOT BAD. NOT BAD AT ALL.
DEVIL... DO YOU OBSERVE, MY BROTHER?

THAT IS WHERE OUR COMRADES HAVE GONE-- OUT TO FORAGE! AND NOW THEY ARE BRINGING TRIBUTE BACK TO THEIR CHIEF!
OBVIOUSLY, IF WE HOPE TO REMAIN AND PROSPER, WE MUST DO THE SAME!
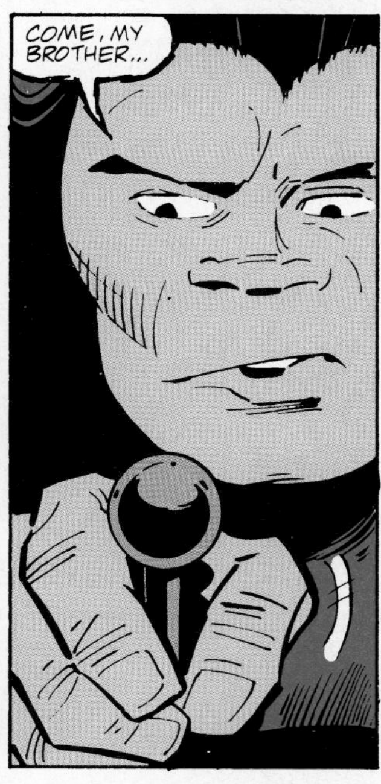
COME, MY BROTHER...

LET US LEARN WHAT WONDERS THIS WORLD MAY HOLD...
...BEYOND THE BOUNDARIES OF BEAT STREET.
WARG

I ASSURE YOU, LOVELY SEÑORINAS, THAT MY FRIEND AND I MEANT NO HARM... BUT... YOU SEE... A LADY WAS CHASING US, AND THE GIRLS WE WERE FOLLOW-ING, THEY...
YOU SHOULD BE ASHAMED OF YOURSELF, YOU LITTLE...
SERIOUSLY, AREN'T YOU A LITTLE BIT YOUNG FOR THIS KIND OF THING?
AND WHAT'S THAT TOY YOU HAVE WITH YOU?
AFFIRMATIVE.

I DO NOT KNOW WHAT YOU MEAN... I WOULD NEVER... A da COSTA RESPECTS LADIES ALWAYS, AND BESIDES, I...I...I...
YOU KNOW, I THINK THEY REALLY ARE TOO YOUNG! YOU'RE RIGHT. I TAKE BACK WHAT I WAS THINKING, TOO. THEY'RE TOO SWEET TO BE PERVERTS.
CLARIFICATION: SELF AND FRIENDBOBBY ARE NOT PERVERTS (QUERY: REF? WILL RESEARCH FURTHER IN FUTURE), BUT MUTANTS.

M-MUTANTS!
CALL X-FACTOR!
LOOK!
I MUST DECIDE LATER WHETHER TO KILL ARIEL, OR CHANCE, OR WARLOCK... OR SIMPLY SETTLE ALL MY PROBLEMS, ONCE AND FOR ALL, BY KILLING MYSELF...

FOR THE MOMENT, I WILL CONTENT MYSELF WITH USING MY STRENGTH AS SUNSPOT TO ARRANGE A HASTY RETREAT FROM THIS PLACE.
COME, WARLOCK, BEFORE THE CLIMATE IN THIS ROOM BECOMES ANY MORE UNHEALTHY THAN IT ALREADY HAS!
?

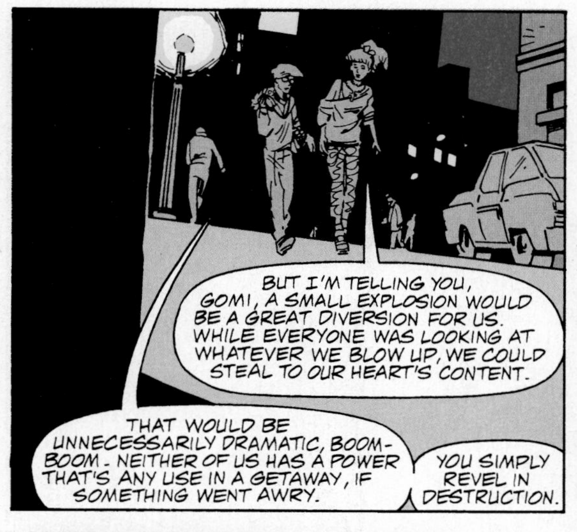
BUT I'M TELLING YOU, GOMI, A SMALL EXPLOSION WOULD BE A GREAT DIVERSION FOR US. WHILE EVERYONE WAS LOOKING AT WHATEVER WE BLOW UP, WE COULD STEAL TO OUR HEART'S CONTENT.
THAT WOULD BE UNNECESSARILY DRAMATIC, BOOM-BOOM. NEITHER OF US HAS A POWER THAT'S ANY USE IN A GETAWAY, IF SOMETHING WENT AWRY.
YOU SIMPLY REVEL IN DESTRUCTION.

I COULD SURE REVEL IN DESTROYING YOU. HOW COME I ALWAYS GET STUCK WITH A TOTAL CREEP, INSTEAD OF--

--HEY, CUTIE, WHAT'RE YOU DOING HERE?

DID YOU GET LONESOME FOR ME?
APPARENTLY NOT.
HEY, COME BACK HERE! I'M TALKING TO YOU, JAMIE MADROX!

THAT'S RIGHT. YOU.
I DON'T KNOW WHAT YOU'RE TALKING ABOUT.
THEN WHY DID YOU STOP WHEN WE SAID YOUR NAME? AND WHY ARE YOU WEARING DIFFERENT CLOTHES THAN YOU WERE AN HOUR AGO?
LEAVE ME ALONE!!
JAMIE!!

I'VE GOT TO BE MYSELF, NO MATTER WHAT PRICE I HAVE TO PAY!

SCHL-
AMM

CATASTROPHIC.
R.I.P.
JAMIE...

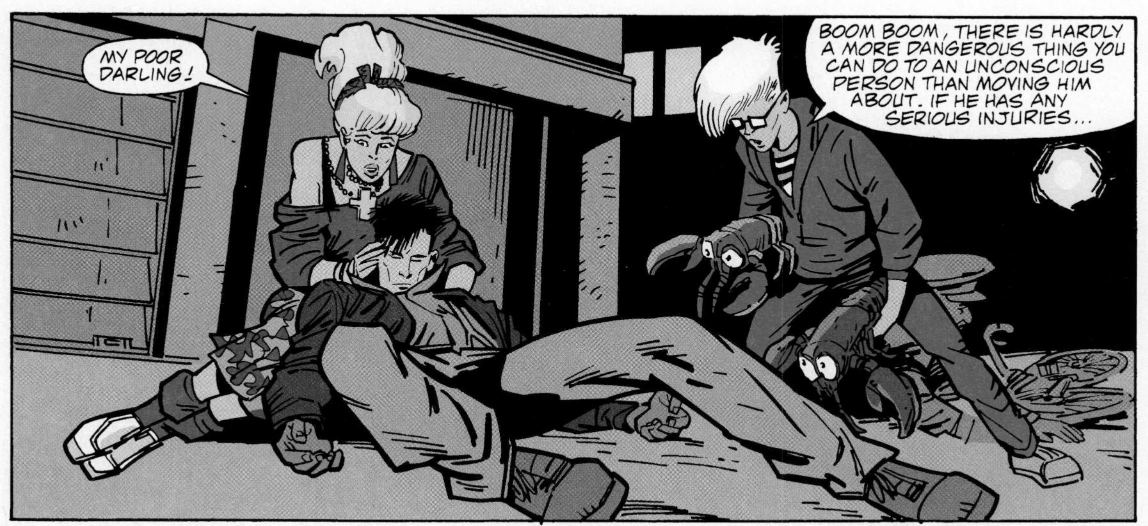
MY POOR DARLING!
BOOM BOOM, THERE IS HARDLY A MORE DANGEROUS THING YOU CAN DO TO AN UNCONSCIOUS PERSON THAN MOVING HIM ABOUT. IF HE HAS ANY SERIOUS INJURIES...

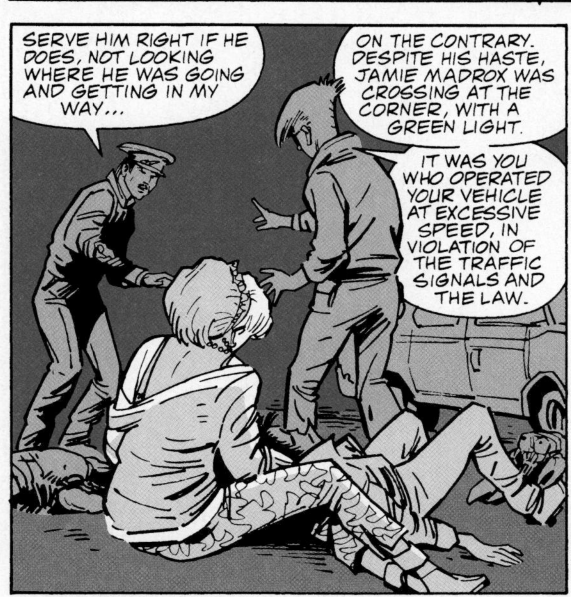
SERVE HIM RIGHT IF HE DOES, NOT LOOKING WHERE HE WAS GOING AND GETTING IN MY WAY...
ON THE CONTRARY. DESPITE HIS HASTE, JAMIE MADROX WAS CROSSING AT THE CORNER, WITH A GREEN LIGHT.
IT WAS YOU WHO OPERATED YOUR VEHICLE AT EXCESSIVE SPEED, IN VIOLATION OF THE TRAFFIC SIGNALS AND THE LAW.

WHAT "VEHICLE"? I WAS ON A BICYCLE!
A BICYCLE IS A VEHICLE, AND SUBJECT TO ALL CURRENT REGULA- TIONS.
LISTEN, WISE GUY, ONE MORE WORD OUTTA YOU, AND I--

--YI-YI-YI-YI!!!
I'M OUTTA HERE!
AND NONE THE WISER, I SEE. WELL, ANOTHER ACCIDENT AWAITS EITHER HIM, OR ANOTHER INNOCENT PEDESTRIAN, THE WAY HE'S GOING.

THAT'S PRETTY BIG TALK FOR A PROFESS-IONAL THIEF.
I NEVER MAKE THE MISTAKE OF CONFUSING SCIENTIFIC PRINCIPLES WITH MORAL ONES. MY OBSERVATIONS ARE BASED ON SIMPLE PROBABILITIES, PLUS A WORKING KNOWLEDGE OF THE LAWS OF CAUSE AND EFFECT.

HOW IS OUR MYSTERIOUSLY WAYWARD FRIEND DOING?

WELL, I DON'T THINK HE'LL BE FIT TO HUG ANYONE FOR A WHILE... BUT I BET HE'S GONNA LIVE!
?

THERE! LOOK AHEAD OF US, DEVIL!
YOU SEE WHERE ALL THE COMMOTION IS! IT IS OUR FRIENDS! LET US JOIN THEM!
THINK OF HOW SURPRISED AND HAPPY THEY WILL BE TO SEE US!!

BUT... ALL OF YOU ARE REINTEGRATED!

ARE WE? I THINK WE MAY BE WRONG ABOUT THAT...

AND I CAN TELL, BY THE INTENSITY OF WHAT I JUST FELT, EXACTLY HOW CLOSE MY OTHER SELF IS! WE CAN BE THERE IN A MINUTE!

HEY, NO FOOLING, BE CAREFUL. I THINK MAYBE YOU HAVE SOME BROKEN RIBS.
AND SOME EXPLAINING TO DO.
PLEASE, WHOEVER YOU ARE, JUST LET ME GO...

NOW, IS THAT ANY WAY TO TALK TO YOUR INTIMATE FRIENDS?
LOOK! YOU WERE RIGHT!
AH! THE LIGHT BEGINS TO DAWN...
SO ONE OF ME DID GO AWOL!

HI. WHEN DID WE LOSE EACH OTHER? THE DAY WE GOT TO TOWN?
THAT'S RIGHT. I DECIDED NOT TO RENDEZVOUS WITH THE REST OF YOU. I WANTED A LIFE OF MY OWN. IF THAT'S SO TERRIBLE.
SHOULDN'T YOU LET YOUR MAIN SELF BE THE JUDGE OF THAT?
SIRYN...SWEETHEART...I THOUGHT YOU LOVED ME. I THOUGHT AT LEAST YOU WOULD UNDERSTAND. I DON'T JUST WANT TO BE A SMOTHERED PART OF A COOKIE CUTTER MAN ANYMORE.
GOING BACK INSIDE OF...HIM...WOULD BE LIKE DYING NOW. I HOPED YOU'D...TALK TO HIM FOR ME...
I...KEEP FORGETTING. ANY ONE OF YOU IS AS... REAL...AS ANY OTHER.
REALLY? THEN I SAY THE MORE THE MERRIER!

YOU KNOW, IF WE MERGED, THOSE BROKEN RIBS WOULD HURT A LOT LESS.
I CAN LIVE WITH THE PAIN.
LET THEM BOTH STICK AROUND, SIRYN. THAT'S ONE FOR EACH OF US.
ON THE CONTRARY. SINCE BOTH MADROXES SHARE THE SAME FEELINGS, IT WILL BE TWO FOR SIRYN, AND NONE FOR YOU, BOOM-BOOM.

LOOK! THERE THEY ARE!
MY FRIENDS! HAVE ANY OF YOU SEEN DEVIL DINOSAUR AND MOON BOY?

WHAT?
HEY, WHO ASKED YOU TO HAVE AN OPINION OF MY LOVE LIFE, ANYWAY?

PLEASE! HOW MANY TIMES MUST I ASK YOU TO BE CAREFUL WHERE YOU'RE PUTTING YOUR FEET?!
YOU ALMOST STEPPED ON BILL.

WHEN WE HAVE TWO SUCH SMALL CREATURES ON THE TEAM, CONSTANT VIGILANCE MUST BE EXERCISED IF WE ARE TO AVOID--!

CRUNCH
SQUIT
!

DON!!
CONTINUED...

#6 IN AN EIGHT-ISSUE LIMITED SERIES
MARVEL®
FALLEN ANGELS™
© 1987 MARVEL ENT. GROUP INC.
75¢ US
95¢ CAN
6
SEPT
CC 02409
APPROVED BY THE COMICS CODE AUTHORITY
MIGNOLA AND WILLIAMSON

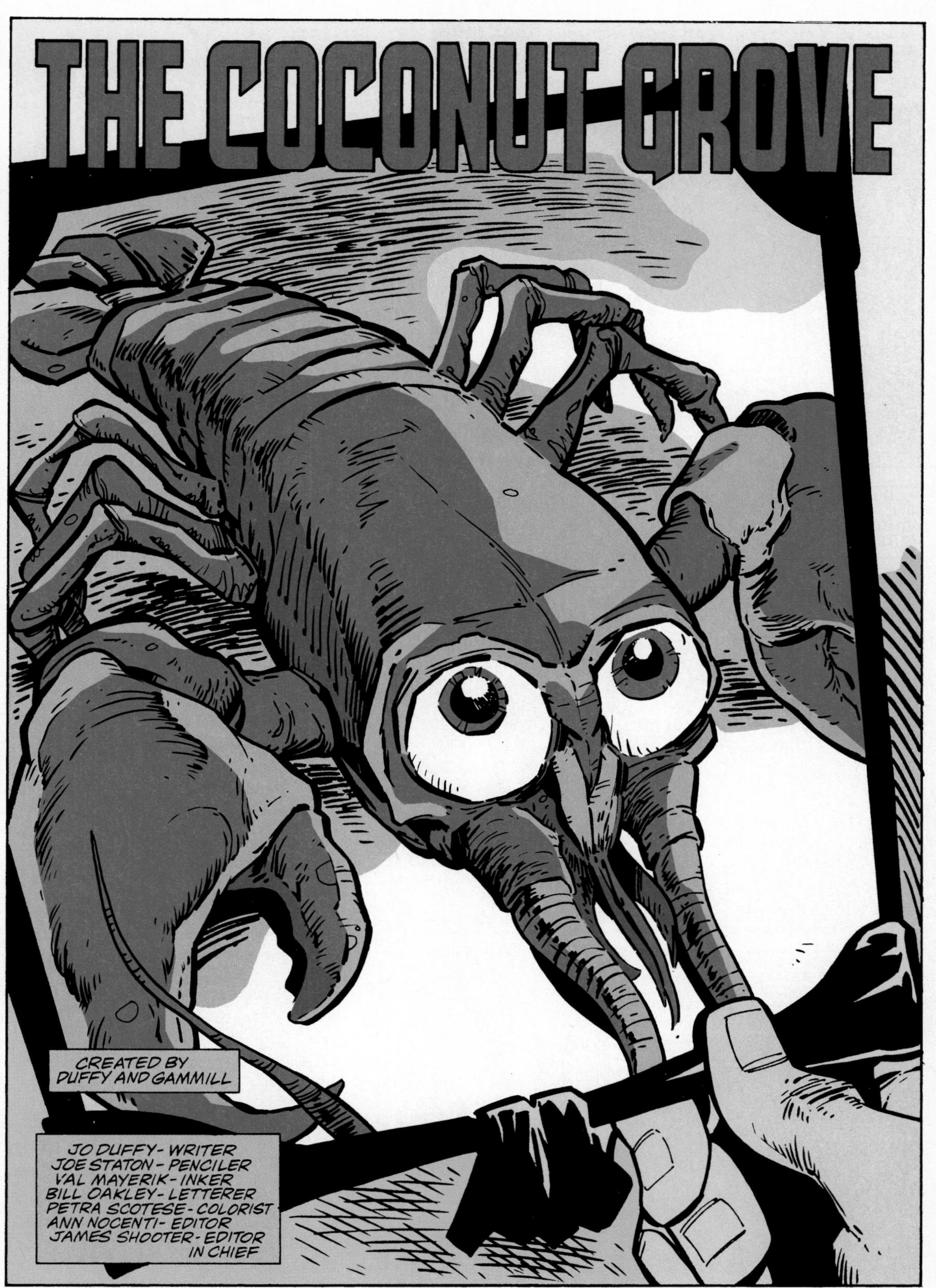
THE COCONUT GROVE
CREATED BY
DUFFY AND GAMMILL
JO DUFFY - WRITER
JOE STATON - PENCILER
VAL MAYERIK - INKER
BILL OAKLEY - LETTERER
PETRA SCOTESE - COLORIST
ANN NOCENTI - EDITOR
JAMES SHOOTER - EDITOR
IN CHIEF

IT WAS A BEAUTIFUL FUNERAL, WASN'T IT, BILL?
POOR DON. HERE TODAY AND GONE TOMORROW. I'M ALWAYS GOING TO REMEMBER HIM THE WAY HE LOOKS RIGHT HERE.

BILL, BILL, BILL... YOU MUSTN'T LET YOUR GRIEF MAKE YOU BITTER. NO ONE COULD FEEL WORSE ABOUT WHAT HAPPENED TO DON THAN DEVIL DINOSAUR DOES.
DON'S DEATH WAS CLEARLY AND CATEGORICALLY AN ACCIDENT.

OUR FELLOW FALLEN ANGELS ARE ALL WE HAVE NOW... THEY ARE OUR FAMILY, AS SURELY AS THE BEAT STREET CLUBHOUSE IS OUR HOME.
ALIENATION FROM THEM WOULD SERVE NO PURPOSE.

MY NAME IS ROBERTO da COSTA. I AM FOURTEEN YEARS OLD, AND I AM A MUTANT, A LIVING SOLAR BATTERY KNOWN AS SUNSPOT.
WITH MY ALIEN FRIEND, WARLOCK, --AN OUTCAST FROM HIS SAVAGE RACE BECAUSE OF HIS ABILITY TO LOVE AND CARE-- I HAVE JOINED THE FALLEN ANGELS.
I DID SO BECAUSE ALL OF THE ANGELS EXCEPT OUR LEADER ARE YOUNG, AND MOST OF US HAVE SOME KIND OF SPECIAL ABILITIES, EITHER MUTANT, CYBORG, OR ALIEN. MORE IMPORTANT, WE ARE... BAD PEOPLE, THIEVES AND LIARS.

THIS IS IMPORTANT TO ME... FOR ONCE, I ASPIRED TO BE A HERO. I WAS ONE OF THE NEW MUTANTS, UNTIL, IN A MOMENT OF PAIN AND ANGER I USED MY STRENGTH AGAINST MY BEST FRIEND... AND NEARLY KILLED HIM.
I DO NOT BELONG AMONG HEROES... AND YET, AS I LISTEN TO THE CYBORGS, GOMI AND BILL, MOURNING THE DEATH OF DON...

...I WONDER IF I HAVE TRULY FLED AWAY FROM LOVE AND FRIENDSHIP...
...OR TOWARD...
...WHAT?

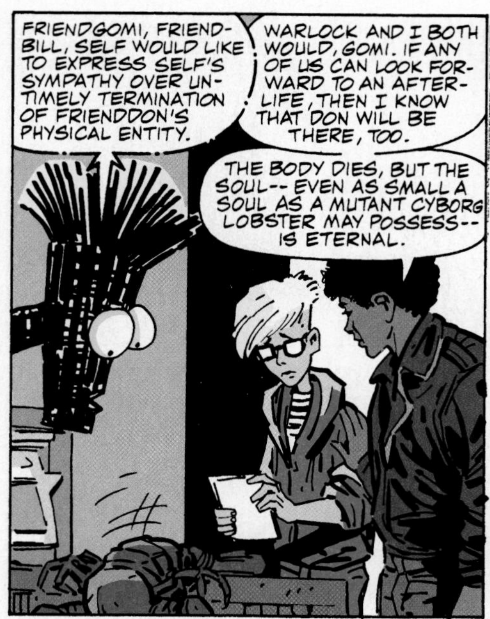
FRIENDGOMI, FRIEND-BILL, SELF WOULD LIKE TO EXPRESS SELF'S SYMPATHY OVER UNTIMELY TERMINATION OF FRIENDDON'S PHYSICAL ENTITY.
WARLOCK AND I BOTH WOULD, GOMI. IF ANY OF US CAN LOOK FORWARD TO AN AFTER-LIFE, THEN I KNOW THAT DON WILL BE THERE, TOO.
THE BODY DIES, BUT THE SOUL-- EVEN AS SMALL A SOUL AS A MUTANT CYBORG LOBSTER MAY POSSESS-- IS ETERNAL.

?

BOBBY, LAD, I DON'T KNOW IF MY PARISH PRIEST WOULD ENDORSE THE UNORTHODOX VIEW OF HEAVEN YOU'VE CONJURED...
BUT AS ONE CATHOLIC TO ANOTHER, IT'S A LOVELY CHRISTIAN THING YOU'RE TRYING TO DO, COMFORTING GOMI.

AND YOU SHOULD BE COMFORTED, LAD. AFTER ALL, YOU STILL HAVE BILL... AND HE NEEDS YOU. WE NEED YOU!
AND DON ALWAYS WAS SUCH A RECKLESS LITTLE THING, HEADING RIGHT INTO SEAFOOD RESTAURANTS, AND WALKIN' INTO THE PATH OF WHOEVER HAD THE BIGGEST FEET...
NOW, YOU KNOW IT'S SO... IF IT HADN'T BEEN DEVIL DINOSAUR, SOMEONE ELSE WOULD HAVE DONE FOR HIM.

NOW, WOULD YOU LIKE US TO LEAVE YOU ALONE?

GOMI?

OH, SIRYN! ≷SOB≶
THAT'S RIGHT, LET IT ALL OUT.
BOB-BEE?
MOON BOY.
SO FAR, NONE OF US CAN FATHOM THE LANGUAGES OF OUR TWO TEAMMATES FROM THE DISTANT DINOSAUR WORLD...
YOU MUST COME AND SEE DEVIL! HE WANTS YOU!
BUT CLEARLY, I AM WANTED ELSEWHERE.

NOT BAD, AS FUNERALS GO, HUNH, VANISHER?
ARE YOU KIDDING, BOOM BOOM? IT'S GREAT! LOOK AT ALL THIS FOOD!
HOW ABOUT YOU, JAMIE?
I'M OKAY.

HUNGRY FOR ANYTHING THAT ISN'T ON THE MENU?
NO!
I WISH SHE'D KNOCK IT OFF!

ARIEL, THERE'S ONLY ENOUGH LIVERWURST LEFT FOR ONE.
OKAY.
THEN LET ME HAVE IT.

WELL, LOOK WHO'S MADE FRIENDS WITH MOON BOY! DON'T THEY LOOK CUTE... TWO LITTLE APES TOGETHER!

CHANCE, IF YOU THINK I RESEMBLE A CREATURE WHO'S MOST OUTSTANDING FEATURE IS HIS LOYALTY...

...I THANK YOU.
FOR MY PART, I PREFER THE COMPANY OF HIM AND DEVIL DINOSAUR TO THOSE OF YOU WHO LEAVE BILL AND GOMI ALONE IN THEIR BEREAVEMENT...
...WHILE YOU GORGE ON THE FUNERAL FEAST!

COME, BOB-BEE INTO THE FINE CAVE OUR FRIENDS HAVE GIVEN ME AND DEVIL, WHILE WE TALK.
WHATEVER YOU'RE SAYING, I CANNOT UNDERSTAND A WORD.
DEVIL HAS ADMIRED YOUR COURAGE ABOVE THAT OF ALL THE OTHERS SINCE WE FIRST MET, AND I KNOW HE WANTS YOUR WISE COUNSEL NOW...

GREAT HAS BEEN MY LARGE BROTHER'S SORROW AND REMORSE SINCE HE INADVERTANTLY TROD UPON THE LITTLE BLUE CLAW MONSTER, AND WE ARE BOTH CONCERNED LEST THE OTHERS OF OUR FRIENDS FAIL TO UNDERSTAND HOW MIGHTY IS OUR GRIEF!
I AM NOT GETTING ANY OF THIS.
YOU MUST HELP US CONVINCE THE LITTLE GREEN CLAW AND HE-WHO-SMITES-HIS-FOES-WITH-OUT-MOVING OF THIS!
CRUNCH CRUNCH CRUNCH
I HOPE WHAT I AM HEARING IS NOT A COMPLAINT ABOUT THE FOOD.

LIFE IS VERY STRANGE, SOMETIMES ... YOU KNOW, MOON BOY, WE ARE NOT SO DIFFERENT, THIS DINOSAUR AND I...
I WONDER WHAT HE IS SAYING.
BOTH OF US HURT OUR COMRADES... AND THOUGH HE INFLICTED THE WORSE INJURY...
SLURF

...MY CRIME WAS THE WORSE OF THE TWO, FOR WHAT HE DID WAS A TRUE ACCIDENT, WHILE I FOLLOWED THE PROMPTINGS OF MY TEMPER.
AND I RAN AWAY... WHILE DEVIL DINOSAUR CAME BACK HERE. HE IS MY SUPERIOR IN MORE THAN SIZE...

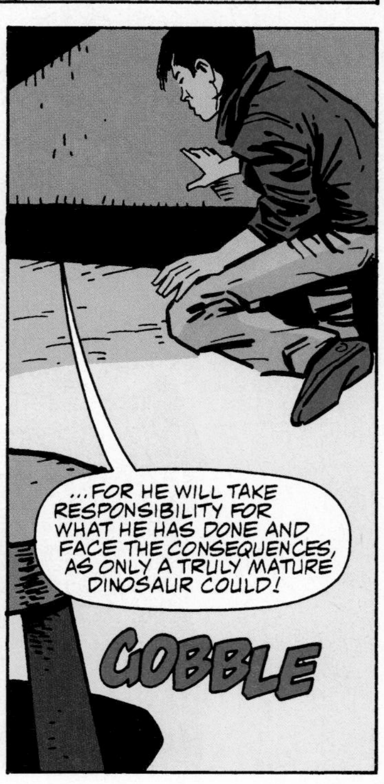
...FOR HE WILL TAKE RESPONSIBILITY FOR WHAT HE HAS DONE AND FACE THE CONSEQUENCES, AS ONLY A TRULY MATURE DINOSAUR COULD!
GOBBLE

CHANCE! WHAT'S WRONG? YOU SEEM RATHER DOWN.
I AM DOWN... ON MYSELF.
NOW, THAT'S NOT RIGHT. YOU'VE JUST LET BOBBY GET UNDER YOUR SKIN.

IT'S NOT LIKE YOU TO GIVE IN TO YOUR CONSCIENCE, YOU KNOW, BUT DON'T WORRY, YOU'LL GET OVER IT.

LOSING THE BLUE LOBSTER LIKE THAT HAS CONVINCED ME THAT WE CAN'T AFFORD TO WASTE ANY MORE TIME. I CAME HERE TO COLLECT MUTANTS, YOU KNOW...

AND IT'S ONLY LUCK THAT ONE OF THOSE GROUPS OF PROFESSIONAL MUTANT KILLERS-- LIKE X-FACTOR OR THE MARAUDERS--HASN'T FOUND US SO FAR. ONE OF THESE DAYS, THEY MAY DECIDE TO NOTICE US...
AND WHERE ARE YOU AND I THEN? WITHOUT ANY MUTANTS TO DELIVER, THE FOLKS WHO SENT ME WON'T PAY US... THAT'S ASSUMING SOMEONE DOESN'T MISTAKE US FOR MUTANTS AND KILL US, TOO.

ARIEL, DON'T YOU EVER HAVE DOUBTS ABOUT WHAT WE'RE PLANNING TO DO?
YOU ARE IN A MOOD, AREN'T YOU? OR HAVE YOU REALLY GONE SOFT? WHAT'S GOT YOU DOWN? BOBBY da COSTA'S LATIN MANNERS AND PRETTY FACE?
DOES HE MEAN MORE TO YOU THAN THE FORTUNE HE'S WORTH TO MY BOSSES?
COME ON... I NEVER THOUGHT I'D SEE THE DAY WHEN "DOUBLE OR NOTHING" HERSELF WAS AFRAID TO GAMBLE.
I...

I NEVER SAID I WAS AFRAID. I JUST WANTED TO MAKE SURE YOU'RE NOT.

WHERE YA GOIN', JAMIE?
I WANT TO SEE HOW OUR INVALID IS DOING. YOU KNOW, THE DOCS WHO X-RAYED HIM AT THE FREE CLINIC SAID THAT HE GOT SOME BROKEN RIBS AND A CONCUSSION WHEN THAT BICYCLIST RAN HIM DOWN.

HOW ABOUT IT, "BROTHER"? CAN I GET YOU SOMETHING... A GLASS OF WATER, OR SOMETHING TO EAT?
I FEEL TOO ROTTEN TO EAT.
I KNOW...

OF COURSE, YOU KNOW... AFTER ALL, WE ARE THE SAME PERSON--JAMIE MADROX, THE MULTIPLE MAN.
YEAH... AND YOU KNOW AS WELL AS I DO THAT WHAT I USUALLY DO WHEN ONE OF ME IS HURT IS HAVE ALL THE DUPLICATES MERGE, SO THAT WE DIVIDE THE INJURY AMONG MYSELVES AND SHARE IT.

ONLY, IN YOUR CASE, I WON'T EVEN SUGGEST IT.
WHY NOT?
BECAUSE FOR THE FIRST TIME I CAN REMEMBER, ONE OF MY SELVES IS SCARED TO REJOIN THE REST OF ME... AND I THINK IT WOULD BE CRUEL TO FORCE YOU TO.

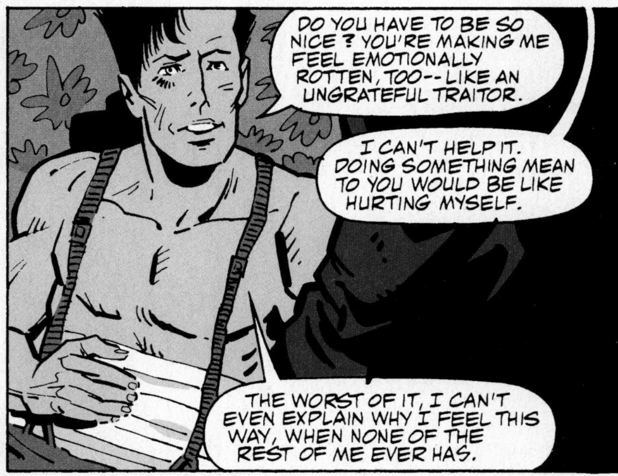
DO YOU HAVE TO BE SO NICE? YOU'RE MAKING ME FEEL EMOTIONALLY ROTTEN, TOO--LIKE AN UNGRATEFUL TRAITOR.
I CAN'T HELP IT. DOING SOMETHING MEAN TO YOU WOULD BE LIKE HURTING MYSELF.
THE WORST OF IT, I CAN'T EVEN EXPLAIN WHY I FEEL THIS WAY, WHEN NONE OF THE REST OF ME EVER HAS.

WELL, I GOT MY POWERS THROUGH A GENETIC MUTATION. MAYBE YOU'RE A MUTATION ON THE MUTATION.
MAYBE.

CHANCE, DID YOU HEAR THAT?
LOOK, GET SOME REST. LATER, IF YOU FEEL UP TO IT, I'LL CALIBRATE THAT LITTLE **CEREBRO** MUTANT SCANNER UNIT AND SEE IF IT DETECTS ANY DIFFERENCE BETWEEN US.

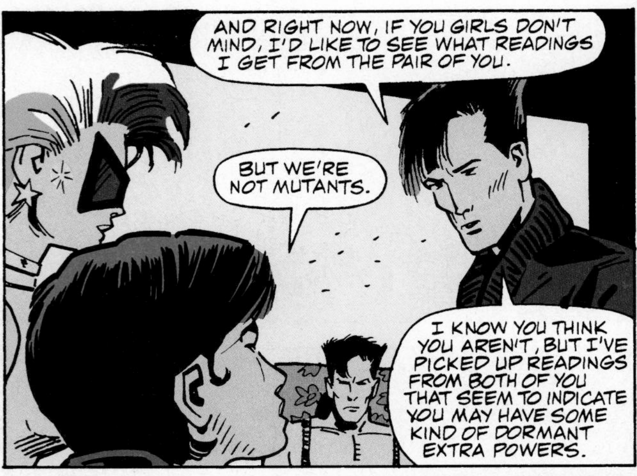
AND RIGHT NOW, IF YOU GIRLS DON'T MIND, I'D LIKE TO SEE WHAT READINGS I GET FROM THE PAIR OF YOU.
BUT WE'RE NOT MUTANTS.
I KNOW YOU THINK YOU AREN'T, BUT I'VE PICKED UP READINGS FROM BOTH OF YOU THAT SEEM TO INDICATE YOU MAY HAVE SOME KIND OF DORMANT EXTRA POWERS.

I DON'T WANT POWERS. BEING HUMAN IS GOOD ENOUGH FOR ME.
JAMIE... YOU'RE SURE HE'LL BE OKAY, AREN'T YOU?
I HOPE SO, ARIEL.

BRAAATT
FEELIN' BETTER?
YES, THANK YOU, SIRYN... BILL AND I ARE BOTH...
CORRECTION: FRIENDBILL IS NO LONGER PRESENT. SELF OBSERVED HIS DEPARTURE IN THE DIRECTION OF THE MAIN PART OF BEAT STREET SOME TIME PAST.

OH, NO.

BILL, DON'T! SENSELESS VIOLENCE IS NO SOLUTION!!

LOOK, BOB-BEE! THE LITTLE GREEN CLAW HAS COME TO VISIT DEVIL! NOW WE CAN SHOW HIM HOW SORRY WE ARE AND BEGIN TO MAKE AMENDS!
?

AAIIEEE!!
MOON BOY!!

BILL, LET HIM GO!!
NO, BILL!!

THIS IS WRONG! YOU'RE STRONGER THAN HE IS! YOU COULD SEVER HIS FOOT!

DEVIL! DEVIL, SAVE ME, MY BROTHER!!

NO!
EVEN IN MY SOLAR-POWERED FORM, I AM NO MATCH FOR AN ANGRY DINOSAUR...
...BUT I CANNOT LET DEVIL GO!
BACK, MY FRIEND. IF I LET YOU HELP YOUR COMRADE, ANOTHER DEATH IS SURE TO RESULT!
HONESTLY, BILL...

WHAT IN THE NAME OF--?
OH.
WELL, A SONIC SCREAM SHOULD SET ALL TO RIGHTS FOR THE MOMENT...

...AND THEY CAN SORT OUT WHO DID WHAT TO WHOM LATER.

WHEEEEEEEN

WHOA!
WHEEEEEEEEEN
VVRRRT

OH, GROSS, LOOK! BODIES EVERYWHERE!
WHAT--?
HUNH?

LET ME OUT OF HERE!
PLINK

MY FOOT! MY FOOT! MY FOOT! MY FOOT!
YOU'LL LIVE TO PLAY "THIS LITTLE PIGGY" ANOTHER DAY--THANKS TO SIRYN'S QUICK THINKING!

I DON'T KNOW WHO TO HELP FIRST. BOOM BOOM, HIT ME A FEW TIMES SO I DON'T HAVE TO MAKE THE CHOICE.

SURE, JAMIE. THE MORE OF YOU, THE BETTER I LIKE IT.

QUERY: WILL FRIEND MOON BOY RECOVER FULL USE OF HIS PEDAL APPENDAGE?
WELL, I DON'T RECOMMEND THAT HE RUN IN ANY MARATHONS FOR THE NEXT FEW DAYS, WARLOCK... BUT I DON'T SEE WHY NOT.

BILL WAS JUST STUNNED, GOMI. HE'LL BE FINE ONCE HE WAKES UP.

HE DIDN'T MEAN ANY HARM, YOU KNOW. HE WAS JUST DEMENTED WITH GRIEF.

UP AND AT 'EM, BOBBY. A KID WHO'S BRAVE ENOUGH TO TACKLE AN ANGRY DINOSAUR SHOULDN'T LET A LITTLE THING LIKE A SONIC BLAST GET HIM DOWN.
BUT... I DID NOTHING. DEVIL ONLY WANTED TO PROTECT MOON BOY, NOT HURT ANYONE.
YOU'LL BE OKAY, BIG FELLA.
I'VE ALWAYS HATED THAT NICKNAME...
BUT HIM IT SUITS.

THANK YOU FOR SAVING ME, MY BROTHER... NO DOUBT OUR NEW FRIENDS WERE REACTING TO THE DEATH OF THE LITTLE BLUE CLAW. I'M SURE IT WON'T HAPPEN AGAIN.

HOW IS HE, GOMI?
ALIVE...
AND WE OWE IT ALL TO YOU!

I WONDER IF SIRYN KNOWS THAT THE MEN IN GOMI'S FAMILY HAVE A FATAL WEAKNESS FOR RED-HAIRED SUPER HEROINES?*
MAYBE SOMEONE OUGHT TO WARN HER.
*GOMI'S KICKY CYBORG TELEKINETIC ABILITIES WERE DESIGNED BY HIS COUSIN, RAMON LIPSCHITZ, CHARTER MEMBER OF THE MARVEL GIRL FAN CLUB--ANN.

DOESN'T LOOK TOO GOOD, DOES HE? HEY, GOMI, YOU SHOULD WRITE A BOOK-- ONE HUNDRED AND ONE USES FOR A LOBSTER.
I CAN THINK OF ONE USE. PUT HIM ON THE TABLE, AND I'LL MELT SOME BUTTER.

PLEASE! DON'T BE VULGAR!

ASSERTION : SERVING AS FODDER FOR VICTOR IS CORRECT USAGE OF FALLEN WARRIOR!

HOW CAN YOU SAY THAT, WARLOCK? I THOUGHT COMPASSION WAS THE MUTATION THAT SET YOU APART FROM YOUR KIND.
COMPASSION IS WASTED ON OPPONENTS.

WARLOCK, I DON'T GET IT.
YEAH, JUST A FEW MINUTES AGO, YOU WERE--

?
JAMIE!

JAMIE, LOVE!
WHERE DID THEY ALL GO?
I DON'T KNOW.

WHAT ARE YOU ALL SO WORRIED ABOUT? I'M SURE THERE'LL BE SOME SOFTIE LEFT TO BABY YOU AND KISS AWAY YOUR BRUISES EVEN IF THE REST OF THE MADROXES VANISH.

GROSS! WHAT A CHEAP THING TO SAY!
HOW COULD YOU?

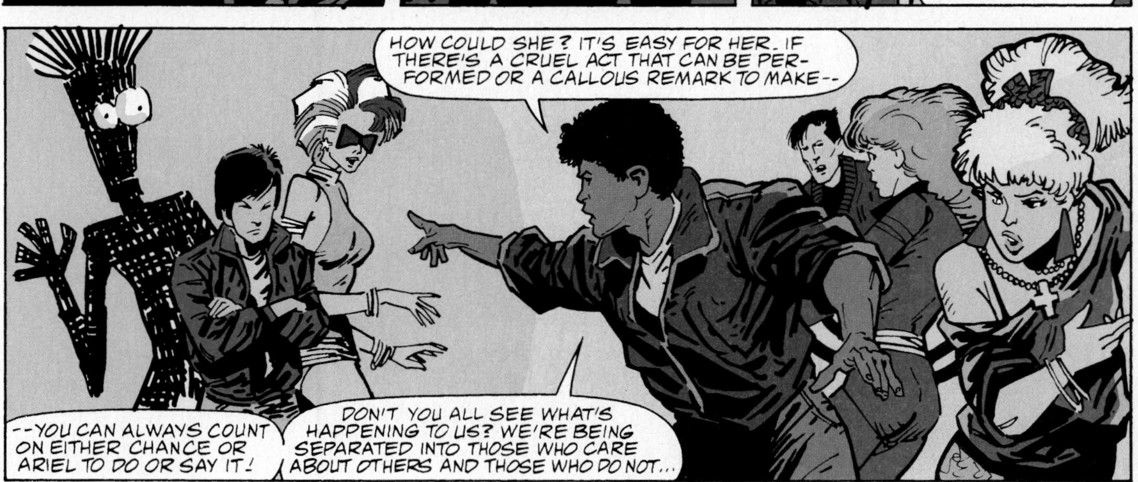
HOW COULD SHE? IT'S EASY FOR HER. IF THERE'S A CRUEL ACT THAT CAN BE PERFORMED OR A CALLOUS REMARK TO MAKE--
--YOU CAN ALWAYS COUNT ON EITHER CHANCE OR ARIEL TO DO OR SAY IT!
DON'T YOU ALL SEE WHAT'S HAPPENING TO US? WE'RE BEING SEPARATED INTO THOSE WHO CARE ABOUT OTHERS AND THOSE WHO DO NOT...

...AND FOR MY PART, I'LL BE HAPPY TO BE GROUPED WITH THE LOBSTERS, DINOSAURS, AND CAVE BOYS!
OKAY... I'VE GOT MY LITTLE ENERGY PACKET ALL MATERIALIZED AND SET TO GO OFF... AND GIVE THAT RATTY CHANCE THE SCARE OF HER LIFE!

NOW, GO AHEAD AND LAUGH AT ME. I, A da COSTA, GIVE YOU PERMISSION.
BEAT SI
JAMIE, NO!

DON'T GET ANY CLOSER TO WHERE YOUR OTHER SELVES DISAPPEARED.
I COULDN'T BEAR TO LOSE YOU...
SO, HOLD ME TIGHT, AKUSHLA.

WELL, I'M BACK. IS EVERYTHING OKAY?
NATURALLY...

OR YOU WOULD NOT HAVE RETURNED.

HEY, CHANCY!! HEADS UP!!
OH, NO! A TIME BOMB!!

ALARM! ALARM!!
UH-OH.
BOOM BOOM, PLEASE, I DON'T WANT TO DIE!

QUERY: WHY HAS THERE BEEN NO EXPLOSION?
IT DIDN'T GO OFF.

HEY, WHAT'S WITH WARLOCK?!
BOOM BOOM!!!

SELF WILL TERMINATE BOOM BOOMENTITY.
HEY, WHAT'S WITH ALL THIS "ENTITY" JAZZ? WHAT HAPPENED TO "FRIENDBOOM BOOM"?
PLEASE... IT WAS ONLY A LITTLE ONE, AND IT DIDN'T GO OFF. I WAS AIMING FOR CHANCE!

WE'VE GOT TO USE OUR POWERS TO STOP HIM!
I'M TRYING, BUT MINE AREN'T WORKING!
NOR MINE!

KILL!

GOMI, YOU GOT YOUR POWERS FROM YOUR MACHINE PARTS AND NOT FROM A MUTATION. MAYBE THEY'RE STILL WORKING!
SAVE ME!!

BOOM
CERTAINLY, BOOM BOOM.

QUERY: WHAT CAME OVER SELF?
THAT SHOULDN'T HAVE HAPPENED. WARLOCK'S PACIFIC DISPOSITION IS THE RESULT OF A GENETIC MUTATION OF HIS ORGANIC CIRCUITRY.
HE REALLY WANTED TO KILL ME.
OH, HE-WHOSE-FORM-CHANGES-LIKE-A-FERN-IN-THE-WIND, ARE YOU WELL? HAS THE MADNESS PASSED?

GEE, IT LOOKS LIKE EVERYONE'S MUTATIONS GOT CANCELED OUT ALL AT ONCE FOR A MOMENT.
OF COURSE, NOT HAVING ANY ABILITIES THAT DEPEND ON MUTATION, THERE WAS NOTHING FOR ME TO BE SCARED OF.

THEN WHY WERE YOU SCREAMING?
YOU MEAN... YOU BELIEVE I WAS AFRAID?
NO. I'M SURE THAT YELLOW STRIPE UP YOUR BACK WAS PUT THERE BY YOUR CLOTHING DESIGNER.

KA-BLOOEY!
ANOTHER COUNTRY HEARD FROM.

HOW ABOUT THAT? IT WASN'T A DUD AFTER ALL!
I SUPPOSE WE HAVE BEEN BEHAVING FOOLISHLY.
AFFIRMATIVE.
"KA-BLOOEY."

SIRYN, COULD YOU AND... UM, I COME HERE, PLEASE?
WHAT'S UP?
WHAT HAVE YOU BEEN DOING WITH THE CEREBRO?

MONITORING WHAT JUST WENT ON... IT DROVE THE SCANNER CRAZY. ONE OF OUR LATENT MUTANTS WAS READING OFF THE SCALE...
...AND THE OTHER ONE DIDN'T SHOW UP AT ALL... BUT I STILL CAN'T FIGURE OUT WHO'S WHICH.

DID YOU NOTICE...? WHEN ALL OF MY OTHER SELVES BLIPPED OUT, BOTH OF US STUCK AROUND.

I'M GLAD... FOR BOTH OF YOU.

THAT'S SOMETHING ELSE THAT'S OFFICIAL. THERE ARE TWO OF US NOW. CEREBRO READS ME SLIGHTLY DIFFERENTLY THAN IT DOES YOU OR ANY OF YOUR DUPLICATES.
SOMEHOW, WHEN I SPLIT OFF FROM THE REST OF YOU, I BECAME A DISTINCT AND AUTONOMOUS ENTITY.

BUT, WE'RE STILL LINKED. YOU FEEL A LOT OF THE SAME THINGS I DO... LIKE ABOUT SIRYN, FOR EXAMPLE.
AND I FELT IT WHEN YOU'D BEEN HURT.

THAT'S OKAY. I KNOW YOU'VE ALWAYS WANTED A BROTHER AS MUCH AS I DO.

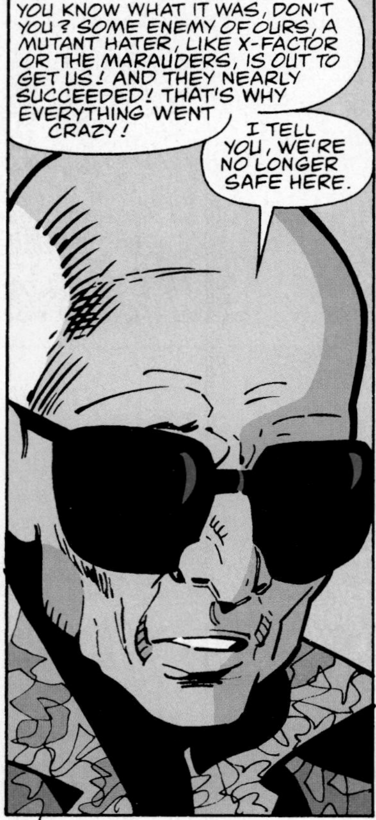
YOU KNOW WHAT IT WAS, DON'T YOU? SOME ENEMY OF OURS, A MUTANT HATER, LIKE X-FACTOR OR THE MARAUDERS, IS OUT TO GET US! AND THEY NEARLY SUCCEEDED! THAT'S WHY EVERYTHING WENT CRAZY!
I TELL YOU, WE'RE NO LONGER SAFE HERE.

BILL, DID YOU HEAR THAT? OUR LEADER BELIEVES THE SECURITY OF BEAT STREET MAY HAVE BEEN BREACHED!

IT'S THE ONLY RATIONAL, INTELLIGENT EXPLANATION.
THEN WHY DID YOU THINK OF IT?
WHAT DO YOU THINK WE SHOULD DO?

I DON'T KNOW...
WE'VE GOT TO GET OUT OF HERE BEFORE WHO-EVER IT IS COMES BACK!
ARIEL'S RIGHT!
AFFIRMATIVE.

YOU MEAN YOU BELIEVE ME?
OF COURSE. WHY SHOULDN'T WE?
I MEAN... I MEAN, OF COURSE YOU CAN BELIEVE ME!

WE'D BE SITTING DUCKS HERE IF ANYONE CAME, ESPECIALLY WHEN SOME OF US ARE WOUNDED.
WE'D BE HELPLESS...
TOTALLY VULNERABLE.

NOW, YOU ALL KNOW THAT MY SPACE-BENDING POWERS ARE SCIENTIFIC RATHER THAN MUTANT, SO THEY SHOULD STILL BE WORKING...
SO I SUGGEST WE ALL CLEAR OUT OF HERE RIGHT NOW FOR SOMEPLACE SAFE!

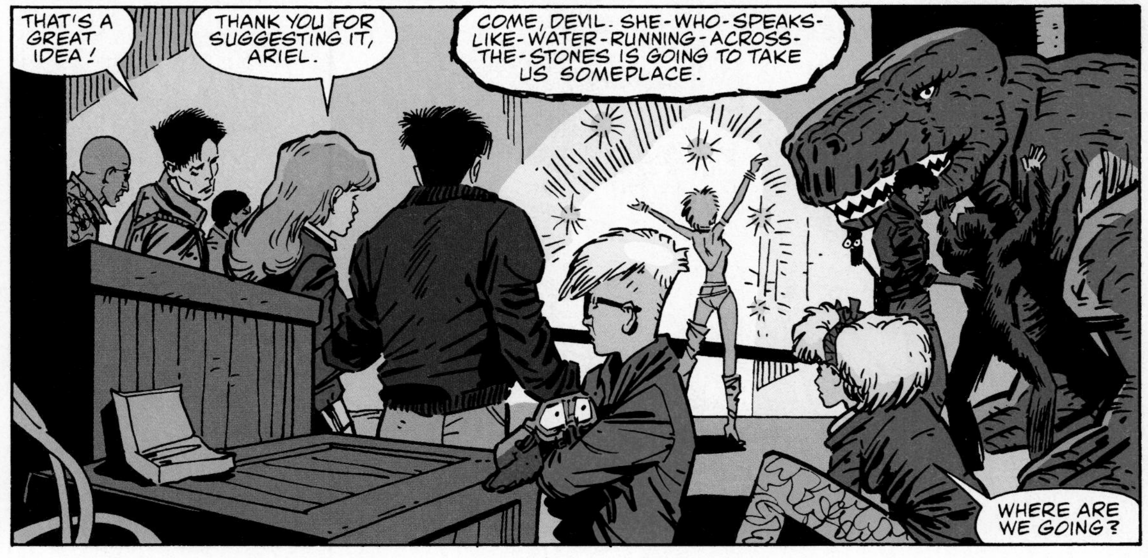
THAT'S A GREAT IDEA!
THANK YOU FOR SUGGESTING IT, ARIEL.
COME, DEVIL. SHE-WHO-SPEAKS-LIKE-WATER-RUNNING-ACROSS-THE-STONES IS GOING TO TAKE US SOMEPLACE.
WHERE ARE WE GOING?

OKAY, EVERYONE, THEY'VE COME A LONG WAY, SO LET'S GIVE THEM ALL A BIG HAND. LET'S HEAR IT FOR THEM--
--DIRECT FROM THE BEAT STREET CLUBHOUSE, THE FALLEN ANGELS!!
FROM BEAT STREET TO MY HOME PLANET, THE COCONUT GROVE, IN ONE EASY STEP!

FRIENDBOBBY... SELF IS EXPERIENCING APPREHENSION.
SO AM I. IT'S A COMFORT TO KNOW THAT WE CAN STILL WALK THROUGH THE DOORWAY BACK TO OUR WORLD, SO LONG AS THAT CURTAIN REMAINS...

NO, WAIT, DON'T--!
⋛SIGH⋚ AND NOW, MY FRIEND, WE ARE TRULY TRAPPED HERE.

HEY, LISTEN TO THAT CROWD. IS THAT AN AUDIENCE, OR WHAT?

IT'S GREAT TO SEE ALL OF YOU!
OW!!

NICE JOB YOU'VE DONE OF MAINTAINING YOUR INDIVIDUAL INTEGRITY, BROTHER. MY COMPLIMENTS...
...TO BOTH OF YOU.
CONTINUED...

#7 IN AN EIGHT-ISSUE LIMITED SERIES
MARVEL®
FALLEN ANGELS™
© 1987 MARVEL ENT. GROUP, INC.
75¢ US
95¢ CAN
7
OCT
CC 02409
APPROVED BY THE COMICS CODE AUTHORITY

TRIPLE CROSS
YOU STAY AWAY FROM ME!
I'M NOT KIDDING!!!
CREATED BY DUFFY AND GAMMILL
JO DUFFY - WRITER
KERRY GAMMILL - BREAKDOWNS
TOM PALMER - FINISHED ART
BILL OAKLEY - LETTERER
PETRA SCOTESE - COLORIST
ANN NOCENTI - EDITOR
JAMES SHOOTER - EDITOR IN CHIEF

WARLOCK, THAT NEW OUTFIT IS YOU! I SHOULD HAVE BROUGHT YOU TO MY HOME PLANET SOONER!

QUERY: FRIENDBOBBY, IS SELF'S NEW ATTIRE APPROPRIATE AND SUITABLE OR DOES SELF PRESENT AN ODD APPEARANCE?

DO NOT WORRY, MY FRIEND. ARIEL IS CORRECT. THAT JACKET MAKES YOU LOOK ALMOST AS SHARP...

...AS I DO MYSELF.

NOOOOO!

EH?

ANALYSIS: ORAL EXPRESSION OF EXTREME FEAR AND DISTRESS.

IDENTIFICATION: CHANCE'S VOICE.

MY NAME IS ROBERTO da COSTA. I AM FOURTEEN YEARS OLD. AND I AM A MUTANT, A LIVING SOLAR BATTERY, ALSO KNOWN AS SUNSPOT.
WITH OUR FELLOW FALLEN ANGELS, A MOSTLY TEENAGED GROUP OF SNEAK THIEVES WITH VARIOUS STRANGE ABILITIES, MY FRIEND WARLOCK AND I HAVE COME TO THE HOMEWORLD OF OUR TEAMMATE, ARIEL.
KNOWN AS THE COCONUT GROVE, THIS IS AS STRANGE A PLACE AS I HAVE EVER BEEN. I THINK IT IS WONDERFUL, AND SINCE WE HAVE ARRIVED...

...I HAVE LET MYSELF HOPE THAT AMIDST SUCH VARIETY EVEN A GROUP AS STRANGE AS THE FALLEN ANGELS MAY FIND A HOME. BUT NOW...
CHANCE?
STOP! WHATEVER YOU ARE DOING TO HER, JUST...

...LET ...HER ...GO.
B-BOBBY?
BUT WE'RE MAKING HER LOOK SO LOVELY!
BOBBY... MAKE THEM STOP...
THIS... IS THE SOURCE OF HER TERROR?

HA HA HA HA HA
AT LAST WE SEE THAT, BEHAVIOR AND APPEARANCE TO THE CONTRARY NOTWITHSTANDING, OUR LITTLE CHANCE IS INDEED A GIRL!
QUERY: ARE NOT ACQUISITION AND TESTING OF NEW GARMENTS GENERALLY CLASSIFIED AS POSITIVE EXPERIENCES?
AMONG NORMAL GIRLS THEY ARE.

STOP LAUGHING AT HER! AND THE REST OF YOU, LET HER GO, NOW!
ARIEL...?
IT'S ALL RIGHT, CHANCE. THEY DIDN'T MEAN ANY HARM. AROUND HERE, THAT'S HOSPITALITY... PEOPLE JUST DON'T THINK SOMETIMES, THAT'S ALL.

LOOK, HERE'S YOUR KNIFE BACK.
THANKS.
FEELING BETTER?
I THINK SO...
FRIENDBOBBY, PLEASE ELUCIDATE.

IT WAS NOTHING TO CONCERN US, WARLOCK. JUST FEMININE WEAKNESS.

REPEAT THAT!!
I AM SORRY, LITTLE MISS, BUT AS A da COSTA AND A GENTLEMAN, I CANNOT RISK HARMING ONE WHO HAS SHOWN HERSELF TO BE SO DELICATE...

...AND FULL OF SENSIBILITY.
FAREWELL, FAIR ONE, THOUGH IT PAINS ME TO SAY SO...
...MORE CONGENIAL COMPANY AWAITS! COME, WARLOCK.

PERHAPS SOMEDAY I SHALL PROVOKE THE LITTLE PEST BY TELLING HER...
...HOW CUTE SHE LOOKS WHEN ANGRY OR AFRAID.

ARE YOU REALLY SURE YOU'RE ALL RIGHT?

ARIEL, SWEETIE-PRECIOUS, WHY DID YOU BUTT IN JUST NOW?
UNIPAR! JUST WHAT DID YOU THINK YOU WERE DOING?
JUST MAKING HER HAPPY... AND KEEPING UP OUR SIDE OF THE BARGAIN.
YOU TOLD US YOU WANTED TO TAKE GOOD CARE OF YOUR FRIENDS AND LET THEM ENJOY THEMSELVES UNTIL...

WELL, THEY'RE NOT MY FRIENDS! THEY'RE YOUR GUESTS.
AND CHANCE IS NOT ONE OF THEM! SHE IS MY FRIEND, AND SHE'S NOT A MUTANT...

...SO YOU JUST LEAVE HER ALONE.
SURE, BABE. ANYTHING YOU SAY.
TOUCHY, TOUCHY, TOUCHY!

YOU KNOW, YOU NEVER REALLY DID EXPLAIN TO ME JUST WHAT WE LURED THE OTHERS HERE FOR...
SHH! THAT'S NOT IMPORTANT NOW...
SOMEONE'S COMING!

BOOM BOOM! YOU LOOK MARVELOUS!
THANKS, GUYS! DO YOU REALLY THINK SO?
UMM... I'VE NEVER SEEN YOU LOOK MORE LIKE YOURSELF!
WOW! THANKS A LOT!

I OVERHEARD WHAT BOBBY SAID TO YOU WHEN HE WAS LEAVING... ARE YOU REALLY GOING TO LET HIM HAVE THE LAST WORD LIKE THAT?
DEPENDS. WHAT HAVE YOU GOT IN MIND?

HOW ABOUT IF I WISH UP ONE OF MY PRE-SET LITTLE SURPRISE PACKAGES... AND LET HIM HAVE IT?
GO TO IT, GIRL!

BOBBY! HEY, BOBBY da COSTA, I'M TALKIN' TO YOU!

WHO'S YOUR TAILOR, BOBBY? I LOVE YOUR OUTFIT!
SLAP!
LOOKIN' GOOD, BOY!

QUERY: HAS NOT BOOM BOOM PREVIOUSLY INDICATED DISTASTE FOR FRIENDBOBBY?
WARLOCK, NO FEMALE CAN BE AROUND A MAN OF CHARM FOR LONG WITHOUT--

BOOM!

YAAAAAAH! GOTCHA!
BOOM BOOM!!!

OH, MOTHER! HELP ME STOP LAUGHING OR I'M GOING TO BE SICK!
HEY, BOBBY, I THOUGHT YOU HAD TO BE AT LEAST EIGHTEEN BEFORE YOU HAD TO WORRY ABOUT THE DRAFT!

CHANCE, I--

--DRAFT?

HA HA HA HA HA HA HA HA
WOO-WOO!
GREAT LEGS!

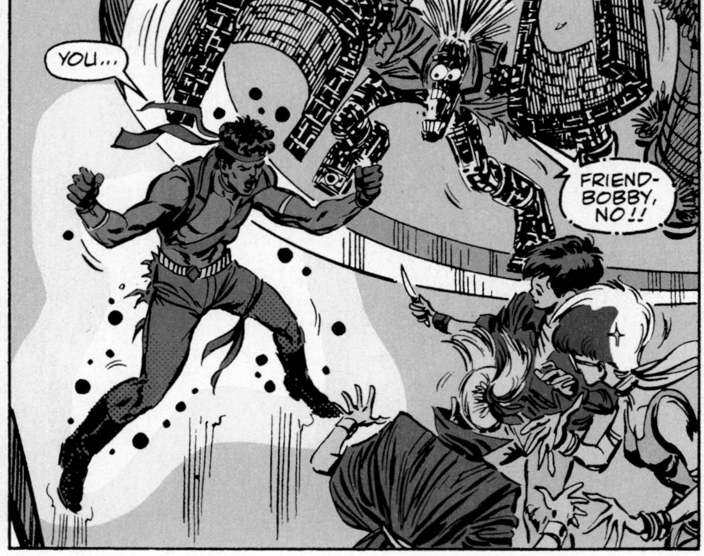
YOU...
FRIEND-BOBBY, NO!!

MY NAME IS ROBERTO da COSTA. I AM FOURTEEN YEARS OLD...
AND ONCE I HAD A BEST FRIEND... A FELLOW MUTANT NAMED SAM.
A NICE FELLOW, SAM, BUT CLUMSY. PLAYING A GAME, HE LOST HIS BALANCE, AND WITH HIS NORMAL HUMAN STRENGTH...
...HE HURT ME BADLY. AND I TURNED TO SUNSPOT...
...AND VERY NEARLY KILLED HIM.
THAT WAS WHY I RAN AWAY FROM MY HOME AND MY FRIENDS--A GROUP OF HEROES CALLED THE NEW MUTANTS--AND JOINED THE FALLEN ANGELS...
BECAUSE I COULD NOT LIVE WITH WHAT I HAD DONE.

NEVER AGAIN.

VERY WELL, LAUGH, IF IT ENTERTAINS YOU!
A MAN HAS MORE IMPORTANT KINDS OF PRIDE THAN THAT WHICH YOU'VE JUST WOUNDED.

YOU ARE NOT WORTH RAISING MY HANDS TO.
FAREWELL!

HE'S REALLY... ARIEL, I THINK MAYBE WE SHOULD APOLOGIZE TO HIM.
WHAT FOR? IT WAS A GREAT STUNT, AND HE DESERVED IT!
YEAH! DESERVED IT!

YOU'RE RIGHT! HE HAD IT COMING!
WE DON'T NEED BOBBY da COSTA!
YEAH! WHO NEEDS HIM?

NOT US!
WE DON'T NEED ANY OF THE FALLEN ANGELS!
YEAH! WHO NEEDS US?

?
?
?

EXCEPT FOR BOOM BOOM, OF COURSE!
OF COURSE, WE COULDN'T GET ALONG WITHOUT BOOM BOOM!
OF COURSE NOT!

AND, OF COURSE, YOU DON'T WANT TO TELL ANY OF THE OTHER ANGELS WE SAID THIS.
OF COURSE NOT! WHY SHOULD I DO THAT?

IN FACT, YOU PROBABLY DON'T EVEN WANT TO REMEMBER THAT THIS CONVERSATION TOOK PLACE.
WHAT CONVERSATION?

NICE SNOW JOB.
SOMETIMES IT'S SO EASY I'M ASHAMED OF MYSELF.
OF COURSE, THE ABILITY TO CONVINCE PEOPLE OF THINGS THEY WOULDN'T ORDINARILY BELIEVE SORT OF RUNS IN MY FAMILY.
IN FACT, WILLIAM SHAKESPEARE USED A RELATIVE OF MINE IN HIS PLAY, THE TEMPEST. THE CHARACTER ARIEL...
...WAS ALWAYS RUNNING CON GAMES AND USING HIS SPACE-BENDING POWERS TO MAKE THINGS AND PEOPLE APPEAR AND DISAPPEAR AT WILL.

THAT'S WHY THE WITCH WAS ABLE TO TRAP HIM FOR ALL THOSE YEARS INSIDE A CLOVEN PINE TREE--NO DOORWAYS, SO NO SPACE-BENDING, AND HE COULDN'T GET OU--

VEEEEEEEEE
HEY!!
--OW!

VEEEEEEEEE
EEEEEEE

HAPPY LANDINGS, JAMIE.
THANKS, SIRYN.
JEEZ, I KNOW SIRYN CAN'T RIDE THE SONIC WAVES LIKE THAT UNLESS SHE GETS UP A LOT OF VOLUME, BUT YOU NEARLY BROKE OUR EARDRUMS!
EVEN FOR YOU, THE RACKET WAS EXCESSIVE!

WELL, I APOLOGIZE TO Y'BOTH... BUT I DON'T KNOW MESELF WHAT CAUSED IT.
I WAS TWICE AS LOUD AS I NEEDED TO BE ...AND I COULDN'T DAMP IT DOWN.

THE VANISHER HAS CALLED A MEETING. HE WANTS EVERYONE THERE.
I HAVEN'T THE LIFT TO FLY EVERYONE BACK...
I WOULDN'T WANT THE FAVOR TILL YOU'VE GOT YOUR POWERS UNDER CONTROL.
NO FIGHTING. DON'T FORGET WHAT I CAN DO...

SURE. BEND SPACE, SO THAT THIS DOOR WILL OPEN INTO THE DOORWAY OF THE ROOM WHERE THE VANISHER IS. JUST LIKE YOUR ANCESTOR IN ***THE TEMPEST.***
THAT WAS ALL A LOT OF HOOEY, WASN'T IT?
NOPE.

ARE YOU SAYING THE CHARACTER IN SHAKESPEARE WAS SOMEONE FROM HERE?
UH-HUH.

BUT, HOW COULD SOMEONE FROM A ZANY PLANET LIKE THIS ONE VISIT A MEDITERRANEAN ISLAND DURING ELIZABETHAN TIMES?

BY DOING THIS. IT'S AS EASY TO GET ACROSS OUTER SPACE AS IT IS A CITY, IF YOU KNOW HOW IT'S DONE.

AND, OF COURSE, AFTER I CLOSE THE DOOR, EVERYTHING GOES BACK TO NORMAL...

...AND OUTSIDE IT REALLY IS WHAT'S OUTSIDE, AND NOT THE PLACE WE JUST LEFT, WHICH IS MILES AND MILES AWAY.

THE ONLY LIMITATION IS, YOU NEED A WORKABLE, CLOSEABLE DOORWAY AT EACH END. NO DOORS, NO SPACE WARP, AND YOU'RE STUCK RIGHT WHERE YOU ARE, WHEREVER THAT IS.

HEY! CHANCE! ARIEL! SIRYN!
JAMIE MADROX! SWEETHEART! DARLING!
I'M COMING, YOU GUYS! WAIT UP!
SLAM

NUTS!

NOW, IF I WANNA KNOW WHAT'S GOING ON, I HAVE TO WALK ALL THE WAY ACROSS TOWN. OTHER-WISE, THEY'LL JUST LEAVE ME OUT!
THEY LEFT YOU HERE... ALL ALONE! OH, YOU POOR DEAR!
I CONDOLE YOU WITH ALL OF MY...

SAVE THE SYMPATHY FOR THEM WHAT NEEDS IT.

LIKE MY FRIENDS...
BLOOEY
...ONCE I CATCH UP WITH THEM.

OH... WHAT A WONDERFUL POWER! HOW DID YOU DO THAT?
I'M A MUTANT. WHY, YOU WANNA MAKE SOMETHING OF IT?
OF COURSE I WANT TO MAKE SOMETHING OF IT! I WANT TO MAKE A FUSS!

YOU WONDERFUL, WONDERFUL GIRL! RARE TREASURE! BLESSED ONE!
GEE... ON EARTH, ALMOST EVERYONE WHO'S NORMAL-- AND MORE THAN A FEW WHO AREN'T-- HATE MUTANTS.
THE FOOLS!
I'LL SAY. PERSONALLY, I THINK IT'S 'CAUSE THEY'RE JEALOUS OF US.

THEY SHOULD GET DOWN ON THEIR KNEES AND THANK THE HEAVENS EVERY TIME A NEW GENETIC MUTATION APPEARS.
I TRIED TELLING THAT TO MY FATHER, AND HE BELTED ME.
CRUEL, FOOLISH MAN! HERE IN THE COCONUT GROVE, WE APPRECIATE MUTANTS... AND WE SELDOM GET A CHANCE TO SHOW IT...
...FOR MUTATIONS ARE RARE HERE. WE HAVE HAD NO SPONTANEOUS GENETIC DEVIATIONS OF EVEN THE MINUTEST SORT FOR MANY MILLIONS OF YOUR EARTH YEARS.

NO KIDDING? ALL THAT APPRECIATION, AND NO ONE TO SHOWER IT UPON. EXCEPT ME.
THEN... YOU'LL LET US SHOW YOU WHAT YOU MEAN TO US? OH, DO!

COME ALONG AND LET US SHOW YOU HOW WONDERFUL WE REALLY THINK YOU ARE!
WELL, IF IT WOULD MEAN ALL THAT MUCH TO YOU...
THAT'S IT. HE'S GIVING US THE SIGNAL.

OUR TEAM IS A VISUAL BABEL TONIGHT, AS WELL AS A LINGUISTIC ONE...

I KNOW NOT WHO LOOK FINER-- DEVIL DINOSAUR AND MOON BOY--

PAR-TEE! PAR-TEE! PAR-TEE!

--OR GOMI AND BILL.

TRUST ME, BILL. LARGE SPECTACLES LEND DISTINCTION TO ANY COUNTENANCE, AS I HAVE REASON TO KNOW.

QUERY: WHAT IS THE NATURE AND PURPOSE OF THE REFRESH-MENTS OTHERFRIENDS ARE CONSUMING?
NACHOS AND PIZZA AND M&M'S AND TWINKIES!
AND HAWAIIAN PUNCH! GREAT STUFF!
THE FOOD IS FREE, AND THE SERVICE IS GREAT!
IT WAS A GREAT IDEA OF MINE, BRINGING US ALL HERE!
RIGHT, VANISHER.

BY THE WAY, DID ANY OF YOU FIND BOOM BOOM? SIRYN AND I COULDN'T.
SHE WA--!
HAVEN'T SEEN HER ALL DAY, BUT I'M SURE SHE'LL BE ALONG SOONER OR LATER.

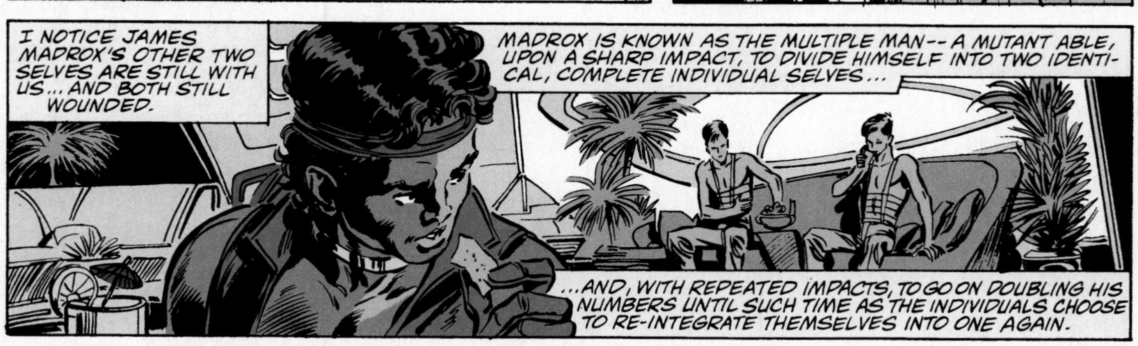
I NOTICE JAMES MADROX'S OTHER TWO SELVES ARE STILL WITH US... AND BOTH STILL WOUNDED.
MADROX IS KNOWN AS THE MULTIPLE MAN-- A MUTANT ABLE, UPON A SHARP IMPACT, TO DIVIDE HIMSELF INTO TWO IDENTI-CAL, COMPLETE INDIVIDUAL SELVES...
...AND, WITH REPEATED IMPACTS, TO GO ON DOUBLING HIS NUMBERS UNTIL SUCH TIME AS THE INDIVIDUALS CHOOSE TO RE-INTEGRATE THEMSELVES INTO ONE AGAIN.

RECENTLY, THE MUTATION MUTATED... THE MAN WITH BROKEN RIBS IS A MADROX WHO SO DIFFERED FROM THE REST OF HIMSELF THAT HE WOULD NOT GO BACK...
HOWEVER, HE RETAINED THE MUTANT TRAITS OF HIS ORIGINAL BODY, AND SO THE RENEGADE INDIVIDUAL HAS BECOME A PAIR OF UNEASY, RENEGADE DUPLICATES.

QUERY: WOULD NOT REJOINING OF MAIN BODY OF JAMES MADROX INVOLVE REDUCING INJURIES TO A FRACTION OF CORPOREAL MASS, FACILITATING HEALING AND DECREASING PAIN?
YEAH, BUT I'M NOT GONNA DO IT.
ME NEITHER.
IT WOULD MEAN GIVING UP MY UNIQUE-NESS.
YEAH... PAIN IS NOTHING, AS LONG AS YOU'RE YOURSELF ...AND AN INDIVIDUAL. WE WON'T EVEN MERGE WITH EACH OTHER.

≶SIGH≷ I WISH I COULD MAKE MYSELVES SEE REASON.
HEY... AS LONG AS YOU TWO ARE BOTH HERE...

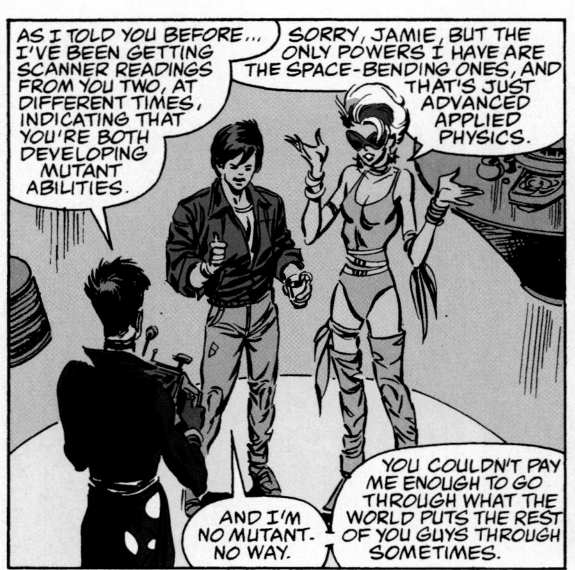
AS I TOLD YOU BEFORE... I'VE BEEN GETTING SCANNER READINGS FROM YOU TWO, AT DIFFERENT TIMES, INDICATING THAT YOU'RE BOTH DEVELOPING MUTANT ABILITIES.
SORRY, JAMIE, BUT THE ONLY POWERS I HAVE ARE THE SPACE-BENDING ONES, AND THAT'S JUST ADVANCED APPLIED PHYSICS.
AND I'M NO MUTANT-- NO WAY.
YOU COULDN'T PAY ME ENOUGH TO GO THROUGH WHAT THE WORLD PUTS THE REST OF YOU GUYS THROUGH SOMETIMES.

AH, BUT YOU MUST ADMIT, THERE ARE COMPENSATIONS ...THOSE EXTRA LITTLE ABILITIES... THE GLAMOUR... THE KNOWING YOU'VE GOT SOMETHING THAT NO ONE ELSE HAS...
BUT WE COCONUT BOYS AND GIRLS DON'T MUTATE. CAN'T BE DONE!
KNOWING THAT YOU MIGHT BE THE BEGINNING FOR A WHOLE NEW EVOLUTIONARY DEVELOPMENT FOR YOUR PEOPLE... I'D LOVE IT!

THAT'S WHY WE BROUGHT YOU ALL HERE... EVEN DEVIL DINOSAUR AND MOON BOY... AND WARLOCK! NONE OF THEM COME FROM EARTH, BUT THEY WERE MUTANTS ON THEIR HOME PLANETS.

EVERYONE HERE-- EXCEPT CHANCE AND I, AND GOMI AND BILL, WHO GET THEIR POWERS FROM HAVING ROBOT BODY PARTS --IS A MUTANT... AND THEREFORE PRECIOUS.

UH... ARIEL, I HATE TO INTERRUPT YOUR SPEECH, BUT RIGHT NOW, I'M GETTING A READING OF FULLY ACTIVE MUTANT POWERS FROM YOU.
WELL, NOTHING'S HAPPENING, IS IT? THE MACHINE IS OBVIOUSLY BROKEN.
DID YOU HEAR THAT?

I GUESS THE CEREBRO MUTANT SCANNER COULD BE FAULTY. SIRYN, I'LL CALIBRATE IT TO READ YOUR POWERS. JUST GIVE ME A SMALL DOSE.
SURE, LOVE.

EEEEEEEE

WAIT A MINUTE ...NOW I'M ALSO GETTING A READING FROM...
EEEEEEEEE

EEEEEEEEE

WARNING: AURAL SENSORS UNDERGOING EXTREME STRESS CAUSED BY OVERLOAD!
AAIEE--

EEE
PLINK

EEEEEEEEE
BUMP
UNBEARABLE...

FOUR MADROXES... FROM AN IMPACT SO SLIGHT THAT NOT EVEN TWO SHOULD HAVE RESULTED!
HAVE EVERYONE'S POWERS RUN WILD?

PEACE AT LAST! I WISH I KNEW THE STRANGE TONGUE THAT ALL OF OUR NEW FRIENDS SPEAK SO THAT THEY COULD TELL DEVIL AND ME WHAT IS GOING ON!
MY GLASSES!
JAMIE, WHAT CAUSED THAT?
I'M NOT SURE... BUT WHEN IT HAPPENED, I GOT A DOUBLED POWER READING FROM SIRYN...

AND A STRONG READING FROM CHANCE.
WHAT ARE YOU LOOKIN' AT ME FOR? I DIDN'T HAVE ANYTHING TO DO WITH IT!
BUT THE TROUBLE DIDN'T START UNTIL YOUR READING DID!

I DON'T HAVE TO LISTEN TO THIS. I'M OUTTA HERE!

WAIT... DON'T GO! NO ONE'S ACCUSING YOU OF ANYTHING. MADROX IS JUST PUZZLED, THAT'S ALL!
TELL HIM TO TAKE IT OUT ON SOMEONE BESIDES ME, THEN.

LIKE YOU, FOR INSTANCE, BOSS MAN! I'M SICK OF YOU TELEPORTING AWAY AND LEAVING THE REST OF US WHENEVER THE GOING GETS TOUGH!
BUT I DIDN'T! AT LEAST, THIS TIME I DIDN'T!
I DIDN'T WANT TO VANISH, BUT I COULDN'T CONTROL MYSELF!

AND THAT HASN'T HAPPENED TO MY POWERS IN YEARS, SINCE THEY FIRST APPEARED WHEN I WAS A TEENAGER!
INTERESTING YOU SHOULD MENTION THE ONSET OF POWERS WITH PUBERTY, BECAUSE FROM MY OBSERVATIONS I HAVE FORMED A HYPOTHESIS, WHICH--!

SORRY, ANGELS, BUT THE PARTY'S OVER! WE GOT ORDERS TO TAKE YOU IN!
IN WHAT?
YOU MAKE US SOUND LIKE A POORLY TAILORED PAIR OF PANTS!

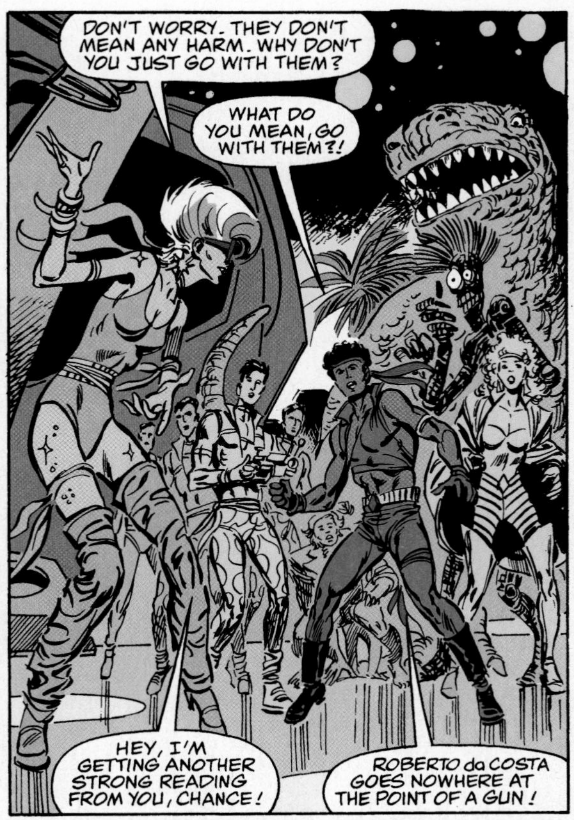
DON'T WORRY. THEY DON'T MEAN ANY HARM. WHY DON'T YOU JUST GO WITH THEM?
WHAT DO YOU MEAN, GO WITH THEM?!
HEY, I'M GETTING ANOTHER STRONG READING FROM YOU, CHANCE!
ROBERTO da COSTA GOES NOWHERE AT THE POINT OF A GUN!

I SUMMON MY SOLAR-CHARGED STRENGTH...
...AND THE RESULT IS... NOTHING.

♩LA!♫
LOVELY. WHY DON'T YOU USE YOUR SONIC BLAST?
I'M TRYING. IT'S NOT THERE!
WHYCAN'TIVANISH? WHYCAN'TIVANISH? WHYCAN'TIVANISH? WHYCAN'TIVANISH?

JAMIE, YOU'RE VANISHING!
WHAT'S HAPPENING TO THE REST OF ME?
THAT'S EVERYONE BUT THE THREE OF US!

EUREKA! AS I SURMISED, IT IS ONLY MUTANT ABILITIES WHICH ARE BEING IMPAIRED HERE! MY BIONIC POWERS OF TELEKINESIS ARE AS FORMIDABLE AS EVER!

DON'T YOU ALL SEE! CHANCE HAS JUST HIT PUBERTY, AND HER MUTANT POWERS HAVE SHOWN THEMSELVES!
UNCONSCIOUSLY, SHE HAS BEEN INTERFERING WITH ALL OF YOU, ALTERNATELY ENHANCING AND INHIBITING YOUR TALENTS!

SELF WILL KILL ALL WHO SEEK TO CAUSE SELF HARM!!
CHANCE, PLEASE! WHATEVER YOU'RE DOING, STOP IT! AT LEAST GO BACK TO HELPING INSTEAD OF HINDERING US!
BUT... I'M NOT ...I CAN'T...

LET'S SEE HOW YOUR ORGANIC CIRCUITRY STANDS UP TO A DISRUPTOR BEAM!
NOT AT ALL WELL.

LET'S SEE HOW YOU STAND UP TO THIS!!
WARLOCK!!

IF YOU CAN TAKE CARE OF GOMI, THE DISRUPTORS WILL HANDLE ALL THE MUTANTS... AND BELIEVE ME, HE CAN ONLY AIM THAT FORCE POWER OF HIS DEAD AHEAD!
RIGHT.
URK

GET THE BIG DINOSAUR! USE YOUR DISRUPTORS ON MAXIMUM!
REEERCH
LET HIM GO!!
YOU GOT IT!

EEEIYAH!
NICE WORK!

YOU IN THE JACKET. GET OVER THERE WITH THE REST OF YOUR FRIENDS.

BUT I'M NOT... ARIEL, TELL HIM!
CHANCE ISN'T ONE OF THE SPECIMENS. SHE'S MY PARTNER. SHE HELPED ME BRING THE REST OF THEM HERE.

NOW, NOW, MY DEAR, THIS IS NO TIME TO BE SENTIMENTAL. WE ALL HEARD WHAT THE LITTLE CYBORG SAID. YOUR PARTNER IS CLEARLY AND UNEQUIVOCALLY A MUTANT.
BUT, UNIPAR, YOU PROMISED ME!

THAT WAS BEFORE I KNEW WHAT SHE WAS. I'M SORRY, ARIEL, BUT THE ENTIRE FUTURE OF THE COCONUT GROVE RESTS ON THE RESEARCH WE ARE CONDUCTING NOW.

FOR THE SAKE OF OUR RACE, WE CANNOT AFFORD TO BECOME SENTIMENTAL ABOUT ANY MUTANT!
NOW, HAVE HER MOVE INTO THE HOLDING AREA WITH THE REST OF THEM.

ARIEL...
...HELP ME.
I...I...
...I'M SORRY.
NO...

I... I HAVE TO GO, UNIPAR. I CAN'T STAY AND WATCH WHAT YOU'RE GOING TO DO TO THEM.
AH... BUT I'M AFRAID I MUST INSIST...
KA-ZIK
...THAT YOU DO.

VREET
A... A FORCE BEAM? I CAN'T GET OUT!

PRECISELY, MY DEAR.
RATHER AN INGENIOUS CHANGE FROM THE TRADITIONAL CLOVEN PINE, DON'T YOU AGREE?
BUT WHY?
BECAUSE I WANTED TO THANK YOU. MY ASSISTANT HAS JUST INFORMED ME THAT YOU'VE BROUGHT US NOT ONE, BUT TWO MORE MUTANTS THAN WE EXPECTED...

...AND I'M AFRAID WE CANNOT AFFORD TO BE SENTIMENTAL ABOUT ANY MUTANT...
...EVEN WHEN THE MUTANT IS YOU!
TO BE CONCLUDED!

MARVEL®
LAST IN AN EIGHT-ISSUE LIMITED SERIES
FALLEN ANGELS
© 1987 MARVEL ENT. GROUP, INC.
TM
75¢ US
95¢ CAN
8
NOV
02409
APPROVED BY THE COMICS CODE AUTHORITY
THE FATE OF
BOOM-BOOM!

GROWNUPS AND CHILDREN
CREATED BY DUFFY & GAMMILL
JO DUFFY-WRITER
JOE STATON-PENCILER
TONY DEZUNIGA-INKER
BILL OAKLEY-LETTERER
PETRA SCOTESE-COLORIST
ANN NOCENTI-EDITOR
TOM DeFALCO-EDITOR IN CHIEF
HIS NAME IS BILL.

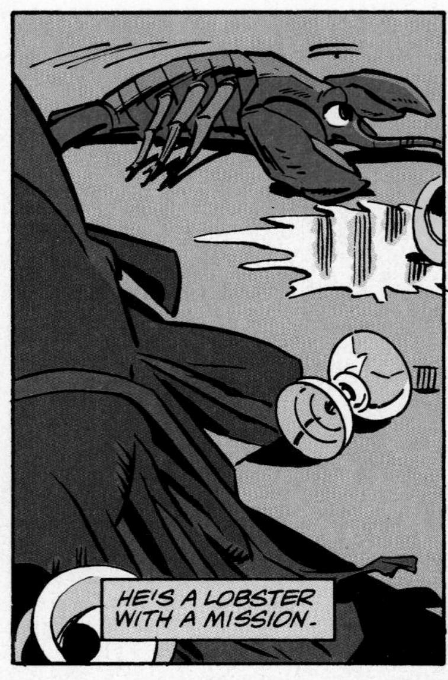
HE'S A LOBSTER WITH A MISSION.

HE'S GOT FRIENDS WHO'VE BEEN BETRAYED. THEY NEED HIS HELP.
HE'S ALSO GOT SOME FRIENDS WHO'VE DIED, AND BILL IS LOOKING FOR REVENGE.

HE'S JUST THE LOBSTER TO GET IT.

BILL IS A CYBORG, PART ANIMAL AND PART ROBOT. IN ADDITION TO INCREASING HIS INTELLIGENCE AND IMPROVING HIS ABILITY TO GO WITHOUT WATER...
...BILL'S MACHINE PARTS HAVE GIVEN HIM SUPER-CRUSTA-CEAN STRENGTH.

THIS IS ONE TOUGH SHELLFISH. AND DETERMINED. TRUE, THE JOB HE'S SET HIMSELF COULD TAKE TIME...

BUT BILL HAS TIME.

AND WHEN HE CUTS LOOSE, EVERYONE IN THE COCONUT GROVE--THIS CRAZY, BEAUTIFUL WORLD WHERE EVERY-ONE'S A STAR AND THE PARTY RUNS ALL NIGHT, AND THEY SMILE AS THEY KNIFE YOU IN THE BACK--

--HAD BETTER WATCH OUT.

MY NAME IS ROBERTO da COSTA. I AM FOURTEEN YEARS OLD.
I AM A MUTANT.
AND I AM IN VERY GRAVE TROUBLE.
MY... FRIENDS, MY COMRADES--THE FALLEN ANGELS--AND I HAVE LET OURSELVES BE TALKED INTO COMING TO THE COCONUT GROVE...
AND, NOW THAT WE ARE HERE, WE HAVE LEARNED, TO OUR HORROR, THAT THE COCONUT GROVE HAS PRODUCED A CIVILIZATION WHERE EVOLUTION IS AT A STANDSTILL.

ITS PEOPLE HAVE LOST THE ABILITY TO MUTATE, AND SO THEY WANT MUTANTS...
...THEIR LEADER, UNIPAR, HAS IMPRISONED US ALL... WE KNOW NOT FOR WHAT.
THAT'S RIGHT... MOVE THEM ALL INTO THE CELL, AND KEEP THE DISRUPTORS TRAINED ON THEM UNTIL WE ACTIVATE THE ENERGY FIELD THAT WILL DAMP THEIR MUTANT POWERS.
THE CYBORG, GOMI, WON'T BE AFFECTED BY THAT, SO DON'T LET HIM REMOVE HIS BLINDFOLD.
THE INNER, REVOLVING CELL IS FOR HIM.

ARIEL, MY DEAR, I REALLY MUST THANK YOU... YOU'VE BROUGHT US SUCH A COLLECTION...
HALF A DOZEN FROM EARTH, THE LITTLE MONKEY BOY AND DINOSAUR FROM THE PRIMITIVE WORLD, AND THE ORGANIC MACHINE, WARLOCK, FROM THE ROBOT WORLD...

AND, OF COURSE, YOURSELF. IF THEY EVER FIND OUT WHAT YOUR MUTATION IS--JUST WHAT SPECIAL, HIDDEN ABILITY OF YOURS WAS SETTING OFF THE CEREBRO MUTATION SCANNER YOUR FRIENDS CARRY--
YOU WILL BE A DEAR AND TELL US, WON'T YOU, SWEETIE?

AND, SPEAKING OF HIDDEN TALENTS, I HAVEN'T FORGOTTEN THAT YOU HAVE THE ABILITY TO BEND SPACE, MAKING DOORWAYS OPEN ONTO ANY PLACE YOU CHOOSE...

...SO YOU GET YOUR OWN LITTLE CELL ALL TO YOURSELF. A FORCE PILLAR, WITH NO DOORWAY. I HOPE YOU'LL BE COMFORTABLE IN IT.

...UNTIL IT'S YOUR TURN FOR WHAT WE HAVE PLANNED.
MEANTIME, CHICKIE-BABY, TAKE CARE OF YOURSELF. I MEAN THAT MOST SINCERELY, FROM THE BOTTOM OF MY HEART.
QUERY: FRIENDBOBBY, WHAT COURSE OF ACTION IS OPEN TO US?
I'M NOT SURE, WARLOCK. I KNOW THE DAMPER FIELD IS WORKING ON ME. I HAVE NO STRENGTH BEYOND THAT OF A NORMAL MAN--
--AND FEEL NO SIGN OF THE POWER OF SUNSPOT--THE SOLAR-ENERGIED MIGHT THAT IS NORMALLY MINE.

SIRYN?
SORRY, LAD. THE ONLY MUSICAL NOTE I'M GETTIN' IS A-FLAT... NOT A SIGN OF A SONIC BLAST.

WHAT ABOUT YOU, JAMIE MADROX?
THE THREE OF US--ONE IN WORKING ORDER AND TWO WITH BROKEN RIBS--ARE ALL YOU'RE GONNA GET, BOBBY. THE MULTIPLE MAN HAS BEEN CUT BACK TO A TRIO.

VANISHER?
I'M STILL HERE, AREN'T I? DO YOU THINK THAT'S BY CHOICE?
OH, WHY DID I EVER DECIDE TO LEAD THIS GROUP?
AND WHY DID I EVER DECIDE TO BETRAY YOU?

CEREBRO JUST CONFIRMS, WHAT WE'VE ALREADY FIGURED OUT BY TRYING--NO ONE IN THIS ROOM IS SHOWING ANY SIGNS OF MUTANT ABILITIES.

DEVIL... MY BROTHER, I SEE THE QUESTION IN YOUR EYES, BUT IN TRUTH, I AM AS PUZZLED AS YOU.
I WOULD TELL YOU WHAT IS TRANSPIRING... BUT THE LANGUAGE BARRIER BETWEEN OUR FRIENDS AND OURSELVES REMAINS AS IMPENETRABLE AS EVER.
I KNOW NOT WHAT THE PEOPLE OF THIS PLACE TRULY WANT OF US, NOR DO I UNDERSTAND WHY THEY HAVE PUT US IN THIS BLEAK CAVE, AFTER GIVING US SUCH A NICE "PAR-TEE"...

BUT THEY HAVE MADE ONE THING CLEAR. IF YOU, WARLOCK, OR GOMI ATTEMPT TO USE YOUR GREAT MIGHT TO FREE US, LESS MIGHTY OF OUR NUMBER SHALL SUFFER FOR IT!
BROTHER... I WISH WE HAD NEVER LEFT THE VALLEY OF THE FLAME. OR AT LEAST THAT WE'D STAYED IN OUR FINE NEW CAVE IN "BEAT STREET."

DRAT--THE WAY THIS PILLAR IS REVOLVING, IF I TRY TO DIRECT MY TELEKINETIC FORCE BLASTS, ODDS ARE THAT I SHALL TOTAL AT LEAST ONE OF YOU.
THEN PLEASE DON'T BE TRYIN' IT, GOMI.
HOWEVER, ALL IS NOT LOST. WE HAVEN'T SEEN BOOM BOOM IN SOME TIME.

PERHAPS SHE IS FREE, AND FORMULATING A PLAN.
BILL, TOO, I WAS HAPPY TO NOTE, EVADED CAPTURE, AND THEREFORE, WE NEED NOT DESPAIR!

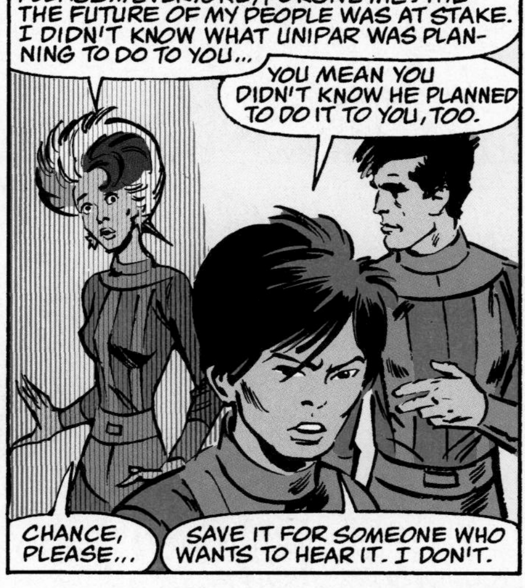
PLEASE... EVERYONE, FORGIVE ME. THE FUTURE OF MY PEOPLE WAS AT STAKE. I DIDN'T KNOW WHAT UNIPAR WAS PLANNING TO DO TO YOU...
YOU MEAN YOU DIDN'T KNOW HE PLANNED TO DO IT TO YOU, TOO.
CHANCE, PLEASE...
SAVE IT FOR SOMEONE WHO WANTS TO HEAR IT. I DON'T.

AND, WILL OUR NEW MYSTERY PRISONER SIGN IN, PLEASE?
TA-DAAA! SEE WHO I'VE BROUGHT YOU?!
BOOM-BOOM!

POOR LASS, YOU LOOK DREADFUL. WHAT HAVE THEY DONE T'YOU?
IT WAS HORRIBLE. IT HURT SO MUCH... DON'T LET THEM...
CUR... TO TORMENT HER, AND THEN LAUGH. BY WHAT RIGHT DO YOU...

YOU'RE PRISONERS HERE, AND ALIENS WITH NO CIVIL RIGHTS. THAT, PLUS OUR NEED, GIVES US THE RIGHT TO DO WHATEVER WE WISH.
SPECIFICALLY, WE ARE DOING MINUTE GENETIC AND CELLULAR EXAMINATIONS OF EACH AND EVERY ONE OF YOU MUTANTS, IN THE HOPE OF ISOLATING JUST WHAT FACTOR ENABLES YOU TO EVOLVE.
IF NEED BE, WE'LL ATTEMPT TO EXTRACT THAT FACTOR FROM YOU, SO THAT IT CAN BE DONATED TO OUR WORTHY YOUNG NATIVE VOLUNTEERS.

FEEL BETTER FOR KNOWING?
HARDLY.

YOU'RE NOT TAKING ANYONE ELSE OUT OF THIS CELL.
NOT WITHOUT COMING THROUGH THE BOTH OF ME, FIRST.
IF THAT'S HOW YOU WANT IT.

FELLA, YOU'RE HURT... DON'T...
SO WE TWO HAVE THE LEAST TO LOSE...

THAT MADROX-- THE WEAK, MOUTHY ONE-- WE'LL DO HIM NEXT.

NO! LET HIM GO, OR I'LL--!

JAMIE!!
NO, YOU FOOL!! THERE WAS NO NEED TO PANIC! WE NEED THESE MUTANTS ALIVE!

NOW, IF ANYONE ELSE TRIES ANYTHING FANCY, WE CAN ALWAYS KILL GOMI, AS WELL. HE'S NO MUTANT, SO WE DON'T REALLY CARE WHERE HIS POWERS COME FROM.
YOU'VE MADE YOUR POINT, BUTCHER.

THE STRAIN OF HAVING ONE OF HIS SELVES DIE HAS BEEN TOO MUCH FOR THE SURVIVING MADROXES...
UH!
JAMIE!

I CAN'T SEE A THING! WHAT'S GOING ON OUT THERE?
ONE OF HE-WHOSE-BODIES-ARE-NUMEROUS-AS-LEAVES-ON-THE-TREES HAS BEEN KILLED!
I'M SORRY, MOON BOY, BUT WHATEVER YOU'RE SAYING, I CAN'T UNDERSTAND A WORD!

ENOUGH OF THIS... BRING ALL THE MADROXES, WHATEVER THEIR CONDITION.

NO! YOU BUTCHERS--!
SUNSPOT, TOO, SINCE HE INSISTS.

HALT! SELF DOES NOT WISH FRIEND-BOBBY TO ACCOMPANY YOU AND SO FACE HARM!
I AM TIRED OF THIS!
WARLOCK...

LISTEN MUTANT, OR ROBOT, OR WHATEVER YOU ARE ... EITHER SUNSPOT LEAVES THIS CELL WITH US, QUIETLY, NOW...
OR HE'S GONNA BE HARMED... BY GETTING BLOWN AWAY, JUST LIKE THAT THIRD MADROX...
I...THANK YOU FOR TRYING MY FRIEND...

QUERY: WHY DOES SELF CARE WHAT BECOMES OF FRIEND BOBBY? AMONG SELF'S RACE, COMPASSION AND ALL GENEROUS EMOTIONS ARE ABERRATIONS.
IN A CELL WHICH NULLIFIES THE EFFECTS OF MUTATION, SELF SHOULD BE CAPABLE ONLY OF SELFISH THOUGHTS AND SAVAGE ACTION.
AH...BUT LOVIN'... CARIN' FOR OTHERS ...WARLOCK, ALL THOSE ARE LEARNED BEHAVIORS.

YOU BEEN CARIN' ABOUT BOBBY AND YOUR OTHER FRIENDS ALMOST SINCE THE DAY YOU WERE BORN. GENETICS OR NOT...
I THINK MAYBE WHAT LIFE'S TAUGHT YOU ABOUT LOVE HAS BECOME SECOND NATURE TO YOU, LADDIE.

HOW YOU FEELING?
NOT WELL, BUT BETTER... AT LEAST TILL WE GET TO THE LITTLE PARTY UNIPAR HAS PLANNED FOR US.
AND SO IT HAS COME... I AND THESE TWO OF MY FRIENDS ARE FACING DEATH...
AND I KNOW THAT IT IS WHAT I DESERVE!

I STILL SEE A WAY OF EVENING THE ODDS A LITTLE...
I DON'T LIKE IT... BUT I UNDER-STAND...

WE'LL BE BACK FOR YOU, ONCE WE'RE THROUGH WITH THE CADAVER...
JAMIE... I LET ONE OF YOU DIE, WITHOUT RAISING A HAND IN HIS DEFENSE...
I AM... VERY DEEPLY ASHAMED.

THERE WAS NOTHING YOU COULD HAVE DONE.
I COULD HAVE TRIED.
AND DIED, LIKE HE DID?
THERE ARE TIMES TO BE A HERO...
WHEN YOU HAVE A CHANCE OF MAYBE HELPING SOMEBODY...
IF YOU TRY WHEN THERE'S NO CHANCE, THEN YOU'RE JUST SHOWING OFF... AND THAT KIND OF EGO TRIP CAN BE PRETTY EXPENSIVE...

I DIDN'T LIFT A HAND TO HELP HIM.
ME, NEITHER... AND IT WAS ME HE DIED TRYING TO SAVE. BUT HE DIDN'T SAVE ME, AND I'M NOT GOING TO GO OFF ON SOME BIG GUILT TRIP...
BECAUSE THAT WOULD JUST BE SHOWING OFF, TOO...

WARLOCK AND I LEFT OUR PREVIOUS TEAMMATES--THE NEW MUTANTS--AND JOINED THE FALLEN ANGELS, BECAUSE, IN A MOMENT OF ANGER, I NEARLY KILLED MY BEST FRIEND, SAM GUTHRIE. IT WAS AN ACCIDENT...
...BUT IT WAS NOT THE ACT OF A HERO... AND I HAVE ALWAYS BELIEVED THAT THE LOT OF AN IMPERFECT HERO IS TO BECOME A VILLAIN.
YET I HAVE LEARNED AMONG THE ANGELS THAT I WOULD BE AN EVEN WORSE VILLAIN THAN I HAVE BEEN A HERO.

IS THAT IT, THEN? TO FAIL IS NOT AN EXCUSE TO GIVE UP...
...BUT A REASON TO TRY ALL THE HARDER.

I UNDERSTAND.
YET, I SEE NO WAY OF AVENGING YOUR OTHER SELF, OR OF HELPING OURSELVES. OUR POWERS ARE STILL DAMPED.

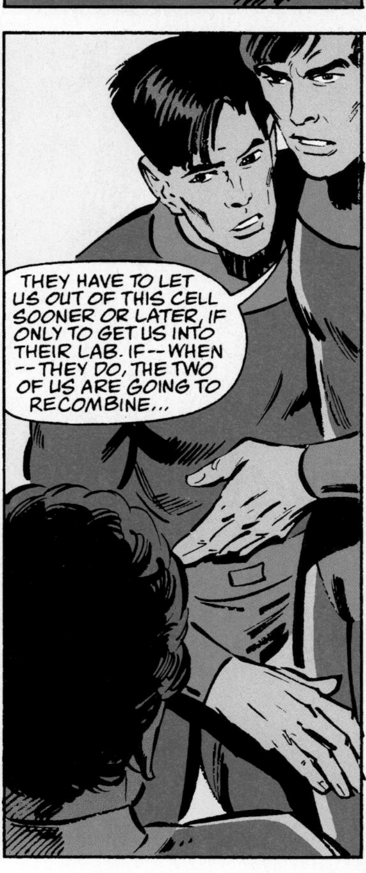
THEY HAVE TO LET US OUT OF THIS CELL SOONER OR LATER, IF ONLY TO GET US INTO THEIR LAB. IF--WHEN--THEY DO, THE TWO OF US ARE GOING TO RECOMBINE...

LOOK...
WHATEVER THE COCONUT GROVE HAS PLANNED FOR US...

IT'S STARTING NOW.

JAMIE, I KNOW THAT AS LONG AS YOU ARE SEPARATED, THE ONE OF YOU WITH THE BROKEN RIBS WILL BE WHAT THEY CALL A SITTING DUCK... BUT I HAVE A SUGGESTION...
WHY DOESN'T THE WELL MADROX DUPLICATE HIMSELF TWENTY OR SO TIMES BEFORE YOU MERGE...? THEN, THE INJURIES OF ONE SHALL BE DIVIDED AMONG DOZENS OF YOU WHEN YOU RECOMBINE...

GOOD FOR YOU, BOBBY. IT'S NOT OFTEN SOMEONE ELSE COMES UP WITH A NEW WAY OF MY USING MY ABILITIES. I LIKE IT!
BUT... THE MORE OF... THEM... HIM I MERGE WITH, THE LESS OF ME THERE'LL BE LEFT IN HIS... OUR COLLECTIVE MIND.
I STILL DON'T UNDERSTAND YOU... A MUTATION OF OUR MUTATION... ALL THE REST OF ME HAVE ALWAYS WELCOMED REJOINING.

PLEASE, JAMIE, YOU MUST... I KNOW IT'S A SACRIFICE... BUT THINK OF THE SACRIFICE YOUR OTHER INDIVIDUALISTIC "BROTHER" MADE FOR YOUR SAKE!
PART OF GROWING UP IS ACCEPTING THAT YOU CAN'T HAVE THINGS JUST AS YOU WOULD WANT THEM!

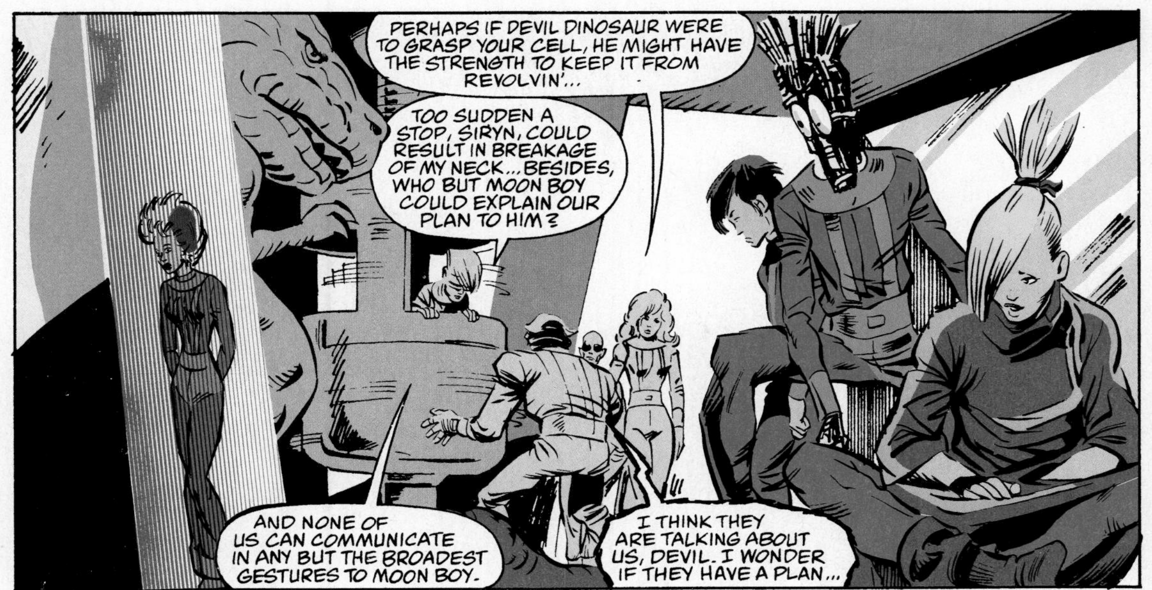
PERHAPS IF DEVIL DINOSAUR WERE TO GRASP YOUR CELL, HE MIGHT HAVE THE STRENGTH TO KEEP IT FROM REVOLVIN'...
TOO SUDDEN A STOP, SIRYN, COULD RESULT IN BREAKAGE OF MY NECK... BESIDES, WHO BUT MOON BOY COULD EXPLAIN OUR PLAN TO HIM?
AND NONE OF US CAN COMMUNICATE IN ANY BUT THE BROADEST GESTURES TO MOON BOY.
I THINK THEY ARE TALKING ABOUT US, DEVIL. I WONDER IF THEY HAVE A PLAN...

WHY AM I BEING SO ROTTEN TO ARIEL...? I WENT ALONG WITH WHAT SHE WANTED... TILL I FOUND OUT I WAS A MUTANT, TOO...
SOMEHOW, UNTIL THEY CAPTURED US, EVERYTHING ARIEL SUGGESTED ALWAYS SOUNDED LIKE SUCH A GOOD IDEA...TO ALL OF US.

IT WAS SUCH A NICE PLAN... SAFE, HARMLESS. GET A BUNCH OF MUTANT KIDS TO STEAL FOR ME... JUST ENOUGH TO BUY A FEW LUXURIES...
SET OURSELVES UP A NICE PLACE--BEAT STREET--IN MANHATTAN... NO SUPER-ENEMIES, NO POLICE, EVEN.
HOW DID IT GO SO WRONG?

AAAIIEEEE!!
WHAT IN THE NAME O' SWEET HEAVEN IS THAT?

NO! HELP! SAVE ME! KEEP BACK!!!

AAIIEEE!!

IT'S BILL!!

AND HE DOESN'T LOOK ANY TOO PLEASED!

NO!!

YIPE!!

KLONG!

ꝏ?
GOMI'S FINE, BILL. YOU CAN FREE HIM--FREE ALL OF US --WITH THOSE KEYS THE GUARD HAS ON HIS BELT!

I THINK THE LOCK'S IN THE BASE O' THE THING.

!

WHOOPS!
QUERY: WOULD NOT FRIENDGOMI'S OCULAR SENSORS FUNCTION MORE EFFICIENTLY IF FRIENDGOMI REMOVED HIS BLINDFOLD?
NATURALLY... I WAS JUST ABOUT TO...

EXIT
!
NATURALLY, BILL. I SHALL BE WITH YOU IN A MOMENT. HOWEVER, WE MUST SEE THAT OUR FRIENDS ARE ALL RELEASED AS WELL!
★✱!!#!!

NOW, BILL, I SYMPATHIZE... MOST SINCERELY I DO...
I MOURN FOR DON AS BITTERLY AS YOU... BUT YOU CANNOT GO ON BLAMING OUR FELLOW ANGELS FOR HIS DEATH...
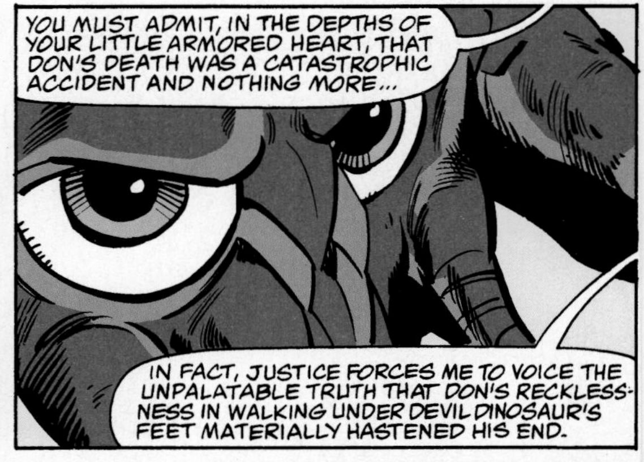
YOU MUST ADMIT, IN THE DEPTHS OF YOUR LITTLE ARMORED HEART, THAT DON'S DEATH WAS A CATASTROPHIC ACCIDENT AND NOTHING MORE...
IN FACT, JUSTICE FORCES ME TO VOICE THE UNPALATABLE TRUTH THAT DON'S RECKLESS-NESS IN WALKING UNDER DEVIL DINOSAUR'S FEET MATERIALLY HASTENED HIS END.

THINK OF DON, BILL. REMEMBER HIS COURAGE... HIS LOYALTY... HE WOULDN'T WANT YOU TO HOLD A GRUDGE. HE'D ENCOURAGE YOU TO SAVE HIS FRIENDS.
IN FACT, I'M CERTAIN, GIVEN THE CHOICE, DON WOULD HAVE SACRI-FICED HIS LIFE TO HELP ANY ONE OF US.
DO IT FOR DON, BILL...
HE'S RIGHT BILL. YOU KNOW HE IS.

CLICK
FRIENDBILL, PERMIT SELF TO EXPRESS SELF'S GRATITUDE...

WAIT, EVERYONE. WHAT ARE WE GOIN' TO DO ABOUT ARIEL?

THERE... DOESN'T APPEAR TO BE ANYTHING ON THIS KEY RING THAT WILL OPEN HER CELL.

SHE DOUBLE-CROSSED US. IT WOULD SERVE HER RIGHT IF WE LEFT HER FOR HER FRIENDS.
I DON'T MIND HELPING HER... UNLESS IT MEANS WE RISK GETTING RECAP-TURED.

LOOK, I'VE ALWAYS DISLIKED THE GIRL MORE THAN ANY OF YOU... I KNEW HER FOR A BAD ONE FROM THE START...
BUT NO ONE'S PERFECT, AFTER ALL. SHE'S SORRY. I SAY THAT DESERVES ANOTHER CHANCE.

I'M WILLING TO FORGIVE HER. AND IF I TAKE A CHANCE ON HER, THE REST OF YOU SHOULD BE ABLE TO. AFTER ALL, SHE BE-TRAYED ME WORSE THAN SHE DID THE REST OF YOU.
YEAH, RIGHT. VERY BELIEVABLE, ONE TRAITOR SPEAKING UP FOR ANOTHER.

Y'KNOW, BOOM BOOM. I'VE NEVER BEEN PERFECT MESELF.
ARE YOU REALLY STANDIN' THERE, EXPECTIN' US ALL TO BELIEVE THAT IN ALL YOUR LIFE, YOU'VE NEVER NEEDED, OR AT LEAST WANTED, SOMEONE ELSE TO FORGIVE YOU?

SHALL WE BE DEMOCRATIC? I SAY WE HELP HER.
SELF CONCURS.

YEAH, SURE, FINE. LET'S JUST HURRY.
OKAY...
THEN, IN THE ABSENCE OF HOSTILE INTERVENTION BY DEVIL DINOSAUR AND MOON BOY, IT WOULD APPEAR TO BE UNANIMOUS...

GOMI, WHAT ARE YOU--? OH, YOUR TELEKINETIC FORCE BLAST...
YOU'VE SHATTERED THE PILLAR! THANK YOU! THANK YOU!

LET'S FIND A DOORWAY. I CAN GET US OFF THIS WORLD AND BACK TO BEAT STREET!
YOU NEVER LEARN, DO YOU? NO WAY!

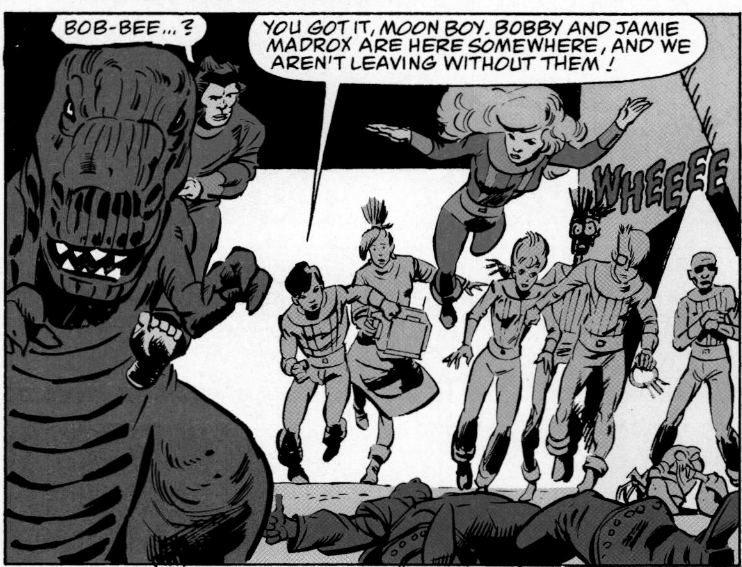
BOB-BEE...?
YOU GOT IT, MOON BOY. BOBBY AND JAMIE MADROX ARE HERE SOMEWHERE, AND WE AREN'T LEAVING WITHOUT THEM!
WHEEEE

WHEEEEE
EH?
AH, SIRYN WISHES TO CONFER WITH ME. NO DOUBT, OUR SELF-APPOINTED LEADER HAS A PLAN.

GET THEM!
DEVIL, MY BROTHER, GET THEM!!
AND A NICE HIGH LEVEL SONIC BLAST SHOULD HELP EVEN MATTERS A BIT!
VORT!

LOOK, THERE HE IS AGAIN! SHOOT HIM!
BUT EVERY TIME WE TAKE AIM, THE GUY DISAPPEARS!
YOO-HOO! NYA-NYAH! CAN'T GET ME!!

OW! MY EARS!!

BOOM-BOOM! WARLOCK! GRAB CEREBRO, AND LET'S TAKE OFF!
IT'S UP TO US TO FIND BOBBY AND JAMIE!!
OKAY. I'LL CALIBRATE THE SCANNER TO READ SPEC-IFICALLY FOR THEIR POWERS.

BY THE WAY... THAT DOUBLE-OR-NOTHING POWER OF YOURS IS READING STRONGLY RIGHT NOW... BUT I CAN'T TELL IF YOU'RE CAN-CELING OTHER PEOPLE'S POWERS...
...OR INCREASING THEM.
WELL, DON'T LOOK AT ME. I JUST FOUND OUT I HAVE IT. I DON'T HAVE A CLUE HOW TO CONTROL IT.

GREAT.
HEY, I THINK I HAVE THEM. WARLOCK, GO WEST!

QUERY: IS THIS THE LOCATION INDICATED BY CEREBRO-SCANNER? FRIENDBOBBY AND FRIENDJAMIE ARE NOT IN EVIDENCE.
THIS IS THE RIGHT PLACE. THEY MUST BE BEHIND THAT LOCKED DOOR.
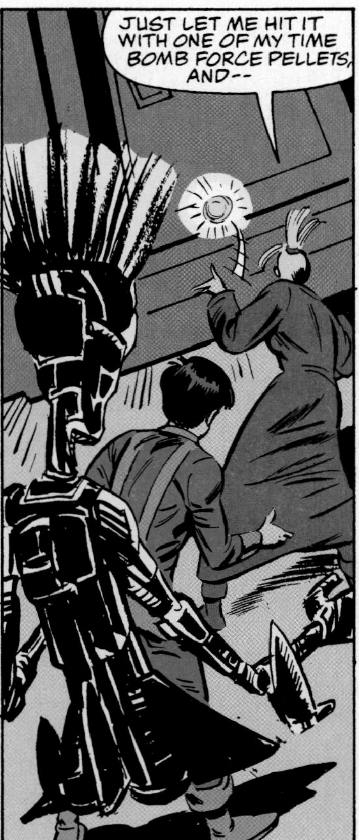
JUST LET ME HIT IT WITH ONE OF MY TIME BOMB FORCE PELLETS, AND--

--NOTHIN'. A DUD.
CHANCE, YOU DOPE, YOU CANCELED OUT MY POWER.

DOPE, AM I? WELL, IF THAT'S HOW IT FEELS TO CANCEL THINGS... THEN THE OTHER STRANGE FEELING I SOMETIMES GET MUST BE THE ONE TO USE...
THE MAKE THINGS DOUBLE STRENGTH!

BLOOEY!!
Y'KNOW, I THINK MAYBE I'M BEGINNING TO GET THE HANG OF THIS.

ACCEPTING THAT YOU HAVE A POWER IS THE FIRST STEP. TRUST ME, I'VE BEEN THERE.
WARNING! SELF SEES HOSTILE COCO-NUT BOYS APPROACHING!

THIS IS A JOB FOR--
--SELF!
ATTA BOY, WARLOCK. THEY'RE ALL YOURS.
WE'LL FIND THE OTHERS.

MADROX! daCOSTA!
BOBBY! JAMIE! JAMIE, DARLING!!
IN HERE!

THEN BACK IT UP, CUTIES, 'CAUSE HERE COMES THE CAVALRY, AND WE'D HATE TO HURT YOU.

WHAT DO YOU SUPPOSE THEY HAVE IN--!

NICE GOING, GIRLS. HIT ME, SO I CAN START DUPLICATING MYSELVES.
YOU GOT IT!

OUR POWERS HAVE RETURNED! THE EXPLOSION MUST HAVE DESTROYED THE DAMPER FIELD! I AM SUNSPOT ONCE MORE!
GREAT! AND NOW TO PULL MYSELVES TOGETHER!

GUARDS! GET IN THERE! CAN'T YOU SEE WHAT'S HAPPENING?!

JAMIE, DO WHAT YOU HAVE TO. I SHALL KEEP WATCH FOR THE GUARDS!
DIVIDE TWENTY GUYS, ONE OF THEM BADLY INJURED, AND THEN PUT 'EM BACK TOGETHER...

WHEW... AND GET ONE KINDA WOOZY GUY... BUT NOW ALL OF ME THAT SURVIVED ARE BACK IN ONE SLIGHTLY DAMAGED PIECE...
CHANCE, I DON'T THINK JAMIE WILL MAKE IT OUT OF HERE ALONE. HE DOES STILL SORT OF LOOK A MESS.
THEN YOU GO WITH HIM, AND HELP HIM IF HE NEEDS IT.
BOBBY AND I CAN TAKE CARE OF THE GUARDS TOGETHER.

YOU... WILL RISK STAYING BEHIND... TO HELP ME?
HEY, WHAT ARE FRIENDS FOR?
ANYWAY, ALONE, YOU'D BE CANNON FODDER. IF YOUR POWER WERE TO, SAY, DOUBLE--
--YOU JUST MIGHT STAND A CHANCE.

AND, IF YOU CANCEL MY SUNSPOT ABILITIES, BY MISTAKE?
ME, I WAS BORN TO GAMBLE.

C'MON... WHAT DO WE REALLY HAVE TO LOSE? IF WE'RE GONNA GO, LET'S GO OUT BIG TIME!

I... DON'T KNOW IF THIS WILL WORK.
I AM FOURTEEN YEARS OLD... AND I DO NOT WANT TO DIE...
BUT, AS SHE HAS SAID, WE HAVE NO CHOICE... AND AT LEAST WE MAY GO DOWN FIGHTING!

SEE? I TOLD YOU!

NEVER HAVE I ENJOYED SUCH POWER!
FLEE NOW, DOGS, AND I'LL LET YOU KEEP YOUR LIVES!!

AH... BUT NONE OF YOU IS INVULNERABLE...
AND, IF WE SHOOT CHANCE, YOUR POWER WILL BE HALVED BACK TO NORMAL.

OH... YOU DON'T REALLY WANT TO DO THAT.

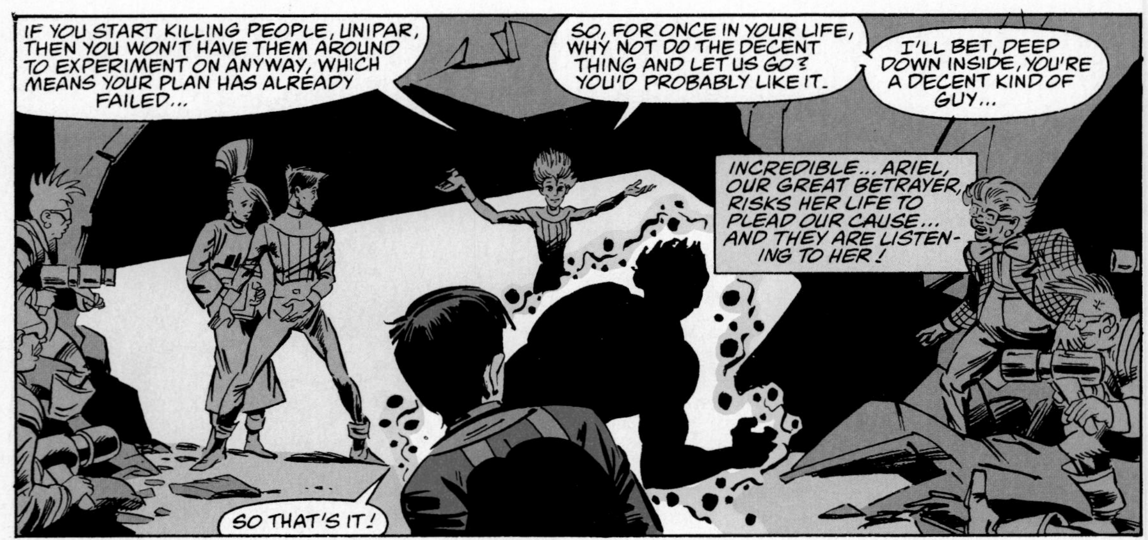
IF YOU START KILLING PEOPLE, UNIPAR, THEN YOU WON'T HAVE THEM AROUND TO EXPERIMENT ON ANYWAY, WHICH MEANS YOUR PLAN HAS ALREADY FAILED...
SO, FOR ONCE IN YOUR LIFE, WHY NOT DO THE DECENT THING AND LET US GO? YOU'D PROBABLY LIKE IT.
I'LL BET, DEEP DOWN INSIDE, YOU'RE A DECENT KIND OF GUY...
INCREDIBLE... ARIEL, OUR GREAT BETRAYER, RISKS HER LIFE TO PLEAD OUR CAUSE... AND THEY ARE LISTENING TO HER!
SO THAT'S IT!

AND, LET ME TELL YOU, IF YOU COULD WIN, WHICH I DOUBT, IT WOULD PROBABLY COST YOU A LOT MORE THAN YOU'RE WILLING TO PAY...
I DON'T GET IT! WHY IS SHE--?

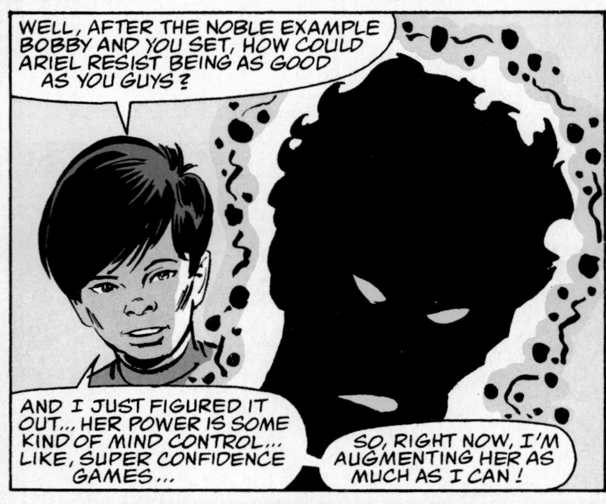
WELL, AFTER THE NOBLE EXAMPLE BOBBY AND YOU SET, HOW COULD ARIEL RESIST BEING AS GOOD AS YOU GUYS?
AND I JUST FIGURED IT OUT... HER POWER IS SOME KIND OF MIND CONTROL... LIKE, SUPER CONFIDENCE GAMES...
SO, RIGHT NOW, I'M AUGMENTING HER AS MUCH AS I CAN!

WHAT THREAT COULD YOU ANGELS POSSIBLY HOLD OVER MY HEAD, ARIEL?

WHY DON'T YOU LOOK UP AND SEE?

CONVINCE THEM, MY BROTHER!
GREETINGS. ARE YOU GOING TO LET OUR FRIENDS GO, OR SHALL WE PULL THIS PLACE DOWN AROUND YOUR EARS?

RAARGH

GOODBYE! WE SURRENDER! SORRY YOU CAN'T STAY! HAVE A GOOD TRIP HOME!!
WE SURRENDER! WE SURRENDER! WE SURRENDER! WE SURRENDER!!

BEFORE WE GO, MY HOST, I FEEL I MUST POINT OUT TO YOU THAT YOU HAVE BEEN NOT ONLY WEAK AND EVIL, BUT A FOOL. ARIEL, A MUTANT, IS A MEMBER OF YOUR RACE.
HENCE, YOU HAVE NOT LOST YOUR ABILITY TO EVOLVE, AND ALL YOUR CRIMES AGAINST US WERE NEEDLESS AND POINTLESS.
IN YOUR ARROGANCE AND DESIRE TO HASTEN THE COURSE OF NATURE, YOU NEARLY DESTROYED THE VERY THING YOU SOUGHT!

ARIEL! PRECIOUS, SWEETIE. YOU WON'T HOLD THAT AGAINST US, WILL YOU?
YOU'RE NOT MAD AT OL' UNIPAR, ARE YOU, MUFFIN? YOU'LL STAY HERE, AND HELP THE OLD COCONUT GROVE.
I'D LIKE TO HELP IT INTO THE MIDDLE OF A BLACK HOLE.

GO SUCK AN EGG, UNIPAR.
I'M TAKING MY FRIENDS HOME--TO BEAT STREET!

PLACE LOOKS GREAT, DOESN'T IT?
DUSTY BUT GREAT!
I'M HUNGRY.
BEATS
ME, TOO. WHO WANTS TO GO OUT AND STEAL US SOME FOOD?
LET'S BE REALLY RADICAL, FOR ONCE. LET'S SEE IF WE CAN GET UP ENOUGH MONEY TO BUY IT.

WELL, THERE ARE AT LEAST TWO DINNERS YOU WON'T BE PAYING FOR. I'VE BEEN THINKING...
...THAT IT'S TIME WARLOCK AND I STOPPED RUNNING AWAY FROM OUR LIVES AND GOT ON WITH LIVING THEM.

WHAT DO YOU SAY? SHALL WE RETURN TO THE NEW MUTANTS?
AFFIRMATIVE! AFFIRMATIVE! AFFIRMATIVE!

BOBBY... TELL YOUR TEACHER ...AND OURS... THAT JAMIE AND I'VE DECIDED TO STAY WITH THE ANGELS A WHILE LONGER. WE KNOW WE CAME HERE IN SEARCH OF YOU...
BUT WE REALLY LIKE THIS GROUP. BESIDES, THEY NEED SOMEONE TO GUIDE THEM BACK ONTO THE STRAIGHT AND NARROW.
PLEASE! NOT TOO NARROW!

HEY, MACHO, COME BACK ANY TIME! ONCE YOU'RE AN ANGEL, YOU CAN NEVER FALL TOO FAR FROM US!
THANK YOU, CHANCE. YOU'LL BE HEARING FROM ME.
AFFIRMATIVE.

WARLOCK, MY FRIEND, THE WORLD HAD BETTER WATCH ITS STEP, NOW THAT THE FALLEN ANGELS ARE BACK!
QUERY: WHAT ABOUT FRIENDBOBBY AND SELF?
WHAT OF US?

LOOK OUT, LIFE, BECAUSE HERE WE COME!!
FIN

MARVEL®
25TH
ANNIVERSARY
© 1986 MARVEL COMICS GROUP
ANNIVERSARY
TM
48
MAR
ONLY
50¢
THE OFFICIAL MARVEL® NEWS MAGAZINE!
MARVEL AGE®
GAMMILL
X-MEN
VS.
AVENGERS!
FALLEN ANGELS!
AND EVEN MORE
NEWS!

HE'S SOME KIND OF FREAK!
WELL, LET'S GET HIM ANYWAY! I AIN'T AFRAID OF NO FREAKS!

Sunspot. Warlock. The Multiple Man. Siryn. A "glitter queen" alien named Ariel. A kid named Gomi, who has two purple and green intelligent lobsters as sidekicks. Devil Dinosaur and Moon Boy. These are the characters that comprise the "FALLEN ANGELS," formerly titled "THE MISFITS," a four-issue limited series written by Jo Duffy and drawn by Kerry Gammill. Jo spoke with MARVEL AGE MAGAZINE regarding this series several months ago (MARVEL AGE MAGAZINE #37), and this month we caught up with Kerry Gammill, who gave us an update on the series, as well as talking about the book from the artist's perspective.

"I've worked with Jo before," Kerry said, "and I ran into her at a convention in Houston earlier in the year. Chris Claremont was there also, and the three of us started talking about a new book that Jo and Ann Nocenti were planning, called THE MISFITS. Jo was excited about borrowing Chris's New Mutants characters. They looked at each other, and then at me, and Jo suggested to Chris that I might be the right one to pencil the series."

At the time of the interview, Kerry was working on penciling issue #2, and he had some interesting views on the characters he's drawing. "I've been mainly doing what you would call 'old standby' characters for the last few years, pretty much your average super hero stuff—which this book really isn't—and this is a good opportunity for me to get into some strange type characters. So far, Warlock has been my favorite character to draw—he's very challenging, because he's basically pure emotion. His whole body expresses what he's thinking. It's tough, because it forces me to think very creatively about emotion, and express it in Warlock's crazy body language."

Because this is a book about teenagers—mutant teenagers, but teenagers nonetheless, the emotions of the characters play a big part in the action of the story. Warlock's body language, Sunspot's outbursts of frustration that sometime lead to violence, and the problems that all kids face when they are confronted with situations that they may not be emotionally old enough to handle give Kerry a unique opportunity to draw kids at,

EEEEEEEEEEEEEEEE
SIRYN IS DOIN' WONDERFULLY WELL, JAMIE, IS SHE NOT? SHE'S BEEN HOLDIN' HERSELF ALOFT ON THE STRENGTH OF THAT ONE NOTE FOR FIVE MINUTES NOW...
...WITH NO SIGNS OF STRAIN.

their worst as well as at their best.

"Ariel, the alien whose people are after her, is very interesting to work with," Kerry told us. "She's not really too alien looking, except that she has a kind of glitter all over her body, and she dresses very flamboyantly—very modern. For reference for the clothes she wears, I had to go to bookstores and buy all the young women's and teen magazines in order to make sure that she's dressed right for the 80's tone of the characters. I haven't kept up really with what the young girls are wearing lately, so that was a fun experience!" In many ways, Kerry indicated, the characters are images of today's kids. They are struggling with today's problems. Only in their case those problems range from what to wear to how to control a mutant power that could potentially be very dangerous. He feels that the popularity of the comics dealing with teenaged mutants is due in great part to the fact that they do appeal to the teens of today—kids going through that transitional time in life.

"Kids today are under a lot of peer pressure—they sometimes need to retreat behind masks of one sort or another to shield them—and the thought that kids like the Fallen Angels are going through some of the same things they are—well, it gives them something to identify with. I'm trying to make the Fallen Angels as much like real kids as possible. Jo's making that very easy for me."

Two of the characters that are in the new series, have made appearances in the X-Men—Jamie Maddrox, the Multiple Man, and Siryn, Banshee's daughter. Kerry is having fun working with these characters. "These are two characters who haven't gotten very much attention, and I'm looking forward to being able to bring them more into the forefront, and giving them their own definitive look, as well as doing some creative stuff with their powers."

"I haven't worked with Devil Dinosaur or Moon Boy yet—they appear in the last two issues—but it should be interesting. I'm over the halfway mark now, and it gets less complicated from here." Less complicated, perhaps. More strange, weird, and exciting—you bet!

—*Sue Flaxman*

THERE ARE SOME KIDS JUST TOO WILD TO HANDLE.
WHEN THEY'RE MUTANTS, IT CAN SPELL *DISASTER*.

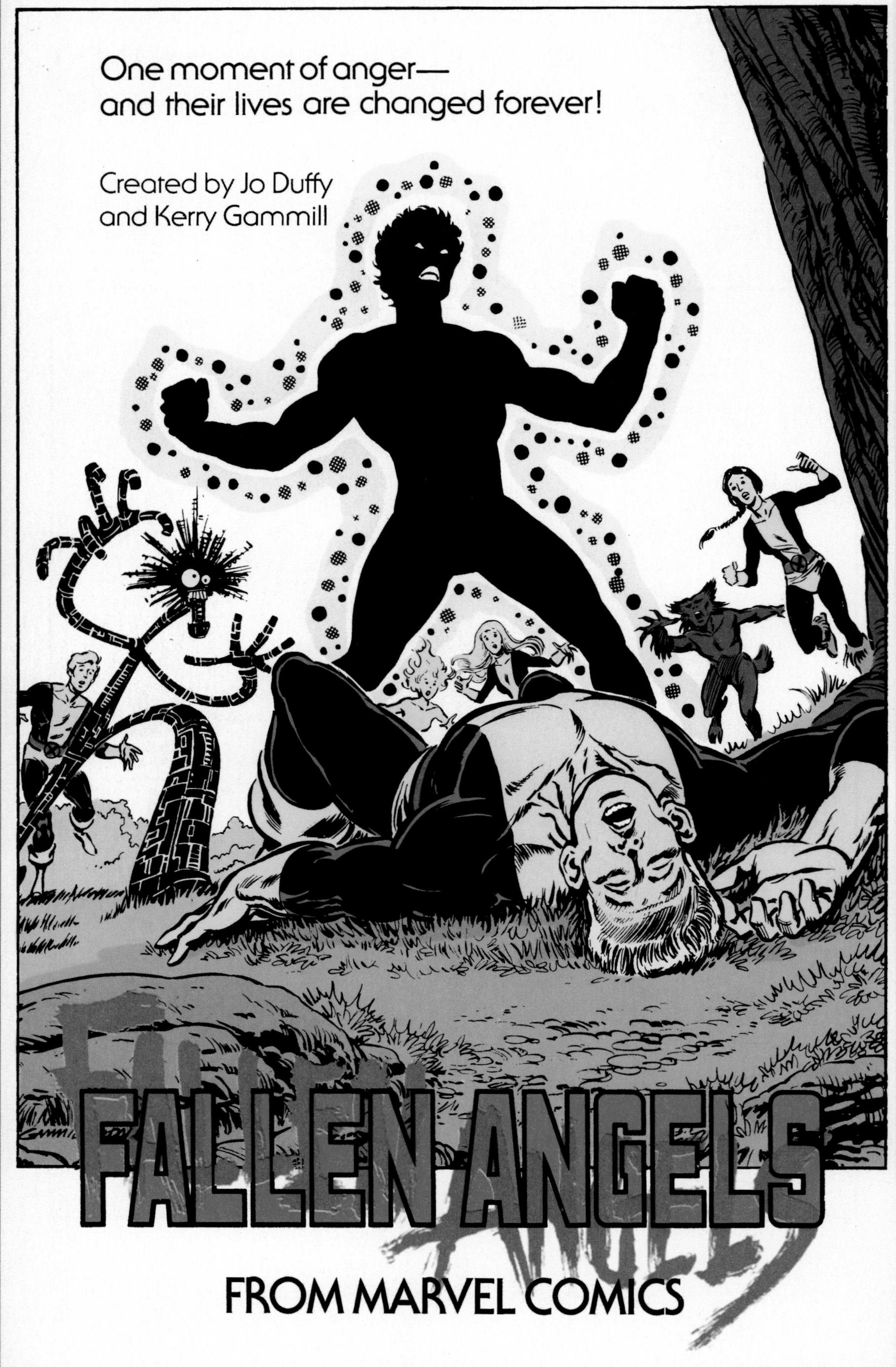
One moment of anger—
and their lives are changed forever!
Created by Jo Duffy
and Kerry Gammill
FALLEN ANGELS
FROM MARVEL COMICS

FALLEN ANGELS

The Fallen Angels is a group of superhuman individuals, primarily made up of adolescent mutants, that is based at the Beat Street Club in Manhattan. Unlike several other organizations of superhuman mutants, the Fallen Angels do not regard themselves primarily as adventurers or as champions of justice. They see themselves as social outsiders and apparently remain together out of their enjoyment of each other's company and need for mutual support.

The Fallen Angels began as a gang of adolescent thieves organized by the adult superhuman mutant criminal known as the Vanisher (see *Vanisher*). Among his recruits were the young mutant Boom Boom, a young female named Ariel, who, unknown to the Vanisher, was actuallly an extraterrestrial from a planet she calls the Coconut Grove, a cyborg named Gomi, who had two cyborg lobsters named Don and Bill, and a young runaway calling herself Chance, who did not know she was herself a superhuman mutant (see *Ariel, Boom Boom, Chance II, Gomi*). Another mutant, Sunspot, left his own team, the New Mutants, in shame over injuring his teammate Cannonball through a reckless use of his superhuman power (see *Cannonball, New Mutants, Sunspot*). He and another fellow teammate, the alien Warlock, ended up joining the Fallen Angels (see *Warlock*). Two other mutants associated with the New Mutants and the X-Men, Madrox and Siryn, joined the Fallen Angels to keep an eye on Sunspot (see *Madrox, Siryn, X-Men*).

Ariel had been secretly assigned by the government of her home planet to gather a collection of superhuman mutants for her planet's scientists to study. Chance was Ariel's accomplice in this plan. Using her superhuman powers, Ariel brought the Fallen Angels to the otherdimensional world where Moon Boy and his companion Devil Dinosaur, both mutants of their own races, lived (see *Devil Dinosaur, Moon Boy*). Moon Boy and Devil Dinosaur accompanied the Fallen Angels back to Earth and became members of their group. (Devil Dinosaur later accidentally killed the cyborg lobster Don by stepping on him.)

Finally, the Fallen Angels journeyed to Ariel's home planet, where they were made captives. Ariel turned against her home planet's ruler Unipar when he took not only her friend Chance but also Ariel herself captive as well, since they both proved to possess superhuman mutant powers. The Fallen Angels succeeded in regaining their freedom and returned to Earth.

Sunspot and Warlock returned to the New Mutants, and Boom Boom went back to X-Factor headquarters and eventually became a member of the team called the X-Terminators (see *X-Factor, X-Terminators*). The other members of the Fallen Angels have remained together as a team.

First appearance: FALLEN ANGELS #1 ■

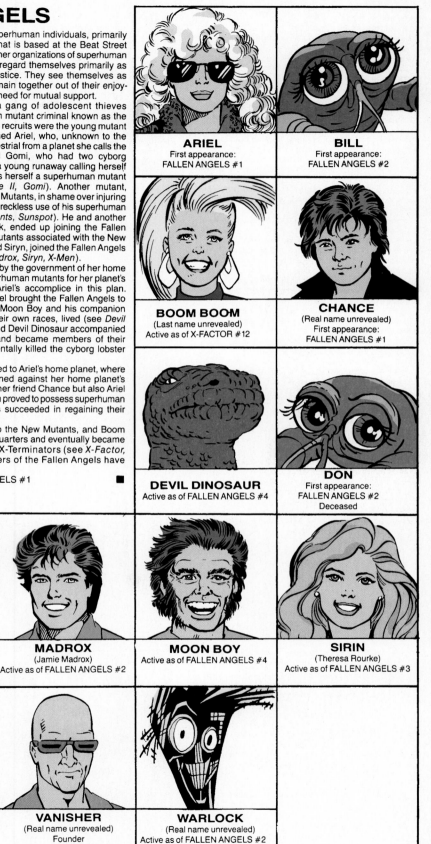

ARIEL
First appearance:
FALLEN ANGELS #1

BILL
First appearance:
FALLEN ANGELS #2

BOOM BOOM
(Last name unrevealed)
Active as of X-FACTOR #12

CHANCE
(Real name unrevealed)
First appearance:
FALLEN ANGELS #1

DEVIL DINOSAUR
Active as of FALLEN ANGELS #4

DON
First appearance:
FALLEN ANGELS #2
Deceased

GOMI
(Real name unrevealed)
First appearance:
FALLEN ANGELS #2

MADROX
(Jamie Madrox)
Active as of FALLEN ANGELS #2

MOON BOY
Active as of FALLEN ANGELS #4

SIRIN
(Theresa Rourke)
Active as of FALLEN ANGELS #3

SUNSPOT
(Roberto de Costa)
Active as of FALLEN ANGELS #2

VANISHER
(Real name unrevealed)
Founder
Active as of X-FACTOR #12

WARLOCK
(Real name unrevealed)
Active as of FALLEN ANGELS #2

ARIEL

Real name: Ariel
Occupation: Thief, adventurer
Identity: The general populace of Earth is unaware that Ariel is an alien.
Legal status: Citizen of the planet known as the Coconut Grove with no known criminal record there
Other aliases: None known
Place of birth: The Coconut Grove
Marital status: Single
Known relatives: Ariel (ancestor, presumed deceased)
Group affiliation: Fallen Angels
Base of operations: Formerly the Coconut Grove, now the Beat Street Clubhouse, New York City
First appearance: FALLEN ANGELS (first series) #1
History: Ariel is an extraterrestrial native to the world known as the Coconut Grove, home of a culture devoted to the pursuit of pleasure. William Shakespeare based the character Ariel in his play *The Tempest* on one of her relatives, who was also named Ariel.

Ariel's race had reached an evolutionary standstill; no mutations had occurred in her race for millions of years. Seeking a means to advance the race's evolution, the leaders of the Coconut Grove assigned Ariel to go to Earth, a world on which superhuman mutants were appearing in great abundance, and bring a number of them back to her home planet in the hope that the factor in their bodies enabling them to mutate could be extracted.

On Earth, Ariel encountered the mutant criminal known as the Vanisher and joined his group of adolescents who worked for him as thieves (see *Vanisher*). Eventually this group became the team of young superhumans known as the Fallen Angels (see *Fallen Angels*). Using her ability to bend space, Ariel transported the Fallen Angels to a distant world, where they encountered Devil Dinosaur and Moon Boy (see *Devil Dinosaur, Moon Boy*). Again through the use of Ariel's powers, the Fallen Angels returned to Earth, joined by Devil Dinosaur and Moon Boy as new recruits to the team.

Finally, Ariel transported the Fallen Angels to her home planet, where they were captured. Ariel was upset, however, that one of the Fallen Angels, Chance, who had become her friend, was also made a prisoner (see *Chance II*). Then Ariel was taken captive as well after being identified as a mutant with a power that, within her race, only she possesses. This was the power to influence minds to compel others to do what she told them. After the Fallen Angels escaped captivity, Ariel used her power to compel Unipar, the leader of the Coconut Grove, to let them return to Earth.

Having changed her loyalties, Ariel accompanied the Fallen Angels to Earth and continues to be a member of the team.
Height: 5'5" **Weight:** 130 lbs.
Eyes: Purple, covered by an opague membrane
Hair: White and pink
Strength level: Ariel possesses the equivalent of the normal human strength of an Earthwoman of her physical age, height, and build who engages in no regular exercise.
Known superhuman powers: Like all members of her extraterrestrial race, Ariel can bend space so that she can create a space warp connecting two points that may otherwise lie great distances apart. There are no known limits on the range that Ariel's space warps may cover; she has created warps that enabled her to travel over interstellar distances from one planet to another in distant solar system. However, Ariel needs an actual doorway that can be opened and closed to serve as a focal point for her power. In addition, there must be another doorway at the receiving end of the warp. By stepping through the doorway, one journeys through the space warp that she has created.

In addition, Ariel is the sole mutant member of her race, possessing the mutant ability to cause others through psionic means to believe what she says or to do what she tells them, whether they would otherwise voluntarily wish to do so or not. ■

CHANCE II

Real name: Unrevealed
Occupation: Thief, adventurer
Identity: Secret
Legal status: Unrevealed, no known criminal record, still a minor
Other aliases: None
Place of birth: South Korea
Marital status: Single
Known relatives: Unnamed parents
Group affiliation: Fallen Angels
Base of operations: The Beat Street Club, New York City
First appearance: FALLEN ANGELS (first series) #1
History: Chance is a 13 year old girl whose parents are members of Reverend Yune Kim Park's Glorification Church. Park brought Chance and her parents to the United States from their homeland, promising to make them American citizens. Instead, he treated them as virtual slaves, and Chance herself was forced to work selling calendars on street corners for the church. Finally, tired of her treatment by the church, Chance ran away.

Chance was recruited by the mutant criminal known as the Vanisher to join the group of teenagers who worked for him as thieves and were known as the Fallen Angels (see *Fallen Angels, Vanisher*). A number of young male and female mutants joined this group.

Chance became the friend and partner of another of the Vanisher's thieves, Ariel, who was actually an extraterrestrial being from a planet called the Coconut Grove (see *Ariel*). For money Chance agreed to help Ariel in her assignment to bring a number of mutants to her home planet, where an attempt was intended to be made to extract the factor from their bodies that enabled them to mutate.

However, after Ariel transported the Fallen Angels to her home world, Ariel and Chance were made prisoners as well, since they too proved to be mutants with unusual powers. Chance's mutant power had only just begun to manifest itself now that she was going through puberty. The Fallen Angels succeeded in regaining their freedom, however, and returned to Earth, where Chance continues to be a member of the team.
Height: 5' 2"
Weight: 97 lbs.
Eyes: Black
Hair: Black
Strength level: Chance possesses the normal human strength of a girl of her age, height, and build who engages in intensive regular exercise.
Known superhuman powers: Chance is a mutant with the superhuman ability to enhance or inhibit the mutant superhuman powers of others. Hence, she can cause another mutant's superhuman power to increase in strength or cause it to cease functioning altogether for as long as she concentrates upon it.
Other abilities: Chance is a formidable street fighter, good at hand-to-hand combat, acrobatics, and in the use of knives as weapons. ■

BOOM BOOM

Real name: Tabitha (last name unrevealed)
Occupation: Adventurer
Identity: Secret
Legal status: Citizen of the United States with no criminal record, still a minor
Other aliases: Time Bomb
Place of birth: Roanoke, Virginia
Marital status: Single
Known relatives: Parents (depicted but names unrevealed)
Group affiliation: Former member of the Fallen Angels and X-Terminators, and member of the New Mutants
Base of operations: Formerly the Beat Street Club, New York City; now X-Factor headquarters, New York City.
First appearance and origin: SECRET WARS II #5
History: A thirteen-year-old girl named Tabitha, nicknamed "Boom Boom," had not gotten along with her parents for most of her life. Tabitha's superhuman mutant power to create balls of explosive concussive energy, which she calls her "time bombs," emerged when she was thirteen, and when her parents discovered them, they were appalled. Resentful towards her father, Boom Boom put a small explosive ball of energy in his lasagna. In retaliation, her father beat her severely. Apparently, Boom Boom's father also beat her on other occasions after he discovered her mutant powers. Somehow learning there was a school for mutants in New York's Westchester County (which was, in fact, Professor Charles Xavier's School for Gifted Youngsters, headquarters for the X-Men and the New Mutants), Boom Boom started journeying there by train (see *New Mutants, Professor X, X-Men, X-Men Headquarters*). She decided to give herself the alias "Time Bomb."

Near Washington D.C. the train was wrecked on a whim by the cosmic entity calling itself the Beyonder (see *Deceased: Beyonder*). Thinking he was a mutant, Boom Boom accompanied him. The Beyonder abandoned her, but then returned and took her to Xavier's school. There the X-Men and New Mutants attacked the Beyonder, who escaped. Boom Boom, frightened and bewildered by witnessing the attack, left, but was later found by the Beyonder, who brought her to a distant planet that he called "World Complex Headquarters" of the alien Celestials (see *Celestials*). There, threatening to destroy the universe, the Beyonder fought and seemingly defeated a number of Celestials. (However, that planet was not truly the Celestials' headquarters, and the Celestials allowed the Beyonder to "defeat" them, presumably in order to observe him in action.) Terrified, Boom Boom demanded that the Beyonder transport her back to Earth and leave her, and the Beyonder complied. Back on Earth, Boom Boom alerted the Avengers about the Beyonder (see *Avengers*). Summoning the Beyonder, Boom Boom thereby led him into an ambush by the Avengers and other costumed champions. The Beyonder, who had regarded Boom Boom as his only friend, allowed the Avengers and their allies to defeat him, but then left. Boom Boom left during the battle.

She eventually encountered the mutant criminal known as the Vanisher, who made her a member of his gang of thieves, and taught her how to steal (see *Vanisher*). Believing that the Vanisher was treating her badly, Boom Boom alerted X-Factor, whom she believed to be a group of mutant hunters, about him (See *X-Factor*). But when two members of X-Factor arrived, who were actually the Beast and Iceman, Boom

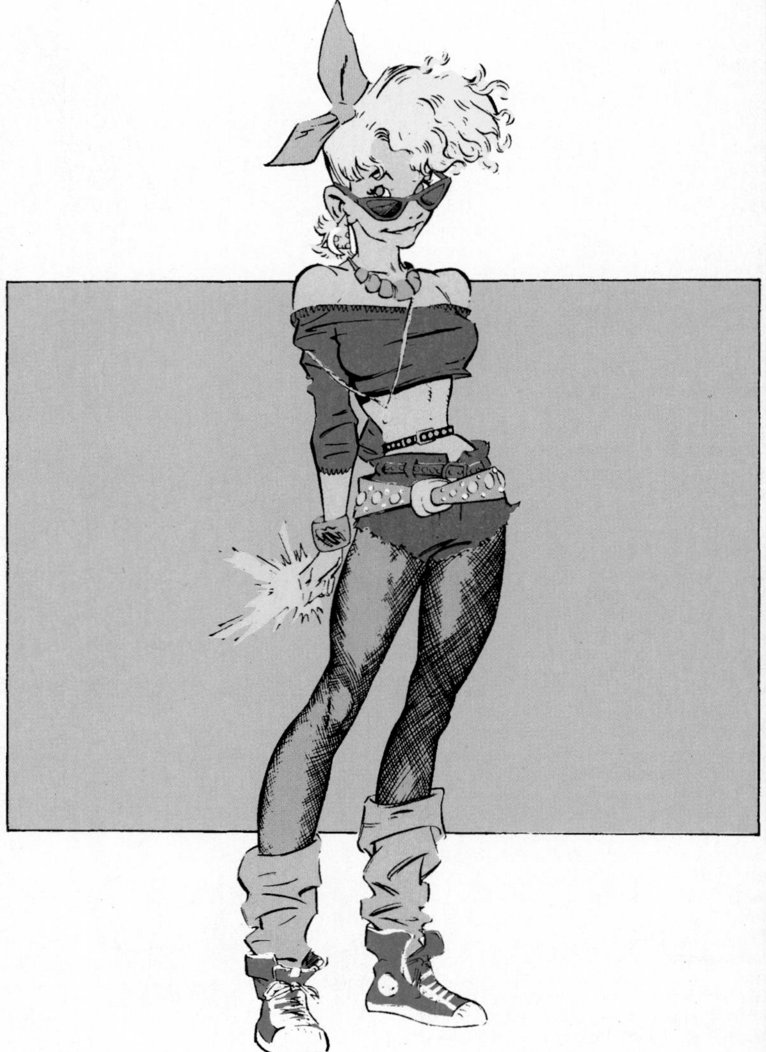

Boom changed her mind about turning in the Vanisher and used her "time bomb" power on the Iceman as a prank (see *Beast, Iceman*). The Beast and Iceman pursued her and caught up to her in their costumed identities. She agreed to leave the Vanisher's gang and live at X-Factor headquarters instead.

Later, after Boom Boom set off another of her "time bombs" in the X-Factor laboratory as a prank, the Iceman pursued her through the headquarters. Another member of the Vanisher's gang, Ariel, used her powers to enable Boom Boom to escape X-Factor headquarters (see *Ariel*). Thereafter, Boom Boom stayed for a time with the Vanisher and his group, who were known as the Fallen Angels (see *Fallen Angels*). After an adventure on another planet with the Fallen Angels, Boom Boom returned to X-Factor headquarters only to be captured by the anti-mutant organization called the Right (see *Right*). Boom Boom and other mutants associated with X-Factor regained their freedom, however, and recently, she and her fellow X-Factor trainees went into action as the team called the X-Terminators (see *X-Terminators*). Currently, Boom Boom is a member of the New Mutants.

Height: 5' 5" **Weight:** 120 lbs.
Eyes: Blue **Hair:** Blond

Strength level: Boom Boom possesses the normal human strength of a girl of her age, height, and build who engages in moderate regular exercise.

Known superhuman powers: Boom Boom can create balls of energy of an unknown kind which she calls her "time bombs." These "bombs" explode with concussive force. She can produce marble-sized "bombs" which have little concussive impact and which she uses for playing pranks. She has produced "time bombs" ranging up to the size of beach balls, which, when they explode, can smash tree trunks and even metal objects. To at least some extent Boom Boom can control the amount of time between the creation of one of her "bombs" and the time it detonates. She can also mentally muffle the sound of the detonation to a limited extent. The limits on her power to create and control her "time bombs" are as yet unknown.

Other abilities: Boom Boom is an excellent player of video games. ■

MOON BOY

Real name: Moon Boy (translated from his native language)
Occupation: None
Identity: Known in the Valley of Flame on his home planet and to the Fallen Angels on Earth
Legal status: None
Other aliases: None known
Place of birth: The Valley of Flame on an unidentified planet
Marital status: Single
Known relatives: None
Group affiliation: Partner of Devil Dinosaur, member of the Fallen Angels
Base of operations: Formerly the Valley of Flame, now New York City
First appearance: DEVIL DINOSAUR #1
History: Moon Boy is a member of a tribe of the "Small-Folk," a furry humanoid race that resembles prehistoric men of Earth, and that lives on an unidentified planet outside Earth's solar system. It was once believed that Moon Boy lived on Earth itself in prehistoric times. However, the Small-Folk do not exactly correspond to any known race of prehistoric men that lived on Earth; moreover, the Small-Folk live at the same time on their world as dinosaurs, which became extinct on Earth (except in the Savage Land and Wakanda) before the coming of early man on Earth (see *Savage Land, Wakanda*). New evidence, however, indicates that Moon Boy is from an unidentified planet and was born in recent times. Presumably the resemblances between Moon Boy's Small-Folk and prehistoric Earthmen are due to parallel evolution.

Besides the diminutive Small-Folk, there are other humanoid races native to Moon Boy's planet. There are two groups, the Hill-Folk and the Killer-Folk, which both are of normal human size and have brown fur; these two groups may belong to the same race. There is also a race of humanoid giants on Moon Boy's world.

Moon Boy was born in the Valley of Flame on his world and was named after the night. On one night, when the rest of his tribe was alseep, Moon Boy went to explore the Fire-Mountain, a volcano in the valley. There he found a group of Killer-Folk who had trapped and slain a female dinosaur of the kind known to the Small-Folk as a "devil-beast" (which resembles Earth's *Tyrannosaurus rex*), and were now slaughtering her young. The last surviving "devil-beast" of the brood wounded many of his assailants, who then tried to kill him with the flames of their torches. Suddenly flame erupted from a pit on the volcano. Moon Boy and the young dinosaur escaped, but he dinosaur was wounded. Moreover, the dinosaur's hide had turned from green to bright red, apparently due to the exposure to fire. The dinosaur collapsed and Moon Boy went to try to help him. Another small dinosaur then attacked Moon Boy, but the wounded "devil-beast" fought the attacker off. The grateful Moon Boy led his rescuer down to the forest and took him to a body of water, which soothed the young dinosaur's pain and began healing his wounds. Moon Boy also brought the dinosaur some food. Thus began the friendship between Moon Boy and the young dinosaur, whom he called "Devil," and who proved to be extraordinarily intelligent (see *Devil Dinosaur*). Riding on Devil's back, Moon Boy returned to the Small-Folk, who, however, fled on seeing the dinosaur. From then on, Moon Boy and Devil Dinosaur lived together in the Valley, aiding each other.

Growing to full size, Devil Dinosaur became the Valley's most powerful denizen and its protector from threats from within and without.

Eventually Moon Boy was reconciled with the Small-Folk, but he continued to live with Devil Dinosaur as his constant companion. At one point Moon Boy and Devil Dinosaur were separated when the dinosaur fell into a pit containing a space warp that transported him to Earth. Devil managed to return to the Valley of Flame by traveling through another space warp. Devil's appearance on Earth was reported in Earth's news media, however, and a movie was made about him.

Through these means the alien Ariel, who was searching for mutants, learned about Devil Dinosaur. She somehow located Devil's home planet and determined that both he and Moon Boy were mutants. Using her space-warping abilities, Ariel transported herself and other members of her group of mutants, the Fallen Angels, from Earth to the Valley of Flame, where they encountered Moon Boy and Devil (see *Fallen Angels*). Moon Boy and Devil Dinosaur traveled back to Earth with the Fallen Agnels, and, as far as is known, they both remain members of the team today and live in Manhattan. However, only the Fallen Angels themselves know that Moon Boy and Devil Dinosaur now dwell on twentieth century Earth. As far as is known, Moon Boy has not yet learned English, but he accepts the other Fallen Angels as his friends.

Height:
Weight:
Eyes:
Hair: Black
Unusual features: Like the rest of his race, Moon Boy has a body nearly entirely covered with fur, with the principal exception of his face.
Strength level: Moon Boy possesses strength roughly equal to that of a normal Earth human being of his physical age, height, and build who engages in intensive regular exercise.
Known superhumanoid powers: Moon Boy is known to be a mutant member of the Small-Folk. Presumably his mutation gave him higher intelligence than other members of his race possess.
Abilities: Moon Boy has great agility, comparable to that of Earth apes.

■

GOMI

Real name: Unrevealed
Occupation: Former laboratory assistant
Identity: Publicly known
Legal status: Citizen of the United States with no known criminal record, still a minor
Other aliases: None known
Place of birth: Unrevealed, presumably somewhere in the United States
Marital status: Single
Known relatives: Ramon Lipschitz (cousin)
Group affiliation: Fallen Angels
Base of operations: The Beat Street Club, New York City
First appearance: FALLEN ANGELS (first series) #2
Origin: FALLEN ANGELS (first series) #3
History: Two students, Ramon Lipschitz and his best friend, Tadashi Fujita, were given a research grant and laboratory facilities near Coney Island in Brooklyn, New York. They hired Lipschitz's cousin as their laboratory assistant, and Fujita named him "Gomi" (the Japanese word for "garbage"). Gomi hated his real name and was content to use this one instead.

Lipschitz and Fujita were doing research into using cybernetics to enhance the abilities of normal living beings by turning them into cyborgs. The two students successfully experimented on two lobsters, who became known as Don and Bill, increasing their intelligence, strength, and ability to live outside of water.

Lipschitz and Fujita were both infatuated with the superhuman mutant Marvel Girl, although they had never met her (see *Marvel Girl*). When the first Phoenix appeared in her stead as a member of the X-Men, Lipschitz and Fujita were shocked (see *Phoenix*). The two students decided to try to recreate the original Marvel Girl by using cybernetic devices to give a woman artificial telekinetic powers similar to Marvel Girl's. Needing a test subject for the experiment, they chloroformed Gomi and implanted the devices in him. As a result, Gomi gained psionic abilities, although they were different from Marvel Girl's.

Not having made enough progress in their real assignment, Lipschitz and Fujita abandoned their laboratory to avoid its inspection by the bureaucrats overseeing their research grant. Gomi was recruited by the Fallen Angels, a team of self-styled misfits and petty criminals, most of whom are mutants. Gomi joined the group, taking Don and Bill with him, and remains a member to this day. Don was killed when another member of the group, Devil Dinosaur, accidentally stepped on him, but Bill remains hale and healthy (see *Devil Dinosaur*).

Height: 5' 5" **Weight:** 107 lbs.
Eyes: Blue **Hair:** Blond
Strength level: Gomi possesses the normal human strength of a boy his age, height, and build who engages in moderate regular exercise.
Known superhuman powers: Gomi is a cyborg possessing artificial psionic powers which enable him to create a pillar of concussive psionic force. The limit of the amount of force that Gomi can generate are as yet unknown.
Pets: Gomi has as a companion a mutant blue lobster named Bill, who has been turned into a cyborg. The cybernetic devices implanted within Bill greatly increased his intelligence and amplified his strength so much that he can knock over a standing human being. The devices also enable Bill to survive outside of water far longer than a normal lobster, and perhaps indefinitely. ■